To Mark
Ylenia
with much love
Nov. '21

VIZCAYA

By
Marco Bronzini

To my mother

Vizcaya – Marco Bronzini

In the end it was all for the love of one woman. Can that be possible? The love of one human being?

ONE

Vincent Jones watched the River Thames from the window of his taxi. The overcast sky on this late November morning gave the water a murky appearance, though even on a sunny day, the Thames never claimed the blues that are plastered on all of London's postcards. He arrived at Waterloo train station after the ten-minute drive from The Savoy Hotel, which is where he stayed and glanced at his cell phone; it was eleven o'clock in the morning. His visits to London were not very frequent, and were mainly for work with Sotheby's, the renowned auction house. He was sometimes called upon to authenticate or appraise an objet d'art, or a painting. Though he did not like to be called 'doctor', he held a PhD from Cornell University in art history. This trip to England was different, and not directly work related. An auction of great importance to him was to take place in a couple of weeks in New York, and he was looking forward to it with anticipation and a certain anxiety. This London trip to him was the prelude to the auction, a public sale of the utmost importance and long overdue.

The typical brouhaha from the station echoed around the large terminal. Vincent looked at the large flap display panel high above the main floor. The departures and arrivals read like a gigantic travel brochure, with destinations from all over the United Kingdom. The train to Portsmouth was leaving in thirty-five minutes, plenty of time for a cup of coffee. Vincent sat down and ordered a cappuccino and watched people coming off the trains and walking away from the platforms. He wondered about their lives. The morning commuters had come and gone, however the station was still very crowded, as one would expect.

"Next stop, Brookwood", announced the voice on the intercom. This was Vincent's stop. The destination was about an hour away from central London. The train came to a full stop. A cemetery was adjacent to the station, and Vincent could already see several headstones. He entered the graveyard through the large wrought iron gate and after a short walk, arrived at the main alleyway and made a left. His heart was racing. The garden for the dead was glittering in the early afternoon light, no doubt after a fair amount of rain. Vincent walked around the puddles of water on the uneven pathway, making his way toward plot 35 in a small circular area called 'The Ring'.

There ought to be only a few things in life that one truly cares for, besides what Vincent would call superficial possessions, like extravagantly expensive cars, or the need to belong to a particular club. Love for the arts, may it be music, literature, painting, is not granted to everyone at birth, it is a gift that few people possess. Though for some, it lays buried deep inside, until it is revealed, hopefully not too late in life, so it can be enjoyed to its fullest. Vincent was lucky, art had been part of his life, like an antidote to mediocrity, since early childhood. This day was a pilgrimage for him. He wanted to be here, in the presence of greatness. For Vincent, there was only certainty, John Singer Sargent was the greatest painter who had ever lived. He stood in front of the headstone, very simple in appearance, one would say almost in a state of abandon. He read the words, carved it seemed, clumsily - *John S. Sargent RA - Born in Florence Jan12th1856 - Died in London April 15th1925*. Vincent stared at the grave, as images of dazzling paintings filled his mind. This was the closest he would ever be to the artist, separated only by a few feet, and yet eternity stood between them. He remained there, pensive, letting his mind go free, letting Sargent's hands accomplish their magic. A robin landed on the headstone, which brought Vincent out of his reveries. He smiled at the tiny creature – the English Robin being a lot smaller than its American counterpart. The bird looked at the intruder, as if to ask, what are you doing here? Vincent marveled at the life before him, and thought about time, the passing years. The bird flew away. Vincent watched him disappear inside a large oak tree and he observed that the cemetery was deserted. Not a single visitor could be seen, not even a groundskeeper. It surprised him. He understood that his passion for Sargent was perhaps excessive, however, the sad state of the headstone and the grave distressed him. Why was it in such neglect, like it had been forgotten. He reached for the stone and touched it, he did not know why, perhaps to create a link with the remains of the great artist. At that moment, a woman with a little girl appeared out of nowhere at a short distance, walking in his direction. It startled him. "Goodbye", he whispered to the grave, and turned around, expecting to see the two visitors. The woman and the little girl were gone, as if they had instantly dissolved. A strange sensation overcame him, he felt a presence, yet the trees and the surrounding graves were the only silent witnesses. He looked around as he walked away, still puzzled at what seemed to be a hallucination. I'm going crazy, he thought, and wanted to dismiss the whole thing as being jet-lagged and having an over imaginative mind. He looked over his shoulder, just in case. Nothing.

Later that night, Vincent sat in his hotel room, the television on mute as the ten o'clock news showed the usual political saga going on in Britain. He got up and helped himself to a couple of Jack Daniel's miniatures from the mini bar, grabbed a piece of paper and a pen from the desk and sat down again. He began to draw. His drawing skills were not very good, however he managed to render an image, slowly. His hand followed a certain pattern, as if his subconscious had power over the lines, dictating their every angle and form. The image represented two figures; a woman and a child, a little girl. Vincent drew the woman, paying attention to shading, applying himself. She wore a long dress, an early 1900's attire, which completely baffled him. He continued a little longer before stopping, questioning his own sanity. It became obvious to him that the two figures on this fairly clumsy sketch, represented the woman and the young girl he saw at the cemetery. In a flash of light, Vincent could swear that the drawing took on a life of its own and he quickly threw the piece of paper on the bed. A burning sensation in his eyes, followed, which alarmed him. His mind wandered. That same sensation again all of a sudden overpowered him, like someone watching him. A ghost, a spirit of some kind, perhaps. He closed his eyes. Forms and faces from the morning at the cemetery performed a strange play in Vincent's head. Though he only saw the woman for a few seconds, he could observe her clearly now, as if she was standing in the room with him. She was a woman of a certain stature, dressed in a richly embroidered silk dress. She approached the grave with questioning eyes, like she longed to speak to him. He could not see the little girl's face. She seemed to be looking over her shoulder, as if she was expecting someone else to join her. Vincent opened his eyes suddenly, confused, looking around the room, as if awake after a heavy sleep. The drawing was on his lap now.

He stared at it before tossing it back on the bed. The signal appeared to be lost on the television; a distorted TV transmission with the color bars, filled the screen with a 'no signal' message. His eyes fell on the digital clock on the bedside table. The red numbers flashed on 12:00 o'clock. He unlocked his cellphone; 12:00 o'clock. "What the hell…". Vincent picked up the receiver to dial the front desk on the hotel phone, only to hear a busy tone. Frustrated, he rushed out of his room, got on the elevator and pressed 'L' for lobby.

The imposing space was deserted and he walked toward the front desk, the sound of his footsteps muffled by an immense Persian rug that covered the whole area. He noticed the drizzle outside through the large glass doors.

"I've tried to call you, but you didn't answer," said Vincent to the concierge as he approached the marble front desk. "Well, that's not entirely true, I got a busy signal."

"I'm sorry, sir," answered the man as he stood up from his stool to welcome Vincent.

"Never mind. Is anything wrong with the internet? Is that the right time?" asked Vincent, amazed at the hour, looking at the clock behind the counter.

"Yes, sir, it's ten-twenty… I don't believe there's anything wrong with the internet."

"Ten-twenty?" Vincent looked toward the main entrance. "It can't be ten twenty," he said with stupefaction, his eyes locked on the front door, framing the darkness of the night beyond. He leaned over the counter and peeked in the concierge's lounge. Images of the last segments of the ten o'clock news were being shown on a small television set. "It can't be ten twenty," he repeated.

"Sir, are you alright?" asked the concierge who felt something was wrong with this guest.

"I'm not getting a signal on the TV in my room," he said, taking his phone out of his pocket. "And… that's weird", he muttered looking at his phone, staring at the numbers 10:22.

"Is everything alright, sir?" asked the night porter.

"Yes… yes… I guess so…" replied Vincent walking away, utterly confused.

"Good night, sir."

"Yes, good night."

Vincent entered his room, feeling anxious. The mind can play strange tricks, especially when the body is tired and one is at a low ebb. The clock read the correct time now, and the television was back on. The drawing was still on the bed. He walked to the window and pushed the heavy curtain to the side. London was quiet. He looked at the black hole, the boundlessness of the night above the city. The rain carved long and glistening furrows on the windows as the drizzle intensified. What bothered him was the fact that he had no recollection of the time elapsed. He was sure he had slept a certain amount of time, and yet no more than twenty minutes had passed. He hesitated to close his eyes again, uncertain why. The drawing was an enigma, and he had absolutely no idea why he made the sketch. He grabbed the piece of paper and stared at the woman he could see so distinctly with his eyes closed. A knock on the door made him jump. He instinctively looked at the digital clock; it was almost eleven o'clock. He felt foolish looking through the peephole. There was no one there. Vincent opened the door, stepped in the hallway and looked to the left and the right, only to see the long, empty corridor. He dialed the front desk. "Have you had any complaints tonight, about people knocking on doors?" Vincent asked the concierge with a certain annoyance in his voice.

"We haven't sir. What seems to be the matter?'

"Well… someone knocked on my door, not five minutes ago. This is The Savoy for God's sake, I expect a little more than this."

"Sorry, sir, I'll make sur—"

"Good night!" Vincent hung up, livid. The fact that he was exhausted only made matters worse. He picked up the drawing and crumpled the piece of paper into a small ball, and tossed it angrily in the waste paper basket. "I have got to sleep!" he told himself. He didn't bother to undress. After kicking off his shoes and turning off the light, he fell backwards on the bed. Eyes wide open, he stared at the ceiling, and in the semi-darkness, asked himself more questions than he had answers. The sound of an ambulance was heard in the distance. He studied the shadowy carvings of the crown moldings around the perimeter of the room, before closing his eyes. Silhouettes, like large ribbons floating in mid-air, advanced toward him. Vincent turned the light back on, jumped out of bed and began pacing the room, struck by an acute case of restlessness. He considered the whole incident at the cemetery. "I did see a woman… and a child. I know what I saw." he pondered out loud, catching his image in the Louis XIV mirror. He hesitated a moment before making a phone call to the States. He scrolled down to 'mother' on his contacts and pressed the number.

"Hello," answered the woman's voice on the other end.

"Miss Brown, it's Vincent Jones. Is my mother available?"

"Yes, she is. Hold on a second."

Vincent thought about what he was going to say to his mother. He was not sure how she would respond. He felt like a young child, lost in a world that showed no latitude for anything outside what is expected of someone in his position. Always parade positiveness, a cheerful disposition, anything within the cubic space of that box one is assigned to, even if the soul is in mourning.

"Vincent?"

"Hello, mother."

"Everything alright? Are you still in London?"

"Yes. At The Savoy."

"It's late for you. Midnight, right?"

"Yes, it's about that time. How's Boston?"

"Cold, but Miss Brown made me some tea. What's wrong?" asked Vincent's mother, her female instinct, stronger and sharper than a diamond at this particular moment in time.

"Well, they're happening again," Vincent said, weary from the hours passed.

"Oh, no. How? When did they start?"

"Hmm, yesterday… I think. I went to see Sargent's grave, you know…"

"And you saw her again."

"And I saw her again. Well… there were two this time. There was a child with her, a little girl."

"A little girl?"

"Yes."

"It's been a while since it happened. And now… a little girl," repeated Vincent's mother.

"Yes, a while," he answered, as his tired mind drifted, consumed by a myriad of thoughts.

"You sound tired. Try to go to sleep. You'll need to go back to Doctor Roberts when you get back. You know that, right?"

"I know. I know."

"He helped you last time."

"I guess so. It's just… just frustrating. Anyway, sorry I called you. I didn't mean to scare you."

"You don't scare me, but I am concerned."

"Don't be. Good night. I'll call you when I get in on Wednesday."

"Hello? Hello? We've been cut off."

"I'm here. Mother. Can you hear me?"

"Ha, it's you. Are you in London?"

"Yes, I am. Can you put Miss Brown on?"

"You need to see Doctor Roberts. He'll help you."

"Mother? Mother? Please give Miss Brown the phone."

"Hello, this is Miss Brown. She was fine just now."

"She seemed alright for a bit," said Vincent, who felt utterly powerless. "How often does it happen now?"

"Three, four times a day. It's never the same."

"Thank you for looking after her. Good night."

"Good night, Dr. Jones."

Not without a great commotion in his head, Vincent finally went back to bed and fell asleep as four empty miniature bottles lay on the table.

TWO

"Good afternoon, ladies and gentlemen and welcome to Sotheby's, New York," said the auctioneer. The room was filled to maximum capacity for this combined sale of Victorian and Edwardian period items, which included, letters, jewelry, paintings and several other collectibles. Some of the memorabilia were estimated as low as one thousand dollars, while others were marked as high as three hundred thousand dollars. This was the case for a watercolor by artist John Singer Sargent. The watercolor, painted in 1917, depicted a landscape the artist had done while he was a guest at Vizcaya, the summer home of James Deering, in Florida. The painting, which measured 15" x 22", was estimated to fetch anything between two and three hundred thousand dollars.

Vincent Jones had been waiting for this sale. His fascination with Vizcaya dated back from his childhood. The connection between Sargent and the great house, was well documented and of historical value, and moreover Sargent's paintings rarely came on the market. Though a lot of his work could be seen in many of the major museums of the world, a great number of paintings and drawings were buried in private collections. This was a very special day for Vincent. Sargent's paintings, may it be his beautiful portraits, or his landscapes, can only be described as exquisite, and the watercolor for sale on this day, was no exception. The artist had captured the very essence of the day at Vizcaya. One could feel the heat of the sun on the Roman marble balustrades, the white statues, sitting against the rich and dark greens bushes. All of it heightened by the deep blue band of the water in the distance.

Soon after he graduated with a Master's degree in art history, Vincent sought employment with Sotheby's. They saw great potential in him and hired him rather quickly, and at age thirty-two, received his Doctorate. Vincent came from a well to do family that made their money in the steel industry in Pittsburgh. His great-grandfather,

Clarence Henry Jones, was the pioneer who gambled his own money in order to achieve his goal; to make steel available quickly, nationwide. His worth was quite considerable and young Vincent, at age three, who was the one and only great-grandchild, inherited a substantial fortune after the death of the ninety-nine-year-old tycoon. Several properties were left to him, which included a penthouse on Fifth Avenue, overlooking Central Park in New York City. Though the object Vincent treasured the most, was a simple mahogany box his own grandfather had bequeathed to him. It was filled with a few items that great-grandfather Clarence had collected during his life. A very small and delicately crafted silver key, had always amused Vincent and had him tell the story that fabulous riches had yet to be uncovered. A letter by John Singer Sargent was one of the treasured pieces.

The auctioneer came to Sargent's watercolor. "Item 95 in your catalogue, the last item of the day," he said with his best auctioneer voice. "A watercolor by John Singer Sargent. This is a very rare painting, ladies and gentlemen, executed while the artist was a guest at Vizcaya, James Deering's summer house in Florida, in 1917." The watercolor had been confined in a private collection until now, and no one really had seen it for over half a century. Vincent sat at the back of the room, anxious and eager to see what price the painting was going to fetch. The bidding started at one hundred thousand dollars. It quickly climbed to one hundred and sixty, then one hundred and eighty. Vincent looked around the room and tried to see who was bidding, but to no avail. There were also bids placed by phone and two people stood near the front, receiver in hand, working for someone who could not make it to the sale. The price increased by five thousand dollars at a time. Now at two hundred and twenty thousand. Vincent held his auction paddle close to his chest; his had the number 153.

"Two hundred and twenty thousand dollars," said the auctioneer. "Fair warning, anymore bids? Anyone? Selling at two hundred and twenty thousand dollars… anyone else?" The room fell silent, as if an announcement of vital importance was to be made. Hearts raced, as they always do in such cases. Of course, art can be irrelevant, like in time of great hardship. People out of work during what is known as the Great Depression, would not have given the renowned artist five cents for his beautiful watercolor. So, what is a painting worth? Well, it is worth whatever someone is willing to pay for it. It is that simple. Today, in Sotheby's, New York, it was worth two hundred and twenty-five thousand dollars. And as Vincent raised his paddle, making sure the auctioneer caught sight of number 153, he and Sargent would forevermore be linked. This is what he wanted. "Sold," said the auctioneer, pointing at Vincent, "for two hundred and twenty-five thousand dollars! Thank you, Mr. Jones." Though Vincent worked for Sotheby's, he was by no means treated like a normal employee. He was well known for his philanthropic qualities, and the art world, as shallow as it can be at times, knew he was a true lover of the arts and they respected him for it.

"Congratulations," said the rather feminine voice behind Vincent.

He turned around. "Oh, you're here" he said, looking at the two piercing blue eyes.

"A little out of my league, but I wouldn't have missed it for the world. But now that I know it's yours… well, I am thrilled for you."

"Thank you. So how have you been?" asked Vincent, more out of politeness than out of genuine interest.

"You know… comme ci, comme ça."

"Right."

"We need to do lunch… soon. I haven't seen you in ages, you wicked man. Call me. Anyway, gotta run. Congrats, really!"

Vincent watched Tracy go - formerly James. He was never quite able to come to terms with the new identity after the procedure known as 'gender reassignment surgery', always stumbling on the name when introductions were required.

"Good evening, Doctor Jones," said the doorman as Vincent walked through the front door of his building.

"Good evening, Grant. Would you like to know what I have here?" asked Vincent, extremely pleased with himself, holding the well wrapped up painting under his arm.

"I would, Sir, if you don't mind."

After carefully taking the brown paper away, Vincent held the picture up, exhibiting it to Grant. "Well? What do you think?" he asked.

"I've never seen anything so beautiful," said Grant, with an unexpected passion in his voice.

"Really? I knew you would appreciate it. I've yet to meet someone who does not love his work," Vincent said, admiring the painting.

"Who painted it, Sir?"

"Sargent. John Singer Sargent. An American artist who lived in Europe, well, France and England, mainly. The greatest of them all!" exclaimed Vincent, who had tears in his eyes. "I just bought it."

"Is the artist still alive?"

"Sadly, no."

"It will look wonderful in your penthouse, Sir."

"Yes." The thought of the painting confined to a wall, his wall, suddenly troubled Vincent. Works of art are meant to be seen, not hidden, and he felt a certain sense of guilt. Private collections are wonderful for the collector; however, one would say, greed and self-indulgence precludes millions of art lovers the pleasures the artwork was created for. "Good night," he told the doorman as he made his way to the elevator.

"Good night, Sir."

Vincent dialed the code to his apartment, which took him to his penthouse on the twenty-eighth floor.

He studied the painting more closely when he finally was able to calm down, sitting in the depth of a large armchair. Sargent's natural gift with both oils and watercolors was clearly evident. Vincent looked at the colors the artist had used and he marveled. The simplicity of the forms and the sunlight, Sargent always seemed to be able to capture in his plein-air work was staggering. Like any true art lover and collector, Vincent had no idea where he was going to put the painting. He had to have it, not because it matched something of no importance somewhere in a room, or its value was going to increase, rather for love alone. He looked around the extensive area of the main room, and found little available space to hang a new painting. The apartment was by no means lacking in art work. Paintings by many different artists in many different styles, graced the walls. A small Sisley hung above the fireplace; a landscape painted along the River Seine in 1878 by the Impressionist master. A pencil drawing by Modigliani on top of Vincent's desk had been placed there, resting against the wall for the last five years. None of the art was arranged to impress friends or visitors, they were bought out of a deeply felt passion for what is beautiful and good. There are prerequisites for such attributes. The

17

handling of paint, the artistry in the gracefulness of a line, a distinctive feel for colors, all of it, contributes to what makes a work of art, in this case a painting, good. Vincent was well aware of this. His taste was not bent toward any particular style or period. He admired a Botticelli like he admired a Picasso.

The lights were on late into the night throughout the penthouse. Vincent had fallen asleep in the armchair, still holding his newly acquired masterpiece against his chest. After several perturbed nights, he had finally conceded defeat. The woman from the cemetery was becoming more and more real to him. What he called his hallucinations, were beginning to take their toll. It affected his work. It affected his life. He was afraid of being alone at night and terrified of going to sleep. The turmoil first began when he was around fifteen years old, though he could not quite pinpoint the exact time. All he knew, was that the apparitions had increased with the years. Doctor Roberts, a noted New York psychiatrist, began to see Vincent when he was in his late teens. His mother, Mrs. Jones, insisted that he see him despite her husband's protests. Vincent's father, William Jones, a weak man, who as they say was born with a silver spoon in his mouth, was no match for the 'matron' of the household. He was absent from Vincent's life, weeks at a time, either on his yacht, or some private resort overseas. He was found dead in a hotel room in Dubai on Vincent's twenty-first birthday. Apparently, overcome by a heart attack. Doctor Roberts, who like any wise psychiatrist would operate, conducted his sessions with young Vincent with the firm intention of keeping his golden goose at bay. By his early twenties, Vincent was much engaged with his studies and he seemed to be getting better, freed from those chains which weighed heavily on his heart. In fact, quite a few years went by without any of the struggle he had known. The labyrinth of his life became smaller, less complex. This is when he met Sarah. Sarah Conti was the island Vincent longed for. He felt secured on its shores, away from all troubles, and sheltered from wind and rain. She was a teller at the Wells Fargo Bank on Madison Avenue, in New York City. Vincent arrived early one hot summer morning at that branch, ten minutes before it opened, in his jeans and T-shirt. He pressed his face against the glass doors, in order to see the inside clearer, only to see Sarah's face inches away on the other side of the glass. They both laughed. She pointed at her watch and mouthed the

words, 'I am sorry', which Vincent found endearing.
walk away, disappeared from her sight and came rigl
backwards. She laughed again. When the bank open
other employees present, Vincent had Sarah to him
minutes, though long enough to find out she was single.
a lot, a must in any relationship. He talked very little abou   ..self and
unlike what most men would have done, spoke nothing of his fortune.
He described Sarah to his mother as a cute little thing, with large round
eyes. He was glad his appearance was more of a workman that day,
than a wealthy philanthropist and a PhD holder. Vincent walked out of
the bank with her phone number and he felt sure, with at least a
fragment of her heart.

There were three texts on Vincent's cell phone when he woke up.
Still in a daze, he could not believe he had fallen asleep with the Sargent
on his knees. "Two hundred and twenty-five thousand dollars," he said
out loud as he stood up from the armchair. "I can't sleep with you
every night!" he smirked, and carefully placed the painting on the floor,
against one of the twelve-foot white Carrara marble columns
supporting the mezzanine. He looked at his phone. One text was from
the head of sales at Sotheby's, congratulating Vincent on his purchase,
the other from Sarah and one from his mother. Sarah was back from
visiting her parents in Seattle, which is where she was from, and wanted
to see Vincent. His mother's text was nothing unusual, a mixture of
thoughts, clashing with one another to the point of making absolutely
no sense. Her mind was an empty vessel at times, like a container,
leaking and dependent on the power of the stream filling it up. It
affected her spirit, her ability to connect with people she was supposed
to love. A hard-headed woman to begin with, who could not accept the
fact that she was diminished, and had become a shadow of her former
self. Miss Brown, who looked after her full time, was a 'true saint', in
Vincent's words. She had no family of her own, and basically
dedicated the last eight years of her life to be of service to a very
demanding woman. Vincent scrolled through his mother's text, but
ended up texting Sarah.
Hello there

Hello

How were your parents and your mother?

Doing better. Did you miss me?

Hmm…

What!?

Of course silly

So did you get it?

Yes I got it

Is it gorgeous?

Fabulous. Can't wait to show it to you

So happy for you. I'll see you tonite. Love you

Love you

Vincent looked at his mother's text again, not at all sure how to reply to it. By all accounts, she was a good mother, though not very affectionate. No lullabies were ever heard in the nursery, no smiling and adoring face leaning over the pram; that indelible image of unconditional love, was absent. All other needs, as irrelevant as they are when the one most craved for is nonexistent, were met, dutifully. Perhaps all had been extinguished in Mrs. Jones's soul after the death of her first born; Vincent's older sister. The infant died at barely three months. It was labeled as an unexplained death, with a name that only showed insensitivity and ignorance – cot death. Such is our sojourn on this earth, with all its cruelties, its exuberances and hopefulness. Five years went by before the Jones's courage returned, and tried to have a second child. Vincent was born. His birth was announced in The New York Times society pages, right next to a column entitled: Parental Disapproval Vital to Our Society; an article dealing with teen-age pregnancies. Vincent turned off his phone.

THREE

Christmas lights lit up the New York City sky on this overcast night. Snow was in the forecast. Fifth Avenue bustled with people rushing in and out of stores, in search of that perfect present, the one item that the beloved one did not possess. Christmas was three weeks away. Hearts are bursting with joy, no matter how young or old; it is the season to give and forgive. Vincent and Sarah were making their way towards Rockefeller Center, the mecca at this time of year. They talked about Sarah's very own devoted mother who had a minor stroke, which prompted the visit to Seattle. Sarah came from a large Italian family. Her father was an amateur tenor, in the true Italian style. He had sung in various local auditoriums, concert halls and weddings. Apparently, his rendition of 'O Sole Mio', either intoxicated or sober, was his signature song, which always pleased a perhaps uncultured crowd. Like in many Italian households, nothing happened without the full knowledge of the entire clan. Though one particular story was not a popular subject of conversation during those massive lunches, where spaghetti reigned. Uncle Luigi, who was accused of manslaughter, had served a short sentence in an American jail in the late nineteen-sixties. Sarah was his favorite niece among the many girls in the Conti family. He had warned Vincent in the form of innuendos, jokes, when the two lovers started to date; Sarah with a broken heart was never going to happen. Vincent had taken the jest with a happy face, though Sarah was under no illusion. She felt confident that no harm would come to her man; they were both very much in love.

The clamor at Rockefeller Center echoed against and around its skyscrapers. Vincent and Sarah stood above the skating rink, below the traditional gigantic tree that would have been at odds with the surroundings at any other time, however, this was Christmas. They watched the crowd on the ice from the terrace of the adjacent café.

"Don't you just love New York this time of year?" asked Sarah, holding Vincent's arm.

"Yes. You never get tired of this," replied Vincent.

Small snowflakes began to fall, like white ashes from a burning forest beyond the clouds. Sarah looked up, watched the particles of ice coming out of the abyss above, as snow emerged out the darkness. She envisioned the Gods perched on high, emptying their cauldrons, like mischievous creatures. She was happy here, with this man. As recently as last Christmas, she roamed the streets of the city, disengaged. She turned to Vincent. "Do you love me?" she asked, her voice commingled with the music and the happy noises on Rockefeller Center.

He looked at her. His face was colorless. His hands held on to the banister as if scared to let go. "What?" he said, hesitantly, in a barely audible whisper.

"My God, are you alright?" asked Sarah, with great concern in her voice.

Vincent had never told Sarah about his hallucinations. He felt foolish, like a child who has nightmares and is unwilling and shy about sharing his afflictions. There she was again, the woman, transcending the physical laws of the universe, entrenched in his life like an ever-present anguish. Barely a month had gone by since the last encounter in England, by Sargent's grave. She seemed to be superimposed on the ice rink, materialized for that split second again, seemingly so real, before vanishing. He watched her, unable to move, taken by a deep sense of fear, almost evil. Yet, nothing appeared sinister about her. On the contrary, she came forth as mournful.

"Vincent!?" Sarah shook Vincent by the shoulder. "Vincent!"

"I'm sorry. I'm sorry," he said, coming out of his delirium.

"What happened?" she asked, more scared than curious. "I thought you were having a heart attack, or something!"

"I'm fine." Vincent looked deep into her eyes. "I have to tell you something. I need to talk to you." he said, with absolutely no idea how to start the conversation, and with the months elapsed since their meeting, now felt more like a confession.

"What is it?" Sarah asked.

He could see the fear in her face, all the anxiety of a woman about to hear it's all over for them; the break up, long time in the making.

"Are you—"

"What?"

"Everything is good with us, right?" inquired Sarah.

"I'm not breaking up with you, silly!"

"I didn't think that…" she murmured, looking away.

"Of course, you did." He held her in his arms, as to reassure her, but also to get the strength he needed. Sarah was a compassionate woman, what did he dread?

"Well? What's the matter?" she asked again.

"I have this… this problem, well, problem is not the right word," he added, still hesitant. "I see people. A woman. I see a woman. It started when I was about fifteen, or so."

"A woman?" repeated Sarah, fixated on the only relevant word she heard during Vincent's admission.

As Vincent poured his soul out, she appeared again. The same little girl from before stood next to her. She remained by the stairs, as if glazed on the stones, like a projected image from a film reel, detached from reality. She held the child by the hand. Vincent froze, again unable to move, like he was being held, pulled down by an anchor. This time, she stayed for what seemed like minutes, staring at Vincent, who was deaf to Sarah's appeals. Then, as if the chains that held him locked in place had been removed, Vincent walked away, angry. He rushed out of the area, Sarah chasing after him, as if the ground they stood upon was going to crumble beneath their feet.

"Vincent!" she shouted, trying to catch up with him.

He turned around, slowed his pace. She saw the turmoil in his eyes. "Let's get out of here!" he said, scared of what he may see behind Sarah.

"My God, Vincent, you're scaring me," she said, fearful and a little out of breath.

They turned left on Fifth Avenue, and Vincent hurried his steps.

Sarah saw Saint Patrick's Cathedral as the refuge who many venerated; its two spires, victoriously upholding the night sky above, like two protectors, covering the innocents. The doors were opened and Sarah wanted to go inside. "Let's go and sit in there for a while," she told Vincent.

"Why?" he asked. "You know I don't believe in any of that nonsense," Vincent added, not at all ready to put his confidence in something he could not grasp and felt was futile.

Sarah knew that, yet she hoped for a transformation within the man she loved. Her very Catholic family had reservations about their daughter dating someone they saw as skeptical of their faith. "Please," she said, tenderly, reaching for his hand. "I know you're angry... at something. Can we go in? I promise you'll do all the talking. I won't say a word."

Vincent looked behind him. He sensed a presence, like that night at The Savoy in London. "For God's sake, leave me alone!" he cried at the air, the empty space before him, making people walking by, uneasy, including Sarah, who did not know how to react. She stared at the man she loved, embarrassed for his sake, for making a spectacle of himself. She was sure now that something was very wrong with him. She had no idea who he was at this moment, though she knew that he was not the reserved person she met all those months ago. He held the sides of his head, like he was struck by a sudden migraine and stood immobile in the middle of the sidewalk. Sarah stayed near him, concerned like a young mother protecting her child from harming himself.

A few minutes passed. The crowded avenue became a world moving in slow motion, like in a dream. Images, like pictures floating by, took on the designs of a magnificent garden.

Sarah noticed that Vincent's demeanor changed. He calmed down slowly. The snow kept falling, and he brushed off the white powder for his shoulders, and looked at Sarah.

"Hi," he said.

"Hi, yourself," she replied, with a faint smile.

"Are you ok?" he asked, almost confused, like someone walking up from anesthesia.

"I should be asking you that question."

"I saw a garden... I think..."

"A garden?" questioned Sarah, at a complete loss. "What about this woman?" she felt compelled to ask. "Is she in this garden?"

"I don't know. I don't know anything."

Sarah grasped Vincent's arm, and led him towards the street, making their way across Fifth Avenue.

"Are you taking me in there?" he asked, pointing at the cathedral.

"Yes, doctor," she answered simply and with a kindness filled with authority.

"Alright, I'm at your mercy."

They climbed the steps of the famed sanctuary, and walked through the imposing bronze doors. Vincent was going to comment on the sculptures of the saints and other religious figures depicted on its surface, nonetheless, he kept silent. It surprised him. Once inside, the celestial silence became the healer, causing in him a metamorphosis Vincent did not anticipate.

"Here, let's seat down," said Sarah, eager to explore Vincent's spirit.

"It's beautiful in here."

"It is."

"And I can see how one could feel infallible inside these walls," he added.

"Infallible?"

Vincent buried his face in his hands, and leaned backwards. "I'm exhausted," he uttered, like a supplication to a higher entity, whose existence he never contemplated.

Sarah sat, turned towards him, her hand on his knee. She waited for him to be willing to speak out. She beheld the ornate ceiling and followed the length of it, the columns and the stained-glass windows.

"I have hallucinations," he suddenly said, looking at her. "I haven't been honest with you. I should've told you about this a long time ago."

"What do you mean…"

"I mean, I think I'm crazy. Not crazy enough to be put away in some madhouse, not a danger to society, but insane enough. I see people who are not there, for God's sake!" He sighed and reached for the side of Sarah's face with the back of his hand. "I'm sorry."

"Don't be. We need to get to the bottom of this," she continued. I assume you've seen someone about this?"

"Doctor Roberts. A psychiatrist. Though I don't think he has a clue."

"Why?"

"I started seeing him when I was about fifteen. You think he'd have an idea about my case. That's twenty years! And I'm not going to talk about the thousands of dollars he made from this… this lunacy."

"Vincent, you're not crazy. You must know this. You're a very bright and clever man, respected by your peers, who—"

"Who's nuts!"

"Don't." Sarah gently ran her fingers through his hair. "So, you keep seeing the same person... a woman?"

"It stopped when I first met you. In fact, it only started again last month, when I was in London. Do you remember, I told you, when I visited Sargent's grave? The painter I love so much?"

"Yes, I remember you telling me."

"There she was. Only this time she had a child with her, a little girl."

"Where did you see this... this apparition?"

"At the cemetery. I was standing in front of Sargent's grave... and I saw her... them. It only lasted a brief... a few seconds, and they were gone. Vanished."

"It sounds like you saw a ghost." Sarah's face lit up. "My God, you see ghosts!"

"Don't be absurd."

"It's not absurd. It's not absurd at all, trust me."

"What. You're an expert on the paranormal, now?" he smiled.

"It's not a joke. There are many studies about this, many references, photos."

"I'm sorry... I just don't buy it. Photos? You mean the kind that are always taken at night, in some dark alleyway? Don't spirits roam in meadows, on bright sunny days?"

"Evidently, they do. You saw it for yourself. The cemetery?" smirked Sarah.

"I'm sorry, I don't believe in that."

"So, you would rather think you're crazy? That's your explanation," she stated.

Vincent considered the years passed, the sleepless nights. Sarah's logic, though far-fetched, made some sense. A little. What if I did see ghosts? He thought.

"I gave you something to think about, haven't I? A challenge for that great brain of yours," she said, kissing him on the cheek.

"Perhaps."

"The garden... I don't get," Sarah pondered. Why a garden?"

"A garden for the insane," replied Vincent.

"Seriously. What's the meaning behind it?"

"I don't know, but I can tell you Doctor Roberts is minus one patient. I think what you said makes more sense than the last twenty years of his bullshit."

"Shhh, Doctor Jones! I don't believe my ears."

"What? I think you may have a point."

"No! I mean you said 'bullshit'… in a church," she murmured, eyes opened wide.

"Oh, sorry."

"I know it's a first for you."

"Well, now you know I see spirits. That has to be a first!" he grinned.

"As long as the woman is a ghost, I don't mind."

"Oh, my God, you're jealous!"

"No!" she insisted. "A little…"

"A ghost! If that's what it is. Really… you're jealous."

"I'm not, but I'm happy you call her a ghost. Not hallucinations."

Vincent nodded.

"I'm glad we had this talk. It was important for you," Sarah maintained.

"Yes, it was. Thank you. Sorry I scared you, earlier," he whispered to her and kissed her forehead. His eyes wandered about the nave. "I must say it's peaceful here. I don't mind it at all."

Sarah looked pleased. "You see…" she said nudging Vincent's shoulder.

"Yes, it's alright."

They stayed like that for a while, free from the outward world, from all its demons. "Well, shall we go, before they kick us out?" he suggested, noticing the last few people heading towards the exit.

"Yes, we should. But this was very helpful for you. Aren't you glad we came in here? Come on."

"I have to admit…"

"Oh, yes, I see the guilt."

"Yes, guilty, though now… onto greater things," he said. "My Sargent. I'm dying to show it to you."

"Here it is," said Vincent, smiling at Sarah, as they made their way into his sitting room. The painting was till leaning against the column below the mezzanine.

"You don't have anywhere to put it, do you!?" exclaimed Sarah, who after months of dating Vincent, understood him so well. Though she found it difficult to come to terms with the art collector's motto, which is essentially to amass items with complete disregard for space; that is, the where and the how the art work shall be displayed.

"Why speak about irrelevance, triviality?" he answered. "But, no... I have no idea where it's going," he confessed, like a spoiled child, though spoiled, he was not.

"That's what I thought."

"So... do you like it?" he asked, beaming.

"It's beautiful."

"Isn't it?"

"It really is. I love the colors." She approached the painting, and knelt down. "Where is this again?"

"Vizcaya."

FOUR

Vincent booked a flight to Florida for Sarah and himself for a short trip before the new year. Sarah had never been to the Sunshine State, and he wanted to take her to one of his favorite places in the world; Vizcaya. He was well acquainted with the house, once a great private estate, and now a museum. His great-grandfather, Clarence Henry Jones was a guest of James Deering's, on several occasions. He met Sargent while the artist was staying at the house in 1917. According to the anecdotes that were passed on from one generation to the next, Sargent was a most agreeable man, very humble and with impeccable manners. James Deering, the owner of Vizcaya and his brother, Charles, were very close to the artist. Vincent had a deep appreciation and love for the house. He knew more about its history than most experts claimed to know. He did not conceal his joy when Sarah told him that she had never heard of it. He showed her pictures of the house on the internet, the night before their departure and gave a brief account of how it all came to be. He spoke with such passion in his voice, that Sarah fell in love with him all over again.

"You really are amazing," she said, listening to him.

"Hold on," he said, and went to fetch the mahogany box. "Look at this."

"What is it?"

"A treasure. It was my great-grandfather's." He unlocked the combination on the cylinder dial with the letters V.I.Z.C.A.Y.A. and opened the box and showed Sarah the contents of it. The intricate locking system fascinated her. She thought the 7-digit combination was funny. A few black and white photographs, showing Vizcaya in an unfinished state, were in immaculate condition. A watercolor brush was kept in a ziploc bag. Vincent said it belonged to Sargent, probably forgotten there when he left the house. A small ivory comb with a tuft of dark hair, which Vincent handled carefully, caught Sarah's attention.

"Wow, interesting, and how romantic. Who do you suppose it was?" she asked with great inquisitiveness.

"Not sure," he replied. "But it must've meant a lot to him." Vincent held up an Art Deco dragonfly brooch, made of platinum, yellow gold, and pink-colored ruby squares, enamel and turquoise. "Quite beautiful, isn't it?" He meticulously unfolded a piece of paper, with a note written on it – *Meet me in the tea house at 10 tonight. Don't be late!*

"Looks like your great-grandfather was up to no good," grinned Sarah.

"Yes, a little cheeky for the day. Look how fragile the paper is. It looks like it was some kind of wrapping paper," said Vincent. Then he picked up an envelope, addressed to Clarence Henry Jones; a three-cent stamp was pasted on the corner. "This letter is from Sargent to my great-grandfather." He opened it delicately, and read the single page.

THE COPLEY-PLAZA
Boston, Massachusetts
July 6, 1918
Dear Mr. Jones,
I have to apologize for not replying to your kind letter sooner. I have been much engaged with the decorations for the Boston Museum. I do remember my stay at Vizcaya with much delight, and the pleasure of meeting you. Mr. Deering was indeed a charming and most generous host.
Yours sincerely,
John S. Sargent

"His handwriting was really bad," remarked Sarah, who tried to read it herself.

"Yes, indecipherable, really."

"Indeciphe... what?"

"Illegible. You know... hard to read," said Vincent folding the letter, and unaware of the impact of his words.

Sarah lowered her gaze. At age twenty-five, ten years his junior, she felt mundane at times when she was with Vincent. Though she was proud of her studies, her two years of community college seemed insignificant. Vincent was a graduate of the highest sort, and in moments like this, she envied him.

"What's the matter?" he asked, mindful of all a sudden.

"Nothing. I bet that letter is your favorite thing in this box," she added.

"Well… I'm not sure… what about this?" he said, producing the small silver key, like a magician, after unfolding the red felt cloth it was kept in. "I think it's the key to a fabulous treasure," he smiled, and handed it to Sarah.

"What a pretty key!" she exclaimed. "But what does it open?"

"I have absolutely no idea."

"But it's in this box."

"Indeed."

She studied the well-crafted key, imagining there was a chest, or a small trunk somewhere in the world for it. "Hmm… I'd love to know why your great-grandfather saved this. It has to be important, right?"

"One would assume so."

"He didn't leave you a clue, somewhere? A note?"

"Nope. Nothing."

She handed him the key. "And this is all from Vizcaya."

"It is."

Sarah noticed another photograph. "Who are these people?" she asked, pointing at a small group standing by a fountain.

"That's James Deering," replied Vincent. "It's at Vizcaya. I'm not sure who the lady is, but that's my great-grandfather," he said, about the young man next to James Deering.

"My God!" Sarah exclaimed, after taking a closer look. "You're his spitting image! Look! It's like… your double. Can't you see?"

Intrigued, Vincent fetched a magnifying glass and studied the face closely. "I guess. I never saw it before. You're right."

"You could be twins. It's amazing," continued Sarah.

"Funny, I never thought about it. I do look just like him."

A short silence followed. "Do you think I'm boring?" she asked.

"Boring? Why would I think that?"

"It's just… sometimes I feel I'm not really the kind of girl someone like you goes for."

Vincent closed the box. "What on earth do you mean?" he asked. "What are you talking about?"

"You know. I don't know much about anything. I'm not educated like you."

"What?"

"I don't know big words."

"Ha, that's what it is… indecipherable!" he affirmed. "It's just a silly word."

"Yes, but I didn't know what it meant."

"You and probably three quarters of the people on this planet. It's irrelevant."

"Maybe… except I'm the one with you."

Vincent reached for Sarah, and hugged her, like a little girl in need to be reassured for the thousandth time that she is beautiful. "I love you, with or without big words."

"Really?"

"Really." He gave her a peck on the cheek. "Are you packed?"

"All ready."

"We'll pick up your bag on the way to the airport," he said.

Though Sarah's family suspected she spent some nights at Vincent's apartment, they very much disapproved. Sarah was not a married woman. Any relationship before marriage was a sin in the eyes of God. It is how they felt; their conscience, seared by centuries of decrees and man's constant pursuit of the unattainable. Sarah had to lie at times about her whereabouts. Spending the night at the penthouse was a daring thing to do. Hiding the truth from her parents was difficult for her. She resigned herself to the fact that she was caught in a mighty conflict; love versus love. Which of the two held the strongest call? Which of the two could be spelled with a capital 'L'? Is platonic love more powerful than lustful love? Sarah's answer to that question varied depending when the question was asked. Before making love to Vincent, the answer would have been an obvious one. After the physical appetites have been gratified, a little culpability always seemed to sneak in. Sarah had learned to live with it. She was content.

On approach to Miami International Airport, Sarah commented on the beauty of the shores below, the color of the ocean, from her window seat. She had never seen water with such hues, as aquamarine and turquoise. After landing, Vincent and Sarah rented a car. The eighty-degree, sunny weather was a welcome sight after New York, and they drove to The Ritz Carlton Hotel on Key Biscayne, a few miles from Vizcaya.

Their room overlooked the ocean.

"Do you like the room?" asked Vincent, who was used to luxurious accommodations, though he rarely noticed anymore.

"How could I not?" said Sarah, coming out of the shower. She opened the closet. "Look, how beautiful those dressing gowns are. Embroidered, too!" she exclaimed.

"What did you say?" Vincent asked, rather abruptly.

"I was saying how beautif—"

"After."

"Embroidered?"

"Yes. Yes, embroidered."

"So?" inquired Sarah, puzzled.

"I see embroideries on her dress. The woman. Her dress is a dress of a rich woman," Vincent alleged, as he sat on the king size bed.

"Well, are you surprised? You meet rich women every day, in your work, your family."

"No… this is different. She is different."

"How?" Sarah sat on the bed, next to Vincent, wearing one of the robes, her hair wrapped in a towel.

Vincent noticed Sarah's nakedness under the dressing gown. "That's not fair," he claimed.

"Don't you like it?" she whispered sensually, opening the front of the gown, and revealing her olive skin and small breasts.

An answer was futile, and they made love. Sarah to immerse herself at this wonderful juncture, and Vincent to forget.

They both fell asleep.

The next day, after a breakfast at the cabana just off the beach, Vincent and Sarah waited for their car to be brought up by the valet.

"That waiter thought Vizcaya was closed today," said Sarah. She stood in a yellow summer dress, and a very elegant straw hat, with matching blue band and shoes.

"You look lovely," Vincent said, noticing Sarah's attention to details for such a special occasion.

She smiled.

"It is closed."

"What. Are we going to break in?" she giggled.

The car arrived at that moment, and Vincent gave the valet a ten-dollar tip, and they drove off.

"No need for that. We have an appointment with the curator. We want to be alone for this, trust me," he told Sarah.

Sarah, who was getting used to the prosperous life Vincent offered her, was amazed, still. "Oh, ok," she simply said, accepting the situation like a normal act, after the surprising news.

"So… imagine all this," he implied with a wide gesture of his arm, "like it was in 1912. Can you do that?"

"I think so." The excitement in his voice was palpable, and Sarah delighted in it. This was the Vincent she knew and loved, not that bizarre character she encountered at Rockefeller Center that night.

He looked at Sarah. "1912, right? Get rid of everything… buildings, roads, people. Imagine the wilderness, all around you. Not many people think about this, or even realize it, but Miami in those days was just a fishing village, of maybe five hundred people. A fishing village!" he exclaimed. "How amazing is that!?" He described how James Deering, in building Vizcaya, his summer home, gave birth to the city of Miami, eventually bringing millions of people here, from every corner of the world. He spoke of how workers from all over the States, and even abroad, came in search of work. They came by the hundreds, stone carvers, builders, gardeners, and later, maids, laundresses, cooks, and so on. One man's single task was to polish the silver each day, another person wiped down the draperies, and yet another, wound all the clocks and checked them for the correct time. Guest bedrooms were given names, like 'Espagnolette, Lady Hamilton'. The estate was the heartbeat of the region. Vincent shook his head. "Just incredible!"

Sarah listened, dumbstruck.

"So, everything you see, came about because a man decided to build his summer home here… in this jungle, as it was."

"Amazing man," Sarah said. Miami should be called Deeringville, or something."

"Ha!" Vincent was amused. "No, you're right. It should be."

"So, was he a grumpy old man?"

"Perhaps, though not so old. He died at sixty-five. In 1925."

"Woah."

"He never saw what's known as the great Miami hurricane of 1926. It damaged the estate. Destroyed many things."

"That is so sad, I wish you hadn't told me."

34

They drove down South Miami Avenue, and arrived at the destination. The gate was closed, but a man opened it, expecting the private visit. "Thank you," said Vincent as he drove down a small length of the driveway. He parked the car in the shade.

Doctor Harmann made his way toward the car. He extended his hand. "Doctor Jones, it's an honor to meet you. I've heard so much about you."

"And I, about you." They shook hands. "This is Sarah Conti."

"Pleased to meet you," said Doctor Harmann. I believe it's your first visit to Vizcaya?" he asked Sarah.

"Yes, I'm afraid it is."

"Well, you have the ultimate guide here," he said, pointing at Vincent. I'm going to let you in, and I'll leave you alone, I'll be back later. Shall we say... 4:30? That should give you about four hours.

"Very kind of you," replied Vincent.

"It's the least we can do for you. Thank you for your generosity."

"Please, don't mention it," said Vincent.

After showing them to the main door, Doctor Harmann left.

Sarah looked at Vincent. She knew about his philanthropic heart, his generous donations, and she realized that he must be a big donor to the museum he loved so much.

"Well, after you, madam," said Vincent, following Sarah in the house, and to the Entrance Hall.

And it began; the sumptuous, the deluge of spirituality mixed with the bedazzling dreams of another era, and the golden age of The Italian Renaissance. The eerie and complete silence took Sarah by surprise. She reached for Vincent's arm, as if something overwhelmed her. She felt a closeness with the house, like a strange call. They walked through the Reception Room, before entering The Courtyard. There, Sarah felt a pinch to the heart. She looked at the main stairway ascending to the gallery above, on the second floor, which gave access to the bedrooms. She admired the small columns lining the full perimeter of the gallery; a perfection of Italian architecture. A glass roof had to be installed several years ago, to protect the contents of the house, but also to provide a location for various museum events.

"Imagine this space, open to the elements and looking right up into the sky," said Vincent, always in awe in here.

"Just beautiful," Sarah murmured in the stillness the house, as if she was in a sacred place of worship.

They walked back to the entrance loggia with its vaulted ceiling and patterned marble floor, and stopped for a few minutes, glad they were alone, before continuing the tour. Each room, each artifact, spoke of an era long gone, erased by the passage of time.

Sarah had tears in her eyes when they stood outside, on the East Terrace, overlooking Biscayne Bay. The magnificent space was but a mere suggestion of what it once was. They stared with sadness at what had been created as a breakwater; a ship made of stone, known as The Barge, humbled and ruined by too many hostile seasons.

"This is the saddest day of my life," she uttered, her eyes locked onto The Barge, the mermaids at the bow and the stern of the ship.

Vincent's joy was complete. "I love you," he said with all of his heart, smiling.

"You're not funny," she said, weeping. This place is amazing, and I'm so sad... I don't know why."

"I know. She has that effect on those who can grasp her."

"She?"

To Vincent, the house was as a great lady, like the matriarch of a family who no longer cared for her. "Yes, I've always referred to this house as 'she'. You feel it, too." He expected that Sarah's sadness was due to this. There was an air of melancholy about the house. "She was never meant to be reduced to this... a backdrop for cheap reunions," he stressed as he contemplated the harmonious lines of her perfect design and proportions.

They remained there for some time, before going to the Venetian bridge, adjacent to the lattice-domed tea house, on the far end of the sea wall promenade.

"By the way, this is the tea house mentioned on that note," Vincent asserted.

"To your great-grandfather?"

"Yes."

"This is too much. I can't stand it." Sarah had never suspected that such emotions could be endured, and reach such a level of sorrow for a house. She imagined life at Vizcaya in its glory days, the tranquility within its grounds. "Wouldn't you love to go back in time?" she asked, letting her mind go.

"Yes. Where is that time machine, when you need one?" replied Vincent.

"The house is amazing," Sarah said with tremendous affection, and as well as she could convey her thoughts. "She is amazing," she smiled. "Thank you."

"You make me very happy," Vincent told her. "I was hoping you'd feel the way I do about all this. I'm pleased."

The four hours went by much too fast. Vincent and Sarah only had time to do a quick survey of the gardens. Vincent knew their every corner, every fountain and statue, and he wanted Sarah to see how magnificent it all was. "There's always another time," he said and held her hand.

Doctor Harmann waited for them by the entrance, as planned. The day had been a good one.

No words were spoken on the drive back to the hotel. As they beheld Miami skyline, both Vincent and Sarah saw the outside world, the modern one, as an intruder, a thief that destroys without any decency or respect for what is beautiful. Indeed, the day was well spent at Vizcaya.

FIVE

Vincent avoided South Beach, the tourist trap, like the plague. He had no intention of going there, however, Sarah had done her very own research; the ultimate mojito was to be found there, on the famous Ocean Drive.

"Talk about heaven and hell," said Vincent as they strolled down the famed street. The only interest he held in South Beach, and it was not a major one, was its art deco buildings. Though some of them were quite banal, he thought.

"I know you hate it here," said Sarah.

"I wouldn't say that. I dislike it intensely," he answered, not without a certain sense of humor.

"It's not Vizcaya," she replied, as a tall and extremely skinny transvestite, crossed paths with them, walking rather clumsily on high heeled shoes.

"Yes, it's hardly Vizcaya," sighed Vincent.

"Oh, don't be such a snob. This is real life."

"I think you mean… the opposite, don't you? This is not real life," he asserted.

"I'm just teasing you!" Sarah chuckled.

"I thought so."

"No, you didn't. You thought I was serious," she laughed.

"Well, perhaps a little."

They sat down at one of the many restaurants, after being chased down by a young girl, showing off just a little too much cleavage and brandishing a menu. Sarah commented on it, saying that Vincent picked her restaurant for two good reasons.

The oversized mojitos, like fish bowls, were brought to them, with a pizza, which seemed to be the wisest choice for food at this touristic and non-gourmet destination. Loud music was coming from every direction, with various drum beats as the predominant sound. No, this was not Vizcaya, far from it, yet the great estate stood not nine miles away by road. Vincent gazed emptily at all the clamor, befitting for

South Beach, and his mind wandered. He stood on Vizcaya's East Terrace again. The glow from the city lights to the north, was like another dawn from a different time. He lingered there, listening to the lapping of the water on the stone wall; The Barge, etched against the night sky, forever remained.

"You're there again, aren't you?" said Sarah with certainty. "With her, I should say," and smiled.

"Sorry, I'm being very antisocial."

"No, it's fine. I drank half of your mojito… so… I'm good."

"You're drunk!" said Vincent, amused.

"Maybe."

"Oh, my God, you definitely are. These things are lethal," he exclaimed, pulling his half empty glass to him. "You, swindler!"

"I'm having a wonderful time."

The waitress came by. "How you guys doing? Do you need another?"

Sarah looked at her. "Yes, pleas—"

"Most definitely not!" said Vincent. The waitress left. "I love the way she asked if we needed more. Needed. A word for an addict, perhaps," he complained.

Sarah's head rested on the brick wall to her side, asleep.

"Ok, young lady, your carriage is waiting. It's way past your bedtime."

The valet helped with Sarah, who struggled to find some sort of balance, when they arrived at the hotel. Vincent managed to take her up to their room, under the amused faces of the night staff. He undressed her; a difficult task with no help at all from her, though she did give out a soft 'that was so much fun', in her slumber.

Vincent lay down next to Sarah. He turned to his side, and observed her profile, the outline of her nose against the curtains, fading in the dimness of the bedroom. He thought of the Christmas party, which Sotheby's gives every year for its employees. It was Sarah's official entrance into Vincent's world. She was a big success, approved by all. Vincent took her on a private tour of the galleries, where artworks are stored before an auction. The large room was like an antique store, filled with wonderful artifacts, paintings and furniture. A sculpture of a head, by Modigliani, fascinated her. The upcoming sale was in a few weeks, and she asked what it was worth. Three to four million dollars, was the answer, which shocked her. Next to the sculpture, hung a charcoal drawing by Henri Matisse. The work was a typical example of his work; a reclining nude figure, estimated at three hundred thousand dollars. Sarah said she was in the wrong business, which Vincent found very endearing.

Vincent was not sleepy and he began to reflect on the day. He would give anything to roam Vizcaya's rooms at this particular moment, with a midnight walk in the gardens. He would sit on the circular basin of one of the fountains, and gaze at the stars, letting the house take him back to the glamour of her past. Yes, he would give just about anything for that.

SIX

Lunch with Tracy was unavoidable. The texts kept coming after the day at the auction, and once back from Florida, Vincent had no alternative and he gave in.

The two met in their last year of college, and the highly intelligent, James, was preparing for his masters, and had full intentions of pursuing his dream of becoming what Vincent is now; a doctor in history. Unfortunately, life had other obstacles for him, the kind that dismantles aspirations, and keeps you tied in a corner. His mother divorced her husband after he abandoned the family, with three young children, and moved in with a young man, some ten years his junior, somewhere in California. Tracy was a bit of an enigma to Vincent, yet he understood the motives behind such a radical action, and the deep resentment he held toward his father.

The transformations that took place, both physical and spiritual, gave Tracy the weapons necessary to face the world, at least the way it was perceived. A self esteem came by at a high price, and Vincent knew that the soul behind the mask would never entirely reveal itself. That, had been a lost cause a long time ago.

They sat at a small French café on Park Avenue, and both ordered a quiche, and a glass of Cabernet.

"Sorry this has to be such a late lunch," said Vincent. "I was at Sotheby's until one o'clock."

"Is this for me?" asked Tracy, eyeing the small and beautifully wrapped gift, next to Vincent's plate.

"No," he answered. "Don't be absurd. It's a Christmas present for Sarah."

"Do I hear wedding bells?"

"Not quite. It's a watch."

"Too bad, I was getting all excited. So... tell me, where did you put that fabulous painting?" asked Tracy. "I'm so jealous."

"So far... it's sitting against a wall."

"How's Sarah?" Tracy asked, totally nonchalant about Vincent's answer. "Tell me all."

"All!? Well… she's doing fine…"

"No, no, no, I mean, what kind of a woman is she? How is she in bed?"

The question embarrassed Vincent, who never shared such particulars with anyone. His private life was not an open book, and his sex life was definitely off limits.

"Jam… Tracy," he floundered, "What a question!" Vincent said, not really shocked by anything coming from the wounded life opposite him.

"Oh, don't be such a prude! You forget we were in college together."

"That's hardly the same," replied Vincent. "Anyway, if you must know, Sarah and I are very good together."

Tracy rolled her eyes. "Fine. But you're being very dull."

"How's your mother?" inquired Vincent, changing the topic.

"Dating."

"That's good, no?"

"I guess. Some guy from Texas… I think he owns cows."

"One would, coming from Texas," smiled Vincent.

The playful retort fell on deaf ears. "I haven't seen my mother happy in so long…"

"I'm sorry. Well, maybe this is the right time for her," said Vincent, genuinely touched by the whole affair, and very mindful of the different destinies between the two of them.

Tracy's demeanor changed, impulsively, as it often did, and with it a drastic change of subject. "By the way, do you know about the secret passageways of Vizcaya?" she asked, enthusiastically. "I read this article. Yes, I'm not impervious to history… anyway, the article mentioned secret tunnels… passageways."

"I'm thrilled you're showing the things you loved, an interest again. I really am. Yes, I know about the passageways. They were kept secret to visitors, during James Deering's life. Only the people who run the estate were made aware. Why are you asking?"

"I don't know," said Tracy, as she moved the chair sideways, and sat crossed legs, showing a split skirt.

Vincent noticed that some customers had been staring. Tracy was six feet two, and all the artificial femininities were still at odds with the natural ones.

"I know you're an expert on Vizcaya, and I just wondered how much you knew about it," continued Tracy. "I wish... I just wish I had gone on... like you." The admission was made with such sadness, that Vincent felt led to reach for his friend's hand. Not at all a natural gesture for him, but he followed his heart.

"You still can, you know. You're only thirty-five years old. If you applied yourself, you could do it in six or seven years."

"You're sweet, but—"

"I'd pay for the whole thing... if I have your guarantee that you'd work hard," affirmed Vincent, as he let go of Tracy's hand.

"Can I give you an answer later?"

"Of course."

"Vizcaya, Vizcaya," said Tracy. "It's like murmuring a poem, isn't it? Oh, how I would've loved to have been there. Imagine all those wonderful guests. And the dresses! Ha, the dresses... divine."

"Yes, I can see you'd feel very comfortable there."

"You mean, gorgeous!"

"I didn't want to say."

Tracy finished the wine. A trace of lipstick stained the brim of the wineglass. Vincent noticed it.

"Seriously, what would you give to be there? To return to Vizcaya."

"Like it was, then?" asked Vincent, whose eyes suddenly lit up, with the thought of seeing her, the house, in full and complete splendor.

"Yes. Like it was. No one to worry about, no guilt. Just a party."

Vincent realized the cry for help. He heard the screaming in Tracy's voice, though the solution visualized here, and dreamt off, was only science fiction. "I would give everything I own to have one day there," he said dreamily, and happy to partake in the fantasy.

"Everything? You say that, because of the impossibility of it coming true."

"No, I can honestly say, if could be beamed there... in 1915, or 16, and the price was everything I have, I would give it all up. Actually, it would have to be 1917... when Sargent was there."

"My, oh my, that's something. Now, you're talking. Sargent. What a day that would be." Tracy looked at Vincent. "You obviously care about this house a lot more than I thought."

"I can't explain it. I have a PhD, and I can't put a simple sentence together to say what this house means to me. Isn't that crazy?"

"Wonderfully."

Speculations about being a guest of James Deering, and everything that it implied, began to form in Vincent's head. What would he say, what would he be wearing? How would he explain his presence? "Anyway... there it is. None of it matters. It's all out of reach... James Deering... Sargent," said Vincent, who allowed himself a small window of pleasure into the past, during this lunch.

Time is a gruesome adversary that brings about decay, and the bones of men who stamped a formidable mark on history. Vincent thought of Sargent. There can never be a return to Vizcaya, like it was discussed so readily during lunch. Dreams were the only mode of access into the realms of time.

"Nothing is impossible to him who believes," said Tracy. I think I've heard it... somewhere."

"That sounds like the Bible," replied Vincent, who never ceased to be amazed by an unpredictable Tracy.

"Oh, yes, that's right, the Bible," she recalled.

"The Bible? Since when—"

"My mother used to read it to us when we were kids," claimed Tracy, in a cynical tone of voice.

"Ha. Well... 'nothing is impossible', is an absurdity, told to boost the morale of those who are weak," replied Vincent, at a total loss.

"You told me earlier that it wasn't too late for me. You said I could go back to my studies..."

"Yes... yes, I'm sorry, you're right, I don't know what came over me."

"That's better. But I'm just fooling with you. You're absolutely right, it should be 'nothing in this damn world is possible'. That, my friend, would be the correct dictum."

They left the restaurant, having stayed much longer than anticipated, wished each other a happy new year, and said goodbye. Vincent watched Tracy go, as the tall figure melted into the early evening crowd of Park Avenue. He was happy they had lunch together. Though some of the conversation amused Vincent, who was not impassive or adverse to a make-believe world, especially a world that allowed Vizcaya's reawakening. However impossible it may be, being a castaway in the illusion of it all, pleased him enormously.

Vincent walked. Night was falling already. Gusts of wind funneled through the buildings, like invisible torrents, and clouds of pewter raced above the city skyline. Someone touched Vincent on the shoulder, and he turned around, expecting to see an acquaintance. There was no one there, and he became afraid. In all the years, this was a first; making actual contact. Or was it all in his head? He hurried his steps, convinced that another hallucination was about to take place. Now, people were staring at him, he knew it. Each face going by, saw the dread in his eyes. Maybe they understood and were witnesses, silenced by this force who crippled him. The Christmas lights only underscored his anguish. He wanted to disappear into a dark hole, hide. A business, closed for renovations, gave him shelter under the scaffoldings by the front window. Vincent stopped there, and hid in the shadow, like a thief. A homeless man, who had claimed that spot weeks before, told Vincent to go. Vincent looked at him, almost envious of his situation.

"This is my place," said the homeless man.

"What? No. I just… I need a minute," replied Vincent, in a daze.

"Let's have a dollar, hey?"

Vincent took his wallet out of his pocket, and gave the man a twenty-dollar bill. "Here. Now leave me alone."

The man noticed Vincent's restlessness. "Cops after you?" he asked, with a smile that showed several teeth missing, and the ones he had managed to keep, stained grey.

"Hardly!" shot Vincent.

"What then? Your wife?" he laughed and coughed.

"None of your business." He looked at the individual in front of him, wrapped up in layers of jackets, scarfs, on this winter evening. The man sat under the carboard he had collected, to make it his lodging. That was his harbor, thought Vincent. He bent down, and saw the figure lying down, ready for another night. "I'm sorry," said Vincent, to the man who had his back turned to him, clamp down for the night.

"I see... ghosts, I guess. At least that's what my girlfriend thinks. More like hallucinations."

The man turned around. "I see ghosts all the time," he said.

"You do?"

"Yes." He pointed at the air behind Vincent. "She's pretty."

Vincent took a quick glance behind him, and fell backwards, almost inside the cardboard cave. "What!?" he exclaimed. "Who's pretty? You see her? She's here?"

The man looked around, rattled, it seemed. "She's gone."

Vincent stood up, brushed off his pants, convinced he had been victim of a prank. "You didn't see anything, did you?" he said, irritated.

The man crawled back into his dwellings, without a word.

Vincent began to walk again, though he looked for a taxi, however, not so easy at five o'clock in the afternoon. He did say 'she', Vincent reflected on the homeless man's words. Why would he say 'She'? Fifty, fifty, I guess. He could've easily said 'he', Vincent continued, quietly torturing his soul. A text from Sarah interrupted his speculations. She wanted to know where he was. Where I am, where I am, Vincent thought to himself, meditating on the words. Not altogether here, was his own answer. He looked behind him at times, really starting to be concerned about his soundness of mind, during those moments of lucidity. He stopped, all of a sudden, like the strength in his legs, abandoned him. Oh, my God, this is it. The obvious came to him, slowly. He signaled a taxi, feeling relieved that his hypothesis made all the sense in the world.

SEVEN

"I see her, the… the woman… ghost, every time I think of Vizcaya," Vincent told Sarah as soon as he entered the apartment, like a statement of the outmost importance, a revelation. "It's like the two go hand in hand… her and the house. Strange."

"What do you mean?" asked Sarah, who had been waiting for Vincent. Are you saying the two are connected?"

"Yes. They must be, right? I'm not crazy, it makes sense. Think about it. In England… by Sargent's grave… what was I doing? Thinking of Vizcaya. With you, when we were at Rockefeller Center… Vizcaya. And now that I think of it, as far back as I can remember, it's always the same. It's the house. That idiot, Doctor Roberts… what a moron." Much agitated, Vincent poured himself a glass of wine from the bottle Sarah opened. "Now all I have to do, is not think about it.

"About the house?"

"Yes. Try to forget it. Never think of it."

"Good luck with that," Sarah murmured to herself.

"It's just a house, right?" questioned Vincent, not at all sure if he could answer that truthfully. "I mean, there are other houses, estates, just as beautiful. Why can't I think about those?"

"I hope you can. I really do. It just… in the many months I've known you, I don't think a day goes by that you don't talk about that house."

"Really? I always talk about it?" whined Vincent, feeling like the boring guest at a party who will not stop talking about his favorite hobby, like collecting stamps.

"You could talk about other houses," said Sarah, trying her best to be logical in a therapeutic way.

"I could," he said, building up his own wall, on which to stand and defend his own life.

"What is it about Vizcaya, and you, anyway?" said Sarah. "It's a gorgeous place, yes, and I felt very emotional there… come to think of it. Hmm… I'm not sure why," continued Sarah, somewhat confused at her own remark.

"If you put a gun to my head, I couldn't tell you why I'm this way with the house. I've had this fascination, since I was… I can't even remember."

"You can't put it into words." Sarah sipped her wine, listening to Vincent, who she thought, was basically telling her he was in love with a house. Nothing to be concerned about. "Maybe you should get rid of everything you have that reminds you of it," she said, unaffected.

"And do what? Throw it away?" he contended with ardor, at the ludicrous words.

"Sorry, I didn't mean that… of course you can't. I don't know why I said that."

Vincent's eyes fell on the Sargent, still leaning on the same spot as it was the night of the auction. He fetched the mahogany box, filled with remnants of another era, memories that no longer mattered to anyone. The collector is a lonely creature, who gathers treasures that quickly become relics. The riches turned vestige, just two generations removed. "What about this?" he asked, opening the box.

"I like the brooch," Sarah smiled.

Vincent stared at the comb, the tuft of hair, entangled in it. His eyes widened.

Sarah picked up on it. "What?" she asked.

"You don't suppose… no, that's crazy," he said, answering his own question. He threw the box on the couch. "I'm a man of science, a PhD for God's sake, I don't believe in the boogeyman!"

Sarah was more curious now than ever. "You thought of something, didn't you?"

"It's nothing. Crazy."

She put her glass of wine on the side table. "Are you sure?" she asked, "because I think we're thinking the same thing."

"What's that?" inquired Vincent, who still could not fathom a world beyond this world.

"I think you know. I can just sense it. You know who that comb belonged to. You know that's her hair. That woman."

"But you see how insane it sounds?" he argued. "And, what… now she's haunting me!?"

Sarah nodded. "Yes," she whispered, eyes wide open.

"Don't be ridiculous."

"Ok, then, explain what you see. This hallucination, like you call it. You told me it's a woman… dressed like in the 1900's, right?"

"And your point is?"

"Can't you see the connection?"

Vincent, who had been pacing the room, sat down next to Sarah. "Ghosts? Come on."

"Yes… and it's beginning to make sense in that head of yours. You're being haunted, followed by a ghost from Vizcaya. Your dreamhouse. All these years. You should be happy," exclaimed Sarah, as if it was matter of fact, while finishing her wine.

"Happy!?"

"Are you kidding? Yes, happy. I would love to be haunted by a gorgeous man from some beautiful and mysterious castle," said Sarah.

"How do you know she's gorgeous," asked Vincent, allowing a bit of humor to flow out of his depleted spirit.

"Well, she has to be, right?"

Vincent realized that the effect of the wine was now dictating just about every word coming out of Sarah's mouth. He leaned back on the sofa, and thought about the strange visitor, the woman, perhaps the figment of his own conception, who had been part of his life for the last twenty years. The logic was slowly replacing the fantastic. Her image now seemed less threatening, and he regarded her as a curiosity, a companion of a peculiar kind. Sarah was asleep. "Light weight," he whispered to her ear and smiled. He closed his eyes, too. This time, he wanted to invite those images, which had caused him great despair in his dreams. He lay down on his side, thinking in the abstract, of forms that cannot be apprehended or understood. He stayed like that, wishing for sleep, willing the ethereal visitor, if that is what she was, to appear.

Sarah had moved to the bedroom, when Vincent woke up. He had a vivid dream, like a memory of the woman, right here, standing in the room. He even got up and walked towards her, unafraid of her forms. He rubbed his eyes, and looked at his phone; it was three in the morning. He got up, knowing it had all been a dream, of course, and saw the little key, lying on the red velvet. Vincent picked it up, and immediately dropped it, as if it burned him, though not from heat, it was from cold. The key felt like it had been left in a freezer. He sat down again, as images from the last hours rushed through his head. The key had not been part of the dream. He knew that much. He looked in vain around the empty room, searching for traces of her presence. She was here, perhaps not at this moment, but she had been here, he knew it. He remembered. She asked him for the key, not verbally, just pointing at the box, and he handed it to her. When she reached for it, he felt her hand. He was certain of it. Did he imagine it, or did he detect an air of sadness about her? She seemed that way, that day by Sargent's grave.

Vincent made his way to the bedroom. Sarah was lying on her stomach, fully dressed.

"Sarah? Sarah?" he breathed in her ear.

She slowly came to, and wondered why she was on top of the covers and dressed. "What is it?" she mumbled.

"She was here. She spoke to me... well, she didn't speak, really, she... she communicated with me. She asked for the key."

Sarah sat up suddenly, like some invisible strings pulled her up. "You saw her."

"I'm telling you, I did."

"And you didn't freak out."

"No."

"That's amazing!" Sarah hugged Vincent. "You know what this means, don't you?" she continued.

"I'm not following..."

"You believe in ghosts. Doctor Jones, PhD, and God knows what else, believes in the afterlife."

"Well... I wouldn—"

Sarah stopped him with her hand on his mouth. "Allow me this one," she said. This is a great teaching moment for me... I never teach you anything."

Vincent sighed. "Fine. I confess, you were right. Ghosts do exist... as irrational as that sounds."

"So... tell me, what happened?"

"You were unconscious..."

"Ok, unconscious... got that," Sarah rolled her eyes. "Then, what?"

"I tried to go to sleep. I wanted to go to sleep. You know the last time that happened?" Vincent looked up at the heavens. "Years."

Sarah looked at the man she loved, maybe against some odds. Some members of her family were not thrilled with her choice. People found him a little emphatic with a certain society. He was not a snob, but he projected the impression of one. He was highly intelligent, and highly educated, yet he was self-effacing in front of a young child. "You need to make contact with her," said Sarah, totally out of the blue.

"You see... you say things like that, and I don't know if you're serious or making fun of me," replied Vincent, who laid down next to Sarah.

"Hundred per cent, serious!" said Sarah, "That's a no-brainer."

"And how am I supposed to do that?"

"You'll figure it out, Doctor. Now can we go to sleep?"

"Go ahead. I can't go to sleep. My head is about to explode."

Vincent turned the lights off. He stared at the ceiling, like he had done thousands of time, unable and scared to fall asleep. He listened for a sound, any sound in the four o'clock in the morning silence, when he felt compelled to look toward the foot of the bed. Here she stood, in the semi-darkness. "Sarah," he whispered, as if the apparition would vanish at the slightest noise.

"I see her," Sarah whispered back. "Oh, my God, I really see her."

"What do I do?" asked Vincent.

"Speak to her."

"What?"

Sarah gently nudged him, "Go on."

The figure appeared as a translucent form, yet, one could discern her likeness, in this prolonged visitation. She possessed an exquisite beauty that mesmerized Vincent. He felt drawn to her, swept in a whirlwind before a mirage. All sense of time was lost. Her eyes were locked onto his eyes. The room became as a tunnel, with the only focus, the only objective, being her. She extended her hand, and he reached for it. There was no fear, no questions about the hereafter, the dreams of long ago.

"Vincent! Vincent!" shouted Sarah, trying to get him out of his daze.

Vincent fell backwards on the floor, bringing him out of his bewilderment.

"My God, you scared me to death!" cried Sarah. "What the hell..."

After a few seconds, Vincent was able to speak. "Did you see that!?"

"Yes, no shit, I saw that! You got up and walked to her... and she vanished... and you went nuts."

"Did you see that?" Vincent asked again, mystified by what just took place. I grabbed her hand... and... wait a minute. Did I dream this?" he asked Sarah. "Did I?"

"No! I tell you, I saw her, too."

"No, I mean, did you see me take her hand?"

"Yes. You got up and walked to her."

"It's impossible." Vincent wrestled with his mind, the visions spewing out of it. "Impossible."

Sarah shook her head. "You had an... an encounter with a ghost. That's amazing! Amazing," she repeated. "So weird."

"I was in the courtyard at Vizcaya, not five minutes ago! That, is weird."

"Whoa, whoa, sit down. Time out," said Sarah, wide-eyed with astonishment. "What?"

"I was there. I'm telling you," said Vincent. "I would have never believed it possible... unless I'm really going crazy. It was like going back in time. Like a dream..."

"That's what you saw?"

"I think I was at the house. I think I was at Vizcaya."

They both looked at each other, trying to digest what transpired; Sarah the excited one, and Vincent, the skeptic.

A couple of days went by, with little said on what had happened that night at the apartment.

EIGHT

"How rich are you?" asked Sarah, casually, as they entered Vincent's building after a dinner party Vincent had to attend.

Vincent wished Grant, the doorman, a good night and a happy new year, and pressed the button of the elevator, to his penthouse. "You know I don't like to talk about that," he replied quietly.

"Well, if I'm going to be Mrs. Jones, you'll have to tell me sooner or later," smiled Sarah, with her hand on her lower stomach.

"Are you?" he asked, looking at her, intensely. "I did notice you only drank fruit juices. I thought that was a bit odd."

She nodded.

They entered the apartment. "We need to celebrate. I'm going to be a father… a dad… amazing."

"Well… before we celebrate, we need to break the news to my parents."

"Damn. Yes, yes, of course."

"My father is going to kill me…"

"And your uncle, kill me. We're both dead."

They both sat down at the dinner table, feeling like badly behaved children.

"I'm serious. How are we going to tell them?" Sarah asked.

"We need a plan…"

"Like… what?" she continued.

"Like… I have no idea."

"Gran Dio, sono morto!" announced Sarah, appropriately in Italian, and with the drama from a leading lady, in the middle of the third act of an opera.

"In English, please," said Vincent.

"I'm dead, I'm dead" she repeated, as if her days had come to an end, and her new baby cast out like a common vandal.

He reached for her hand. "We're going to be parents," he said, softly. "You have nothing to worry about. I'll talk to your father." The look in Vincent's eyes, conveyed a sweet message, one of love and forgiveness. This new life was going to give him a purpose. He would be the great father, so wished for by every child. Sarah, he knew, would be a wonderful mother. He had a little hint of her maternal instincts, during some of his 'episodes'.

Vincent opened the drawer, and placed Sarah's present on the table. "Merry Christmas. Sorry I don't have a tree."

Sarah smiled a smile of total happiness.

Vincent suddenly realized the huge mistake he had made, in choosing such a small box; a square box at that! No! his mind screamed, what have I done? "It's not... it's a... It's just a watch," he quickly said to extinguish the flames of passion, before the point of no return.

Sarah opened the present. "Thank you," she said, putting on the gold watch on her wrist.

"You're not disappointed?"

"Why should I be? No. I love it."

Vincent heard the hushed anticlimax in Sarah's voice.

"Your present is on its way. I had to order it on Amazon," she declared, not willing to say anymore.

"Thank you. So... you like the watch," inquired Vincent.

"I do. Cartier?"

"It is a Cartier. The best," he said.

"Are these...?"

"Diamonds. Yes."

"So... how rich are you?" Sarah asked Vincent again, her head resting on the table.

"You look like Ann Boleyn at the chopping block," he smiled.

"And my dad holds the axe!" She said, looking at Vincent. "It's ok if you don't want to talk about money. I shouldn't ask anyway. We're not married, yet."

"I have money," said Vincent, obviously uncomfortable talking about his wealth.

"Will I go on working?"

"Ha! That's up to you."

"Well, you're working, right?" she asserted.

Their conversation was interrupted by a noise, coming from the mezzanine, the bedrooms above.

"Did you hear that?" asked Vincent, looking toward to source of the noise.

"I did."

"She's here, again," Vincent uttered, ready for yet more strife.

Vincent's mother appeared on the top landing at that moment.

"Mother!" Vincent exclaimed, utterly surprised. What are you doing, here? Did Grant let you in?"

"Yes, he did." she said coming down the steps in her silk dressing gown, Greta Garbo style, straight out of a 1940's film.

"She likes to make an entrance," Vincent whispered to Sarah, who had never met the now future mother-in-law.

Sarah stared at the distinguished figure.

"I'm only staying the night. Well, aren't you going to introduce me to this pretty girl?" asked Mrs. Jones.

"Yes, yes, of course. Mother, this is Sarah."

"How are you, Mrs. Jones," inquired Sarah, extending her hand, not quite sure about the 'protocol' of the American upper class on the first meeting, which can feel more like an audition.

"You are a cute little thing," Mrs. Jones replied, and gave Sarah a peck on the cheek. She hugged her son, and sat down on the largest couch by the fireplace.

"You call your mom, mother?" murmured Sarah from the corner of her mouth.

Vincent looked at her, surprised and confused at the question, "yes… always have." He sat next to his mother and Sarah sat in the adjacent armchair, quiet as a mouse.

"When did you arrive? I'm very upset that you didn't tell me you were coming. I would've met you at the airport," said Vincent.

"I'm very capable."

"And Miss Brown? Where is she? Is she in town, too?" asked Vincent.

"I was worried about you," said Mrs. Jones. "I haven't heard from you since you called me from London. Did you go see Doctor Roberts?"

"No, I had—"

"What is your name again, sweetie?" Mrs. Jones asked Sarah.

Sarah sat up straight, as if her posture meant a great deal to the woman in front of her. A woman she had never met, who terrified her.

Vincent had mentioned that his mother was diagnosed with the first symptoms of Alzheimer. Sarah could see first-hand, the ravaging effects of the disease.

"Sarah," she answered. "My name is Sarah."

"Mother, where is Miss Brown?" Vincent asked again, worried.

"Miss Brown? I'm not... well, where is she?"

Vincent looked at Sarah, as they both witnessed the cruel certainty of what lay ahead, ready to ambush. They waited for the crisis to pass. It sometimes took minutes, other times hours, to subside.

"She's staying with a friend," she suddenly said. "Don't worry, she's here with me," she continued, lucid again.

Vincent was reassured. "It's late, shouldn't you be going to bed. You must be tired. We are," pleaded Vincent.

"Yes... I guess..." she replied, vacantly.

Mrs. Jones grew up in the 1950's; the age of Christian Dior, Coco Chanel, Marilyn Monroe and Marlon Brando. Her father, James Walker, worked for the government, more precisely for the Internal Revenue Service; the three most dreaded words in the English language. His young daughter, Patricia, was told never to breathe a word at school about her father's occupation. For years, she thought he was some kind of a gangster, but because he always wore a suit, she made him to be the head of a fabulous criminal organization. By her early twenties, and of course, well aware of her father's job, she was about to meet a very neatly dressed, young man, one day during her lunch break from a summer job at the National Gallery of Art. Patricia walked into her father's office, and there he was, elegant, tall and fairly handsome; William Jones. It was love, unpredictable and contrary, yet love all the same for her.

Vincent's mother was lucid again, and he smiled at her.

"Sarah, please call me Patricia," she said.

"Can I get you a drink?" asked Sarah, now feeling a little more comfortable.

Vincent looked at Sarah, and gave her a 'no, no' gesture with the hand.

"She obviously doesn't want to go to bed," said Sarah.

"I do not," replied Patricia.

"Very well," Vincent ceded, and lay down, taking the full length of a smaller couch.

Sarah returned from the kitchen with two glasses, one with white wine, the other with apple juice, a good substitute, color wise, with chardonnay. "You like wine, right?" she asked, Patricia.

"Of course."

Vincent was already asleep.

"Way past his bedtime," laughed Sarah. "Cheers."

"Cheers. It that the watercolor he bought? The Sargent?" asked Patricia, after she noticed the painting against the column.

"Yes. His new baby," said Sarah, smiling inwardly, sipping on the apple juice, and taking the 'alcohol-free pregnancy' to a whole new level.

"He's always had this fascination with that house, what is it called again… some odd Spanish name…"

"Vizcaya," answered Sarah.

"Yes. I don't know what it is about that place. Some strange legend, or something."

"It's beautiful. I think it's Vincent's special spot."

"It is." Patricia looked around the vast room, the oversized windows. "I don't think he's ever had a Christmas tree in here," she sighed. "Tell me, how long have you known my son?"

"Almost a year."

"Have you seen him having these… hallucinations? I guess that's what they're called."

"I have." Sarah was hesitant about mentioning what Vincent called them now; visits from the grave. It did sound a little weird, perhaps idiotic to some. "He's had a few bad days," Sarah simply said.

"His father had the same problem."

"What!?" Sarah exclaimed, astonished by the unexpected answer. "You mean… Vincent's dad saw her, too?"

"Saw, who?" inquired a bewildered Patricia.

"I meant, did he have them, too… the hallucinations?"

"He most certainly did. I thought he was going mad. He thought he was being followed by a woman, a ghost, as he called it. Imagine that?"

"Yes, imagine that," Sarah repeated the words, looking at Vincent, totally unaware and fast asleep.

"It only lasted a couple of years… maybe more… I'm not positive," mumbled Patricia.

They spoke for more than an hour. Sarah enjoyed the time with her future mother-in-law, though she had no idea about her unborn grand-child. She liked her colorful spirit, and felt a deep sense of sorrow, at the idea that none of this would matter, or would be remembered.

Vincent was snoring on the couch when both women went to bed. They laughed.

Do I have news for you in the morning! Thought Sarah, looking at Vincent.

Depending on the day, the term 'hallucinations', which can imply an unstable state of mind, was ignored, and the word 'ghost', assumed the more sensible alternative. It did however, change constantly. Vincent felt the full force of his encounters. People were open to the ghost stories, finding them amusing in a creepy sort of way. Hallucinations were frowned upon, and audiences were allergic to such horrific curses. Vincent, who hid his 'condition' from everyone, was thrilled about the ghost's fables taking center stage. He still doubted the existence of such manifestations, yet, he could not explain them. He knew that most people considered stories from beyond the grave, as foolish, and more like fairy tales, entertaining anecdotes at cocktail parties. Some people give credence to the fact that there are other forms of intelligence in our universe. Why is it so hard to accept the presence of other forms, spirits from an afterlife? To him, it was like being removed from reality. It was unreal, yet it felt genuine. It was laughable, yet he showed no smile. Time moves onward, like a train, and Vincent sat by the window, confounded at the world going by.

"Good morning," said Vincent, in front of his laptop. He sat at the enormous island in his kitchen.

"Is your mother up?" asked Sarah, as she walked in.

"No, not yet."

"I had a nice time with her… after you went unconscious."

"Sorry about that."

"She's very sweet."

Vincent was preoccupied with the internet. "I have to be in Cairo in a couple of weeks," said Vincent, scrolling through his emails.

"Your father saw the same woman you keep seeing. Same apparitions," Sarah said, waiting for Vincent's reaction.

"Mm-hmm," interjected Vincent, his eyes fixed on his computer screen.

"And she looks like your mother, but she's bold... eight feet tall, and missing one arm."

"What?"

"You didn't hear a word I said, did you?"

"I did. You said somebody is missing an arm."

Sarah punched him on the shoulder. "You're unbearable!"

"Ouch! I heard you. I know all about it. My father told me about his 'visions'. I thought it was due to his drinking." Vincent's confession took Sarah by surprise.

"Your dad was an alcoholic?"

Vincent closed his laptop. "Maybe not officially. I don't know... he consumed a large amount of alcohol. I wasn't very close to him. I've never been close to my mother, either. We're not like your family. Far from it. You're lucky."

Sarah gave Vincent a tender hug. "We'll bring up this child, Italian style," said Sarah, in a most positive tone.

"What child," inquired Patricia, joining the impromptu conversation, in that same dressing gown.

"We might as well tell her," shrugged Vincent. "Sarah is pregnant, mother."

"Pregnant? How wonderful." Patricia turned to Sarah. "Are you pregnant?"

"Yes. Yes, I am."

"I was pregnant, too. A long time ago. But... I'm not sure... um... Vincent is younger."

"Sit down, mother. I'll make you a cup of coffee."

"Yes... a cup of coffee would be nice," Patricia smiled with an empty glare, as if life had been scooped out of her.

A sad glance passed between Vincent and Sarah. Cheerlessness weighed heavy in the room, and all exultance from the miracle of a new life, was smothered.

NINE

New Year's Eve was spent reading. What could be more engaging? In previous years, when bothered, Vincent watched the countdown to the new year, the ruckus of the city below, on his television, or from the roof of his building. He was not fond of noises or crowds, and Times Square was most definitely out of the question. Vincent longed for peace. His bruised spirit needed to hide in a safe place, and he rejected the world and all of its celebrations.

Sarah had left in the morning to spend a few days with her parents in Seattle. No plans had been made as of yet, to inform them about the upcoming addition to the Jones and Conti families. The news would have to wait a little longer.

Vincent curled up in his armchair, reading *Making the Mummies Dance*; Thomas Hoving's memoir. Thomas Hoving, the former director of the Metropolitan Museum of Art, had met Vincent several times, and had given him invaluable tips. The book was very well written and full of amusing accounts. It told the story of a man who took on the huge challenges of running a world class museum, and at the same time, tried to please wealthy, demanding, and often clueless donors. Vincent had read the book before, however, he relished the idea of a second read.

The wind howled and he sank lower into the armchair. Bursts of lights, like multicolored blossoms, smeared the night at regular intervals, as fireworks displays began. He entertained little meditations about the crowds awaiting the last vanishing seconds that separate a year from another, in frigid temperatures. He glanced casually at the antique clock sitting on the mantle; five minutes after midnight. He took a sip of his special Remy Martin Cognac and wished himself a happy new year, in the quietness of the room. An amusing passage in the book made him laugh. Without warning, and as if someone had turned off the lights, the room plunged into darkness. Vincent closed his book. Except for the dim flashes of colors from the distant fireworks, the penthouse was in total darkness. "I know, you're here," he said softly, his back turned to the main space of the room. "I'm not scared of you." A cold sensation ran throughout his entire body, apprehensive of the next seconds. He sat there, unable to move and in fear of what he might see, if he turned around. He reached for the light switch on the lamp by the side table, and felt a touch to his wrist. He closed his eyes, as if to separate himself from an affliction that plagued the last twenty years of his life. He knew when his eyes were opened again that she would stand in front of him. He could sense it. He could sense her. Vincent was not thinking about Vizcaya when the penthouse plunged into darkness. All previous reasoning on what brought on those apparitions, were null and void. He had argued the contrary, though evidently, he was wrong. He was cursed, that's what it was, he thought, and he opened his eyes, indifferent of the outcome.

The manifestation of a figure, enveloped by a white incandescence, floated motionless, a foot above the marble floor, right in front of him. Vincent was silent, like the lesser being, a slave waiting for his fearsome master's voice. He watched her, the woman, the same one as before. This time she seemed to have almost materialized, in the flesh, yet reaching for her was unthinkable. The room opened up and a black cloud formed as a pillar, moving upwards, arching the full circle of the sky. Vincent was hurled forward, through the moving walls of his penthouse, as images of forgotten dreams held him captive. It was the house. The house spoke. Vincent absorbed its pain, her pain. Vizcaya breathed, she breathed a long sigh of despair, as the impenetrable essence of her was about to bring forth life again.

The walls had not been pulverized, the penthouse was intact. A single light shone in the far corner of the room. Vincent tried to get up, staggering like the mere mortal that he was. The antique clock stopped his eyes from meandering. He managed to get to the window. Fireworks displays splattered the night sky to the south, and on the horizon. He looked around the room, as if to reconcile fiction with reality. No time had elapsed. It was 12:06, January first. He recalled the room at The Savoy, and his dilemma, accepting what is unacceptable to a sound mind. This was the second time he faced such a deep state of trance. A text from Sarah, wishing him a happy new year, was his only foothold. He walked to the guest bathroom, and stood in front of the mirror. He stared at his face, questioning his very own existence, searching for some kind of logic, a scientific truth that would awake him from this ordeal. Nothing made sense. Nothing came to him, not even a hint of comfort. I have to go back there, he thought. I do, he continued in this self-examination. "The key", he said out loud. "Where's the key?" He had no idea why it was such a significant part of the mystery all of a sudden. That small piece of metal, granted very attractive, became the prime element, which held his entire world together. The mahogany box rested on an ottoman. He hesitated, before opening it. As soon as he held the key in his hand, an image, clear as a bright summer day, took on forms he knew only too well; the complex and sophisticated enigma that Vizcaya is. He stood there, swaddled by a great sense of peace, like he had not known in more than twenty years. It was as if the curse had been lifted. Now. She was never coming back to haunt him. That woman. He had to go to her.

TEN

The invitation to the opening of a new wing at the Cairo Museum of Antiquities, in Egypt, was quite an honor. Sarah who had hoped to go, showed her disappointment when Vincent cancelled the trip. The request for Doctor Jones's presence came from the Director of the Museum, a friend of Vincent, and himself a great admirer of Vizcaya. Vincent's mind transferred all previous routines of his life, into the unknown. His reasoning, ordinarily conservative, logical, was thrown into the abyss of the unexplained. He tried to resume his normal habits, his work with Sotheby's and with other associations. The confrontations between reality and the world of delusion that consumed him, raged as battles in the depth of his soul. The truce was over. The handful of unperturbed weeks were over, and Sarah would not come to his rescue. Vincent's colleagues had become aware of his mood change, his temper, which grew more and more as one of an impatient man. Vincent was disassociating himself from the world. At night, his breathing was brisk, like a runner at the end of a race. He seldom slept, anxious for the morning. The apparitions stopped, however, strange scenes of out-of-body experiences, often took place. They always were the same; Vincent leaving his body, and desperately trying to reconnect with it, as a force pulled him away. He knew who caused all this unrest. It was her, the house. She was never going to give him rest. She demanded all, from those who loved her.

Sarah arrived at the penthouse one day after shopping in the city. "Vincent?" she called, as she walked in. She noticed the Amazon unopened box by the front door. "You didn't even open your present," she murmured to herself.

"Up here," he shouted.

She stepped in the bedroom, and saw Vincent lying on the bed. She noticed the mahogany box on the bedside table. "Are you okay?" she asked. "I haven't heard from you in three days."

"I'm fine."

"I've never seen you in bed at five o'clock in the afternoon."

"Oh, well. Five o'clock... ten o'clock, midnight, what's the difference?" he said, reaching for the key in the box. "This... is the key to everything," he stated, looking at it closely, "no pun intended."

"I don't know what you mean," replied Sarah, somewhat anxious at Vincent's attitude.

"No one knows. No one has known... for a hundred years. But I know. I know. You see... this key, this insignificant piece of metal, holds all the secrets of Vizcaya," he said, twirling the key in his hand.

Sarah was afraid now. Afraid that Vincent was having a nervous breakdown. His mother's illness also concerned her. Alzheimer's and nervous breakdowns were two very separate conditions, yet Sarah was at a loss for anything helpful. She watched Vincent turn away from her and completely ignored the fact that she was here.

"I've got to sleep now," he simply said.

She caressed his hair, gently, and left the room. Once in the lobby, she gave Grant, the doorman, her phone number, and asked him to let her know if Doctor Jones needed anything. What she really wanted to tell him, was to let her know if Vincent went out, and in what state he was. However, that would have caused all kind of gossip in the building.

Fresh snow covered the sidewalk. Trees in Central Park appeared in silvery tones and as a grey misty form, dense and suspended above an emitting light coming off the ground. The faint outline of the buildings beyond the park, like watermarks, framed the perfect winter scene.

Sarah looked up towards the penthouse, before waving a taxi, which took her to Rockefeller subway station. From there, she connected with another line to Queens, which is where her small studio apartment was located.

She cranked up the heat of her window air conditioning unit. The single room was cold, and uninviting. After making a cup of chamomile tea, Sarah sat down in front of her small television set, and held the remote control in her hand, without clicking on the power button. She watched her reflection in the dark screen, and felt her stomach, considering time and the weeks already gone by. She also thought about the joy a woman should feel during such times, yet such happiness was overshadowed by emotions she could scarcely ignore. Yes, her father was the ogre of the family, though a gentle one, and one that could be reasoned with, smoothed over with batting eyes and kisses, like when she was a little girl. No, this emotional upsurge was of another kind, one that lurks beneath all good intentions of the heart. What is to become of us? Sarah questioned herself, imagining a new life in the depth of her womb. She feared that her feelings had rushed ahead of her, and that perhaps some decisions were made too hastily. She confessed that Vincent's wealth may have influenced her young heart, a little. She never talked about it, though her parents eventually congratulated her on her choice, with that one condition Sarah was only too conscious of; no sex before marriage. How is that possible? How can anyone have such self-control? She put up no resistance, not even a semblance of it. And now… she talked about a baby. Sarah sipped her luke warm tea. That woman, the visitor from beyond time, bothered her less than the impact she had on Vincent. Ghosts are ghosts, Sarah pondered in her youthful exuberance. Though the church condemned such beliefs, she never denied their presence. Where is the danger in that? Many people witness strange phenomenon, and some, or most of them inexplainable, but for a life beyond this life. And Vizcaya, how did it figure in the equation? A haunted house? That seemed a little childish. How, then, could one explain all the paranormal activities? There had to be a connection between Vincent's ancestors and the house, and the wooden box filled with effects from another time. Two generations of Jones's suffered identical grievances. Sarah found that very unusual. For all she knew, Vincent's grandfather was part of the curse, just like his father before him. When did it all start? Now, Sarah considered having a child. She caressed her stomach, gently. Vizcaya, she thought. Vizcaya. "That house is cursed," she said out loud, like she needed to be heard. Heard by whom, or by what, was uncertain. She looked around her small room, perhaps waiting for a sign, a manifestation of her very own. Crazy. "Are you here?" she asked the empty space in front of her. "You don't scare me, bitch." Sarah was ready to clash with a shadow, fully aware of the futility of such confrontations.

She got up and took her tea mug to the sink. Her phone rang. It was Vincent and she quickly picked up the phone. "Hello."

"Sarah… hi. I… I'm on my way to JFK. Catching a late flight," Vincent managed to spill out.

"What? You are!?"

"I think you know where I'm going," he said, not quite sure how to act. "I've got to see for myself. You understand."

"You're going to Florida, right? Vizcaya," affirmed Sarah, listening to a conversation like she was a third party, removed from the process of decision making.

"Yes. It makes sense to me now… I think it does… I don't know," Vincent moaned. "It's like a long dream, and I feel it's about to end. You know what I mean?"

"You're going to get there, and then what?"

"I don't know," lamented Vincent. "As sure as I know I'm talking to you, I just know I have to go there."

"Does Doctor Hoffman, the director of Vizcaya, know you're going?" inquired Sarah.

"No, he doesn't. He wouldn't understand. This visit has to be done… in secret, I guess."

"When do you think you'll be back?" asked Sarah, trying to keep Vincent on the line for as long as possible. Premonitions are seldom taken seriously. When they are, they can really overtake one's life, and alter one's behavior. Sarah felt the full force of a horrible intuition. "I'm worried about you," she cried. "I wish I could come with you. I could fly down tomorrow. We could meet in the gardens you love so much," pleaded Sarah. "Please?"

"No… I need to do this by myself. Please, let me do this. I'm sorry." Vincent could hear Sarah sniffle. He hated to make her cry. "You did open my eyes, you know that, right? It was you, who made me unafraid. You."

"I know," Sarah blubbered, as her sniffling became louder.

"You made me a believer, me, who didn't believe in anything."

"I know."

"You realize how long this has been going on… this… this curse. It's got to stop. I have to meet her face to face." Vincent weighed his next words carefully. "I think she's waiting for me."

Sarah calmed down a little, her crying was less audible. "I don't understand. What do you mean, waiting for you?"

"Her. That woman." Vincent still wavered on the word 'ghost'. "She's willing me to come to her. I know it now. And I know you can guess where she is."

"Vizcaya."

"Right."

"Are you even thinking of our baby?" asked Sarah, trying a last line of defense.

"That is all I'm thinking about. Do you think I want this child to grow up and… and be followed by a ghost? Haunted? I don't think so."

Sarah screamed.

"Sarah? Sarah?" shouted Vincent, after he heard the scream and a commotion, like furniture being pushed around. "Stop the car," he told the taxi driver.

Sarah came back on the line. "Vincent, she was here!" said Sarah with a trembling voice. "I fell backwards… she pushed me. I know she did."

"I'm turning around."

"No. Go. Go, I'll be fine. She just surprised me. I didn't expect her to come here."

"Are you sure?"

"Yes. I mean, she can't hurt me… she's a fucking ghost!"

"I wish I had you all those years ago. You're amazing," said Vincent, though somewhat surprised by the language.

"Fucking ghost! Do you hear me?" shouted Sarah in the emptiness of her room.

"Sarah. I don't believe my ears," said Vincent, remembering the night in Saint Patrick's Cathedral. "You do shock me."

"Well, no more mister nice guy," she replied. "This bitch is beginning to piss me off. This is war!"

Vincent listened, somewhat unsettled by Sarah's high-spirited attitude; a side of her he had never seen. "Are you going to be ok?" he finally asked again.

"Piece of cake."

"Right, then. I'll go. I'll text you later. Oh, thank you for my present," he quickly added. "I haven't had time to open it… sorry, it's very inconsiderate of me."

"That's alright."

"No, I mean it, I'm sorry. Do you want to tell me what it is?"

"It's nothing. An encyclopedia of architecture," she said. "It's five books."

"How sweet of you. Thank you. I know I'll enjoy it."

"I thought so."

"Ok, I'll be in touch." He told the taxi driver to go on, and texted Sarah a heart emoji, his first ever, which made him smile.

By the time Vincent arrived at The Ritz-Carlton, the same hotel he stayed at with Sarah, it was three o'clock in the morning. The carry-on luggage contained enough clothes for a short stay, as he had no intention of being here longer than he had to. He also brought with him the mahogany box and all its contents. He opened it up, and placed it on the bed, next to where he was going to lie. After brushing his teeth, he turned the lights off and went to bed. He waited. This, he felt was the breakthrough of twenty years, or more in the making. This was for his father, possibly his grandfather, and now he realized probably his great-grandfather. Aren't we blessed, he thought, with much sarcasm. Our very own ghost. A family legacy. No more hallucinations. I know what you are, Vincent continued. I am quite fed up with you. He reached for the ivory comb, and played with the tuft of hair. "Well… where are you?" he enticed the hollowness of the room. "I'm waiting for you." Mild shivers crawled the whole length of his body, like minuscule insects, which made him think of an Egyptian curse. He tried to appear in control of whatever circumstance, yet years of dismay prevailed and fear installed itself in him, like a loathsome guest. "I hate you… I hate you…" Vincent repeated in a faint voice, as he slowly fell asleep.

ELEVEN

It was raining. Vincent looked out of his hotel window. Fine curtains of rain bled over the horizon, like a vast painting. The typical sunny intervals in the distance, reminded Vincent of the mild Floridian winters. His phone rang. It was Sarah.

"I'm fine," he answered right away.

"I thought you were going to text me when you got in," she said.

"It was three in the morning!"

"I miss you."

"I haven't been gone twelve hours." Vincent regretted the heartless answer. "Sorry. You know I miss you, too."

"Liar. But yes, I know."

"Did you sleep well… after… you know…"

"Yes," answered Sarah. "She didn't bother me after that. I think she was pissed at me. Damn ghost. Anyway, when are you going?"

"In a bit. It opens at 9:30." Vincent considered his answer. "I hate to refer to Vizcaya as a 'it'. That really upsets me," he said.

"You are strange."

"I know."

"Will you keep me posted, please? I want to know if anything happens. Promise?" she implored.

"Promise. I love you."

"I love you."

After placing the mahogany box in the hotel safe, the following morning, Vincent helped himself to a cup of coffee in the lobby, before leaving. Wednesday was a good day to be at Vizcaya, he thought. Weekends were far too crowded. No, this was a good day. He could feel it.

"Eighteen dollars, please," said the young man in the kiosk. A light rain began to fall, yet several people were already in line under their umbrellas, for a ticket. Vincent gave the man twenty dollars and realized this was the first time he paid the entrance fee. In the last few years, he had given more than five million dollars to the museum, and yet, he had never actually paid for a ticket. It amused him. "Keep the change," he told the baffled young man, unaware of Vincent's identity.

Here she was. The house. Vincent walked the length of what was once the entrance drive to the house, flanked by sculptured stone water courses, cascading downwards, and now a walkway for tourists. The magnificent architecture slowly emerged through the trees. How easily one could lose oneself in the bedazzling and exquisite dream of her. Something was about to take place. Surely. Vincent followed the same itinerary as he did with Sarah, expecting something to happen. In possession of certain facts, he proceeded meticulously throughout the house, like an adult playing hide and seek with a child. Under the gloomy sky, a dispirited courtyard stopped Vincent in his tracks. Such melancholy, he thought; a space that must have been the center of all social gatherings, in Vizcaya's prosperous days, now in mourning. Vincent visualized James Deering, the nonconformist millionaire. He pictured him sitting under the vaulted loggia, a cup of tea in hand, looking up at the open roof of his courtyard. A courtyard he loved so much. A couple of people walked in, unaware, disturbing the calming silence. Vincent looked up; the glass roof brought back all sense of reality. He hated that. He recalled his conversation with Tracy during that lunch, the fanciful talks about time and the yearning for the past, and for the things that could have been. What is so compelling, so alluring about the past, that man will theorize ways to transport himself back in time? The romantic spirit will conceptualize perfect love, unconditional, and preferably in a faraway place. Though not opposite to the notion of time travel, the pragmatist will consider carefully the fallouts of a world without technology, medicine; 'the good old days.' Still, there is love to think about. That Goddess, languishing in a dungeon. Time. Vincent thought about that word, and juxtaposed it to 'present'. Present time. There is no such thing, he thought. A moment that passes, what we call the present, instantly becomes the past. Only the future can be anticipated, he kept on. Only the future is real.

The wide stairway led him to the second floor, as relentless notions still puzzled him. He leaned over the balcony, right outside James Deering's bedroom, and admired the courtyard below, envisioning guests of that epoch, like shadows. An odd sensation behind him, as if someone was going to push him over the edge, made Vincent turn around. She looked straight at him, standing not three feet away. "Are you real?" he murmured, confused, yet strangely happy that she was here. He extended his hand towards her. Touched her. She remained immobile, like the transient fragment of a dream. Vincent's hand felt nothing but empty air around her, yet she appeared tangible, more so than ever before. A young couple walked by and glanced at Vincent, who waited for a reaction from the two tourists. None came. She was invisible, inaccessible to the rest of the world. Vincent was prepared to stay there, waiting for a sign, conscious of his newly found poise.

More people walked by, continuing their visit. Vincent was blind to them. He only saw her, and was captivated by her countenance. They were both in a trance, it seemed. Each looking at the other. One, here, the other, unattainable on the other side of time. Vincent observed her garments, the stunning sage-green and golden-yellow silk-chiffon gown, laced with delicate embroideries. His eyes lingered around the low-cut V-neckline corset, which revealed her alabaster skin. And then, all of a sudden, nothing, only the unoccupied space where she tarried. Her sudden departure, bothered Vincent. He wondered why he thought of Sarah, as pandemonium encroached itself in Vincent's wearied mind. He made his way into the next bedroom, known as Espagnolette, with its eighteenth-century Rococo opulence. Vincent knew that one of the secret passageways was located in this bedroom. A small group strolled around the room, evidently fascinated. Vincent waited, pretending to read an information label on the wall, like a criminal about to break the law. As soon as they left, he began looking for the secret door, hidden behind a silk-embroidered panel with a palm tree motif. There it was. Vincent stepped out of the room and took a quick look around. Fortunately, the mid-week day and the rain prevented a lot of people from being here. The coast was clear. He knew that what he was about to do could cause trouble, perhaps even legal problems, Doctor Jones or not.

He carefully moved the small Louis XVI table to the side, and ran his finger along the narrow groove of the well-concealed door. In doing so, he noticed a small key hole, barely a quarter of an inch in diameter, located far too low to attract attention, and normally camouflaged by the table. He took a step back, stunned by the discovery. He quickly moved the small table back in its place. It can't be that simple, he thought, as more people came in the room. It wouldn't be, he continued in his speculations. Two generations of Jones, and no one, no one at all, thought of this? he said to himself. He exited the bedroom, on the lookout. "Where are you?" he whispered walking along the galleries above the courtyard. He presumed that she was constantly by his side, just not always willing to show herself. She was like a secret friend, really. He wished he had felt that way about her all these years ago. He thought about Doctor Roberts. What a buffoon. What would he think about all this? He probably would ask again about Vincent's youth, if there was anything there he had not admitted to, and on and on it would go. Now Vincent was possessive, attached to an illusion, a ghost of his very own, and Doctor Roberts's ignorance left Vincent indifferent.

Undeterred by the drizzle and seeking some kind of solace, Vincent descended the wide steps of the terrace, and walked the length of Vizcaya's garden. Only a handful of people were braving the elements, scattered around the various terraces and areas of the vast Italian Renaissance landscape. He followed the edge of the central basin, wet, yet happy, and watched the infinite tiny circles forming on the surface of the water. On the east side of the estate, The Rose Garden, almost hidden, seemed to be waiting for a visitor. The large marble fountain, was a sad vision, silenced from neglect and probably from lack of funds. Vincent was drenched, and he sat on the circular edge. Moisture on the bottom of the empty pool, allowed moss and some tiny wild flowers to take residence there. There is nothing in this world so heartbreaking as a dead fountain, he thought and cast a languid eye over the whole spectacle, as the rain increased. Tomorrow he would come back with the key.

After returning to the hotel, Vincent took a bath and called Sarah. The explanations made some sense, though she seemed to disapprove of the sneaky way Vincent acted in finding the hidden door. Like him, Sarah was amazed at the simplicity of what seemed to be the answer to the century old curse. A conversation about what could lay beyond, on the other side of the secret door, ensued. Doubts, of course were part of the sentiments. What if? And the key... still so much in the unknown. Sarah kept the skepticism alive and well, saying Vincent's treasured key was not necessarily the one for that door; a revelation that exasperated him. His bath was getting a little cold, and he ran the hot water. He asked Sarah if she thought the ghost was standing next to him, watching him. The question made Sarah laugh. Her answer was, yes, of course, which made Vincent uncomfortable. He looked around the bathroom, hoping the steam from the hot water would cause her to materialize. But no luck. Discussions about the afterlife, took on much lighthearted tones in the last few weeks. Yet, if Vincent really stopped and thought about it, he retreated from an authenticity that had all the resemblance of an imaginary world. That, scared him.

"Do you think I'm crazy?" he asked Sarah. "Did you really see her that night?"

Sarah abruptly changed the subject. "I know you're busy… and not really in the mood to talk about this, but… when do think you'll talk to my dad? About the baby."

"Oh, my God, yes, soon. Actually, as soon as I get back," he replied, as he came out of the tub and dried himself.

"Don't you think we should take a quick trip to Seattle?" she asked. "You know… see him in person."

"Absolutely. No, you're right. It's not something that can be done on the phone."

"Ok. I was just wondering. That's all."

A short pause followed. "You didn't answer my question… am I crazy?" Vincent finally asked again, looking into the bathroom mirror.

"No."

The single word reply fell like a deceptive report. "Right," he uttered, and said goodnight, despondent. A warmth, like breath on the back of his neck, caused him to smile at his own reflection. He knew she was here. And now, as never before, he could feel her.

TWELVE

A pale Floridian winter sky in shades of pinks and milky whites, saluted Vincent. The key was on the bedside table, just as he left it before going to sleep. He checked the weather on his phone. No rain today. That meant more visitors at Vizcaya. He felt like saying good morning, his voice directed somewhere in the room. He assumed she was here, again. Perhaps she had never left his side.

He gently placed the ivory comb in an envelope, so as not to disturb the tuft of hair caught in it, and put it in his pocket. With the key lodged in his wallet, Vincent left his room, powerful emotions sailing ahead.

As anticipated, visitors were in higher numbers. Vincent made his way directly to the bedroom, only to find it closed to the public. He looked for one of the museum's guards. "Excuse me," he said to the man in uniform. "Why is Espagnolette bedroom closed?"

"There's a problem, a water leak coming from Mr. Deerings's bathroom. It's closed indefinitely."

Vincent smiled inwardly. "Ha, ok, thank you." There was no doubt in his mind who the Culprit was, though he shook his head, giving the word coincidence a whole new meaning. He walked back to the entrance of the bedroom, had a quick look around, and unhooked the red rope blocking the way in. Once the rope was hooked back on, he went straight to the secret door. This was it. Would the key fit? Vincent's heart was beating at a crazy pace. All the years, all the heartaches, the nightmares, could it all end here? He held the small key in front of the keyhole. He felt like a daring bank robber, nervous about what he would find behind a dark entryway, and too excited to give a single thought about being caught. The key slid perfectly into the aperture. Now all he had to do was turn it. A quick glance over his shoulder, showed an empty room. This was the moment. He turned the key, and the door was unlocked. Just like that. He pulled the panel towards him, and a glacial air rushed out, as if an unearthed crate which had been kept locked for centuries, had been opened. Vincent stepped inside the narrow passage and pulled the door closed behind him. He reached for his phone, to put on the flashlight, but his pocket was empty. The comb was gone, as well as his wallet, which utterly confused him, and put even more doubts in his head. Only the key remained, and he held it tightly in his hand. Was he even here, in Vizcaya? His eyes slowly became accustomed to the darkness, and a faint glow several feet away, guided him. He noticed the musty odor, like one would find in the depth of a cave, though it reminded him more of some ancient tomb. The walls of the passageway felt rough, void of any of the attentions the rest of the house enjoyed. About thirty feet into the tunnel, Vincent thought he heard voices, and he could make out a dim light not far from him. He stopped. The muffled sound of people talking, unnerved him. The tunnel had to lead to another room, where the only thing he would find, was a group of dismayed tourists. Then, all this was in vain. He took a few more steps. The voices stopped. The passageway made a sharp turn to the right, and Vincent found himself in front of another door. A yellow light filtered through the fine slot. He hesitated, before pushing it open. Were the police on the other side, waiting for him? He could just imagine the papers and their headlines; 'Eccentric millionaire caught red-handed!' or, 'Vizcaya pillaged!' Not sure which was the more appropriate one. He pushed the door slightly ajar, which opened into a bedroom. A man was in bed, reading The New York Herald. The headlines read: *THE TSAR OF RUSSIA ABDICATES*. Vincent held his breath, astonished and suddenly terrified.

Another figure came into view; a woman, dressed elegantly in a long colorful silk gown. "Will you unbutton me?" she asked the man. "Who do you suppose commissioned Mr. Sargent, to paint Julia?" she asked, as she approached the bed.

Vincent felt a deep pain in his chest, suffocated by an overpowering fright. Quietly closing the door, he felt it was crucial to rush back to the point of entry. That much he knew was real! In complete disbelief of what he just witnessed, he made his way back in the semi-darkness.

Anxious and mystified, he saw that the red rope was gone when he peaked through a small opening of the door. That meant the bedroom was open to the public again, though no one was in it. Strange, thought Vincent, having been told by the guard that the room would remain closed indefinitely. He locked the door behind him, and put the small table back in its place. He reached in his pocket. The phone was in it.

Vincent held the device in his hand, at a total loss. The battery was dead. He felt the comb in the other pocket, and his wallet; all of which had disappeared when he entered the passageway.

Vincent crept out of the bedroom, into the galleries. He was struck by the total lack of inactivity. No one in sight, not on this floor, nor on the ground floor below. Nothing, but absolute silence. The glass roof above the courtyard showed a night sky. He also realized that only about half of the lights were on in the house. Vincent froze. Vizcaya was closed. Now what, he wondered, unsure of anything. After descending the main staircase, he stood under the loggia, expecting an alarm to go off at any second. Silence. Slow footsteps reverberated near the entrance. Vincent hid in a dark corner, and saw the night guard making his rounds. This gave him hope that at least one door would be unlocked, which he found. He ran up the driveway, and to the street entrance of Vizcaya. He waited for a taxi. One hour, then two, until finally one drove by.

"Where to?" asked the driver.

"The Ritz-Carlton, Key Biscayne, please. What time is it?" he asked.

"Quarter after three," said the taxi driver.

That's ridiculous, thought Vincent. I couldn't have been there for fifteen hours! "Did you notice anything strange?" he asked the cab driver.

"Strange? Like what?"

"I don't know... a bright light... something," continued Vincent, shaken by the experience.

The driver glanced at Vincent in the rear-view mirror.

Vincent caught the man staring at him. "Don't worry I'm not crazy," he simply said.

The taxi dropped Vincent off.

"Good morning, Sir," said the concierge, as Vincent walked in the lobby.

"Good morning," he answered. "I need a new key, I think I've lost the one I was given," said Vincent, genuinely unaware of its whereabouts.

"What's the name?" inquired the concierge.

"Jones. Doctor Jones."

The concierge checked the computer. "Excuse me, Sir, I don't believe you're a guest."

"Don't be absurd," answered Vincent, somewhat annoyed. "I'm in room 1206. Check again. Doctor Jones."

"I don't' think so, Sir," said the concierge with all the politeness due.

One of the managers approached the counter. "What seems to be the problem?" he asked.

Vincent stared at the man. "What day is this?" he suddenly felt compelled to ask.

"It's Wednesday," the manager answered.

"Wednesday." Vincent was scared to ask another question, as he knew the terrifying answer.

"Doctor Jones," said the concierge, after checking the reservations again.

"Yes?"

"You were here last week, and you left without paying for the room. We have all your belongings in storage. Sorry about the misunderstanding."

The manager walked away, knowing the situation was resolved.

"I've been gone a week?" said Vincent.

"Six days, to be correct," answered the concierge, somewhat puzzled.

Vincent lowered his head, in utter disbelief.

"A Sarah Conti phoned several times, I see on the computer notes," added the man.

"Oh, my God."

The Ritz-Carlton staff are highly trained, and asking personal questions is absolutely unthinkable. The concierge knew something was wrong, yet all he could do was mind his own business.

Vincent sat in the lobby, with a cup of coffee; his luggage and the mahogany box by his feet. The cell phone was charging and he was being overwhelmed by the sheer thought of what just transpired. Five minutes through that door, was as a week. And what did he experience there? Did I really go back in time? he wondered. A great sense of fear, and an equally strong sentiment of excitement enveloped him. Call Sarah? Then what? Going back to New York seemed irrelevant.

Call her and say some unforeseen business has to be dealt with, and how sorry he is for not calling sooner. Maybe not. Vincent dialed Sarah's phone number. He became frustrated, after several attempts and getting some interference noises.

"May I use a phone?" he asked the concierge.

"Right this way, sir," said the man, pointing at the end of the counter.

"Hello," said the tired voice, answering the call. "Oh, my God, is that you?! Vincent!"

"I know, I know, I'm so sorry."

Vincent heard Sarah bursting into tears. "Vincent. You can't disappear for days and not tell me where you are. That's not fair."

"I'm sorry," he repeated, feeling guilty for not telling her the truth.

"Where have you been?"

"I wouldn't know where to start," he answered.

"Where did you go after your day at Vizcaya? Where are you, now? You're not still in Miami, are you?"

"I am."

"There's something you're not telling me. I can hear it in your voice. Is everything alright?" Sarah asked, showing her insecurity, as any young woman would ask of her boyfriend after a week of absence.

"Look, I can't tell you. It's too incredible, even for you to believe."

"Madre mia! now, you have got to tell me!" she said, frantically. "What did you do?"

Vincent hesitated a moment. If anyone would understand, it would be Sarah. "Alright, alright. I think, well, this is insane. I went back… in time. I think I did. I know I did. I found the passageway."

"So, you were right. That key was the big secret."

"Did you hear what I just said?" asked Vincent, amazed at Sarah's nonchalant observation.

"You went back in time."

And you don't think that's unbelievable? Amazing? I don't know, pick an adjective."

"I think it's the most incredible thing I've ever heard of."

"You just amaze me," said Vincent. "Yes. I went through the hidden door, and it took me down a long… like a tunnel. My phone was gone, my wallet was gone. My pockets were empty, even the little comb was gone. That's when I started to panic."

"Then what?"

"It led me to a bedroom. There were people in bed. Do you hear me? People in that room were from… the woman talked about Sargent, as if he slept in the room next door. Sargent!" he exclaimed. "Do you realize I was only there for five minutes? Five minutes… and a week went by," he pondered out loud. "Incredible."

"When are you coming back to New York?"

"I don't know. I need to stay a little longer."

"What do you want me to do with your mail?" asked Sarah. "One is from the Museum of Antiquities in Egypt. Do you want me to open it?"

"No, it can wait." Egypt was the furthest thing from Vincent's mind at this moment. "I'll call you later. Promise."

"You're going to try to go back there?" inquired Sarah.

"I have to, don't I?"

"I suppose," she replied.

"You sound strange. Like you don't believe a word of what I said."

"I'm just tired. Sorry."

"No, I am sorry. I forgot I woke you up. Go back to sleep, we'll talk later." Vincent felt guilty for not asking about her health. "How's the baby? Growing… I trust."

"You're too much. Yes, growing… I hope. Which means my belly will start showing… which means, you know what."

"What?"

"My father!" she sighed. "My father. He has to be told."

"Shit. Yes… I need to do that."

"Yes, you do."

"I've got to go," Vincent suddenly said. He hung up. She was here. The apparition he welcomed now. She stood right in front of him, three feet away. He stared at her, before taking the comb out of his pocket. He removed it from the envelope which he had kept it in, and showed it to her. She instantly disappeared, as if the object terrified her. Nothing seemed real now. What was he supposed to put his faith in? Am I deranged? A passing, yet reoccurring thought, which consumed him for years. Vincent wondered if the comb he held in his hand was even real. Am I really seeing this? he kept asking himself. He picked up the mahogany box, with all its treasures, and he held the Sargent letter in his hand. "I know, you're real," he said out loud.

The hotel concierge approached him. "Are you planning to stay a little longer with us, Sir?"

"Actually, yes. You have a room, right?"

"We do, sir."

"When can I get it?"

"Right now, if you like."

"Perfect."

"Will you need help with your luggage?"

"No, thank you." Vincent walked to the front desk and took a credit card out of his wallet. "Here, charge me for a week," he told the man behind the counter. Going back to New York was probably the wise thing to do, Vincent speculated. However, what defines wisdom? One reasonable answer would be things one dislikes to do, or are contrary to one's desire. The brain acts in odd ways when it is challenged. Situations that would normally be regarded as harmful, become palatable, as the boundary of self-serving lies become vague.

The new hotel room overlooked the ocean. Distant clouds, way out over the Atlantic, showed a hint of color. A faint orange light, smudged on the lower sky, announced the new day. What would it bring? Perhaps more confusion, more questions. Sarah's reaction surprised Vincent. As juvenile as the topic of science fiction may sound, something extraordinary happened; a passage through time, to put it simply. A glimpse into another era. Vincent thought of all the minds past and present, studying the effect of time. He thought about the men who had invested their whole life, searching for that one elusive power; how to control time. He considered all the books and films about time travels, and time machines and various contraptions. "And here I am, with a single key," he said, holding it in his hand. "That simple." He looked at the silver ocean, meditating how easy it was to travel to the other side. To Africa, or Europe. He visualized a rocket, launched from the beach in front of the hotel. He superimposed his finger on the horizon line, pointing toward the south east. "Probably Senegal, here," he said. Then pointing to the north east, "and Portugal, here," he mused. He feared going through that secret door again. What if coming back was impossible? The question was not where it led to, he knew the location. The question was, where in time?

THIRTEEN

A week went by, then another, and another. New Yorkers were looking forward to Spring, though one more month of below average temperatures was announced. Sarah's visit to the penthouse seemed less and less frequent. Due to a large amount of work Vincent had to deal with, the Seattle trip was postponed several times, which upset Sarah. She kept pressing Vincent to do 'the right thing', speak to the family, and then get married. Her parents were put on a 'waiting list' were Vincent's not very thoughtful words. More than three months into the pregnancy, Sarah did not appear to show any trace of the physical transformations all women go through. The only thing Vincent noticed, was her intransigent mood swings. When asked about the fact that she showed no signs of her tummy getting bigger, Sarah replied that her mother was just the same. Give it time, was her answer.

Though Vincent was 'old school' in many ways, and asking a father permission to marry his daughter was important to him, he nevertheless refused to allow such customs to stand in his way. After all, this was the twenty first century. Sarah was pregnant, and that was that. Asking permission was ludicrous, and in time, the Conti family would have to accept the facts as they were; an unmarried daughter with child, yet, also adding to the equation, the wealth coming to her, through such a union.

The Sargent watercolor was yet to be hung on a wall. It remained on the floor, lying against one of the columns. Little about Vizcaya had been discussed in the last few weeks. In fact, that name had not been mentioned at all. Vincent sat in an armchair and stared at the painting. The cup of coffee on the side table, was cold, forgotten hours before. Somehow, he felt lonely. Strange how the mind operates. He missed her. The woman. He missed her more than Sarah. His last visit to Vizcaya, was the last time he encountered her. Why? Why wasn't she here? he wondered. Apprehensions, like he would have never thought possible, were taking hold of him; what if she was never to return? What if the last time he saw her, was, the last time? After a life of restlessness, unsure of anything, she was the only thing real to him now. "Why are you not haunting me!?" he shouted at the emptiness around him. "Why?"

He fetched a large coffee table book on Sargent's work from his library. He became curious about that name; Julia. "Who are you? Julia. Julia," he repeated, as he thumbed through the book, searching for a painting with that name. Nothing. He sat down at his desk and googled the name. Several images appeared, yet none that corresponded with the Sargent. He kept looking. Finally, a small picture showed up. The file was very small. He zoomed in as much as the image allowed it, though it did not show him anything, except that the woman in question was indeed painted by Sargent in 1918; titled Lady Julia Montagu. The low resolution of the image hid any kind of detail Vincent was seeking. After 'digging' a little further, Vincent discovered that the painting was in a private collection in England - the collection of Edward Montagu, Earl of Halifax.

Vincent was anxious to learn more about the painting. He grabbed his phone, to call the Head of Sotheby's and Sarah rushed in at that moment, sobbing.

"What's going on?" asked Vincent, panicking.

"I lost it! I lost it!" she burst out crying.

"What? Lost what?"

"The baby! The baby!" she said falling to Vincent's knees, inconsolable.

"Oh…" Vincent caressed her head, trying to appease her.

"God punished me!" she cried. "He's punishing us for not taking him seriously."

Vincent pulled away. "What!?" he replied angrily.

"You should've talked to my parents. To my father."

"God, you really believe that, don't you? You really think God killed your baby because we didn't go to Seattle!"

Sarah stopped crying all of a sudden. She looked up at Vincent as she stood up. "Yes," she said, with fire in her eyes.

Vincent paced the room. "Well, I don't believe in that." He searched for the right words, as not to offend Sarah, whose anger, it seemed, was mounting. None came. "It's a bunch of crap," he shouted, fed up with the religious aspect the conversation was taking.

"You don't believe in anything," she answered, following him around the room. "Well, excuse me, you do, really, you believe in that stupid ghost. That's the only thing you believe in."

"At least, she's real."

"Real? Real? Do you hear yourself? She's a fucking ghost!" Sarah exclaimed. "A fucking ghost!"

"Here it is again, that foul language coming out of your mouth! I have to say, I'm shocked at you," Vincent asserted, surprised at Sarah's blustering words. "What do you think your God will say about that?" he said in a sarcastic tone.

"What are you talking about?"

"And what about you?" Vincent continued, not sure if he was ready for the imminent dispute.

"What about me?" she asked, looking deep into his eyes. "What?"

He shook his head, as in disbelief of what he was about to say. "Were you really pregnant?" The words came out too fast. They could never be taken back. The sentiment was out for the taking, to destroy and cause irreversible damage.

Sarah's fury, which lay dormant, and the likes of which he had never known, came forth. She looked at the precious Sargent watercolor and looked back at Vincent.

"Don't you dare," he said, his voice trembling at the prospect of what Sarah was thinking of doing. The Italian blood runs very hot, and Sarah's was at boiling point.

"Your precious Vizcaya," she uttered with disdain, and rushed to the other side of the room.

"Sarah!" Vincent shouted, going after her, though it was too late. Sarah grabbed the painting and holding it with both hands, she smashed it against the very column that it had been resting against since the day of the auction.

"No. No," he cried. "Why did you?" he whimpered, like a wounded child, kneeling down by the shuttered glass and the broken frame. He turned around with tears in his eyes, holding the exposed watercolor, safeguarding it on his chest. Sarah was gone.

Through the moisture of his eyes, Vincent examined the painting for any damage. Such analyses were common in his work, and he carefully looked at it. Except for a very small scratch in the lower section on the landscape, the painting appeared fine. He turned it around, to check out the back of the paper. Written with a pencil, he found Sargent's signature with the inscription *Vizcaya*, and a date: *April 5, 1917.* Below that, another inscription took Vincent by surprise – *To Lady Julia, in friendship.* "Here you are again. Julia," Vincent murmured to himself. "So, he gave it to you," he continued, staring at Sargent's dedication. April 5th. 1917. He considered the date, the people staying in that room and the newspapers headlines about the Tsar abdicating. "Who are you?" he asked, looking at the inscription. It was unusual for Sargent to sign the back of his watercolors, and even more unusual to dedicate it to someone. He thought it strange that the auctioneer never mentioned it, since it adds great value to the work. Still, no one can see it, so what was the point of stating it, he continued in his deliberations. Perhaps no one was aware of it. The painting was framed in the 1930's, and the inscription had been forgotten. That was the only logical explanation.

Why should I make the first move? wondered Vincent, as he walked down Madison Avenue. Sarah had not contacted him since that crazy night, which was at least a month ago. He realized also that he slept better, and the absence of any kind of apparitions, actually brought peace. Sarah's bank was on the other side of the street. "What am I doing?" he asked audibly. His steps had taken him to Sarah's place of work. After a short hesitation, he crossed the street and walked inside the bank.

"Hello," said one of the tellers, "Welcome to Wells Fargo. How can I help you?"

"Actually, I'm looking for Sarah. Sarah Conti. Is she in today?"

"Sarah doesn't work here anymore. She quit at least six months ago."

"She did?" Vincent looked around the room. "Six months ago?" he repeated, like a broken-down automaton.

"Yes. I'm sorry." The teller seemed to recognize Vincent. "Aren't you her fiancé?" she asked.

"I am… well… boyfriend, though I'm not sure now."

"Oh, sorry."

"Did she say why she was leaving?"

The teller looked down, as if she wanted to giggle without being seen. "She said she was coming into a lot of money soon, and she didn't need to work," she shrugged, with all the credulity in her young countenance.

"I see," said Vincent, much more disappointed than he cared to show, and taken aback by the answer. "Well, thank you."

The sun outside blinded him, and as Vincent strolled nonchalantly away from the bank, his heart felt the full force of betrayal. Abandonment is a heavy cross to bear. It is one of the essential components required for a full-fledged broken heart, and Vincent fell victim to it. He loved Sarah. At least he thought so. None of the things the teller told him made sense. Sarah Conti; a con artist? Was she really after the money, like a common thief? Not possible. "She's so sweet," he found himself saying out loud, and having forgiven her for trying to destroy the painting. He turned back, and rushed inside the bank again. The same young girl watched him come toward her.

"You forgot something?" she asked.

"Yes." He leaned forward over the counter. "Did she ever tell anyone here why she had an abortion?" he asked, almost whispering.

"An abortion?" she answered, lowering her voice.

Vincent stared at the teller. "Yes, why would she do that? Do you know?"

"Sarah was not pregnant… why would she… oh, I see…"

Vincent shook his head. "That's what I thought," he said, his faith in humanity having sank a little lower. "Are you absolutely sure she was not expecting?" he inquired one more time, as a last act of forgiveness.

"Yes. We told each other everything. She was engaged to my brother before she met you. So… you see…"

Vincent was dumbfounded.

"I'm sorry. I really am," continued the girl. "Sarah is different… to say the least."

Vincent took a deep breath, and left as quickly as he came. He walked, his eyes fixed somewhere into the distance. The truth is, he was lost in a maze, a maze of deceitfulness. The sidewalk became a moving carpet, the avenue, an unknown gateway leading to nowhere.

"Good afternoon, sir," said Grant, opening the door for Vincent. The doorman noticed Vincent's somber mood; an unusual sight.

Vincent proceeded through the lobby, and turned around. He walked back towards Grant. "What do you think of Miss Conti?" he asked.

A puzzled Grant, who had never been asked anything remotely personal, stood still behind the marble counter; his safe and very own morsel of Fifth Avenue. "Sir?" he muttered.

"Come out from there," Vincent continued. "I need you to just be Grant, not the building concierge. Alright?"

Grant obeyed. He stepped out of his safety zone.

"Did Miss Conti ever say anything out of the ordinary to you? Anything?"

"Not that I can recall," said Grant.

"Nothing at all."

"Well… she did ask me about your penthouse, how much it was worth. I thought that was a bit unusual. I told her I had no idea," continued Grant. "Then she said, it's got to be worth millions."

"Thank you. Thank you for your honesty," said Vincent. "You have a good evening."

"You, too, sir," replied Grant, as he watched Vincent take the elevator.

Vincent reached in his pocket for his front door key, and entered his apartment. With an automatic gesture, he flung the key in a small antique Chinese plate that sat on a small table and looked up. The full and clear apparition startled him. Here, she stood, again, after weeks of absence. The woman; both spirit and so very real, to him now. This time he walked straight to her, unafraid, like he had been expecting her. He felt a slight ache in his heart, as he neared her. No more than four feet separated them. A trace of strange scent made her presence even more authentic this time. She remained there, in the middle of the room, looking spectacular in her long garment. He approached her, extending his hand, but she backed up. Vincent fetched the watercolor lying on his desk, and held it up with both hands, as he approached her again. The Sargent was in full view for her to see; Vizcaya. She stared at the painting, it seemed. Vincent felt somewhat foolish, however he wanted to speak to her. "Do you want me to be there?" he asked, pointing at the watercolor. "Is this where I'm supposed to be?" All of a sudden, with supernatural speed and power, her face came within inches of Vincent's, and he froze. He closed his eyes, overtaken by a great fear, engulfed by the sheer existence of her. He knew she was still there, around him, inside him. He opened his eyes slowly, and felt the substance of her, like the warmth of a summer sun on the skin. And that scent again, filled his nostrils. Her eyes were like the agate stone; a cobalt, translucent blue, and her hair seemed to flow, as if blown by the softest wind. Vincent did not move. He liked how she made him feel. Alive. Perhaps, more than that. A sensation, more powerful than anything he had ever known, made him quiver, as she dissolved, passing through him. He turned around, startled, yet filled with wonder. She was gone.

FOURTEEN

Summer arrived in New York, finally. Central Park turned to more cheerful colors, and people filled its space. Vincent had spent the last few months like a social outcast, staying away from any gatherings. Invitations for various parties just piled up on his desk. He did, however, enjoy his work again, and was called upon many times, including to appraise an important collection of fifteenth century drawings for an upcoming sale. To say Vincent was happy was perhaps untrue, however, he saw the breakup with Sarah as a good thing. Having dismissed the notion of becoming a father, he slowly returned to the bachelor's life. Now and again, the thought of looking into a baby's eyes, did haunt him, convinced that he would have been a wonderful parent.

Having written a letter to the current Earl of Halifax, he eventually received a reply from his daughter, Lady Charlotte Montagu. The return address was in Philadelphia. The letter was most distressing. The painting of her great-grandmother, Lady Julia, had sadly been destroyed in a fire, only the charcoal sketch Sargent had made of her, remained. A phone number was given at the bottom of the letter, encouraging Vincent to call, should he desire to do so.

Vincent grabbed his phone and dialed the number.

"Hello?" answered the voice on the other end.

"Hello, this is Doctor Jones, Calling from New York. Is this Lady Charlotte Montagu?"

"Doctor Jones! Hi. Please call me Charlotte."

"Charlotte. I'm sorry to bother you, and I really thank you for your letter."

"I'm sorry it wasn't the news you expected."

"So sad. I'm so sorry," said Vincent.

"Yes. It was a terrible accident. Several other works of art were lost to the fire, though the Sargent was the most painful loss," Charlotte affirmed.

"Just terrible. I can't imagine how I would feel. Such a masterpiece."

"It is what it is, right?"

"Yes." A moment of indecision followed. "I'm calling to ask a favor of you," he voiced, finally. "Would it be possible for you to send me an image of the sketch? I believe you have my email address. I know, I'm asking a lot."

"Of course, it's not a problem. So, you're doing some research? Why are you interested in my great-grandmother? she inquired.

Vincent was caught off guard. He hesitated, before giving an answer. "I am doing a little research about a house and the people who were guests there."

"Wait a minute… do you mean Vizcaya?" she asked.

"Yes! Yes," he replied, like he had just found a partner, an accomplice to some fantastic adventure. "You know the house?" he asked, excited.

"Mais, bien sur," she replied in French, which gave her that 'discreet charm of the bourgeoisie.' "Of course, I know Vizcaya. Who doesn't?" she claimed with assurance.

"You'd be surprised."

The call lasted more than an hour, as neither Vincent or Charlotte were willing to hang up, it seemed. Vizcaya was part of the conversation, though other topics, some quite personal, were discussed.

Well, I am so pleased that I called," Vincent said, eventually. "It was wonderful talking to you. May I bother you again, sometime?" Vincent felt like he had gone too far, after a silence ensued. "I'm sorry, I didn't mean—"

"You may." Charlotte smiled. She was thrilled. The phone call was her ray of sunlight on a gloomy day. Like Vincent, she tried to visualize a face to go with the voice; an activity that is very rarely successful. "Please call again," Charlotte blurted out. "I'd like that. I'd like that very much."

"Very well. I will. I look forward to your email."

"Goodbye."

"Goodbye."

It took Charlotte less than two days, to get back to Vincent. The email, with an image attached, simply said 'I hope to hear from you soon.' Vincent opened the file. He stared at the drawing, staring right back at him, like he peered into a mirror, a door that led to nowhere. He recognized her at once. She was the one who tormented him, pursued him, unrelentingly. At last he knew her name. The charcoal rendition showed the elegant and refined Julia. The depiction matched every encounter Vincent ever had. "Julia. Julia," he muttered under his breath, looking at her face, her eyes fixated on him, incandescent like two burning suns.

Vincent closed his laptop, as to escape her gaze. Unsure of how he felt, he delayed his much anticipated phone call to Charlotte. He felt as if he had broken the spell, finally; the enigma that had been the bane of his existence. He remained sitting there for a long time, indecisive about how to react. The face, the shadow, had a name now; Julia. A name he could call out. He turned around, looking around the room. "Are you here, Julia?" he asked in the silence of the penthouse.

Miss Brown called the next day, to tell Vincent that his mother had passed away. She died peacefully in the night, without much of a fight, like a dying flame deprived of oxygen. Vincent listened to the news, waiting for an emotion which never came. He became sad. The sadness was not due to the loss of his mother, of that, he had no illusion and knew was just a matter of time, because of her illness. His distress was due to his lack of grief.

A call from the family lawyer, came, as well as a deluge of texts and emails. Everyone sending condolences, and prayers. 'She was loved', were the most used words. The lawyer needed Vincent to be present for the reading of the will, within the next few weeks. Vincent let the voice mail pick up all the messages. He was in no mood to talk to anyone.

Later that night, Tracy called. The contact number on the cell phone, read 'James', as to not confuse Vincent. He decided to pick up. "Hello, Tracy," he said with a tired voice.

Only someone crying could be heard.

"Tracy!"

"Yes." Still, the crying went on.

"Put yourself together," said Vincent.

"I can't believe she's gone. I just can't believe it."

Vincent sighed. "I know."

"How are you doing," Tracy asked, having calmed down a little. "I mean—"

"She died peacefully," interrupted Vincent, not really knowing what to say.

"I loved her. She was so sweet to me, so understanding. You know?"

"I remember. She defended you, whenever someone talked unkindly about you. She really loved you."

"When is the funeral going to be?"

"It hasn't been decided yet. I'll let you know."

"Please. I assume it will be in Boston? Maybe we can go together."

"Yes, Boston. Sure."

"I'm really broken-hearted. Good night. May your dreams be filled with happy thoughts," Tracy added, still crying.

Vincent shook his head, knowing the opposite was the most likely scenario; dreams filled with images of Julia, in a never-ending cycle. "Good night," he answered Tracy.

The funeral took place on a Friday. It rained all day. Umbrellas dotted the entrance of the Trinity Church, in downtown Boston; a stunning piece of architecture, built in the late 1800's. Vincent sat on the front pew, next to a couple of cousins he had not seen in years, and whose names he could not remember.

He sat there, his mother's casket not twelve feet away from him. The speaker, apparently a friend of the family, mumbled some words of comfort, and elevated the deceased to sainthood; a plea for the skeptics in this diverse congregation. Vincent's mind drifted. His eyes fell on the magnificent stained glass above the altar, before returning his glance to an empty podium. He quickly picked up his notes, and walked to the microphone. The solemn hour came; Vincent's very own eulogy. He watched the expecting faces, perhaps a hundred, and realized that he only knew a handful of people present. Someone coughed at the back, like a cue. After a long silence, Vincent began to speak. He rummaged through his notes, before folding the pieces of paper. He looked straight ahead. His eyes hovered above the crowd, as if he was alone. Vincent smiled, and he began to speak, and his voice echoed around the church.

"It's been said that not a single stone will remain standing. Not one. The great matriarch of our time is gone, yet... yet, one can still salute her. One can still love her, unconditionally. Her compassion for those who love her is eternal. Her life is like a great gift, designed for the pleasure of those around her."

Some people looked at each other, unsure about what Vincent was alluding to. A certain discomfort could be felt.

"She is waiting, and I shall join her soon," Vincent continued, as a gasp ran the width and length of the nave. "In her solitude, she cries, as those who don't understand her, abuse her." He stopped and looked at the cherry veneer wooden box that held his mother. "Mother, I know now," he whispered, staring at the casket, and looking more and more like a man who needed to be rescued. Rescued from what, was unclear. "That which was hidden," he further said, "has now been burst wide open." Vincent glanced around the church, expecting to see Julia. Did she feel any sorrow for his loss? Tracy was crying, sitting in the third row of pews, grief-stricken. Miss Brown wiped her eyes. She sat on the second row of pews. Of all the people present, she was the only person Vincent truly cared for. This was the end of an era for her, for him. He knew he would take care of her financially.

The Vicar in charge of the funeral, looked at Vincent, and his demeanor changed to uneasiness when he noticed the quiet dismay in the sanctuary. After what seemed like an eternity, he finally stood up, and Vincent simply walked off the altar, and sat down. The eulogy made no sense to anyone, which meant, either Vincent had lost his mind, or the message was meant for someone, or something beyond anyone's comprehension. He took the decision to skip the traditional get together after a funeral, and decided to return to Boston only for the reading of the will.

After saying goodbye to Tracy and Miss Brown, Vincent walked towards his car, and heard his name being called. The rain had decreased, and now a fine drizzle fell any which way, blown by a sudden wind. He turned around. A woman in a wheelchair approached him.

"Doctor Jones," she said. "It's Charlotte. Charlotte Montagu."

Confounded, Vincent tried to associate the voice he heard on the phone, and the crude image he had concocted in his head, during the conversations. None of it matched. "Hi," he answered. "How… how did—"

"How did I know about the funeral?" she asked.

Vincent noticed a man in the distance looking at them, as if he was waiting for Charlotte to return. "Sorry, I… I didn't expect to meet you under these circumstances." He looked at her. Her hair was pulled back, covered by a headscarf. A rain coat was thrown over her shoulders.

"It was in the papers," she continued. "I liked your eulogy," she added. "Different. Your sense of spirituality is to be applauded."

"Very discerning of you." Vincent made every effort to ignore the wheelchair, yet he caught himself glancing at it at intervals. "I meant to call you, after you sent the Sargent," he conveyed to her. "It was very kind of you."

Charlotte stared at Vincent. She felt the awkwardness he projected. "I'm sorry. This is probably a bad time for you. Not very thoughtful of me."

"Not at all. I was looking forward to meeting you."

Charlotte noticed that Vincent kept looking at the man behind her, on the other side of the street. The wind disturbed her headscarf, and she rearranged her hair, which showed the absence of any kind of rings on her fingers. "He's my chauffeur," she said. "As you can clearly see…" she stated, "I'm not what you might call self-dependent, but I'm sorry, I think I've bothered you long enough."

"Will you have coffee with me?" Vincent asked out of the blue. He saw the surprise on Charlotte's face.

"Now?"

"Of course, if you're not free—"

"Yes, I would love that," she answered without a trace of hesitation.

"Good. Good. Do I take you there, or… is your chauffeur going to send a hit man if I drive you?"

Charlotte laughed. "He's very sweet. I know he looks lethal, but he's a lamb."

Vincent was not convinced. The man in question looked like a character straight out of a film noir.

"It will be easier if he drives me," she said. "He's used to this contraption. We'll follow you. Is that ok?"

"Absolutely."

Vincent kept looking in the rearview mirror, making sure Charlotte's car was following. What are we going to talk about, he wondered. I'm such an idiot. Will you have coffee with me? That's the best you've got? he questioned himself, waiting for a light to turn green.

The two cars pulled into a small parking lot, adjacent to a coffee shop Vincent knew. He stepped out his car, and walked to Charlotte's back door, to open it for her, however, the chauffeur got there before him. The wind had chased away most of the rain, and the drizzle stopped. Avoiding the puddles, Vincent continued toward the entrance of the shop, and waited for Charlotte to be pushed inside.

"Thank you, Dimitri," she told the chauffeur. "I'll take it from here."

Dimitri went back to the car.

"Dimitri. Your chauffeur is Russian," remarked Vincent.

"Yes, born in the U.S. though."

Vincent sat at one of the small tables, and Charlotte pulled in her wheelchair. Two coffees were ordered, for two strangers, now face to face.

Charlotte spoke first. "I'm sorry, I didn't mean to embarrass you," she said, and removed her headscarf. She took off the hair tie, and let her long blond hair fall around her, onto the black dress.

Vincent watched the perfect display of femininity, silently.

"What?" she asked, aware, really.

"Nothing. Yes, actually. I'll regret it, if I don't say it now. I'm sorry. I'm sorry for staring at your wheelchair earlier. You caught me off guard."

"No, it's my fault," she insisted. "I shouldn't have come. This is not how I wanted to meet you," she affirmed.

"Well, here we are. How do you do? I'm Doctor Jones," Vincent said, extending his hand.

"I'm Lady Charlotte Montagu," she replied, extending hers.

"Lady Charlotte, it's a pleasure."

She laughed that same laugh again, showing that willingness to revel in a moment of happiness, perhaps caused by infrequent joy, Vincent thought. He tried to dismiss that last opinion. A few seconds of silence befell, and they stared at each other. Charlotte's blue eyes, like a probe, searched the depth of Vincent's mind. What was it about her that attracted him? He could not quite put his finger on it. Life was complicated enough as it was. No need to add more conflict, he thought, which put Charlotte's friendship in jeopardy.

"I'm curious about your eulogy," she said, breaking the silence.

"How so?"

"It looked you were speaking off the cuff," she explained. "Were you?"

"I was. I don't know what came over me... I know it was a little strange."

"It wasn't, at least not to me." She sipped her warm coffee. "One day, you'll have to tell me what it was all about," she said, simply, as if this was the start of a great friendship.

Vincent just smiled. Finally, he asked the question he longed to ask. "Why did you come to my mother's funeral? I mean, you didn't know her. You barely know me."

Charlotte sighed. "You know... I have no idea why. I had to be here," she uttered, looking at the table, downcast. "Why did you want to have coffee with me?" she asked, boldly, like a rebuttal.

"Guilty," Vincent answered, putting his hands up. "I admit it, I wanted to spend time with you. God! Why does it have to be so hard?"

"What?" she asked.

"This." He looked at her. "Why can't we just agree to the obvious, that we like each other. I mean we spoke for an hour on the phone, before we even met. That should tell you something. Right? When was the last time you did that? Well... perhaps you have, but I... I don't speak to anyone." He drank some of his coffee. "Whoa, that's really disgusting," he asserted, all stirred up.

"My turn now," Charlotte announced. "I do like you, and I have to admit, I was trying to find an excuse to come to New York, to see you. To meet you." She spoke without any reservations. Her calm and quiet demeanor, showed great command in the midst of sensitive situations. Her confinement to a wheelchair gave her the fortitude, otherwise often lacking in circumstances such as these. "I realize a friendship is all I can expect from this, and I don't want you to think I gave this a lot of thought, I really mean this," she stopped and weighed her next words carefully. "Your friendship would mean the world to me. There, I said it."

"You have it," said Vincent, and he reached for her hand. Her teary eyes denoted much about her assertions. They remained there, for a long time. Vincent inquired about Charlotte's family, how the painting of her great-grandmother came about, and the tragedy of the fire.

He felt more comfortable now, and her infirmity departed from her, empowering the beautiful woman she was inside, to go free from any physical afflictions. The two cups of coffee, barely touched, ended up serving just as props.

FIFTEEN

By late August, the restlessness began again. Vincent no longer wished to be left alone, as he had pleaded during all those years. Every night he waited for a visit, anxious to find Julia standing at the end of his bed, like before. Standing anywhere. Every night, he yearned for her. The thought of her consumed him now, more and more. Her powers seemed limitless. Here, or not, she dictated his whole being. Books about the afterlife, the enigmas that lay beyond the grave, were scattered around the penthouse. Most of them were purchased in the last few months. Sarah was definitely instrumental in Vincent's way of thinking, and now certain facts were explained and made more sense. Now that fiction became reality, he needed more of it, like a drug. Vincent thought about only one thing – returning to Vizcaya.

Phone calls to Charlotte were the only reprieve Vincent enjoyed. She became the voice of his logical thoughts, as if she was sent to him to save him from himself. Conversations lasting more than an hour, were not unusual.

He dialed Charlotte's number late one night, before noticing the time on his digital clock on the bedside table. She answered her phone before he could hang up. "I'm sorry, I just noticed the time," apologized Vincent.

"I wasn't asleep. It's ok. Is everything alright?" she asked. The languor in her voice, only added to Vincent's self-reproach for the late call.

"Yes, everything is fine."

"But?" continued Charlotte, now more attentive.

"Ha! And here's the reason why women are smarter than men," he said, as if it was a matter of fact. "You're more intuitive. That's it. You're wiser, and can see the troubles ahead."

"Well, I can't disagree with that analogy." Charlotte sat in bed, pulling herself up into her pillows.

Vincent heard the laborious effort required for that simple motion. "Did you just sit up?"

"Yes. Quite a circus, I'm sorry. So… women are smarter than men. Can we expand on that?" she chuckled.

Vincent liked making her laugh. He liked the sound of her voice. In fact, he liked everything about her if he was being honest with himself.

"When are you going to ask me why I'm in a wheelchair?" Charlotte's voice changed to a more depleted tone. The acceptance of her condition came at a very high price. The five-foot eight figure brought down to her knees, never to stand straight again, had contemplated suicide, to cheat fate.

"Do you want to talk about it?" inquired Vincent, reluctantly.

"I do."

Vincent waited for Charlotte to speak.

"You need to ask me," she suddenly said, breaking a hush, Vincent found heart-breaking.

"Alright. Why are you—"

"I had a riding accident." Silence again. "You know, it was the dumbest thing," she said. "My horse came to a sliding stop, just like that. We think a rabbit may have scared him. A stupid rabbit. Anyway, he stopped, abruptly and I kept going. Landed on my head. The doctors said I was lucky I had my helmet on, or I'd be dead. Can you imagine that? No helmet, no wheelchair," she exclaimed, tearful, her voice expressing hopelessness and pessimism.

"I'm so, so sorry, Charlotte." Vincent thought how inadequate his words were, how pathetic.

"Needless to say, my fiancé at the time, suddenly developed amnesia and a fear of commitment. Well, can't blame him. Good old Geoffrey, he never had much courage, or gallantry for that matter."

"You were engaged?"

"I was. Five years ago," she declared. "Though now it seems like I dreamt it all. How about you? Were you ever engaged?" she asked, in need to stir the conversation away from her.

"Well, now, there's a question. I was. I was, though, not officially."

"What happened?" Charlotte felt entitled to ask. After all, she devulged something extremely personal; a time of her life she was very much unwilling to share.

Vincent's account of his relationship with Sarah, saddened Charlotte. The fake pregnancy upset her. Vincent spoke freely, like the two had known each other their whole lives. As a little more was revealed, both realized their dependence on each other. Inwardly, words like affection, devotedness, were being thrown around, though neither Vincent, nor Charlotte, felt anywhere near ready to say them out loud; Charlotte, detained in her minute world, and Vincent adrift in his own phantasmic universe.

The day of the funeral was the only time Vincent spent in person with Charlotte. They appreciated the only form of communication available to them, and little by little, their lives became an open book. Charlotte spoke about the electrical fire that destroyed the painting and damaged a great part of her childhood home. The cost of the tragedy was massive, though no lives were lost. Vincent talked about periods of his life he had not spoken about for a long time. Yet, nothing was ever said about his troubles, and his intentions regarding Vizcaya. Sure, the house was talked about, however, never to the point of the extreme questions of time travel. Vincent was not ready to talk about that with Charlotte. At least not yet.

Lady Charlotte Montagu came from a family that dated back to King Henry VIII. Not in a very distant past, her ancestors owned more than five thousand acres in Yorkshire, a region to the north of London, in England. Wheat, barley and oats had been the primary source of income for generations, as well as rents from several farms and houses. Charlotte grew up on a large country estate, with stables and a vast conservatory for a multitude of plants that were used for the house, mainly. Hunting parties and various fundraisers at the estate, kept the staff of more than twenty, occupied, during the summer months. Charlotte was the youngest daughter of the Earl of Halifax. His grand-mother was Julia. Lady Julia spent a lot of time in the United States, enjoying a life of leisure. She had invested some of her money in the productions of films during the silent era, and lived for a short period of time in Hollywood, in its infancy. Her travels to the East coast in

1916, gave her access to the American high society, a much-needed change for young Lady Julia. She met James Deering at a party thrown by his brother, Charles. Vizcaya loomed in the distance, and with it the conception of a fabulous dream.

Vincent's anxiety about the fact that Charlotte was related to Julia, made matters even worse. That, he kept to himself. How to begin to speak about such a world? A world not from this world. A world inhabited by visitors from another time. And Julia. Julia. How could Vincent explain the fascination from her shadow. The seduction? How to put logic, in an utterly illogical thought? Can anyone apprehend such a concept? The PhD was at a loss.

No other details about Sargent's painting of Julia, were available. The internet was a dead-end, and not a single art book, or any other publication, mentioned the art work. Even the Heads of Sotheby's were perplexed about the lack of archives on the subject. The painting, which measured at least seven feet by four, should have a place in history. Yet, records of the full-length portrait remained as obscure as the subject herself. What was known about Lady Julia? Not much. Even Charlotte could not help.

Vincent laid on his couch, holding a print of the painting in his hand. "What is it about you?" he asked the indistinct image on the piece of paper. The reproduction was poor, and blurry, though he could tell how magnificent of a model Julia must have been. The garment selected for the portrait was breathtaking; a pale gold silk, trained satin evening dress, with paste jewels. Could the print of the painting, and the photo Charlotte sent of the charcoal sketch, be the only trace left of a life once lived to the fullest?

A text from Charlotte popped up on Vincent's phone. The text just said that she needed to speak to him, and that he should call her whenever convenient. Vincent dialed Charlotte's number right away.

"Hi," she answered. "That was quick."

"It sounded urgent. Is everything alright?"

"Yes, yes, I just need to tell you something. It's a bit embarrassing... I mean I should've told you before."

Vincent sat up, curious about Charlotte's message. "Tell me."

"I've never told a soul about this, not even my parents, although they probably suspected it." Charlotte gave a big sigh, as if what she was about to confess had weighed heavily on her. "I caused the fire that burned the Sargent… and a great part of the house."

"Ooh, my dear Charlotte."

"I was six years old. I took the candles from the dinner table… they only got used one time, and I stole them before the butler cleared the table." Charlotte became emotional. Her voice trembled.

"I'm sorry," murmured Vincent. "You don't have to say anymore."

"I do. I need this. I'm grateful I can tell you. It will be our secret."

"Okay."

"Thank you." Charlotte went on to explain how the fire started. She told Vincent how

her 'Princess' dress caught on fire, and that she had seconds to take it off. The curtains of her bedroom ignited soon after, as flames were rapidly lapping upward. The ancient beams and the old woodwork, only made the fire more ferocious, which quickly turned everything in its path into ashes, including Julia's portrait.

"I'm glad you felt like could you tell me this," said Vincent. "It was a tragedy, and you were just a little girl." He heard Charlotte sniffing back a sob. "Thank you for your trust."

"Aah," she sighed, "I don't know why I'm so emotional!" she exclaimed. "It's not like it happened yesterday."

"Yes, still, it's the first time you spoke about it," Vincent replied, "right?"

"It is. You're a sweet friend. I'm happy we share this… this secret."

"Me too. Now go a pour yourself a large gin and tonic!" he exclaimed.

"I'm way ahead of you," she laughed, sipping her cocktail.

After they hung up, Vincent looked at the print of the painting again, amazed at the revelation. He smiled.

From then on, Vincent prepared himself, at least mentally, for a return to Vizcaya; to 1917. He began to wonder about his presence at the house, as he sat on a bench in Central Park. How would he explain his arrival to James Deering and what sort of clothing he would need? How long could he stay? So many questions filled his mind. Some trivial? Perhaps. One question, though, he had not asked himself before; what if the access into the past was closed to him now. What if the last time was a fluke? It could happen, Vincent thought, with a certain nostalgia, and his logic still at odds with the supernatural. The secret door now would only lead to a dusty and spiderweb covered passage. No more Sargent. Gone would be the glorious elegance of those long-forgotten times, and Vizcaya in its full grandeur. Vizcaya sealed forever. How tragic. An image began to form in Vincent's head. He stood up, and started to walk, uncomfortable with his meditations. He tried to dismiss the forms etched against the walls of his mind, her forms, her. Julia. She was there, waiting for him, beyond time, yet he could feel her. He walked aimlessly. Being unable to cross the time barrier, now distressed him. Never in his wildest dreams had he imagined to be in this situation, in that thinking process. Everything he knew, was in direct contradiction with what slowly became reality to him. A reality so absurd, so ridiculous, that he dreaded to speak to anyone about it. Such was his life now; consumed by a once sumptuous house, now inconsequential, and a shadow who roams the earth. Scientific? What does that even mean? he thought. I know what I saw, he continued, still pensive and yet decisive about the future. Those voices I heard, he kept thinking, those people are in that bedroom. As sure as I stand here, he continued, trying to grasp the idea of time and the displacement of anything three-dimensional. They are there, "right?" he said out loud, and stared at the entrance to The Museum of Natural History on the other side of Central Park. Several hours had passed, and the late afternoon light cast an orange glow behind the skyline. Vincent simply turned around and began to walk in the opposite direction. The secret passage was the most important thing in his life now. He knew it. That secret passage was his sweet certainty. The woman, whose name he knew now, would welcome him with open arms, and the house, full of life, would celebrate the visitor from another era.

SIXTEEN

Break into Vizcaya? Unthinkable. Vincent lay on his bed, the penthouse plunged into darkness, as Vincent entertained the idea that Julia favored the absence of light. He weighed all options of literally breaking and entering, yet very much unable to come to terms with such inconceivable reality. His reasoning powers blocked the way for anything remotely non-scientific. Even as a child, documentaries were far more appealing to him, than any kind of super hero, or anything to do with make-believe space crafts. An ill-fitted teacher, once told Vincent's mother that her son would not amount to anything, if he considered himself as being too advanced for her class; 'above the common man', were her very words. Mrs. Jones laughed at the spinster, and promptly removed her ten-year old son from that school. The truth is, Vincent was far more accomplished than he cared to show. This, of course, can have a reverse effect on a young child's life. Bicycles, soccer balls, toy bows and arrows, were never found under the Christmas tree. Some happy-go-lucky people play and have fun in those innocent early years, oblivious of life's cash register lurking somewhere in the future. Others, study or work hard on their gifts, excluded from soccer camp, and endless hours spent in arcades. Yet, those can usually afford a life of leisure, having prepared for it. There is no right or wrong. Vincent did everything he was supposed to do. Why was he persecuted during all those years? And why was he chosen to partake in a most incredible journey? True, he loved art beyond just about anything, even so, Vincent did not possess a very creative spirit. What was he meant to achieve? And that creature, that woman, who was abducting his mind, what was her role in haunting him?

Returning to Vizcaya without being seen. A dilemma. The Jones family ran the risk of becoming the center of attention, and start a crisis of monumental proportions with the media.

Vincent had to return there. Like a lover, languishing while away from the beloved, he could only hear the agony of his heart. He felt drawn to the house by an irresistible force. Why deny it? A flight was booked for the next day. The Sargent watercolor, which had been re-framed, rested on the floor, still. Vincent picked it up, and looked for a suitable place to hang it. He paced the main room, and finally settled on a spot, near the fireplace. A small drawing by Barbara Hepworth had to be removed. The space seemed perfect. He stared at the painting after he hung it, and approached it. This is it, he pondered, imagining the artist, his favorite artist, sitting there and composing Vizcaya, like a symphony and as if by magic.

"Good morning, Sir. It's good to see you again. How long do you plan to stay with us?" asked the concierge of The Ritz Carlton.

That, Vincent could not answer. An eternity, he thought, maybe… he smiled inwardly. "I'm not sure. A few days," he said.

"I have to advise you, there's a storm coming our way. A hurricane. Hurricane Irma," said the concierge. "We shouldn't have accepted your reservation, really."

"Yes, I saw it on the news. Well, those storms can turn away so fast," he replied.

"I'm not sure this one will. We may have to evacuate."

"Really? Evacuate?"

"Yes, Sir. I'm sorry."

"Not your fault. Not your fault," replied Vincent, deep in thought.

Vincent walked by the hotel pool, where parents and children splashed the hours away. Maybe just relax, enjoy the rest of the week, he thought, and go back on Tuesday, when the house is closed to the public. No one can know about this, he told himself. Vizcaya's director would be dismayed at such an incoherent, preposterous theory coming from Vincent. The secret passages were one thing, however, that they led you back to another time, was a concept worthy of serious doubts on one's mental health. It could not be so.

"What would you like to drink?" asked the waiter at the beach cabana.

"I guess, a mojito," Vincent replied, thinking of his weekend with Sarah and South Beach.

The salty wind coming from the water relaxed him, and Vincent found it hard to imagine that a hurricane was brewing beyond the horizon line. A couple of cruise ships, lacking all elegance, headed out to sea in the late afternoon light, no doubt to get away from the storm.

Vincent checked his phone, and he found the absence of a single call or text, perplexing. "Excuse me," he called the barman, "can you call my phone? I'm not sure it's working." Vincent gave the man his number, and waited while he dialed it.

"I just hear some weird noises," said the waiter. "Are you sure you don't have it on silent?" he asked, trying to sound logical.

"I'm sure. It's alright, thanks." said Vincent. His intellect shushed everything. The phone had eventually become an empty shell, all technologies nullified when it crossed the threshold of time. Vincent removed himself from the physical state of being there, on this beach; his subconscious in full alert. The willing participant, and now a witness, was ushered into the past. Such was his life now, a crusade to rekindle the ashes of what was once Vizcaya. He felt spoiled, in a way. Had he been given a choice, not knowing what he knew now, he would sacrifice everything for this. Tracy's words during their lunch in New York, played in his head, like a malicious game. How prophetic they all were, and how accepting Vincent had become. Still, the possibility of being lost within the black hole of time, and unable to return to the present, scared him. He saw Charlotte's face, and sipped on the mojito.

By midnight on Friday, it became obvious that Florida was going to be hit again by a major storm. Every television set throughout the hotel were tuned to The Weather Channel. The so-called cone of uncertainty, looked categorically frightening, and most definitely certain of its objective. Category 3 and 4 were mentioned much too often for comfort. Vincent's first thought was for Vizcaya. How much damage and beating the house would have to endure. The thought made him very angry. However, a terrible idea came to him. An idea so devious, that he had to hide from a hotel employee coming his way the following morning.

"Can I get you anything, sir?" asked the unsuspecting girl.

"No, I think I'm all set. Thank you." Vincent headed towards the main counter. "Any news about an evacuation?" he inquired to the hotel manager, who seemed very uptight.

"I'm afraid, it's very likely, yes. A landfall is scheduled for tomorrow... sometime in the early afternoon."

Vincent's mind was made up. This was the day. The hurricane would be his ally. An irrational idea in the head of a brilliant man, is not an uncommon occurrence. Vincent tried to justify navigating in murky waters. He had never been even reprimanded for anything in his entire life. Not only was he going to break the law, but the deed would be done in the middle of a raging storm. How could it go wrong?

Irma was now a category 5 hurricane, according to the National Hurricane Center, a few miles down the road. Still a full day away from striking the coast of Florida, and already the effects of the storm were visible. The hotel staff were running in all directions, trying to appease the nervous guests and at the same time, do their work. Everything had to be put away, or secured. The pool deck was empty of people, and the choppy water was lapping against the edges. Vincent looked up at the charcoal sky, and watched the clouds moving in a counter-clockwise pattern.

By 5:30 the next morning, the lobby had become a vast waiting room, and tens of people waited for the buses, to evacuate. Flip-flops and Ferragamo shoes, all shoved into the same arena, regardless of people's stations in life. It was amusing to watch. Strangers were becoming instantaneous friends, notwithstanding the fact that forty-eight hours earlier, such camaraderie would have been insufferable. However, desperate times call for venturesome measures, as the weather was deteriorating by the minute.

"Do you think you could get me a taxi?" Vincent asked one of the many people behind the front desk.

"I can try, but I don't know if you'll get one."

"That bad, hey?"

"I'm afraid so."

"I'll need to leave some things in storage," said Vincent.

"Very good. Just bring whatever you need to keep here to me. A couple of phone messages were left for you. Did you get them?" asked the concierge.

The messages had to be from Charlotte. No, they were from Sarah, which surprised Vincent. "May I?" he asked, pointing at the hotel phone.

"Of course."

Vincent dialed Sarah's number, and listened to the short statement; "I'm not here right now, if you know what I mean… leave a message."

"Hi… it's Vincent. I'm not sure why you're calling me. I'm safe… the hotel is bringing in buses, and we're evacuating. By the way, my phone is dead." Vincent hung up, not at all sure of his own heart. He had forgotten Sarah. That bothered him, yet not as much as it should, and that really concerned him. He dialed Charlotte's number, and left a voicemail, saying his phone was acting up, and that he was in Miami for a few days.

After giving his luggage to the concierge, Vincent waited for his taxi. Apparently, a few were still operating. He sat outside, beneath the covered entrance, and watched several buses arrive. The evacuation had begun.

The taxi arrived. People stared at Vincent as he climbed into the car, perhaps a little perturbed. The mind can act in strange ways during an awesome act of nature. A mighty wind is supposed to drive people crazy, if you believe some legends. A category 5 hurricane would definitely qualify.

"Where to?" asked the cab driver. "You're my last ride. All hell is gonna break lose."

"It seems that way," answered Vincent, desperately trying to pluck up his courage. "Just leave me outside Vizcaya, you know where that is, right? on south Miami Avenue," he finally said. "Someone's picking me up." The lie came naturally. It embarrassed him.

"That house is gonna get pummeled again. That's too bad."

"You like that house?" asked Vincent, interested and curious about what the man was going to say.

"Yes, it's a beautiful place. Magical."

"It is." He liked the word 'magical'. In layman's terms, it did describe the spirit of Vizcaya.

"My great-grandfather worked there. He was a stone carver, from Italy.

"Really?" said Vincent, amazed, his senses on high alert, now.

"Yeah, a lot of people came looking for work."

"What's your name?"

"Stefano. Stefano Moretti, of the Moretti family. God bless their souls," he said, crossing himself.

"Glad to meet you, Stefano. I'm Vincent Jones. And by the way, thank you for picking me up."

"No sweat."

"Do you happen to know what your great-grandfather worked on?" asked Vincent, getting excited at the thought of that 'degrees of separation theory'.

"No, sorry. I just remember that name… Vizcaya, Vizcaya, when I was growing up."

The wind had increased in the last few hours, and its effects were being felt on the car.

"I hope you'll be picked up soon," said Stefano. "It's gonna get ugly," he added, as the car stopped in front of Vizcaya's main entrance.

Vincent paid the fare. "Do you believe in ghosts?" he felt compelled to ask.

Stefano put the car in 'park' and turned around. "Of course. Why?"

"Just curious. Don't tell anyone, but this house…" he said pointing towards the entrance, "is haunted. I'm serious."

"I know. I heard stories."

"Right? Like a beautiful woman roaming the land…" suggested Vincent.

"No, nothing like that. A beautiful woman? I'd like a piece of that," said Stefano, showing his less than poetic tendencies, and certainly not being a true descendant of what Vincent pictured an artist from Italy to be; even a common stone carver.

"Right."

"You wait in the car if you want… you know, until your ride gets here."

"I'll be fine, thank you. You better go."

"Suit yourself. Good luck," said Stefano, and departed.

A powerful gust of wind shook the whole gathering of trees by the main gate. Vincent stood there, watching the day worsening fast. The avenue was deserted, except for a couple of cars in the distance. Clouds speeding across the ominous sky in a vast circular motion, grew even darker. A huge flock of birds darkened a large portion of the sky above the horizon, moving haphazardly, like a delicate silk veil lost to the wind. A police car stopped. Vincent panicked.

"What are you doing here? You can't stay here," shouted the officer, his face red as a beetroot.

How demeaning it is to be in the wrong. Vincent's presence here was inexplicable, at least to this police officer.

"Keep moving. Go home," he asserted, and sped away, no doubt to some manmade disturbance, as the criminal spirit in men shines best in times like these.

The main gate was open. The name 'Vizcaya' carved vertically on both stone pillars, seemed to invite Vincent, who had lost his nerve. He felt the key in his right pocket, twirling it, like a good luck charm.

SEVENTEEN

The estate seemed deserted, abandoned to the upcoming fury of Irma. Vincent walked toward the house, close to the trees, like a common thief. Guilt and anxiety took turn in causing great anguish in him. Still, another aspect had to be considered; the emotion of being another, removed from what he knew to be real. He felt that same sensation again, the fervent desire to be here, to be spellbound.

Unaware, he looked for her, the woman. Julia. Was she waiting for him on the other side of time? She had to be. Vincent reached the main terrace. Still, no one around. The Barge waited; the ship made of stone, anchored there for eternity. He looked at the winged stone mermaids on its bow and stern; the creatures of strange legends, holding the ship up, victoriously, invulnerable. A passing thought for Charlotte made him question his intentions, of literally breaking into a museum. Then, there was the other predicament, the likes of which remained nonsensical; a return to 1917. Going back in time. A complete reversal of the aging process curse; the despair deeply rooted in every man. The fear of wrinkled forehead, the fear of boredom. Could this small plot of land, this insignificant speck, be the passage to another dimension? Was any of it true? Had it all been in his head? In those moments of complete lucidity, fiction and reality really scared Vincent.

The water level in the bay had risen. Choppy little waves lapped furiously, like angry little demons, against the sea wall. The wind had increased, too. Strong bursts in small tornadoes rushed through, as nature's chaos reigned triumphant. Vincent surveyed the whole area around him as Vizcaya was preparing for the worst. It was time to find shelter, leave, it was not too late to stop this madness. The house seemed to confront him at that very moment. Should he ignore what appears factual and step into that other dimension? Become the visitor into another time? His mind was made up.

Vincent began to walk around the house, in search of an unlocked door, or perhaps the wind had already damaged a window from which he could enter. Bands of heavy rain were making the quest perilous. Another gust of wind forced Vincent against a side wall, and he stood there in awe of nature's ferocity, as horizontal spears of rain and sand pounded his entire body. The white linen slacks and the ivory cotton shirt were soaked and getting dirty beyond recognition. Both garments were bought as an ensemble, in the hope to assume the role about to be played. He could see the gardens from his vantage point. Many trees had already lost branches, and debris was being thrown indiscriminately as chaos increased, like a pestilence. The wind rushed through the property, stronger and more destructive, still. How much more could Vizcaya endure? Vincent felt hopeless and could only be a witness to the carnage before him. A marble statue was knocked off its pedestal by a large tree limb, as the deafening roar of a thousand blenders suddenly whipped the air with stinging wind and water.

Irma was about to make landfall, and Vizcaya would never be the same again. Like a defenseless child, the house stood against the savage storm. An invisible sea monster coming to shore, was about to trample through the gardens, blindly knocking vases off their pedestals, flinging marble statues to the soggy ground, breaking and smashing without any concessions. Vincent knew the water surge was going to flood the lower part of the house and the half-basement rooms, ruthlessly, suffocating the very soul of Vizcaya with several feet of sea water. How does anything of beauty, created by man, survive the passage of time? Between wars and natural disasters, which are the most lethal ones? A question Vincent could not really give a definitive answer to. And he watched a little piece of history going to ruins.

A few steps away, a small window was missing its glass. This is it, thought Vincent. He crawled through the cramped space, though not before taking another look over his shoulder. If he was not deceiving himself and if logic took no part in it, a peaceful Vizcaya awaited him on the other side of time.

The water marks from Vincent's white canvas shoes, betrayed his presence inside the house. The rooms were empty of life, and he continued toward the courtyard; the heart of Vizcaya. His gaze rested on the balcony. Where are you? he pondered, climbing the main stairway, expecting to see the apparition and took the key out of his pocket. The world outside seemed far removed from Vincent's reality, as in a bad dream. And he looked up and watched the whirlwind, the pandemonium beyond the glass roof, with the eyes of a small and scared creature. The walls trembled, as Irma overshadowed Vizcaya with an unrivaled strength in a one-sided combat. One, the peacemaker with all beauty and grace, the other, the aggressor, a bully sent to abuse and destroy with far too much strength. All the money in the world, could not alter the course of this hurricane, which it seemed had made this place 'her' objective.

Vincent's mind wandered. He noticed the quietness inside the house. He closed his eyes for a second and noticed the silence, yet Irma was just behind those walls. The power was gone and soon darkness was going to make moving around, difficult. He heard a sound, like someone was moving furniture. The noise came from upstairs. He climbed the stairs, and walked in the bedroom. She stood in front of the secret door. The woman. Julia. She was here, waiting for him. Vincent stopped in his tracks. How did he feel now? He didn't really know. Did he fear her, or was he simply in awe of her? He approached her, slowly. How many ghost stories had he heard in his life? Tales from other worlds, from beyond the grave and beyond our comprehension. None came close to the phenomenon he was witnessing. With all certainty, this was no hallucination. This was as real as it gets. Vincent reached for her, in a moment of passion for what he had weathered all his life. His hand went through the hologram, like he was trying to apprehend a fragment of a dream, and she vanished. All he had to do was to go through that door; that hidden passage. He stared at the key in his hand and thought of Charlotte again. The house was silent, as it was waiting for his decision. Irma, outside, was causing havoc. Vincent's heart was beating fast, and the thought of crossing the barrier of time with the possibility of no return, frightened him. It alarmed him, and at the same time enthralled him. Then there was that other factor, one he would never admit to; that woman, the companion of his youth. He knew now that she had beguiled him all his life, calling him in his dreams to finally meet outside this door. This was her plan all along. She was inviting him into her domain, in her time. Why hesitate? Fear. It was fear. Fear of the unknown, the threatening thoughts of what we cannot see. Vincent's analytical reasoning process was very much at odds with such foolishness. Yet, he had seen her. He had experienced her. He smiled. Sargent, too, was on the other side. James Deering. He placed the key in the key hole, and wished with all his heart, giving no room for rationality, for this miracle to take him to April of 1917. He turned the key, without another trace of hesitation, and opened the door. That same cold draft as before, enveloped him.

EIGHTEEN

What is more heartwarming for one who seeks tranquility, a magnificent view of a mountain range, or the embrace of a loved one? Can solitude heal the wounded heart? Possibly. Vincent's solace lay within the walls of Vizcaya. He was prepared to abandon all, for the sake of his peculiar attachment to a house. From his first visit to Vizcaya, as a teenager, Vincent discerned the spirit of the place. It was as if the house was conscious of him being there, and brought the past into the present. Every room, filled with shadows from days long-passed, welcomed him as one of their own. From that day on, a strong bond was formed, forged together like two components, to become inseparable; one made of flesh, the other of stone.

As soon as he entered the passageway, Vincent felt his pockets, and just like before, the phone and wallet were gone. Though he figured this would happen, he was petrified. This was really the doorway into another dimension. His clothes were perfectly clean, which he found amusing. Eyes closed, the wish to return to a particular month in 1917, did appear to be impossible. April 1917, is when Sargent was a guest, Vincent told himself. Why would I choose another time? He realized his demands were outrageous and had to conclude that he could easily end up just about anywhere in time. Yet, the hope of being here for Julia, at her request, really restored his faith and he thought his appeal was perhaps not that ridiculous.

The door was closed behind him now; leaving the present on the other side. His future was ahead of him, at the end of this passageway. Vincent took a few steps toward that other bedroom. He heard some music, perhaps a brass band.

Though at the moment the bedroom was unoccupied, the scent of a perfume confirmed the fact that someone was staying here. A silk dressing gown lay on the unmade bed and a magnificent pink faience vase with fresh white roses, stood on the chest of drawers. Vincent wondered what time it was, and more specifically, where in time. He walked to the window. The brightness of the day amazed him. Several people were gathered on the terrace below, enjoying the sun, unaware of the storm raging around them. Irma was humbled, eradicated by a simple turn of a key. A brass band at the back of the garden's main alleyway, entertained a fairly large group of people. Vincent knew that from time to time, James Deering opened his estate to the public. Though he never participated in the festivities, he enjoyed watching those happy assemblies from the comfort of his house.

A book with a bookmark in it, resting on the bedside table, caught Vincent's attention; a novel by Edgar Rice Burroughs – The Lost Continent. The sound of voices came from the ground floor and Vincent imagined a gathering of some sort in the courtyard; perhaps lunch, or breakfast? "What now?" he murmured to himself. He stepped carefully toward the bedroom door and opened it slightly. His outfit caused him great anxiety all of a sudden and he approached a mirror. He stared at his own reflection, wondering if anyone would be fooled by his presence. "What have I got to lose?" he said out loud. "Hmm, let's see… you'd be kicked out and sent to jail," he continued, talking to his reflection. He brushed off his sleeves, and ran his fingers through his hair. "Well… here we go."

Vincent stepped outside the bedroom and looked straight up at the open roof. A sensation of bliss and fear ran throughout his entire being. I'm really here. I'm really back in time, he acknowledged, as a couple of white clouds slowly passed above the house. More voices were heard coming from the ground floor, though Vincent could not see anyone in the immediate vicinity. He approached the main staircase, stood beneath the vaulted archway and looked at the courtyard below, the slender palms in each corner, and the flowering shrubs in huge jardinière pots. The high carved fountain, trickled water into an ancient basin. Vincent had never seen it in action. "My God," he exclaimed in a whisper, "what am I doing?" Vincent became acutely conscious of what was happening to him. I cannot be seen, he thought. Now he wanted a way out. Now fear took over anything he previously saw as a fantastic journey, the pursuit of a capricious dream. He looked up at the open roof again, in awe of the moment. He stood there, alone with his thoughts and as the intruder now, a ghost from another world. Vincent had to know what year this was and what month. His curiosity took hold of him. He knew that his first visit took place in March of

1917. The New York Herald headlines about the Russian revolution, and the Czar abdicating, told him that. That was then; March 15, 1917. What about now? The sound of the brass band stopped.

Vincent had no time to anticipate the utter stupefaction about to befall on him. Suddenly, out of nowhere, James Deering appeared at the bottom of the stairs, dressed in immaculate white linen. Vincent recognized him at once. "Mr. Jones," he exclaimed. "When did you arrive? I wasn't sure you'd be joining us this time." Vincent could swear Deering felt suspicious. "Lunch will be served shortly. You might want to change."

Still under the total shock of seeing James Deering in the flesh, Vincent remained speechless in the seconds that followed. "My luggage seems to have been lost at the station." The words finally came out of his mouth with a frankness that surprised him, as if they were edited and spoken by someone else.

"Well, we can't have that, Mr. Jones," said Deering as the great host that he was. "The housekeeper will show you to your bedroom. You'll be in Lady Hamilton," he added, and headed to the terrace.

"I can't believe I just spoke to James Deering. This is crazy!" uttered Vincent, between his teeth, as his self-confidence tumbled down the steps, crumbling a little more. "He called me Mr. Jones!" he repeated quietly and mystified. "Mr. Jones?" His mind wandered. Vincent felt nothing but misgivings about his presence here, when Sarah's face came forward, like a light in the depth of a cave. He remembered her remarks about his physical resemblance to his great-grandfather. Vincent had given little thought about his '1917 identity', how he would explain his presence, or indeed his arrival at the house. No, he had never meditated on those rather important points. James Deering was convinced that Clarence Henry Jones was in his house. He had been a guest on several occasions before, so why not this time? Assuming the character of his great-grandfather was perhaps an insane notion, yet, James Deering was fooled, so it seemed. The problem was, the 'real' Clarence Henry Jones. Where was he right now? At home in Pittsburgh, on his way to Vizcaya? The latter being a formidable disaster, not to mention Vincent's encounter with his own ancestor!

"Please follow me, Mr. Jones," said the housekeeper.

"You're Cecilia Adair, right?" inquired Vincent, as they made their way toward the assigned bedroom.

"I am, Sir. How kind of you to remember my name," she replied, convinced the guest was Clarence Jones.

Cecilia Adair was the well-documented housekeeper of Vizcaya. Vincent knew everything about her. He knew when she was born, and when she would die. He felt a certain sense of power, and at the same time, a sense of frailty. "Tell me, what day is this?" he asked. I've been so busy, I've lost of sense of time."

"It's Tuesday, sir. Here it is," she said, and opened the bedroom door for Vincent. He looked puzzled. Is there anything wrong, Sir?"

"No, I'm fine, thank you. I would love a newspaper, though. Thank you."

"I'll bring one up. Your clothes will be brought up, too," said the housekeeper, and left.

Vincent became conscious of the room, the delicate fresh smell of flowers and clean linen. He looked down at the embroidered wool rug he stood upon, with obelisks, birds and flower motifs. The colors around the room were so much more vivid, not the faded hues of the museum Vizcaya would become. His eyes fell on the lacquered and painted bed, with silk upholstered head, blue silk and ribbony floral garlands. Two gilt cupids, on top of the headboard, stared vacantly at the bed. Vincent's sensitivity took the full force of such a display of charm and elegance, doomed, and eventually lost to its own destiny.

Several outfits were brought to Vincent's bedroom, even a swimming suit. One could only be impressed with James Deering's hospitality and his sense of details to keep his guests comfortable and not lacking anything. Where did those clothes come from? Vincent had no idea. He looked through the closet, and found an outfit for just about any social activity. After changing into a white linen suit, which fitted him well enough, Vincent looked in the bathroom for some kind of gel for his hair. He found a small bottle with a label that read: *Colgate's Brilliantine – A preparation that imparts a greaseless luster to hair. It keeps hair in place and makes it soft and glossy. Colgate & Co. New York, USA.* He poured some of the gel on the tip of his fingers, intrigued, though not at all convinced of the result, spread it on both hands, and greased his hair. "I look like a mobster," he said, looking into the mirror, combing his hair back, Rudolph Valentino style. The bathroom was supplied with everything a guest might need; a silver toothbrush and a silver moustache brush, really took Vincent by surprise. The infinite details and the luxurious commodities struck Vincent. James Deering was an eccentric of the most wonderful kind.

Vincent noticed that a newspaper had been left for him – The Tampa Times, a newspaper that went out of business in 1959. He looked at the date, nervous – Monday, April 2, 1917 – yesterday's paper, due to distance for delivery, Vincent pondered. He grabbed the paper, and held it up, as in a triumphant gesture. He wanted to scream for joy, such was his happiness, however, that would have been a bad idea. He looked at the date again, as to confirm the reality of this momentous event. "April 2, 1917," he said in the quietness of the room. Not quite three weeks after his first visit. If a few minutes were as one week, like the first time, what would several days at Vizcaya in 1917, turn into in the present? A week? A month? Five years? There was no way of knowing, and Vincent's fear returned, unannounced, like an ember inside his head. If he stayed for too long, would the gateway back to the present be closed for ever? How long was too long? His life in New York, though not too exciting he found himself admitting, was nevertheless, a good life. He was a respected member of society. He focused on Clarence Henry Jones's clone in the mirror, when the reflection of a woman standing by the door, appeared behind him. Vincent turned around. "Hello," he said, startled.

"I don't believe we've met. I'm Marion Davies," said the young and attractive woman, still standing in the doorway. She wore a stunning silk chiffon emerald green afternoon dress, that fell just below her knees. Her short blonde wavy hair outlined her bright face, on which two large dazzling blue eyes, shimmered.

Vincent knew exactly who Marion Davies was; a famous film actress from the silent era, who also appeared in Broadway musicals. He had seen a couple of her silent films, though he had never had the chance to see her in the talkies, which she transitioned into successfully. He was also aware that she had been a guest of James Deering. "I'm Vince... I'm Clarence... Henry Jones," he managed to blurt out, astounded by the young film star. Here she was, in the flesh and in full color. Vincent noticed the tone of her voice, never having heard it before. His mind raced at such a speed, that he was unsure about his ability to control anything coherent coming out of his mouth. Marion Davies! he exclaimed in his soul, as he shook her hand. For a split second, Charlotte's image came forward. It confused him.

"I think Mr. Deering is expecting us for drinks," she said, smiling.

"We wouldn't want to make him wait, would we?" he answered, now more confident of himself, though still a little apprehensive about a certain family ancestor arriving unexpectedly.

Marion Davies held Vincent's arm, and they made their way downstairs to the courtyard.

Several lacy white iron tables were placed around a particular area, under the galleries, and guests were enjoying James Deering's philanthropic lifestyle. Vincent counted at least eight of them. Some people were talking and laughing, others seemed to be attentive to some of the plants and flowers beneath the upper galleries. James Deering liked drinks and lunches served in his beloved courtyard. Vincent could not help himself, and had to look up at the open roof again, as if it was the indisputable proof of his presence here, now. The fragrance of flowers and blossoms was an enchanting addition to the miracle, emphasized by the warm breeze coming from the bay through the three opened, arched doors.

Drinks, from white wine, cider and whiskey, were served before lunch, which consisted of fish and fresh vegetables, grown just across the street, on Vizcaya's very own extensive farm. Tables were garnished with bowls of fruit, and chunks of cheddar cheese. Marion Davies appeared to be the guest of honor, and stories about her latest film dominated the conversations. Vincent was pleased to listen, and keep a low profile, as servants promptly removed plates, and replenished glasses.

A few of the men lingered over brandy and cigars, after lunch. Vincent felt he had to join them, though during lunch, and since his arrival, he wanted to step outside. Images of The Barge kept clouding his mind. He wanted to see the ship of stone, he so admired, in its authentic and most beautiful state. The sound of an organ, that had been set to play mechanically, filled the house with the music of Mozart and Handel. James Deering had retired to another room, perhaps the music room, thought Vincent. Some of the men asked about the steel industry, how business was going. Fortunately, Vincent was well versed in the family affairs, and he came across as legitimate. Though Deering told Mr. Jones, during lunch, that he had lost some weight, since his last visit.

Marion Davies returned to the table, like a breath of fresh air and asked Vincent if he would like to join her in the gardens. He did.

She held his arm again. "This is only my second visit here," she said. "You've been a guest many times, haven't you?"

"A few times, yes," Vincent replied. "Do you mind if we go this way?" he asked, pointing towards the East Terrace.

They stepped outside. Vincent marveled quietly at the sunny day, Irma in the back of his mind. He thought about space and time, and the fact that right here, right now, exactly a hundred years away, a raging storm was destroying the very landscape he was looking at.

Marion Davies and Vincent stood on the terrace, the barge before them, adorned with shrubbery, palms and fountains. Vincent admired the small summer house on board, with its lattice dome roof. Such artistry. He had never imagined it to be so beautiful, and that he would feel so sad.

"Ugly thing," she said.

"The Barge?"

"Don't you think it's ugly? I was here last year… it was still under construction," she added, with such indifference in her voice, that Vincent found it hard to ignore. He would give anything to witness the construction of the famed ship. "You like it?" she asked.

"I think it's magnificent."

"Magnificent?"

"Yes," he uttered, his mind on things to come; Vizcaya in disarray and the terrible years ahead, which any day would include a world war. He observed the beautiful expanse of lawn that covered the terrace, an aspect of the house that would disappear in the years ahead, replaced by stone. He had only seen it depicted in one of Sargent's watercolor.

Marion looked at Vincent. "You are strange," she said, with that voice, Vincent found rather pleasing. Soft.

"How so?" he asked.

"I can't put my finger on it." She held his arm a little tighter. "But I will."

They both walked down to the water's edge. Vincent looked toward the North, where the Miami skyline eventually would emerge.

"What are you looking at?" Marion asked.

"How peaceful everything is. How clean."

"If you want peaceful, this is it," she remarked.

"You miss Hollywood?" he asked.

"No," she asserted, with vigor. "I miss my work, but I don't miss the shark infested waters," she added.

"I'd imagine it's not easy."

"It's easy enough if you're pretty and have no morals."

"I see."

"Let's not talk about all that. Look, we're here, in this strange paradise."

They made their way to the main garden. The brass band was gone, as well as members of the public. Their few hours spent at Vizcaya, were no doubt the highlight of the day, or perhaps it was something they would cherish forever. Several men were working in the garden, attending to the hundreds of plants, flowers, and countless vases on pedestals.

It was hard to assimilate the substantiality of what Vincent was witnessing. As he walked arm in arm with Marion Davies, herself a shadow from the past, Vincent became all too conscious of his own mortality.

NINETEEN

After a light dinner and a few more cigars and brandy, guests slowly began to say good night. Marion kissed Vincent on the cheek, and wished him sweet dreams. The last of the dirty dishes were removed. James Deering had gone to bed early. The servants, too, were gone. The house became silent, all life removed. Vincent stood on the balcony, outside his bedroom, watching the courtyard below. Stars filled the open roof, brighter than ever before, in the unpolluted Florida sky. He closed the door of his bedroom and sat on the bed, still amazed at what took place. He wondered if he dared head back toward the door, the secret door, that led him here. Perhaps it was time. He had seen enough. Marion Davies was a delightful encounter, and yet one that could never materialize into anything. "What am I saying?" he expressed quietly. "Have you lost your mind?" He hesitated before lying on the bed, fully dressed. Somehow, the idea of being inside the sheets, made him feel weird, as if he was meddling with part of an exhibit. Mr. Director of the museum would not be amused, Vincent thought, as he finally lay on the Lady Hamilton bed, which the bedroom was named after. He tried to fall asleep, unsuccessfully. Sargent should be arriving soon, Vincent thought. The notion, far too absurd to analyze at this point, terrorized him. He lay, hands on his chest, listening to the silence. An image he had not thought about all day, ever since he stepped through time, came forth, powerfully. Julia. Her face appeared in his head, and only one thought consumed him for the rest of the night; where was she?

The bright light of a new day, awoke Vincent. For a short moment, his mind played tricks with him, and he looked around the strange surroundings. He wiped his eyes, and sat in bed. He wondered what time it was. The muffled sound of voices coming from downstairs, meant people were up, and Vincent walked to the bathroom and ran a bath.

A small group of guests were already in the breakfast room, on the second floor, and adjacent to some of the bedrooms. A large round table, that could accommodate at least twelve people, sat in the middle of the room. Vincent admired the view of the gardens from the open windows that telescoped back into the wall. Filling the full length of the wall, the open space became a loggia, and a lovely cool morning breeze could be felt. Again, he was deeply moved at the sight of the room, filled with joviality and life.

The breakfast, buffet style, included fresh fruit, eggs, bacon, cereal of all kinds, orange juice and tomato juice. Several newspapers were lying around. Vincent glanced at the dates, just to make sure, before sitting at the table. There was an air of relaxation about the place, no one seemed to be rushing, or asking questions, simply to be polite. No, it was a wonderful house to be in, and James Deering was its wonderful owner. The plates, cups and saucers, that will sit behind locked cabinets in the years ahead, became a subject of contemplation for Vincent.

Casual conversations took place, though a couple of more serious topics were discussed about the Russian Revolution, the abdication of the Czar. Vincent found it odd that no one was talking about the conflict taking place in Europe. In a few days, a declaration of war from President Wilson would be announced, and the United Sates would be at war with Germany. At the risk of sounding more like a fortune-teller, than a well-informed man, Vincent considered mentioning it, however, he decided not to.

A boat trip was planned, and Vincent looked forward to it. He had never seen Vizcaya from the bay.

"Mr. Sargent is supposed to arrive, today," said one of the guests, impeccably dressed.

"I believe he's staying with Mr. Deering's brother, Charles," said another.

History was correct, and Vincent, who became as intoxicated all of a sudden, knew it well. Sargent was indeed staying at Charles Deering's estate, about ten miles to the south. So today, was the day. Today, he and the great artist he admired for so long, would breathe the same air, under the same roof. This was too much. This was more than a miracle. Vincent's excitement had to show. He became like a child on a Christmas morning; a smile affixed on his face.

"Do you know the artist in question, Mr. Jones?" asked one of the two remaining guests.

"I do. Though, I have not met him," said Vincent. "I've seen his work. He's extremely gifted."

"So I hear," said the other man, who looked like he was in his early twenties.

Marion Davies walked in at that moment. "I slept like a log," she said, standing by the buffet in her tailored purple blouse and long white skirt. She looked magnificent, and so very cute at the same time. Her hair perfectly styled, she appeared to have spent the time to make herself look beautiful. She was, after all, a film star, and like all film stars, she had to look perfect at all times. "What were you all talking about?" she inquired.

"We were talking about Mr. Sargent's arrival today," answered Vincent, looking at Marion. He was quite taken by her. At barely twenty years of age, she was the little girl in a world of adults. Children are jubilant, adults are dull. She radiated that sweet innocence adulthood wipes out along the way.

She helped herself to some fresh orange juice, and sat next to Vincent. The two other men left. "I scared them off," she smiled.

"Why would you say that?" Vincent asked, not quite sure how serious she was.

"They're lovers," Marion whispered, as if the secret was to remain hidden.

"They're g… they're homosexuals?"

She nodded with a giggle. "I'm afraid so."

A change of subject was wise. "Do you know Sargent, the artist?" inquired Vincent.

"Of course. He's been commissioned to paint my good friend, Lady Julia. She's coming."

Vincent tried to put up a face of impassivity, as he stood up, startled by the revelation. He walked to the open window, to hide the shock on his face.

"It's a beautiful day," Marion stated, as she approached Vincent. The gardens glowed in the late morning light, and leaves rustled in the gentle sea breeze.

Images of Julia, the apparition, Julia, both the ominous and the nostalgic, flashed through Vincent's head. He had traveled the

124

unbelievable road of a once fictional world to be with her, to meet her. Now he was about to encounter her, as if he had woken up from a very long sleep and held hostage with dreams of her. Marion's lips moved, yet Vincent was unable to hear her speak. He kept his gaze toward the gardens, incapacitated, his mind focused on a single hope; that his presence here would not be in vain.

The rapture passed, slowly. Vincent stood alone in the breakfast room. How long did he stand there? He could not say, though he noticed the dishes were cleared from the table, and Marion was gone. He looked outside again. A cool movement of the air brought the exotic scent from a thousand flowers.

TWENTY

Approaching Vizcaya from the bay was a rare treat. Deering loved giving tours to his guests on one of his boats. Reflections from the house, in pink streaks, moved slowly in the tranquility of the air. Again, Marion sat next to Vincent, along with five other people, including James Deering. No one spoke. There was no need for that. The sheer beauty of the place spoke about all the grace and elegance much more adequately than anyone competent enough to do so, or any poet would. The boat circled The Barge, as Vincent soaked in the architectural excellence of the structure. He looked up, as the boat neared the 'vessel', and admired the summer house with the lattice roof on the deck. If James Deering could only see how time erodes and destroys, thought Vincent, torn between what he knew, and what he was witnessing.

Vincent could not believe how much had been lost to the passing years. He knew it was a great deal, yet seeing it for himself, was quite shocking for him. Deering's boat leisurely passed by the delightful Tea House, a treasure of architecture, with its lattice-domed roof and Venetian bridge leading to it. The pink façade of The Casino, on top of the mound, in the southern part of the gardens, loomed through the trees and the mangroves. A path that led into the deep shade of the woods, could be seen from the boat. Small islands in the south lagoon, were linked by little bridges. An oriental overtone was evident, and reflection of the main Chinese bridge formed an 'O' in the water, before the boat distorted it, as it approached the landing. None of this remained today and Vincent's sorrow returned. Vizcaya was bound for neglect, and nature surrounded her unmercifully, showing no clemency in the years ahead. Vizcaya, like an illusion, would be abandoned, before her partial re-birth as a museum.

Lunch was served late. Clouds gave sunny intervals, which brought relief from the heat in the afternoon. A full twenty-four hours had passed since Vincent's 'arrival', and he felt nothing but excitement about his decision to be here, now. Of course, any unpredictability, like the arrival of the real Clarence Henry Jones, would be disastrous. Vincent hoped that luck was on his side, and perhaps destiny as well. As he pondered those things, he realized how much he had changed in the last few months. The logical man, made room for the free-spirited one. As a nonconformist, Vincent saw the world as an artist would, more colorful, more exciting. Creativity had never been his strength, though his work demanded a certain amount of it, he dismissed it. Now, he felt like an outburst of enthusiasm, as if a new breath had taken place in the core of his very soul. He saw with new eyes, new sensitivities, and not just on the subject of Vizcaya, which he was most passionate about, rather with everything else.

His meanderings took him to the gardens, and he walked along the shaded alleyway. The fountains were in full display and the sound of water spewing and cascading, gave Vincent an immense joy. Vizcaya was alive and well, and she was exhibiting all the splendor she possessed, though perhaps only for a short chapter of her existence. Still, here I am, Vincent reflected. "Here I am," he said out loud. Memories of being here with Sarah, bothered him, as if he had shown an intruder his innermost sacred and prized refuge. He thought about Tracy, and Charlotte. Where were they? He also thought about his mother, the years spent avoiding her. One can speculate on things that could have been, yet life passes by, without making any excuses for its impetuous course. Regrets came knocking at Vincent's door, many times, only to be discounted as the natural stages of one's life. How foolish it all sounded now. How irrelevant. Vizcaya, the forgiver, the harbor for lost souls, had welcomed Vincent with her renewed strength and prestige. That was indisputable. He really was here, in this paradise, in 1917. The city of Miami was but a speck on the horizon, a mere fishing town. The sound of jet engines from overhead airplanes, would not be heard for many decades to come. Vincent sat on the steps of The Casino, the miniature building meant to be a pause for a walk in the garden. The furnishings, the decorations, fresh from the blueprints, amazed Vincent. He looked behind him, through the open loggia, and pictured the waterways beyond, as it would become; a complete disappearance and destruction of the site.

He watched Marion in the distance heading his way. He watched her with a certain smile. Vincent liked her.

"What are you doing here, alone?" she asked, happy to have found him. "Do you know how hot it is? It's 87 degrees," she answered her own question.

"It does feel rather warm."

"So, you're just going to sit on those steps," she said, looking at The Casino. "I had tea in there, last time I was here."

Vincent had to ask. "Is that when your friend, Lady Julia was here?"

"Yes." Marion looked at Vincent. "Come on," she said, extending her hand to him, "let's go for a swim."

The thought of swimming in the pool, made all the sense in the world. Not only because of the heat, but because Vizcaya's pool had been admired for years. The pool extends to the exterior, in the sunlight, from a marvelously decorated arched grotto beneath the house. Who is the visitor who has not conjured up a swim in its clear water?

"Wonderful idea," replied Vincent. And they walked toward the house; Julia very much in the forefront of Vincent's speculations.

Some of the guests were swimming, others were sitting on the stone benches in the coolness of the shade in the grotto, drinks in hand.

"Tea will be served in the Tea House, if anyone cares for it," announced Deering, peeking through the door of the billiard room, adjacent to the pool.

The Tea House was another architectural marvel, at the south end of the sea wall promenade. Vincent hoped for his very own mystery to be resolved, soon; the note kept in his mahogany box, written to his great-grandfather, about a certain clandestine meeting there. Maybe it was written by Marion. He looked at her in her blue bathing suit with short sleeves and legs ending at mid-thigh. She looked quite modern, he thought, and quite daring for 1917. He found it hard to reconcile the Marion Davies here and now, and the Marion Davies who passed away in 1961. He glanced at his own bathing suit, and imagined the staff at Sotheby's making fun of him. The black and white horizontal stripes made him look like a convict.

The day lingered, as indolent guests removed from their habitual tedious lives, savored the luxurious intermission given to them so generously.

The 18th century French clock in the Reception Room, read 6:30. Vincent wondered if Sargent would ever come. And Julia. Where was she? He walked to the east terrace, and watched the late afternoon light casting its warm colors towards the bay and on the barge. Not a building in sight, as far as the eye could see. Not a hint of civilization, near or far, to falsify his presence. Vincent stood in awe again.

At eight o'clock, dinner was served in the great dining hall. Deering sat at the head of the table, with a few new guests Vincent had not seen during the day. Marion sat five people away from him. He really missed her close company. This time, the troubles in Europe were talked about. Some of the guests said if war was declared, it would not last for more than a few months, which seemed to please Deering. He had quite a bit more artifacts coming from Italy, and a war would make things difficult to get. Vincent listened, mainly, until one of the men asked him what he thought of the whole thing.

"I'm not sure," replied Vincent, "though a war may last longer than you think."

"Unfortunately, I agree with Mr. Jones," said Deering, from the head of the table. "It may go on longer than we want."

"You have a lot riding on this, don't you, Mr. Deering?" Vincent asked the question, of which he knew the answer only too well. An entire shipment of 17th and 18th century furnishings, as well as several antique statues, would soon be lost at sea, torpedoed in the middle of the Atlantic Ocean by a German submarine. Vincent was not sure if the question was too delicate to ask. Everyone looked at Deering.

"Well, Mr. Jones, it seems there's not much I can do about it. And yes, I may end up spending a lot of money, and get nothing in return. Things may be held up until after the war. Who knows?"

The women quickly turned the conversation to more cheerful subjects, such as fashion and Broadway shows. Marion became the center of attention.

After dinner, brandy, crème de menthe and coffees in fragile little cups were served. The lace tablecloth showed signs of candle grease, and crudely folded napkins lay here and there, as the chatter from a pleasant dinner party continued.

Music from the organ filtered through to the courtyard, where people gathered after dinner. Cigars were lit, and Vincent watched their smoke climb up to the open roof. Guests were sitting, savoring the rest of the evening, as a few clouds drifted above in the dark night sky.

TWENTY ONE

A restless night caused Vincent to wake up late the next morning. He even got up in the middle of the night and stood outside his bedroom door, listening for anything unusual. He had accepted Julia, the apparition, to the point of awaiting her presence. However, Julia, the guest, threw Vincent into a quandary. The last time he saw her was on this very spot, when she appeared to him. He knew absolutely nothing about her, except that which was captured by Sargent. Would she know me? Vincent wondered. She had spent a lifetime with him, by his side and at times nearer than anyone. What Vincent was really asking, was simple, and yet ridiculously complex; would she feel any admiration, any love, he dared to meditate, for him? And would he feel the same toward her?

Once out of bed, Vincent got ready for the day. Another outfit was selected in the closet, and this one fit him just as well as the first one. He held up some of the clothes; all seemed tailored made for his size. He shook his head, puzzled.

The breakfast room was empty, due to the late hour; it was almost eleven o'clock in the morning. Miss Adair, the housekeeper, straightened the chairs around the table.

"Good morning, Miss Adair," said Vincent.

"Good morning, Sir. Do you need anything?" she asked.

"No. I was wondering... where is everyone?"

"Everyone is in the garden. Mr. Sargent arrived this morning."

How odd those words sounded. How casually they were uttered. Sargent was here, in Vizcaya, as sure as Vincent was standing in the middle of James Deering's breakfast room in 1917. Speechless, he looked at the housekeeper with eyes that unnerved her. She had nothing to fear, of course, Vincent being the great pacifist acknowledged by everyone, yet the small woman eyed the doorway.

"Are you feeling alright?" she asked, finally, not too sure if her question was relevant or not.

"Yes?" Vincent answered with an empty gaze. "Did you say Mr. Sargent arrived? He's here. Here... in the garden?" he mumbled.

"He is, sir. Would you like a cup of tea, or coffee?" she asked, anxious to leave the room.

"I'm sorry. I didn't mean... I didn't sleep well last night. No, thank you, I think I'll join the other guests,"

Vincent made his way downstairs, uneasy, afraid, really. The sun-drenched east terrace was deserted. Vincent walked to the water's edge, and saw some of the guests sitting in the shade by the tea house, talking. Marion was there, too. She waved at him. He turned, and looked towards the boat landing, on the north side of the sea wall promenade. It looked like someone was there, perhaps more people strolling in that part of the garden. Vincent took a few steps before he came to a standstill. There he was. Sargent. The great John Singer Sargent, sitting on a short stool, painting, dressed in a brown suit and a straw hat. An umbrella was placed directly above the painting, to block the direct sunlight. So, it came true, like a wish made by a child before an assembly of cynics. A wish, more like a dream, made by a young boy born in the wrong time, the wrong century. Vincent's soul came alive with a loud scream within him. He took a few more steps, the bravest ones he had ever taken. He felt an ache in his chest, as the idea of being face to face with the great artist, had become reality. Vincent's breathing also seemed to accelerate at an alarming rate, every atom of his body about to explode. How is one deserving of another life, another destiny? The cemetery in England, the grave, all that was erased, put on hold for several more years. Here, in Vizcaya, one could defraud time, even reverse it, thought Vincent. How many re-entries would he be allowed to make through that secret door? What remained a mystery, was the passing of time on the 'outside'. For all he knew, a whole year may have gone by, in the space of the last forty-eight hours.

Vincent watched, as Sargent's brush glided effortlessly on the paper of his watercolor. He stood there, silent, watching what millions of people wished they could witness. A tap on his shoulder, startled Vincent.

"What are you doing?" whispered Marion. She was like the little mischievous girl at a birthday party, who knows the content of every present.

"Look. That's him. That's Sargent," Vincent whispered back.

"I know. We're all waiting to see Mr. Sargent's painting. Mr. Deering has invited him to stay as long as he likes."

"He'll stay about two months," Vincent said with too much haste.

"Two months? How do you know?" Marion inquired, looking at Sargent.

"Oh, it's just... just a guess." Vincent kept staring at his favorite artist, who now, sat not fifty feet away from him. "I wish I could get closer," he continued, shaking his head in disbelief.

"You are strange," said Marion, now looking straight into Vincent's eyes. "I've never met anyone like you."

"If you knew how great this man is..." Vincent whispered at Marion, wishing he could say more.

Sargent stood up at that moment and took a few steps back, looking at his work.

Vincent was only able to see a small section of the watercolor through the shrubbery. Here goes at least 250,000 dollars, he thought, but he quickly was appalled at such meditations.

Sargent turned around and saw Vincent and Marion, and he returned to his painting.

"I think we better go back with the others," said Vincent who tried to appear as unemotional as he could, after he peered into Sargent's penetrating eyes.

At a certain moment in time, a specific pair of eyes was providentially appointed to encounter another, like an unwritten alliance. Some would use the word destiny, as the answer for anything inexplicable. Others would suggest that life is a sweepstake, and destiny its ever rolling dice. Though that first encounter was brief, Vincent would forever be changed by the short-lived communion. It would abide in him, as his most treasured memory.

"Right now, for instance, what are you thinking about?" asked Marion, as she and Vincent walked away from Sargent.

"Do you believe in destiny?" he asked.

"Absolutely."

"Yes. Me, too," he went on. "I know... I'm strange," he smiled.

"You are!" she replied, attracted by Vincent's attitude, which seemed at odds with everything she knew. "I'd like you to visit me in California next month," she whispered in Vincent's ear as they drew near the other guests.

"Next month…" Vincent answered, his mind diverted by such a proposition. He liked Marion, with all the exuberance of her youth, and he looked at her. He gave her a faint smile, a sorrowful countenance on his face. Marion was dust, as was everyone here, in this oasis of silence. Vincent's spirit plummeted down from a great height, like a mighty stone rolling down the hillside towards the precipice. The passage of time. Time, and all its secrets, the hysteria and the insatiable desire to get to the 'other side' was beginning to suffocate Vincent. Had he made a mistake in coming here, to this long-forgotten area? Yes, perhaps, though he had yet to meet the woman, Julia, the one who drove him out of his mind, on the other side of time. Where was she? Was she really coming? Marion joined the few guests in the tea house. Vincent looked at her with an empty gaze.

A light wind started to blow across the bay. The barge seemed to be floating all of a sudden, as the water surrounding it broke up in streaks of gold in the sunlight. Vincent imagined the 'vessel' breaking free from its moorings, guided out to sea by the awoken stone mermaids on its bow and stern.

"Mr. Jones," called out Deering from the tea house, "I'm sure Mr. Sargent will be delighted to show you his work later on."

"Yes, I guess I was a little too eager there," answered Vincent. "I'm a great admirer of his," he continued, making sure nothing was said inadvertently.

Some people sat in the shade of the royal palms. Others sat in the tea house, beneath the wooden trellis, looking at the bay through the arched openings of their cool retreat. There was a peace to be held dear here, a soothing calm about Vizcaya, like a hideaway, mysterious and invisible to the unbelieving eye. Vincent had found it. He had come across it, a little by luck, much because of love, and his life was changing before his eyes.

About half an hour later, Deering, who had briefly returned to the house, came back to the tea house with Sargent. The artist seemed to be carrying what looked like a watercolor under his arm. Vincent became excited, and he watched them approaching, like a scene from a movie about the life at Vizcaya. Sargent and Deering, both played by particular Hollywood actors, who with the right make up, bore some resemblance. But this was not a scene from a movie, and nothing about the set was fake. Vincent was about to be introduced to his great artistic hero.

"This is Mr. Sargent," said Deering to his guests, and handshakes followed.

Vincent came forward, his enthusiasm at war with his lack of courage, as if none of this could possibly be happening. The heavy-set man with a goatee before him, was not just a mere mortal. This was the great John Singer Sargent, whose grave Vincent had recently seen and touched in a cemetery in England. Again, time was the annihilator, the instigator of misfortune. How he had wished for this moment, though not as a PhD, whose world is confined to the literal, rather as a dreamer, whose scope is so much broader.

"I'm Clarence Jones," uttered Vincent, desperately waiting to see the painting. "It's an honor to meet you, Mr. Sargent."

"Thank you. The honor is mine, Mr. Jones."

And just like that, without so much of the sound of trumpets, coming from the grandstands above, the appointed time, came. The manifestation. The dream. Vincent was in awe. He had so much to ask, like a child, anxious to learn, yet unable to speak. He observed Sargent's hands. He studied them, their every form, as the artist spoke to some of the guests. The amazement was clearly obvious, at least to Marion, who seemed confounded by Vincent's reaction. She had some knowledge about Sargent's fame, but she struggled to make a connection between the life of the artist and the exaltation shown in Vincent's behavior.

"Will we be allowed to see your work, Mr. Sargent?" inquired Vincent. Marion stood behind the small group of people, halfway in the shade of the tea house. She listened.

"Of course. If you like," replied Sargent, and he held up the watercolor for everyone to see. Some of the trivial remarks by the guests, amused Sargent, but an astounded Vincent felt like he was in the final tumult of an intensely visual dream, as he beheld the very watercolor he had purchased at the auction. There it was, fresh from the brush, unhindered by time, brilliant, sublime.

"Well, Mr. Jones, what do you think?" asked Deering.

"It appears Mr. Jones is speechless," said Marion, who looked straight into Vincent's eyes.

Vincent stared at the artwork. "I think it is... fabulous. Simply fabulous," he asserted, powerfully impacted by the certainty of the moment. This was perhaps the most compelling evidence of all for Vincent. The painting which hangs in his penthouse this very day, was plucked out, as a complete reversal of events took place, to end up one more time in the hands of its creator. "You are indeed a genius," said Vincent, letting his emotions go free. "Thank you for showing it to me."

Sargent, though used to various forms of accolades, was taken aback. He never really expected someone staying at Vizcaya to be such an enthusiast of his work. "My dear Mr. Jones," he said, "I find myself humbled by your passionate comments. I sincerely am."

"I say, Mr. Jones, you do surprise me," interjected Deering. "I didn't realize you were so dedicated to the arts."

"I am. It is what I truly love." Vincent was almost in tears, and felt like he had to apologize for his fervent display. One is not supposed to exhibit any kind of euphoria when one holds a certain station in life. It is regarded as unrefined, even though the arts are the highest calling one could hope to have. Vincent knew this. Sargent certainly knew it, yet he approached Vincent after most of the guests had dispersed.

"I was touched by your fervency," said Sargent, as Vincent struggled to accept the fact that Sargent stood in front of him, and was speaking from the heart, like he would to his most beloved friend.

"I believe a cup of tea is in order," said Deering, heading inside the Tea House.

"I think you're wonderful," Marion whispered to Vincent, who felt supremely happy. She placed a small piece of paper in his hand when no one was looking, and smiled.

Somewhat curious, Vincent held the paper in his hand wondering what Marion had given him. He suspected a secret note of some kind; a queer feeling about Marion's eccentricities and her young heart, absorbed him. He distanced himself from the guests, unfolded the paper and read the note. He looked at Marion, who had joined another group of people, though she had watched Vincent for his reaction from the moment he read the note.

Vincent gave Marion a tender smile. His mind engrossed by the years that belonged to another season, another era, when the author of that piece of paper was unknown. *'Meet me in the tea house at 10 tonight. Don't be late!'* He read it again. Vincent felt a little relieved and a little disappointed. The freshly written and hand delivered note impacted him forcefully; he had hoped that it came from Julia.

A light dinner was served that evening. The long tedious journey by train from New York City to Miami, was discussed. The situation in Europe was talked about, as well. Sargent had returned from Italy a few weeks ago, where apparently the situation was quickly deteriorating, with much fighting to the north of the country. Vincent was engaged in most of the conversations among the twelve guests sitting at the table. It was clear that Vincent was accepted as Clarence Henry Jones, the young tycoon from Pittsburgh. His 'rebirth' as his great-grandfather happened so naturally, so quickly, that Vincent had no time to analyze any of the problems that would have followed, if caught as an impostor. He made the effort not to ask anything remotely artistic, to anyone, during dinner. James Deering's brother, Charles, a good friend of Sargent, was expected for lunch in a day or two.

Sargent's manners were impeccable, which complied with historical accounts about his life. He seemed to be a humble man, not full of words, like one would expect someone of his stature to be. Vincent fervently waited to hear about the portrait of Lady Julia that Sargent was commissioned to paint. He heard it mentioned the first time he walked through the secret passage. That seemed like an eternity ago, thought Vincent. From time to time, he turned his gaze towards the dining room door, expecting Julia to suddenly appear.

Marion, watchful and still puzzled as ever, was amused by Vincent's theatricals. She smiled at him when she left the table with the other women, as brandy and cigars were passed around.

Not a mention of the portrait was made. Instead, the subject of money and the stock market took precedent over anything cultural and brilliant. Were these people sitting around this table, that disinterested about the presence of a great artist in their midst? Vincent blamed their insensitivity on the lack of insight he was privy to. He smiled inwardly at the irony of the conversations taking place in this magnificent dinning room; mainly money. Here sat Sargent, whose paintings would fetch millions of dollars in the years ahead, and all those shrewd business men were ignorant of it. Talking about investing your money, thought Vincent. Here was the opportunity of a lifetime, a legacy for the grandchildren, who would forever praise their ancestors.

"Mr. Jones." Vincent heard his name. "Mr. Jones, I believe you reside in Pittsburgh?" asked Sargent.

Vincent had never realized the impact of a shadowy figure in a dream, coming to life, would have on him. Sargent looked at him straight in the eyes, expecting an answer from James Deering's guest. "Mr. Jones?" Sargent called out the name again. "Are you not well?"

"I'm sorry," Vincent replied finally. "As you can see I was lost in a dream," he said, raising his glass of brandy, "a dream about this charming estate. Forgive me." He took a sip of the golden drink, as did Deering. "I do live in the great city of Pittsburgh," said Vincent, "though I travel a lot. I was in Boston recently," he added, not quite sure why, though perhaps to tell himself that he was like an invincible creature, caught between the axels of time, and that no one could find. Actually, having a conversation with Sargent was like listening to two people speak, deduced Vincent, yet one of them was himself. The words uttered, were not his own, so it seemed, except earlier this afternoon, when he spoke so openly. Images of his life in New York, began to surface in Vincent's mind. Had his mother's funeral, now so far removed from his new reality, even happened? And Charlotte. What about her? Her face came forth for a split second, as if she was calling out for him. A 'dear Charlotte', came to the forefront of his meditations.

Perhaps brought on by the consumption of wine and brandy, Sargent appeared more at ease talking about himself. A far more fascinating discussion began about his travels abroad, painting in Switzerland, Italy, and Spain. He had greatly reduced the number of portraits and commissions, which had brought him fame and fortune, and turned his focus to landscape, producing a huge number of works in oil and watercolor. He talked about his architectural paintings of gardens, fountains and statues. Venice was among his favorite places, and he described how he enjoyed painting the canals, the boats and the intricate facades of the city. Vincent held on to every precious word.

A few minutes before ten o'clock, Vincent made his way to the tea house. He crossed the east terrace as lamps from the bedroom windows above, projected warm beams of light onto the lawn. The moonless night plunged the gardens into total darkness. He felt a little awkward about this clandestine rendezvous, and though he was fond of Marion, she could never take Julia's place in his life.

The tea house was empty and appeared desolate at this hour of night. The sound of crickets and frogs in the nearby lagoons broke the absolute stillness of the night. Vincent looked out towards the bay and his mind began to wander, when he heard the sound of light footsteps approaching.

Marion walked right up to Vincent, and without saying a word, kissed him passionately. The long kiss was not refused, on the contrary, it increased in fervor. Marion was a very desirable young woman, and obviously willing to give herself to Vincent. Yet, Vincent gently drew back from her.

"You didn't like it?" Marion asked in a soft whisper. "I had to kiss you. I couldn't stand it, any longer."

"I liked it, that's the problem," replied Vincent.

"Come to California," she said, all rules of conduct broken by the kiss.

"We have to stop this. This cannot happen, said Vincent. You're a wonderful person, and I am very fond of you, but there's someone else."

"Oh."

"I'm sorry."

"Don't be. I'm the one who's making a fool of herself."

"You're not making a fool of yourself. If things were different..."

"Yes, if only..."

Vincent's eyes became accustomed to the night, and he saw her more clearly now.

"This other woman... this person... is she in love with you?" asked Marion.

Vincent shrugged, searching for an answer that would make sense to him. "I don't know," he had to say.

Marion stared at him. "So, it's like that. You are a bigger fool than I am," Marion said. Her whole face lit up.

"Can we be friends?" asked Vincent, with a genuine enthusiasm.

"Sure. Friends."

"I think we should head back to the house." Vincent extended his hand to Marion. "Come on."

She smiled and held his hand tight.

The account of Sargent's life, told from his own lips at dinner, was Vincent's culmination of a life given to the arts and its history. He thought about Marion as he undressed to go to bed. It was almost midnight. The incident of the tea house had to remain just that; an incident, as awful as the word may be. Marion was many things a man desires. She was beautiful, rich and famous, yet she lacked that one ingredient, or rather Vincent did; love.

Under the covers, and alone with his thoughts, Vincent relived the dinner and the conversation with the great artist. He knew all about Sargent's work, down to the smallest sketch. How he wished he could have talked freely to him, and in greater depth, to get to know the man behind the mere mortal with a gift given from above.

TWENTY TWO

The only sound in the courtyard, was the soft pitter-patter of the rain. The faint glow of the early morning light outlined the open roof and Vincent watched from the galleries, standing in his silk dressing gown outside his bedroom, enthralled by the spectacle. He remembered being here as a young boy, before the glass and steel pyramid cover was installed. However, he had never experienced the delightful sound of the rain within these walls. He just stood there, mesmerized. Not even a clatter from the kitchen could be heard. What else could he ask for? This extraordinary moment in time for Vincent, was to be treasured. Alone, as if everyone had vanished, Vizcaya was giving back some of her enchantment. It was her reward, and Vincent bowed before her beauty and grace.

After breakfast, some of the guests took another boat ride. The weather had cleared up on this bright April day, and the refreshed gardens echoed with the chirping of happy birds.

Vincent crossed the courtyard and walked out to the sundrenched east terrace. A woman stood by the water, looking at The Barge. She was elegantly dressed and held a white lace parasol. Vincent's heart began to race, after he first assumed that she was a guest who had just arrived. The woman turned around at the sounds of footsteps coming towards her. Julia's unmistakable gaze caused Vincent utter dismay. Any premonitions about anything, became groundless. Nothing could have prepared him for this, not a dream, not a wish, not even the lonely years awaiting her arrival in his life. Julia lowered her parasol, which revealed her face, free from any inclement shadows. The eyes from Sargent's charcoal drawing were locked into his. He could reach out to her now. He could touch her. The years spent trying to avoid her, afraid of what she represented and before Vincent began to seek her presence, had come to this. They both had travelled far, deep into the realm of time and of the universe. Vincent was afraid to speak. He looked to the left and to the right, anxious for no one, and not willing to share this hour with the rest of the world. Julia remained silent. She looked at him with an intensity as profound as his conviction of her existence, and the soul-wearying promise of this day.

"You came back." Julia's voice materialized the countenance of her, and gave her the breath of life.

Filled with an immeasurable joy, Vincent took a few more steps towards her, as twenty years of his life came crashing at his feet. Any reasoning now would obliterate this moment, and reduce it and Vizcaya to rubble, Vincent felt. He walked to her, and stretched his arm to touch her.

The barge behind Julia began to dissolve into its current state of ruin. The new stonework, the mermaids slowly broke up into the bay. The sky grew darker as clouds appeared in a whirlwind with a roar of a thousand lions. Vincent felt the touch of Julia's hand, the warmth of her skin. She tried to hold on to him, and she smiled a smile of mournfulness, before everything turned to black, like a boundless space around him.

TWENTY THREE

"Julia… Julia," muttered the semi-conscious man on the stretcher. Vincent's chart read 'John Doe' under the line 'patient's name'. He was being transferred from the emergency room to a bed on the fourth floor of Mount Sinai Hospital, in New York City. A jogger found him in Central Park, in the early morning hours of this cold April day. The soiled linen outfit he wore, pointed to a homeless person, though his hands were clean and well-manicured.

"Where am I?" Vincent asked Nurse Lena Wozniac who had just walked into the room.

"You're in Mount Sinai Hospital," she replied. "You were in bad shape. What happened to you? Were you mugged?"

"No. No, I wasn't mugged. Are we… why am I here?"

"I told you—"

"No, I mean… why am I not in Miami?" he asked, his voice crying silently.

"Sir, you're in New York," answered the nurse, who was starting to think her patient was on the wrong floor.

"Not possible. Not possible… I'm in Miami, in Miami, with her."

Doctor Ajay Badal entered the room at that moment, upbeat, and very much in charge of his department. "What have we here?" he inquired, looking at Vincent. "So, you spent the night in the park?" he continued, looking at the chart.

"I'm Doctor Jones," said Vincent, not at all convinced of his own confirmation.

"You're a doctor?" And you say your name is Jones?" asked Doctor Badal.

"Yes, Jones. Vincent Jones." Vincent held the side of his head.

"Your head hurts?" observed the doctor. He took a flashlight out of his pocket and shone the light into Vincent's eyes. "Who is Julia?" inquired Doctor Badal, "your wife, girlfriend?"

"She's…" The utterance remained unfinished, like a thought, a yearning that could never reach the pledged state of exuberance.

"I think what you need is a good rest. I've given you something for that, and let's see in a few hours. Meanwhile, this nice lady here will take care of you," said Doctor Badal, pointing at Nurse Wozniac. The doctor took the nurse to the door, spoke to her, and left.

A reproduction of a painting by Renoir, the great impressionist, hung next to the window, on the right side of Vincent's bed. The painting titled 'Ball at the Moulin de la Galette', was perhaps with Van Gogh's 'Starry Night', one of the more popular images in the world of prints. Vincent kept looking at it, and the nurse noticed it.

"You like that painting?" she asked, securing the IV-line in place.

"I do like Renoir, though he's never been my favorite," answered Vincent. "The print is backwards."

"Backwards?"

"Yes, the image has been printed backwards. In other words, that group of people sitting on the left, should be on the right. Typical mistake made by an industry who has zero interest in fine art," he added with a certain disgust in his tone.

"I see," said the nurse, looking at the painting, mystified, though more about her patient than the Renoir.

"Don't take my word for it, look for the signature."

After a short hesitation, she approached the picture, and searched for Renoir's signature. "Wow," she exclaimed, "you're right, it's here," she pointed, "and it's reversed."

Vincent nodded, and closed his eyes. Confusing forms floated in the dimness of his thoughts. A young girl's face kept coming forward. She walked the length of shaded path, hiding at times behind a long line of columns that led to a raging sea in the distance. Other faces, more abstract, appeared in his medically induced sleep.

Several hours later, Doctor Badal came back to check on Vincent, who was sitting up. "You should feel better. You've been resting. All your tests came back negative, so there's no reason for you to be here."

"Where are my things? My belongings?" asked Vincent.

"You didn't have anything with you, except the clothes on your back. No ID, nothing."

Nurse Wozniac entered the room.

Doctor Badal continued. "I've checked the internet… I couldn't find a Doctor Vincent Jones anywhere. I'm sorry. Are sure that's your name? Anyway, we can't keep you here. There's nothing wrong with you."

Vincent noticed that Doctor Badal held a BlackBerry phone in his hand. "You still use a BlackBerry, I see?" Vincent asked, as a dreadful feeling suddenly overcame him. "What year is this?" he asked, now fearful and looking around the room, knowing the question would provoke more strife, still. The outdated television set anchored to the wall, confirmed his dismay.   Vincent pressed the 'on' button on the remote control, and waited for the image to appear. Footage of Pope Benedict XVI showed the Pontiff at Ground Zero in New York City.

"It's 2008," replied Doctor Badal, who looked at the nurse, shrugging. "The Pope was at Ground Zero this morning. Why?"

"2008. 2008," Vincent repeated. "No. It can't be," he moaned.

Nurse Wozniac put her hand to Vincent's forehead, like a mother would to take the temperature of her sick child. Doctor Badal was not quite sure what to make of his patient. Was he simply crazy? Was he suffering from amnesia? The obvious, and habitual 'by the book' diagnostics had been talked about, away from Vincent with other colleagues. Time traveler, is one explanation that was never brought up. Doctor Badal left the room, saying that he would be right back.

"I'm not sick, really," Vincent said softly to the nurse. The television was on mute, and images of President George W. Bush, played like the scenes from a decade old video.

"My shift is ending," said the nurse. "I need to go, I'm sorry."

"Of course. Of course. Thank you for taking care of me," Vincent said.

She smiled at him.

"I'm not crazy. And I don't have amnesia. I am Doctor Jones, and I live just a few blocks from here. Really."

"I'd be in such trouble," said the nurse, who read Vincent's mind. "I can't release you."

"I'm not asking you to do that. I need you to find a friend for me. Just one phone call. Her name is Charlotte Montagu. She lives in Philadelphia. Of course, I don't remember her number, that's the problem with smart phones, it makes everybody stupid." Vincent stared at the nurse. "Please, Lena."

As far as Lena was concerned, this patient was obviously disturbed, though there was something about him that told another story. In her nine years working in this hospital, not one person pointed out the blunder with the Renoir print. Though the picture had been seen by thousands of people, patients and visitors in the last nine years, no one noticed. Vincent Jones puzzled her. "You're an enigma," she said. "Okay, I'll try to find her. Give me a few minutes," said Lena, and she walked out of the room.

Now alone with his thoughts, Vincent tried to understand what happened to him. He remembered touching Julia's hand, feeling her, and then… what? And why 2008? What was the meaning of all this? Nothing about Doctor Vincent Jones? Impossible. A cycle of uninterrupted schemes crisscrossed his mind, like an unstoppable wild horse, running through a thick fog and blind to the oncoming obstacles.

Lena came back in the room. "There is a Charlotte Montagu in Philadelphia, but no one's answering." Lena watched Vincent's despair on his face. "I'm sorry. Here, that's her number," she said, giving Vincent a piece of paper. "I'm so not allowed to do this!"

"Thank you. You've been so kind to me." Vincent looked at the young woman before him. "I'm going to tell you something, but this is just for you, you understand?"

"What is it?" asked Lena, distancing herself from Vincent.

"I'm not a huge sporting fan, I'm more… in the arts, if you will, history and such… but next February, put all your money, all of it, borrow if you have to, on the Pittsburgh Steelers winning the Super Bowl. Trust me."

The confidential statement, outrageous to say the least, reaffirmed Lena's diagnosis; that her patient was deranged in some way.

Vincent saw the skepticism on Lena's face. "I'm from Pittsburgh and it's… never mind." He looked at her. "I can't quite recall the score—"

"Recall?! It hasn't happened yet," she answered with much suspicion.

"It has for me."

"You can see how this sounds… well, crazy, really."

"I do. But you'll regret it for the rest of your life if you don't do what I tell you." Vincent closed his eyes. "I'm not crazy," he said, attempting to grasp a sense of reality. Everything pointed to the sad truth, that something was wrong. This hospital room, the nurse, were they even real? And Julia. Was she a dream, too?

"Vincent," said Lena, on first name basis now. She felt sorry for him. "Do you have any recollection of what happened to you?" she asked.

"Well, I have to go now." The answer implied a false composure. Vincent spirit was crying out for help, yet faceless onlookers were watching him drown.

"You should wait for Doctor Badal. He'll discharge you," said Lena.

"No, I think I'll discharge myself," said Vincent, feeling isolated, removed from a world who seemed to reject him.

"Goodbye," said Lena. "I hope you find your friend." She felt she should shake Vincent's hand, and the impromptu move surprised her. "Good luck. I mean it," she said extending her hand.

"Thank you," replied Vincent, shaking her hand.

"You sure have soft hands for a homeless person," said Lena.

"Perhaps it's because I'm not homeless," answered Vincent, with a touch of sarcasm in his voice.

"Okay, so who are you?" Lena inquired. She sat down, determined to find out more.

"Aren't you leaving?" asked Vincent.

"My shift is over, I'm just a visitor now. Who are you? Are you really a doctor?"

"If I told you, you'd really think I'm crazy, and probably call security, or something."

"Well, I know you're not homeless, that's obvious. You're probably well-to-do… maybe finance… maybe something to do with art. You have an art gallery!" she exclaimed. "You have an art gallery and you were robbed… and left for dead in the park. Am I right?"

"You certainly have a vivid imagination, but you're going to have to do better than that." Vincent stared at Lena. "Much better than that."

"Tell me."

"I can't. I'm not even sure what to make of this… me being here… 2008."

"You did have a key in your pocket."

"A key!? I had the key with me!?" exclaimed Vincent, as if the loose lifeline suddenly had been connected to solid ground again.

Lena walked to the closet. "Here," she said. She opened the ziploc bag and held up the silver key.

"You don't know what this means," cried Vincent, whose strength had left him, until now.

"It's just a key," Lena mumbled, looking at the small silver key, and confused by Vincent's reaction.

"Yes, just a small key, but if you knew what it opens!" said Vincent. "I have to go. This changes everything," he said getting out of bed.

"Don't get up too fast!" intervened Lena, as Vincent found it hard to find his balance for a split second.

"Wow, I didn't think I was that knocked out," said Vincent.

"Sit down, I'll give you your clothes."

Vincent held the key in his hand. He shook his head, staring at it, flustered. His speculations took him to a land of quicksand, a land of desolation. Vizcaya was real. There it was, several hundred miles to the south. That, was not a dream. That, was real. What crime did I commit, to be cast away like this? Vincent stared at the ancient key, and questioned his own reasoning about its purpose, and its function in his own life. The gates of hell, versus that other opening, the one that gives life, though he did not have much confidence on that subject. A brief thought for Sarah, took him by surprise. If she does even exist, she must be a teenager, he thought, engrossed by the idea.

"Who's Julia?" asked Lena. "You kept asking for a Julia. Who is she? Your wife?"

Vincent felt trapped, unable to give a direct answer. Who was Julia? She was the unexplained force in his life, the reason for his existence. He knew that much, now.

"You don't remember?" Lena insisted.

"She's someone far away."

Doctor Badal returned at that moment. "You can go, you're discharged," he said, not even noticing Lena's presence in the room. "I've written you a prescription for your headaches. Something mild. Well, good luck," he felt he had to add.

"Thank you." Vincent took the prescription and tore it up as soon as the doctor was gone. "Idiot."

"That's not very nice," said Lena.

"There are all kinds of headaches. Pills will do nothing to mine. It's a headache from another world," he whispered to himself.

"I'll walk out with you, if you like," said Lena, and they both walked to the elevator.

"What about you?" asked Vincent. "Why are you being so nice to me?"

"A little out of boredom. A little out of curiosity. I don't know… you seem legit, I think." They reached the lobby. "There's no one waiting for me at home… well, home is a big word, in my four hundred square foot studio."

"That is small. So, I amuse you," Vincent asked, smiling.

"No, no, I didn't mean that at all."

They stood outside the hospital's main entrance, neither one willing to say goodbye. It is strange how life will thrust people in one's path. Some are a curse, others a gift. Lena Wozniac was the gift. She was the shadow that comes and goes, at times unnoticed, ignored and rarely rewarded for anything that is good and decent. She had the best intentions for Vincent's welfare.

They headed towards Fifth Avenue, like two friends walking home from work. The clear blue sky masked a deceptive chill in the air, and Vincent felt its bite. The linen shirt, perfectly suitable for Miami, was impractical in New York City in the month of April. The sunny side of Fifth Avenue was welcomed.

"Where are you from in Poland?" asked Vincent, after a lengthy, yet comfortable silence.

Lena looked at Vincent, somewhat baffled. "Warsaw," she answered. "I was born there, and we moved to another city, which I'm sure you never heard of. My father found work there."

"Which city?"

Not entirely sure what to make of him, Lena looked at Vincent. The stranger fascinated her, though she had no idea why. "Well, maybe you know it. Zamosc. Have you heard of it?"

"I have. Very pretty. There's a great market square, one of the most beautiful in Europe," Vincent continued. "It's very Italian, very Renaissance."

"Now you're going to tell me you've been there," Lena smiled.

"As a matter of fact, I have. And Warsaw, of course. Great museum in Warsaw, with a wonderful collection of ancient Egyptian art."

Lena stopped in her track. "Okay, okay," she interrupted, "you're not just some bum... so, who are you?"

"Ha. Now you believe me," joked Vincent. "Are you impressed enough to trust me, though?" He looked at Lena.

She shrugged. "I've known you twenty-four hours." Lena's demeanor changed. "Look, I have to go now. I think you're a very sweet guy."

"Yes, you should go home. Thank you for keeping me company."

Lena looked up to the sky, and took a deep breath. "Where are you going to go?" she asked, the nurse in her coming to the rescue of a wounded soul, yet also a little bit out of her own loneliness.

"I was going to my building... to see if... I don't know."

"How far is it?"

"A couple of blocks south of The Met. Fifth and Seventy-Fifth street."

"You mean the museum?"

"Yes, sorry, The Metropolitan Museum."

Lena stared at the ground. "Okay, I'll come with you... if you want... If you need more company."

"Are you sure? It would be lovely if you walked with me."

Lovely, thought Lena. Never would she have used that word in that way. Vincent and the mystery around him, became murkier.

TWENTY FOUR

The building remained unchanged. Vincent was not sure if it even existed, such was his perplexity about the last twenty-four hours.

"I'll wait outside," said Lena. "I'll be here."

"Alright," replied Vincent, looking at the front door, the familiar entrance to his penthouse. He went inside.

Once in the lobby, the concierge approached him. "Can I help you?" he asked, giving Vincent a look of antipathy.

"I don't suppose you know where Grant is? Do you?"

"Grant? There's no one by that name here."

Vincent studied the whole area, the front desk, the spectacular flower arrangement on the round table, in the middle of the lobby.

"I think you better leave," said the doorman. "You obviously have the wrong address."

"Who lives in the penthouse?" Vincent inquired, knowing full well the information could never be divulged.

"I'm sorry—"

"I know, you can't say." Vincent saw Lena outside, waiting for him. "One more question, and I'll go. Does the name Doctor Jones mean anything to you? Have you heard it before?"

"I haven't."

"Okay… thank you." Vincent's worst fears were becoming much too real. The gates of time seemed to have closed for him, only to throw him back in some alien life, removed from everything he knew and loved. Julia screamed for him from the top of her voice, but the muted shadow would never return. It was finished. Vincent felt the silver key in his pocket, the once spellbinding instrument of his wishes turned mythical.

"Not good news, hey?" said Lena, after Vincent came back out.

"No, not good news at all."

"I can cook you something. You could stay with me for a while."

Vincent gave Lena a faint smile; a smile of capitulation, and a smile of thankfulness. He knew his options were non-existent, and without this stranger coming to his rescue, reality was bleak. "I don't know what I'd do if you weren't here," said Vincent. "I'll make it up to you, that, I promise."

"Great. Well... let's go. We need to catch a bus, then a train. I live in Brooklyn."

"I find myself in an awkward situation," said Vincent. "I don't have any money.'

"I know."

"So, tell me about this Super Bowl thing," Lena asked, during the half hour-long commute to Brooklyn.

"I knew you were paying attention."

"Are you for real?" she questioned Vincent.

"I'll tell you when we get to your apartment."

"Don't get too excited, it's just a small studio," she replied, her eyes searching for anything amiss with Vincent, as some level of anxiety took hold of her.

Both looked at the houses going by, after the train surfaced from the underground tunnels. Night was falling. Vincent leaned his head onto the cold window glass, and thought about Vizcaya. He thought about 1917. He thought about Sargent, and the others. Marion Davies. All had vanished under the cover of time. They spent the portion of life allotted to them, to each one, with complete disregard for fame, fortune, or anonymity. Images on film reels, paintings in dusty museums, and passages in various books in the libraries of the world, was all that was left of them. Mere thoughts. What to do now? Do I even exist? Vincent interrogated himself.

Lena's studio apartment was located above a dry cleaner and a pawn shop. The narrow wooden staircase that led to the third floor, cracked under their feet, and Vincent followed Lena, who was conspicuously silent. She opened the front door. The cramped space with a single window over the street, was neat and well organized. A small bunch of yellow artificial flowers added color to an otherwise austere room.

"Well, this is it," she said. "It's not much, but it's home," Lena claimed, kicking off her shoes.

"It's perfect," replied Vincent, who was genuinely thankful.

"I'll make some tea. You do drink tea, right?"

"Yes. Thank you." Vincent looked around the room, the minute kitchen at the back of it.

"The restroom is through that door, if you need it," said Lena, pointing at the only other door in the room.

They sat on the sofa, which Lena said was bought at the great bargain price of fifty dollars from a thrift store. She let her long black hair down, smiling at Vincent. "So, do you want to watch TV, or just talk?" she asked. "You can you tell me who you are, at least what you can remember."

"Do you mind if I close my eyes for a bit. I'm tired."

"Sure." Lena made her way to the kitchen sink, and rinsed her cup. "Vincent, I need to tell you something," she declared in the quietness of the room.

"What is it?" questioned Vincent, half asleep already.

"Never mind. I'll tell you later."

"Okay," mumbled Vincent, as the silhouette of Vizcaya's Tea House loomed in the distance, against the fiery sky of his mind. A figure stood still beneath the royal palms, when a powerful wind blasted through the exquisiteness of the grounds, leaving nothing behind its path, but desolation.

Lena watched the stranger she knew nothing about, wrestle with his own demons in his troubled rest. The name 'Julia' kept being repeated, like a bad omen. Vincent's body convulsed and he clutched one of the pillows, as if he was hanging onto a wreckage. He calmed down, finally. Lena studied his features, which she found very pleasing and approved of the unshaven face. A single lamp gave a warm light, casting soft shadows against the pale grey walls. Night had fallen, and Lena felt the full weight of the hours spent at work. She curled up in the small armchair, and fell asleep.

The clock on the stove read 2:35 when Vincent woke up. The disarray of the last forty-eight hours took their toll. Never had he reached such a low ebb. The complete chaos that he witnessed and had created in his life, primarily due to his pursuit of entities that cannot be, brought ruin. Doctor Vincent Jones, never existed. Gone was everything he worked for, loved, and cherished. The PhD made to bow down to his knees. He glanced at Lena, the accidental guest into his life. Someone who he would have passed by on the street, unremarkable and hidden from him, from a self-inflicted prejudice of selection.

Lena stirred. She turned toward him. Vincent looked at her hands, those unassuming hands, not beautified by anything artificial, and so taken for granted. What miracles had they performed, through those unselfish years?

"You're awake?" Lena whispered.

"Yes. I've been awake for a while."

"What time is it?" she inquired, whipping her eyes.

"Late... or early, depending how you look a it. It's almost three o'clock."

She ran her fingers through her hair. "I'm sorry, I fell asleep."

"Why are you sorry? I'm sure you need the rest."

"I'm wide awake now. Perks of being a nurse," she smirked, "never need more than two hours of sleep."

"That can't be true."

"Your dreamt about Julia, again. You kept saying her name. Who is she? Is it that you can't remember her?"

Vincent shut his eyes. "She comes in the night, searching for my soul," he answered. For a brief instant Vincent stood on the East Terrace at Vizcaya, speechless, his eyes filled with tears of joy, and Julia waited with open arms. The sound of a siren in the distance, abruptly brought Vincent back to the present, and he opened his eyes.

Lena remained silent, having eliminated anything logical about Vincent's state of mind, like drugs, concussion, or worse, amnesia.

"I'm terribly sorry, you must think I've lost my mind," Vincent told Lena.

"No. I don't."

"I apologize for taking your sofa," he quickly added, standing up, and not anxious to talk about Julia.

"It's okay. It opens up to a bed, you know," she blushed. "I mean... we could both use it... lie down, I'm just saying..."

"What did you want to tell me... earlier? I think I fell asleep in the middle of our discussion," inquired Vincent, who needed another topic being discussed.

"Oh, that. Yes... I wanted to tell you back at the hospital, but I didn't have the nerve, I guess."

Vincent listened.

"I phoned your friend, Charlotte, and… she answered the phone. Well, I spoke to her, and she said she never heard of you."

"Did you give her my name? Did you say Doctor Jones?"

"I did."

"She thought it was a prank call. I'm sorry."

"What am I going to do?" Vincent murmured to himself.

"I am sorry. I have a friend who's a cop, I think you need to speak to him. He can search the data base for missing persons. It's a start."

There was nothing to find for the police. How can one find something that does not exist? "I really don't know what I'm going to do," he told Lena, staring at her. "I've never been in that predicament before. I've lost everything." He pointed at his clothes, "this is all I have, and do you know what the amusing thing is, this was not even mine. This outfit was given to me."

"Who gave it to you? Maybe they can help."

"My dear Lena…"

"What?"

Vincent sighed, deeply, and shook his head. "Alright. I'll tell you. I'll tell you who I am. But you won't believe me, and you will surely not trust me after this."

"Try me."

For the next forty-five minutes, Lena listened to Vincent's narrative about his life. Some of it made sense, especially the fact that he was an educated man, however, the more fictional accounts about hallucinations turned ghosts, fell on deaf hears. Stories about Vizcaya thrilled Lena, who listened intently at Vincent's description of the estate, which she had never heard of. Vincent looked at her, happy as always to speak about his beloved house, though he felt Lena was not ready to hear more. He concluded not to disclose anything about his whereabouts before he was found in the park.

Vincent had delayed trying to call his mother. The fear of what he may find out, terrified him. He hated what reality had become and dreaded what it was about to show him. "I need to call my mother," he told Lena. "May I borrow your phone?"

He dialed the number, apprehensive. Lena sat opposite him, waiting.

"Hello?" said the voice with an accent that sounded Hispanic.

"Hello, may I please speak to Mrs. Jones?"

"No Mrs. Jones here," the man replied, and hung up.

"Well, that was rude," Vincent said, and dialed the number again.

"Hello?" This time it was a woman's voice.

Vincent could hear a lot of noise in the background, like children crying, and other voices talking. "Hello? Is this 617-555-0123?" Vincent asked.

"Si, but no Mrs. Jones. Please!"

Vincent hung up. "Maybe you should talk to your policeman friend. I'd like him to look into a missing person for me."

"Your mother?"

"Yes. Patricia Jones," Vincent said, though already knowing the result of the search. Vizcaya had given and Vizcaya had taken away. Vincent's life, at least in this century, never was. His mark, his influence, good or bad on the life of others, had been erased, like a terrible story that no one is prepared to listen. It did confuse him. How can life feel so real, and yet be so false? How can one be born and never exist?

Lena hugged Vincent. Her kind spirit took the full burden of his pain. "It will be okay," she said.

"Well, it is what it is," muttered Vincent. "We should talk about your future," he continued, as if nothing happened. "Money. I can make you lots of money," he said, like a reprisal against the twists of fate. "Money!" he smiled, hiding his melancholy.

"Why would you tell me to bet money on the Super Bowl?" she asked. "You're not a crook, are you? You don't seem like one."

Vincent smiled. "No, I'm not."

"Those hallucinations you have, or had... did you ever see a doctor, of psychiatrist about that?" inquired Lena, with all the concerns of a skillful and attentive nurse.

"For many years. But I tell you they're not hallucinations. I thought they were, but there's more to it."

"I'm sorry... ghosts? I just..."

"I know. I was like you, once," said Vincent. "Look, we can do something, if you like. I never thought it would come to this. But... what if I could prove something to you? Would you help me after?"

"Sure. What is it?"

Vincent breathed deeply, like a secret was about to be revealed.

TWENTY FIVE

A couple of days went by. Lena was the angel who saved Vincent from self-destruction. She took care of him, knowing that he was probably mentally unstable, and that he would walk out of her life one day, never to return. The sofa was never shared at night, Vincent insisting on sleeping on the armchair. Still, she paid for his food, and after a few trips to the thrift store, bought him several outfits to wear.

Lena had absolutely no interest in horse racing, and when Vincent told her about the Triple Crown races, her eyes wandered about the room.

"I don't care much for any sports, really, though I do enjoy going to the races," he explained. "If you can bear with me for a couple more weeks, you'll make some money."

"How? Horseracing?"

"Yes, horseracing," Vincent replied.

"Vincent, I don't have money to bet. I'm not a gambler. I'm just a nurse."

"Trust me. Just bet a couple hundred dollars, that's all, for the time being."

"When is the race?"

"It's coming up. May third. And you're going to bet on a horse named Big Brown."

Lena shook her head. "Big Brown. I must be crazy. Okay, I'll do it," she said, her doubts on high alert.

The day of the race arrived. Lena took the cash out of her checking account, all crisp twenty-dollar notes, and placed the bet at one of the locations she and Vincent found online. By six o'clock in the evening, both sat in front of the television set.

"I must say, this is kind of exciting," she exclaimed, with a glass of Cabernet in her hand.

"You'll see."

Lena looked at Vincent. "You're not nervous?"
"Why should I be? I know the result."

Vincent watched Lena's euphoria, as Big Brown took the lead to easily win the race.
"Oh, my God!" she screamed. "We won, we won! I can't believe it. How did..." she looked at Vincent, intensely. "Who are you?" she asked. "Come on, you just guessed, right?"
Vincent shrugged. "Who knows."
"So, how much did I win?"
"More than you make in a month."
Lena watched the screen, as Big Brown made his way to the 'winner's circle', surrounded by the press. "What's next?" asked Lena.
"The second race of course, in two weeks. Just trust me."
"Which horse on that one?"
"Same one. Big Brown."
"Really? Are you sure?"
"As sure as I stand here. Bet at least a thousand dollars this time."

May seventeenth. Both Lena and Vincent watched the race as before, and Big Brown won again, which dumbfounded Lena.

On June seventh, Lena placed a bet of eight thousand dollars on a horse she had no idea existed twenty-four hours earlier. Da'Tara won the race and upset Big Brown's bid to win the Triple Crown. Lena had never felt that way. She had made more money in the last three weeks than she had made in her entire life. She was intoxicated with that manufactured joy, spawned from material possessions and money. Vincent knew only too well how it felt, and he was glad for her.

"You're not happy?" she asked the following evening, as they celebrated in a local Italian restaurant.
"I am very happy for you," he replied.
"Well, I guess you have my attention, now."
Lena wore a red low-cut dress for the occasion, which revealed her cleavage. Her long black hair tied up in a bun, gave her a high society allure.

Vincent found it hard to concentrate all of a sudden. "You look beautiful," he uttered, mindful not to over-praise.

"Thank you."

"I came back from the year 1917, when they found me... in the park, that's what I've been trying to tell you," he blurted out.

Lena laughed. "That's the last thing I expected from you," she declared. "Come on. What are you... like a time traveler?"

"I guess so, if you want to call it that."

Though not exactly accepting his story as the truth, Lena was still puzzled about Vincent's foreknowledge of the three races. "Okay, let's say I believe you. So, what happens... do you just come and go?"

"Why don't we forget that for the moment and enjoy the evening."

Lena's eyes sparkled, as she sipped a little more wine. The free-spirited girl and her bohemian ways, comforted Vincent who felt at ease with her.

"What makes you happy?" she asked.

"I don't quite know," he replied.

"That's sad," she asserted, tearful.

Vincent was not being honest; not with Lena, and certainly not with himself. "The thought of tomorrow," he said all of a sudden, letting his guard down. The bitter taste of absence rendered him powerless. Tomorrow she would come. Julia. She came for him before, and she would again. She held on to him for that precious second. He felt her long-awaited touch, and all he had to do was to keep that memory alive. Being here was only temporary, like the day that follows the night.

"What about tomorrow?" Lena asked, not quite grasping Vincent's distress and his meaning of the word 'tomorrow'. "You'll be leaving?"

"I need to find another friend. We went to college together," said Vincent, referring to Tracy, who he hoped to find, if anything, to attest of his existence. Vincent's mind drifted, and he thought about Charlotte and Sarah.

"I want to believe you," Lena affirmed. "I really want to, but how can you explain going through... time? I know you know how crazy that sounds."

Vincent reached for the silver key in his pocket, which he made sure was always in his possession, and showed it to Lena. He explained to her in greater depth this time, about his family and the connection with Vizcaya. He described the mahogany box and its contents; the ivory comb, the note and the rendezvous at the tea house. And he talked passionately about Julia; who she was, her presence in his life, and how she appeared to him.

The contest was lost for Lena. She could not compete against the woman Vincent portrayed. Living or dead, actual or fictitious, she had his heart. A woman can tell those things, and Lena became acutely aware of her defeat.

"So, this key opens up a door," she contended, willing to go along with Vincent's claims.

"I told you everything," he said. "I know you probably don't believe me, and I don't blame you. It's insane."

The conversation continued on the way back to Lena's studio apartment. They walked slowly, Lena hanging on Vincent's arm. She made it clear that she did not believe in the afterlife, in whatever form it may take. Lena had witnessed medically inexplicable happenings in her line of work, like near-death experiences in some patients. She knew all about the bright light on the other side, mentioned in every case. Yet, she remained unaffected by it all. The notion of ghosts was to scare children and stupid grown-ups, she said. Vincent did not have the strength to argue with Lena, and he respected her too much to force his now definitive point of view on her.

When they finally sat on the sofa, Vincent promised that he would never talk about his life again, and he moved close to her. Lena saw tears in Vincent's eyes. They hugged for a long time, like two people who know they will never see one another again. Both felt blessed to have found themselves within the sphere of each other's lives, even for that brief moment. Each heart is given the task to profoundly affect another and become indispensable, and though the art of love requires no training, the true disciples are few. Lena hoped for a different outcome, and confessed to Vincent that she felt attracted to him, the minute she laid eyes on him. She joked that the money she won was a good substitute, and that she would be forever in his debt.

Lena wore her scrubs, ready to go to work. The Cinderella tale ended today. She stood in the middle of the room, as Vincent folded the pullout sofa. They looked at each other.

"Thank you so much!" Vincent said, his hands folded as a thank you gesture. "You saved my life."

"You've got all you need?" Lena asked, pointing at the small duffle bag she gave Vincent.

"Yes, all packed. Thank you."

"Keep in touch, if you can. Maybe I'll hear something about your mother. You've got my address and phone number," said Lena, softly. "And you're welcome."

Vincent nodded. They both knew the probability of meeting again was nonexistent. There are things that do not need to be explained, things that are too painful to try to comprehend. And hope remains, like a floatation device, adrift and subject to the endless currents.

"I'll write down the details for the Super Bowl, before I leave," said Vincent. "You can bet as soon as the teams are announced. Don't forget. Bet as much as you can."

"I will."

"Alright. Take care," he murmured, feeling the sadness of something much stronger than just two friends separating permanently.

The sunrise light filtered through the venetian blinds, highlighting Lena's face. A tear shone like a single precious stone on the side of her cheek, and she gave Vincent a tender hug and a kiss on his forehead.

TWENTY SIX

Vincent stood on the sidewalk, across the street from Sotheby's, and watched people go in and out of the building he knew so well. In real time, barely a week had gone by since he walked through that front entrance, yet the year was 2008, and now no one there would know his name. The sale of the Sargent watercolor of Vizcaya, would not take place for another nine years. Where was it now? Vincent wondered.

He started to cross the street and stopped abruptly, shocked to see Tracy walk out of the building. "Tracy!" he called. "Is that you?" Vincent asked, doubting now, as the person in question was dressed very conservatively. He approached. "Tracy?"

"Excuse me?" replied the man, turning around.

"I'm sorry… you look just like… are you James?" inquired Vincent, flustered by the likeness between the man before him and his college friend.

"I am James. I'm sorry… who are you?"

"Vincent." The irrelevance of the name was lost to the wind, like an unwanted sound which has become bothersome. "Vincent Jones," Vincent added, with all the anticipated despair.

"I'm terribly sorry, you have the wrong person," said the man, looking at Vincent intensely before he departed, a briefcase under his arm.

"He didn't know me," said Vincent out loud, as if he wanted to confirm that fact. "It's as if I never existed," he continued. Vincent felt like an outcast at that moment, and he remembered his encounter with the homeless man who claimed to see Julia's ghost, that night, long ago. Julia. "Where are you? What am I supposed to do?" Vincent whispered, like no one else was meant to hear his plea. Alone and left with his memories, Vincent considered his life, his work, which now was insignificant. A life wasted, pursuing the study of art and artists, men and women who by definition are at best contemptuous, and for what? For the love of what? For things that are beautiful? That passes. Things that are new? Such things have already become relics. Then what? Vincent did not have an answer. Thousands of people besieged him, like an army of shadows from a life that was no longer his own.

Vincent's fascination with Vizcaya came with a price, when he made the choice to walk through that secret passage. No one took him there by force, he was fully aware of the risks involved; the uncertainty of what he would find beyond time. He realized this. He understood that withdrawing from everything he knew to be real and giving himself up, a hostage to time, was perhaps ill-considered. He gambled and lost. It was that simple, and help would not come. Vincent walked the streets of New York City, like a man without hope. He was destitute, his spirit bankrupted. The lights at Vizcaya were covered up with the blanket of forgetfulness, never to shine again.

Philadelphia was not that far. Vincent considered going there. Seeing Charlotte face to face perhaps would awake something in her. What did he have to lose? Lena gave him two thousand dollars in cash, which he kept in his belt, like a drug dealer. Though she insisted, he refused to take more money from her. Vincent caught his own reflection in the store window. He stared at himself, the unrecognizable figure, the unsung traveler, and he walked away, sorrowful. The Greyhound Bus Station on Broadway, was only a few blocks away. Vincent lifted the collar of his jacket, and headed in that direction. He walked past Trump Tower and was diverted to see people freely enter the famous building. No barricades, no police presence, simply a normal place of business, and this for another eight years. Vincent looked up at the skyscraper, realizing the potentiality of his knowledge. Knowing the future is an uncommon and very powerful asset, granted to supreme beings, and one that could be destructive for the wrong group. However, Vincent showed no interest in such games, and he smiled, taking his secret with him.

The bus station was crowded, and much larger than Vincent imagined, never having been in one. He sat down on a wooden bench, ticket in hand. An old woman asked him where he was going. Philadelphia, he replied. She was on her way to Richmond, Virginia, to visit her daughter, whose husband had abandoned with three children. Her words were very much matter of fact, unvarnished and true. Her tired voice had uttered similar words her whole life, except perhaps on birthdays, or a Mother's Day, as the ever-present smell of barbecue sweetened the day. Vincent looked around him. How many stories were there, like this one? Too many, he thought. Yet, this was real life. This was not a fantasy buried in a fictional book. His mind wanted to escape this moment, this crowd, flaunting their misery at his feet. He closed his eyes, trying to visualize the east terrace at Vizcaya, where Julia stood, but the noise from the bus terminal came crashing, victorious in its impartial quest and brought Vincent back to reality. Charlotte would come to his rescue. She had to. Someone on this planet has to remember my life, Vincent moaned, in the depth of his delusions.

The roughly three-hour trip to Philadelphia allowed Vincent to get a much-needed sleep. The bus ride was comfortable, which surprised him. Just before exiting the bus, Vincent approached the old woman who sat four rows behind him. He took five hundred dollars out of his belt and placed the money in her hand. "It's not much," he said, "but it will help... a little."

The old woman looked at him, as if she beheld an angel, as tears came flowing out of her wearied eyes. Vincent smiled at her, and left. She leaned over in the aisle and watched him go. Her gratitude needed no utterance, it was marked by the shining countenance on her wrinkled face.

A taxi took Vincent to the address he found on Lena's computer. The car pulled up to a large wrought iron gate.

The long driveway, flanked by large oak trees, led to a beautiful Georgian-style house. Vincent dropped his duffle bag on the ground, and leaned against the grills. He saw a woman leading a horse to a structure that looked like stables. An intercom was fixed onto the side of the gate, although before Vincent could use it, the woman spotted him and headed his way.

"Can I help you? Are you a salesman?" she asked, as she drew near Vincent.

Her identity was unmistakable; Charlotte stood on the other side of the gate. Vincent was taken aback to see her on her feet. Of course, her riding accident was not to take place for another four years, or so.

"Can I help you?" she repeated, somewhat irritated.

"Hello." Vincent had no idea how to begin the next sentence. Charlotte was attractive, and shadows from the foliage above, undulated on her shirt and skin, in the soft tones of Springtime. "No, I'm not selling anything. We've... we've met before," he said. "You're Lady Charlotte Montagu, are you not?"

"We've never met," she replied, coldly. "I think you better leave."

"You came to my mother's funeral in Boston."

"When?" she inquired, doubtful.

The slight hesitation was enough to make Charlotte walk away. Vincent had no way to explain that the funeral was eight years down the road.

"Please leave, or I'll call the police," Charlotte said, as she distanced herself.

"Lady Julia's portrait burned. It was lost in the fire at your childhood home... in England," Vincent shouted, desperate to convince Charlotte.

Charlotte stopped. She turned around, looking at the stranger standing at her gate. "How do you know this? Did you look it up on the internet?"

"That info is not on the internet, in fact it's nowhere to be found. You told me."

"So, what else did I tell you?"

"That your fiancé..."

"What?"

"I... nothing." The riding accident could not be mentioned, at least not yet. "Your chauffeur's name is Dimitri," Vincent nodded, "he's Russian."

"Well, he would be with a name like Dimitri, except I don't have a chauffeur."

A man approached the gate with a garden rake in his hand. "My Lady, is there a problem?" he asked.

"Yes," she said, "call the police if this man hasn't left in the next thirty seconds," Charlotte told the man who was her gardener.

"Please, Charlotte, please, I'm desperate. I need your help," he implored her, but she walked away. "I know how the fire started!" Vincent said, looking at the gardener.

"Go away," said the gardener, brandishing the rake.

"It's okay," said Charlotte, appeasing the man with a gesture of her hand. "What did you say?" she asked Vincent, close to him, again.

"I said, I know how the fire started," he told her in a quiet voice.

Charlotte was three feet away from Vincent now.

"You started it," he whispered, so the gardener would not hear. "You said were six years old. You took the candles from the dinner tables—"

"How could you know this?" she asked, baffled.

"I know it sounds crazy, but we've met... before," Vincent floundered, "we were friends. My name is Vincent Jones, and you told me about the fire. Please, let me explain. Can I have a moment of your time?"

"I'm Doctor Jones, I work... I used to work for Sotheby's among other places." Vincent sat in Charlotte's bright sitting room. His outfit bought from the thrift store seemed at odds with the beauty of the décor. He knew Charlotte had to be aware of it. Everything about the house displayed the elegance and taste of 'old money', which did not surprise Vincent. Several paintings caught his eye, including a great portrait by American painter William Merritt Chase. Charlotte said it was one of her favorites in her collection.

A small painting by Modigliani hung on the far wall of the room. It represented a woman sitting on a chair, a subject prevalent with the artist. "That's where it is," said Vincent, happy about the discovery. "I knew this Modigliani was in a private collection, but I didn't know it was yours. Beautiful painting," he added.

"You obviously know about art," Charlotte answered, as she glanced at the painting. "And you obviously know about the Sargent I destroyed," she added, looking at Vincent. "What else?"

"I would love to see Julia's drawing. The charcoal, Sargent did of her."

Charlotte's sentiment became one of acceptance. This man, indeed, was telling the truth, as inconceivable as it sounded. "So, you know about that, too," she said.

"You emailed me a picture of it, after I requested it."

"It's in my bedroom." She stared at him. "You don't seem dangerous. Follow me," she uttered, no longer sure of anything.

The drawing hang above a chest of drawers. It was a typical charcoal drawing by Sargent; a life-size portrait, which the artist usually executed as a study, before a painting. Julia's resolute stare caught Vincent's eyes, as soon as he entered the bedroom, as if she had been expecting him. He stood by the door, with all the respect due to a woman's privacy in her own bedroom. Seeing the original moved him, deeply. Vincent succumbed to the absolute likeness of Julia's image, yielding to her every wish.

"You can go in," she said.

"May I?"

"Please."

Vincent entered the large room, and felt the soft rug under his feet. Charlotte drew the heavy drapes open, letting the late afternoon light penetrate the room, through the octagonal bay window. She stood there, silent, considering the moment and what she was told.

Vincent approached the portrait. The same commotion as before, conquered him. Julia's piercing eyes mesmerized him, and hijacked his thoughts, to cast him out of the present. Vizcaya waited. The barge waited.

Almost an hour went by. Tea was served in the sitting room, and the subject of Vizcaya kept the conversation to normal, until the notion of time travel was raised.

Charlotte put her tea cup down. "What are you saying?" she asked.

"I've just came back from 1917."

"Doctor Jones, Doctor Jones," she said, "and just when I was starting to like you! How do you expect me to interpret that?" she sighed. "That we were friends, this I can believe, you seemed to know something I've never told anyone, but that you went... travelled back in time, that I can't swallow."

"And if I can prove it?"

"How?"

"What if I could prove to you that it is possible to be back there, in 1917?"

Charlotte shook her head. "I wish you would stop talking about this."

"I tell you, I touched her. She held on to me. She was real," Vincent said.

None of the assertions made sense. "Who was real? Who is this?" Charlotte insisted.

Vincent lowered his gaze. The Charlotte he remembered would have embraced such theories, however improbable they may have sounded. He wondered if something had been altered in the course of what had come to pass. How much had been transformed to line up with the new present? Hard to tell, though no one he crossed paths with, seemed to recollect him. "It's my life," Vincent said. "I'm sorry, I'll leave. Thank you for seeing me, and listening to me. It was good to get it off my chest."

"You're welcome."

This was the last hope, the last stop Vincent admitted to himself. He stood up and extended his hand. "Well, goodbye."

"Just a minute. You mentioned something about my fiancé…"

Vincent stared vacantly at Charlotte. "Yes… yes, you were engaged… well, you will be," he corrected himself, "if you know what I mean."

"No, I don't know what you mean. Help me understand."

"We used to talk a lot, phone conversations mainly, at times we spoke for hours. I loved our talks. You did, too. You were engaged… oh, what was his name…" Vincent closed his eyes… Geoffrey!" he exclaimed. "That, was his name. Do you know a Geoffrey?" Vincent asked, cautiously.

"I do, actually." Charlotte was dumbfounded. "I do," she repeated and sat down again, amazed at the revelation. "Please sit down," she told Vincent.

"You're alright?" he inquired, seeing the shock on Charlotte's face. Now Vincent had to contend with another dilemma; the Charlotte of the future was in a wheelchair. He looked at her, all glamor and class, a lovely woman in the prime of her life. He remembered that day at the café, after the funeral. He should have fallen in love with her, then. She was beautiful that day. Wet from the rain, she removed her headscarf and let her hair fall down. Yes, she was beautiful.

"Geoffrey is an old flame, he's been after me for a while now." Charlotte hesitated. "I don't really love him," she said softly, and also a little surprised at herself for disclosing it. She looked at Vincent who sat opposite her, listening.

"I need to tell you something. Something really important," declared Vincent.

"Stay for dinner," Charlotte said, all of a sudden, like a radical change had taken place in her. Though a lot of what Vincent had shared, was beyond comprehension, she perceived the same affection as he claimed they held for each other. "You can stay, right? Or do you have to be flying off somewhere, to a more exotic time?" she joked. "Sorry, not funny."

"It's alright," he shrugged, "it was quite funny, actually."

"Let's have a drink. Wine? Whiskey?"

"A glass of wine, thank you." Vincent felt very comfortable with Charlotte. This felt natural, and could easily be a trip from New York to see his friend, a week or two after the funeral in Boston. None of the events of the last few days took place. No Vizcaya. No Julia. Nothing to contend with, but the pleasure of being alive. Now.

"It's the cook's night off, so I hope you like scrambled eggs," said Charlotte.

They both sat at the kitchen countertop, like two friends enjoying a casual evening. Though it could scarcely be said that the house was neat, on the contrary it appeared well lived in, it was nevertheless silent, devoid of any of the sounds of children, other family members. Vincent noticed a large library, visible from the arched kitchen door. Bookshelves reached the ceiling, on both sides of a stone fireplace.

"You live alone?" Vincent asked.

"I do. Prince Charming has yet to call on me," she said, though not without a trace of lament in her voice. "I have to admit something. I do know a Dimitri, though he's not my chauffeur," she added, while finishing her gin and tonic. "His family came from Russia many years ago, and he's done some work for me, around the house, you know... bits and pieces."

"Thank you for that." Vincent was pleased. He had misgivings about coming here, trying to convince Charlotte that he was sane.

"So, I told you about the fire," she asserted. "Amazing how I have absolutely no memory of this. What else? And what did you want to tell me that's so important?"

"Oh... I'm not sure how to say this."

"Just say it. Wait, you need more wine."

Vincent watched her pour the wine. He observed the grace of her hands, and felt a tremendous sense of hopelessness.

Charlotte put the bottle down. "There, that's better. Now, tell me, what is it?"

"You're going to have a riding accident."

The expression on Charlotte's face was one of skepticism, and yet also of certainty. The man sitting in her kitchen was either mad, though incredibly well informed, or he was telling the truth. "When does this… accident supposed to happen?" she questioned Vincent.

"I'm not sure, but probably sometime in 2012, maybe 2011. You just said at the time, it happened five years ago. And we were in 2017."

"How bad was the accident?" she asked, showing the temerity often found among the English upper-class.

"Bad. You were in a wheelchair. I'm sorry."

Charlotte emptied her second glass. "Good God, a wheelchair! A riding accident, you say?" She tapped the countertop with a regular beat with her finger. "But, wait. You just changed that," she said, at the simple solution. "I won't go riding that year. That's it, right?"

"I'm not sure… it can't be that simple," said Vincent.

"Sure, it is."

"Perhaps…"

"You saved my life." Charlotte gazed into Vincent's eyes, not immune to his good looks, and somewhat influenced by two large gin and tonics. "You are telling the truth, aren't you? You are who you say you are, and you did go back in time, didn't you?"

Vincent nodded.

"Are you hungry?" she asked.

"Famished, actually."

"Well, be prepared for the best scrambled eggs, ever," Charlotte declared, a little unsure on her legs.

"Why don't I make that?" Vincent proposed, smiling.

"Yes, I think you'd better."

"You saved my life," she repeated, sitting down, watching Vincent search for a frying pan. "I'm so glad you're here," she divulged, faintly, like if the admission came at a cost. Learning about her future, bound to a device on wheels, tormented her. Charlotte was not the type to exhibit her own hardship for everyone to see. She did not need to draw attention to herself. Yet, knowing the prospects of a life endured, as supposed to one acquitted of all physical pain, did not leave her unaffected. She grabbed Vincent's hand. "What am I going to do?" she asked. "I don't want to end up in a wheelchair," she cried.

"I know."

It was about midnight. Vincent and Charlotte sat outside, on a canopied love swing. The full moon lit up the garden with a blue mist. Almost everything that needed to be disclosed, had been said, and Vincent was at peace with whatever the outcome. Charlotte leaned back and gave a little push with her feet, which caused the swing to gently rock.

"Do you want to spend the night?" she asked, looking up at the sky.

"Yes, I would love that. If you want me to."

"Separate rooms, of course," she emphasized.

"Of course."

"Why did you want to be back to 1917?" Charlotte inquired. "Why 1917? What's so special about that year? I realize Vizcaya must have been a delight, but why that year?"

"Because of Julia," he felt he had to answer quickly, before his bravery abandoned him.

"Julia? My Julia? My great-grandmother?"

"Yes."

"I'm definitely not letting you go now. What's all this about?"

The explanations followed, down to the smallest details. Vincent talked about Sargent's grave in England, and the strange hallucinations. The years spent dreading Julia's apparitions, to the months of desperation, waiting and yearning for her presence. Vizcaya. The secret passage that led him to the past, and his desire to meet Sargent. Vincent described his encounter with Julia, her touch, and how everything ceased.

Charlotte listened. She believed. "You're in love with my great-grandmother," she said softly. "That's something."

Vincent nodded. "Except, I don't think I'm able to return there."

"I have a couple of photos. I'll show them to you tomorrow. Why do you say that? There must be a way," she insisted, seemingly reformed, now.

"I hope so," Vincent said, dreamingly.

"I'm so happy you came looking for me," she murmured in the stillness of the night.

They both stared at the moon, playing hide and seek with the clouds coming from the east. Far, far to the south, the same moon shone above Biscayne Bay, glistening in the water around the stone barge and shinning down on the courtyard for the pleasure of Vizcaya's ghosts.

TWENTY SEVEN

Julia cried. She stared at the very spot where seconds ago, Clarence stood. She felt like the gates of hell opened up again, stealing and ravaging, without any compromise. Having once been granted the ability to roam the earth throughout eternity, Julia was now isolated, and a great divide, like a gaping hole, barred the way. Clarence was again on the other side of time, and Julia no longer had access to him. All her powers had been used to bring him here, to Vizcaya, now. She possessed a knowledge that no one would comprehend, not here at Vizcaya, nor anywhere in this world. She watched her life slowly fade away, to eventually become spirit, until a window into the afterlife was opened to her. She did not know why, or how. It just was. Clarence Henry Jones was the great love of Julia's life. Through some mischievous ordinance, tragedy redefined the trajectory of her existence, and propelled her somewhere into the twenty first century. Vincent Jones, a fabrication of fate itself, a coincidence of the paranormal kind, came into being for her. Julia's own untimely death, inexplicably brought her to him as a vision, a shadow. She pursued Vincent Jones and made it her purpose to dwell in his very own life and soul. Though Vincent was not aware that he and Clarence were the same person, she guided him to that secret passage, willing him to come to her. Vincent was the result of the preordained, placed on the wrong course. His very life was like a figure made of clay, unfinished and without an armature to consolidate its forms, doomed to collapse under its own weight. It is as if some things never were, the cycle of time inverted, to unite the destinies of two men; Clarence and Vincent. One was nothing without the other.

The capricious consequence of time, the mysteries of the universe and existence, had created Vincent. The purpose was unknown. Why were Julia and Clarence denied access to each other again? Why the separation? That purpose remained unknown as well.

Lady Julia, hailed for her beauty and self-reliance, was just a fraud, with a single hope; to be reunited with Clarence. But at what cost? He was in her grasp, here at Vizcaya, and the grounds became their miraculous realm, after a hundred years of infinite grief. Now, he vanished, clutched by the predatory hands of circumstance.

The guests were coming back from their boat ride. Julia watched them, her mind searching aimlessly for a way to return to her metaphysical forms. Could her death take her back to that state again? Could it? She did not think so. The portal of the ages had dissipated, like a nebulous thought. She would never see Clarence Henry Jones again.

"Good morning, Lady Julia," said Deering, from the back of the boat. "Did you just arrive?"

"Yes," Julia replied, trying to compose herself. "Just now."

Deering introduced his guests to Julia as they came to shore. They all headed to the house, no doubt to cool off. Deering stayed behind, not entirely unaffected by Julia's sad demeanor.

"What seems to be the matter?" he asked, really breaking all etiquette conduct.

"It's nothing. Perhaps the heat is getting to me." She held up her parasol and walked to the house. Deering followed her, not at all convinced.

"Ah, here you are," said Deering, looking at Sargent as he and Julia entered the courtyard. The difference of temperature was at least twenty degrees with the outside. The breeze, coming from the south, disturbed ever so slightly the palms standing tall in each corner. "This is Lady Julia," Deering told Sargent.

"Hello, Mr. Sargent," Julia said, folding her parasol.

"I am delighted to make your acquaintance, Lady Julia," said Sargent.

"Please, just Julia," she insisted.

Most of the guests had gathered in the courtyard, as drinks were being served before lunch.

"I was looking forward to meeting you," said Sargent. "I usually like to spend a bit of time with my subjects," he continued, looking at her. "I'm sorry, I don't mean to make you uncomfortable."

"I don't mind," Julia replied.

"Has anyone seen Mr. Jones?" inquired Deering.

Julia looked at Deering. No one was aware of her relationship with Clarence, least of all James Deering, who was a very private man. How she wanted to divulge the depth of her emotion to him, her heartache, like a daughter to a father, yet she could not.

"I'm sure you'll want to change," said Deering to Julia. "Miss Adair will show you to your room."

"This is the most beautiful house I have ever seen," said Julia, transported by the magic of Vizcaya. "It truly is magnificent."

"Thank you. It has been a bit of a headache at times, but it's finally coming together."

Marion came in from the garden at that moment. "Julia!" she exclaimed. "You're here. I'm so happy to see you."

Both women hugged. Their friendship began in California, in Hollywood, more precisely, when young Marion Davies was unknown and just starting her career. They were good friends, yet not quite close enough to share the anxieties of their hearts.

"How are you?" asked the always good-humored Marion.

"Well enough," said Julia. "How about you?"

"Bored," Marion whispered. She took Julia to a more remote part of the courtyard, making sure her host was at a certain distance. "There's nothing to do, except eat and drink, and you know what that does to a woman," she maintained, putting her hands on her hips. "I've got to be back in Hollywood next month. Mr. Vidor is doing a new picture, with me in the lead role."

"I don't think you have anything to worry about," said Julia. She listened to Marion, the uncomplicated life she enjoyed. Stardom is not something Julia envied, though at this moment she would have exchanged her life for the movie star's.

"I did meet someone. Someone staying here. In fact, I'm not sure where he is," said Marion, looking around the courtyard, curious about Vincent's whereabouts. "Well, you'll meet him later."

"That's exciting. What's his name?"

"Clarence Jones. He's wonderful. Different. But I don't know…"

"Clarence Jones?" Julia asked, baffled. "Clarence Henry Jones?"

"Yes. Do you know him?"

Julia's face lost all color. She had to sit down.

"Oh, my God, you know him," said Marion, who sat next to Julia.

One of the guests, a Miss Brown, a middle-aged spinster from Ohio, came in their direction. "Let's have it," she uttered. "What are we gossiping about?" she continued with that very irritating high-pitched voice.

"We were just talking about Mr. Sargent's portrait of Julia," intervened Marion, quick as a flash.

"Ah, yes... very nice," said Miss Brown, disappointed by the subject under discussion, which she found tiresome. She politely excused herself, and returned to the small group she was previously part of.

"Disagreeable woman," said Marion, "how can she be acquainted with Mr. Deering?"

Julia remained in a daze. "I know Mr. Jones," she finally said. "We've known each other for about two years."

"I didn't know," explained Marion. "He never said anything about it, he just kept asking when you were coming," she continued. "Come to think of it, I thought it was a bit annoying." Marion looked at Julia, conscious all of a sudden of Julia and Clarence's relationship. "Oh. It's you..."

"When did he arrive?" asked Julia, longing to know how and when Clarence had made the passage through time.

"I'm not sure," said Marion. "He just arrived..." she added, perplexed. Marion had no concept about Vincent Jones, and Clarence Jones as being one and the same. "But you are that other woman. Aren't you?"

"If you can say that." Julia stood up. "I need to go and change. I've been in these clothes for too long."

"Okay. Okay, but we need to talk," said Marion.

"Of course."

After thanking Mrs. Adair, the housekeeper, Julia closed her bedroom door. Her luggage had been brought up, and she just stared at it. It represented a life she had no wish to be a part of, a life away from everything she had such confidence in; the width and depth of true love. Love experienced, love without end. Lady Julia and all her accolades, had become as inconsequential as the first day of spring when summer arrives. She ran a bath and began to undress, slowly removing all her clothing, while looking at her own reflection in the mirror. She stood in the middle of the bathroom, naked, her feet against the cool marble floor. Clarence's hands caressed her body again, and she shut her eyes to be closer to him, to feel him.

Julia stepped in the tub. The hot water relaxed her body, and she let the water hold her up as her dreamlike fantasy continued in the stillness of the day. She caressed her breasts and ran her hands the length of her thighs. She laid in the tub for a while, remembering…

Julia closed her eyes again. She wanted to return to that happy winter of 1915…

"This is Lady Julia," said the hostess of the crowded Christmas party. Clarence Jones, dressed in an immaculate formal tailcoat, approached.

"How do you do," Clarence said, saluting the woman who would forever change the course of his life.

"Mr. Jones is a young entrepreneur, I dare say," continued the hostess.

"I'm very happy to meet you," replied Julia.

"What brings you to Pittsburgh?" Clarence asked.

The hostess excused herself, to attend to other guests that were arriving.

"I have family in Boston. I'm just passing through," said Julia, removing her gloves.

"I hope you won't be in too much of a hurry," Clarence smiled. "Would you like a drink?" he asked, anxious to keep her close to him.

"Champagne, thank you."

Clarence returned quickly from the bar, avoiding eye contact with anyone who might stop him for a chat. The room was fairly crowded, and too many single men were in attendance, and all too willing to come to Lady Julia's rescue. "Here you are," he said, conquered already by the dazzling young Julia. He watched her take a sip of her champagne and dove into the azure of her eyes, losing himself to the magnetism of her.

"So, what is it that you do, exactly, Mr. Jones?" she asked, with that voice he knew he would find impossible to forget.

"I'm in the steel industry. Nothing very creative," he added.

"Well, that's not strictly true," she said, "one has to be creative in other ways, perhaps, but creative all the same."

"I like that," Clarence declared. I like that very much."

"I was told Mr. Deering would be here, this evening," Julia asserted. "Do you happen to know him?" she asked, her eyes wandering about the room.

"I do. I believe he is coming."

"I would love to see his new house in Florida. Vizcaya, I think it's called."

"Yes, Vizcaya. It's magnificent. I'm sure you'll get an invitation," Clarence said, feeling James Deering would succumb to Julia's charms.

"Oh, you've been there?" she inquired.

"I have. Mr. Deering has been kind enough to ask me to stay there, on two occasions. It's not quite finished yet, but I believe it will be spectacular when it is."

"I'm told it's the most perfect house."

"It is more than that," said Clarence…

The bath water was cold. Julia opened her eyes to face the certainty of the day, the muted sound of reality, alone in this bathroom in Vizcaya. Clarence was right, Vizcaya was more than a house. She grabbed a towel, wrapped it around her body and let her long black hair down. Her mother called it her crown of glory, for it was like a veil of rare and fabulous beauty, black like the deepest night.

Julia knew about the secret passage that led to that other dimension. She guided Clarence there. She is the one who caused the water leak that day at the museum, so the bedroom would be closed to the public. Now, she wondered… would she have to go after him again?

A knock on the bedroom door startled Julia. "Yes?" she questioned the intrusion.

"Julia. It's Marion. Are you coming down to lunch?" she asked.

Julia stared at her face in the mirror.

"Julia! Are you in there?"

"I'll be down in a minute."

Deering asked the housekeeper if Mr. Jones had left abruptly. She replied that his belongings were still in his room. Everyone concluded that an emergency, perhaps at one of his factories, had occurred and that Mr. Jones had left without a chance to thank his host, or say goodbye.

TWENTY EIGHT

Charlotte knocked on the bedroom door. "Vincent? Are you awake? I have a cup of tea for you."

"Oh, thank you," muttered Vincent waking up from a deep sleep. "Come in, come in," he said.

Charlotte entered the bedroom. "I have to tell you, this is very strange indeed," she said, placing the cup and a small saucer with two biscuits on the night table.

"Well, thank you. I didn't expect tea in bed."

"What am I going to do with you?" Charlotte exclaimed. "What's your plan?"

"I'm afraid I don't have one." Vincent took a sip of tea. "Aah, so civilized," he murmured, eyes closed, savoring the English tea.

"It's a mixture of Darjeeling and Assam," she said, before returning to a more critical issue. "I'm serious. You can't stay here."

"I know. I have no such intention." Vincent looked at Charlotte. "I have no idea about what's going to happen to me next." He took another sip of tea. "You know... you should come with me."

"Where?" she inquired, not quite sure she wanted to know the answer.

"To Vizcaya."

"No, no, no," she answered. "I don't think so."

"I can prove to you that I'm telling the truth."

"I already know you are... I think..."

"Ah, you see. You're not sure," said Vincent, pointing his finger at her.

"You can hardly blame me. The whole thing sounds ridiculous."

"You want to believe, but... there's that little thing, called rationality, logic, and it's putting up a massive wall in front of you."

"Perhaps," said Charlotte.

"I was just like you... once. I didn't believe in anything I couldn't see, anything I couldn't touch. And then I learned. I was shown."

Charlotte sat on the bed, and gazed at the morning light through the window. Both she and Vincent kept silent. A ray of sunlight shone on a blue vase filled with daisies on the corner desk, setting it ablaze in bright sapphire shades. "Look at that," she said, pointing at the flowers. "The simple beauty of everyday life, and yet so many people miss it. And it passes." A cloud obscured the sun, and Charlotte's point was made the more powerful. "I was thinking about this accident... I'm supposed to have."

"Yes?"

"Is that my destiny? Can one stop what has been predestined?" she asked.

"Maybe I'm the living proof of that. Don't you think?"

"I don't know..." she wondered. "How do you know you didn't follow the path you were meant to follow in the first place, the roadmap of your very own destiny?"

"I told you last night, my life was well-structured, methodical, I never dreamt about anything like this. Only someone insane would follow such an idea, something that leads to another time."

"And yet, here you are. You did take that road." Charlotte became anxious. "I want you to help me. I don't want the accident to happen. Do you understand?"

"I know," Vincent said, nodding. "I'll try."

Charlotte stood up from the bed. "I'm still puzzled as why my great-grandmother pursued you... that her ghost pursued you, I should say. That is so strange."

"That your great-grandmother pursued me, or that I was pursued by a ghost, that happened to be your great-grandmother?" smiled Vincent.

"Both!" Charlotte exclaimed, as she left the room. "Okay, get ready, we're going to go for a nice walk," she shouted from the hallway.

"Yes, ma'am!"

Charlotte's five-acre property was in Gladwyne, a suburban community about twenty miles to the northwest of Philadelphia. Vincent walked next to her, receptive to the natural beauty of the surroundings. Neither one spoke. New leaves and wild flowers marked the landscape with bright and festive colors on this early summer morning. Rolling hills reminded Vincent that this was not south Florida. The lack of humidity made that point as well. He smiled.

"What's so funny?" Charlotte asked.

"Oh, nothing."

She pointed at a particular spot in the distance. "You can see downtown Philly from the top of that hill."

"You have a wonderful property," Vincent said. "You seem to have a good life here," he added. "You're lucky."

"Evidently, not that lucky. Remember, I'm supposed to end up in a wheelchair?"

"God, I'm sorry about that."

"What the hell!" she moaned. "Why me?"

Vincent could not answer that. His own life had taken so many turns, plagued by confrontations so destructive at times, that he thought the word 'destiny' was laughable. A word used by people with no aspiration for anything; and destiny comes along, like a crutch on which they stagger along. No, Vincent was definitely not an authority on the subject of life.

The top of the hill was reached. "Look, how peaceful it is," Charlotte said as she gazed into the distance. Downtown Philadelphia rose above the morning mist, like an illusion. Not a whisper of air disturbed the silence. High in the sky, a couple of birds circled above.

Vincent nodded. They both stood there, in a field of wild grass and dandelions.

"You can stay if you want," said Charlotte, still looking towards the city.

"I'm—"

"Don't answer that," she quickly added. "I don't know what came over me." Charlotte looked at Vincent. "Oh, alright. Can you? Can you stay?"

"You don't want me here," answered Vincent, shaking his head.

"Why not?"

He stared at her. All actions changed, unexpectedly, and with it, the mood. The morning walk, the stillness of the day, became immaterial. "I'm not sure how to answer that," Vincent said.

"I'm alone. You're alone. We have similar interests."

"I can't perform miracles," asserted Vincent.

"What? You really think this has something to do with my accident," she replied, expressing her frustration by making quotation marks with her fingers on the word accident. "It's not, I can assure you. Maybe we should head back to the house."

A short, uncomfortable quiet, followed. Vincent admired the vast expanse of the sky and was on the verge of mentioning it, but refrained from it at the risk of sounding trivial. "I'm sorry," he uttered, finally. "I didn't mean to sound so rude."

"All sins forgiven," Charlotte replied.

"Did you really mean what you said?"

"I did. But it doesn't matter now. I should've never said that. It's not fair to you."

Vincent looked at Charlotte. She wore a headscarf, just like she did the first time they met. He was not impervious to her charms then, and he surely was not now. Yes, that was fine, thought Vincent. This life suited him well enough. The allurement of all complications made simple, with one hand clap, was hard to pass. All this would be true, if two names were wiped off the blackboard of his life. Merely two names, two little words, and a complete life reversal would occur. Two little words; Julia and Vizcaya. Those few syllables were etched in the depth of him, in the core of his being, and nothing could amend that.

By the time they returned to the house, a voiceless accord was made. It seemed love was absent and regardless of how much respect and ardor is poured out, even without restrain, the soul will not withstand the sorrow. The inner beast of unbridled passion would slowly devour its illegitimate offspring. Charlotte knew this. Yet, loneliness makes for a powerful argument.

Vincent sat down. "I'll leave this morning," he said, as Charlotte paced the room. "I'm happy I came, and thrilled you took me in, and that you believed what I said."

"What will you do? You're going back to Florida?"

"I must. I have nothing here." Vincent saw the disappointment on Charlotte's face. "I lost everything. I don't even have an ID. I don't exist. All I have left is a small key," Vincent said, as he reached for it in his pocket. "And I'm not even sure it will help now."

"Do you want to see the few pictures I have of my great-grandmother?"

"I would love to."

Charlotte fetched a large leather-bound photo album and sat next to Vincent. She turned the over-sized pages to the last ones. Several black and white as well as sepia images were pasted onto the page. "This is one of the best shots I have of her," said Charlotte, pointing at a beautiful picture of Julia.

Vincent looked at it. "May I?" he asked, wanting to hold the book closer to him. Julia posed in a studio, in front of a New York City backdrop. The photo was taken around 1915, thought Charlotte. "This is odd," said Vincent. "I think I just figured something out."

"What is it?" she asked.

"I just had this... this weird vision. It's like a dream I keep having, and I have a feeling it happens when I think about her," Vincent exclaimed, pointing at Julia.

"That is strange!"

"Don't you think?"

"What is this dream you keep having?" inquired Charlotte.

"I'm drowning. I fall off... a boat, I think it's a boat and I sink deeper and deeper. I cannot get back to the surface."

"Oh, dear. That sounds awful."

"Strange," continued Vincent in his reflections. A second photo showed a younger Julia with a little girl by her side. They sat by a fountain. "Julia looks very young in this one," said Vincent. "And who is this little girl?"

"That was her younger sister, Elisabeth. She died a few months after that photo was taken."

"Oh, how sad. What happened?" asked Vincent.

"Pneumonia, I think."

"Terrible."

"Yes. Nothing was a sure thing in those days."

Another photo, smaller, this one, intrigued Vincent. Julia stood at a train station, holding a little girl by the hand. "Who's this little girl?" asked Vincent.

"That's my grandmother. Julia's daughter."

"She has... had a daughter?" exclaimed Vincent, apparently surprised by the revelation.

"Yes."

"I didn't know that," said Vincent, stunned.

"Why would you?" answered Charlotte.

Vincent leaned over and looked at the photo closely. He stared at the young child and sat up abruptly, like he became conscious of something he had forgotten.

"What?" questioned Charlotte.

"She looks like the little girl I saw at Sargent's grave. I didn't tell you about that." Vincent held the photo album as he spoke about that day at the cemetery. Charlotte, who had heard most of what Vincent had to say, was conflicted and confused by the continuous haunting Julia inflicted on him. "You do realize that you're the only person in this world who thinks I'm not crazy, who think this actually happened to me."

"I know," replied Charlotte.

Vincent kept staring at the photo of Julia with the little girl.

Charlotte paced the room, as if something was amiss, something that did not make sense. "Yes?" The question was more of a remark.

"I didn't say anything," said Vincent.

"Oh, but you did." Charlotte very much believed in the afterlife. She felt quite sure that spirits roamed the earth, and although much was beyond comprehension, such apparitions took place. Her question was why would a spirit pursue someone so incessantly.

"You don't suppose…" wondered Vincent, whose own conclusion left him mystified.

"Oh… what? Wait. Are you? What are you suggesting?"

"I'm not suggesting anything. Trust me, I don't know anything."

Charlotte approached Vincent, and took the photo album from him. "This is going to sound absolutely crazy! I mean, crazy!" she exclaimed. "She's my great-grandmother, for God's sake! I can't believe I'm going to say this." She stared at Vincent.

"What?" he wondered.

"Did you sleep with her? Did you sleep with Julia? While you were… you know… back there, in time?

"No!" Vincent replied forcefully. "Absolutely not. I was with her maybe a minute."

"You know, that's the only thing that makes sense. This little girl… you know who she is, don't you?"

"No," said Vincent, shaking his head. "How's that possible?"

"I think you know who she is."

Vincent buried his face in his hands. "Oh, God, I'm afraid, I do… maybe."

"Why are you afraid? She could be your daughter, Vincent. That's why Julia has been making your life a misery."

"If that were true, that would make you—"

"Your great-granddaughter! Technically," answered Charlotte, eyes wide open.

"Oh, my!"

"I know. Crazy, right? Who's going to believe that?"

"I'm amazed you don't have a problem even considering it," said Vincent.

"So… if you didn't have any relations with her when you were in Vizcaya this time, it means the two of you were together another time." Charlotte sat down. Her mind explored the wild implications that were made. She seemed to enjoy the challenge, like something exciting was going to occupy her days. "Am I right?"

"You lost me at she's your daughter," said Vincent. "How is that even possible? And how did I miss it? All those years, and I never thought of it. Not once."

"But this is incredible. Can't you see? You've been places at different time. You can… whatever you want to call it… travel through time. That's incredible!"

"Even though I have no recollection of it at all," argued Vincent.

"Yes, it's wonderful."

"Yes, wonderful," replied Vincent sarcastically. "Look at me, the great time traveler. Don't I look fabulous?"

"Oh, stop feeling sorry for yourself, I wish I were that fortunate."

"That's the problem with you Brits, you have no compassion… you just make fun of people."

"That's how we endured the war, my dear. No compassion and lots of tea," laughed Charlotte.

The lack of more photographs of Julia prompted him to ask for the album again. "May I see the photos again?" asked Vincent.

"Sure, but I don't have any more photographs of her. This is all there is. She died young, I think she was twenty-five or twenty-six."

"Twenty-five, twenty-six!?" cried Vincent. "What are you saying?" he lamented.

"She died young. I'm not sure…"

Vincent stared at the photo of Julia with the New York City backdrop. He stared into her eyes, as if to attempt to reach her, to speak to her. Vincent looked up at Charlotte. "This makes no sense," he said, confused by too many events that led him to too many dead ends. "When was I with her, then?"

Charlotte's demeanor changed, like something terrified her. "Oh, my God!" she exclaimed, vacantly staring into the distance. "She died in a boating accident. I just made the connection. I mean, I haven't thought about this in ages."

"Oh. That is incredible! Are you sure that's how she died?"

"Positive. I don't know why I didn't make the connection sooner. I must be crazy. Do you think this is related to your dreams?" asked Charlotte.

"It must be. Right? That changes everything."

"It certainly does. Oh, my God."

"What about your grandmother? Her daughter?"

"She lived to an old age. Eighty-two, I believe." Charlotte sat next to Vincent. He could tell Charlotte had something else to divulge. "Unless..."

"What is it?"

"Julia was engaged to a Captain, whose name escapes me, but I can look it up for you."

"She was engaged? This is getting worse."

"I'm sorry, but she was."

"And?" questioned Vincent, on the verge of losing his mind.

"She could be his daughter... the Captain. I mean, who knows?"

"Right."

"He was killed in Verdun." Charlotte shook her head. "What a waste."

"I think I need a drink now," said Vincent.

"Absolument!" she said in her perfect French. "We definitely need a drink."

Vincent closed the photo album, unsure of his very existence and the reason of him being here, sitting on this couch.

"Well, great-granddad... I'm coming with you," she smiled. "Off to Florida."

"Great-granddad... maybe," he asserted. "Let's not jump to conclusions."

"Of course, but I'm still coming with you."

"You really are?" asked Vincent, who felt very happy about the news, mainly because he loved Charlotte's company, but also because she legitimized his claims.

A strong storm moved inland, and a heavy rain began to fall, with drops the size of marbles. The sitting room became dim, and a wonderful display of lightning intermittently lit up the room. Charlotte and Vincent sat on the couch, next to each other, witnessing the spectacle. Tomorrow, on to Vizcaya.

TWENTY NINE

The passing of time. How many cycles around the sun does the earth have to make to soothe our spirit? A rock, once sat on and a view of indescribable beauty, takes our thoughts floating on a nomadic journey. A path that leads to that small patio, where so many memories, joyful and oppressive, are holding us caged in. One remembers. Some things are hard to let go. We want to see the unblemished picture as we try to rebuild something that never really was, but we try, and we make it stronger, better, in our effort to salvage an inescapable outcome. Yet, that somewhere, as significant as it appeared, will be like the autumn leaves that fall from the very tree that once harbored and nurtured them, and are scattered, never to be remembered again.

Vizcaya, lifeless. Vizcaya, widowed. Vizcaya, separated from what was hers; a claim to eminence, immortality. Vincent had to return there. Even if going back to one's roots can end up being a terrible mistake, Vincent had to return to Vizcaya. Like the unwavering migrating bird who returns to a kinder climate, the presumption of something no less noble than absolute love, would guide him once more. Vincent was ready. He believed this time, even though lives were turned upside down, erased.

A hundred years is but a minute, when everything is made clear. Clarence Henry Jones was reborn, and a woman and a child were anxiously waiting for him.

THIRTY

"Ah! Lady Julia, here you are," said Sargent as Julia came down the stairway into the courtyard. "You look spectacular, my dear," he continued. Deering nodded with that subtle smile that some misguided people confused with a scorn.

Other guests chose to ignore Julia's entrance, which was never meant to be so arresting in the first place. She abhorred being the center of attention and she discreetly joined Sargent, who stood up from his chair for her. Julia's indigo dress showed the stark contrast of her unblemished ivory skin. Her thick long hair worn down, cascaded in thick waves. Sargent could not take his eyes off her.

Drinks were being served, with lunch to follow at the usual small tables under the galleries. Marion who sat two tables away from Julia, felt like she had been abandoned by her friend. She tried to draw Julia's focus on her, but to no avail.

The after lunch lethargic afternoon began, with very little to do, except become lizard-like and soak up the opulence of the day.

"Why are you ignoring me?" Marion asked Julia, after most of the guests had moved to various parts of the house.

"Truly, I'm not," replied Julia. I wanted to sit with Mr. Sargent, who as you know has been commissioned to do my portrait.

Marion listened. "Are you sure? Because I'm sorry if I did anything wrong. Mr. Jones doesn't mean anything to me."

"I know."

"So, we are friends?"

"Of course."

"When is Mr. Sargent going to do your portrait?" asked Marion.

"Probably next month."

"Are you excited? Who commissioned him?"

"I think Clarence did. Yes, I'm very excited." Julia felt she already had said too much and she regretted what was divulged. The five thousand dollars Clarence would have to pay for the commission, made her feel uneasy. She knew about the devastation of the war in Europe and luxuries like having a portrait done at such a cost, was something she was not willing to talk about. Marion, she sensed, would inquire about the dollar amount, yet she never did. The Hollywood star showed a certain amount of class, which surprised and pleased Julia at the same time. As the only true blue-blood at Vizcaya, Julia was brought up with that British upper-class, 'mind your own business' attitude. She never knew what to expect when staying with people. It became habitual for her; she would either be lavishly entertained, or completely ignored. Some individuals were intimidated by her title, a title which she did not like to flaunt about, yet there are those took care of that matter and acted like the rooster in the chicken coop. Most vulgar, she thought.

Marion appeared startled by the news that Clarence commissioned the painting. She had no idea about Sargent's fee for a portrait, though she imagined it was quite a lot. "He must really care for you," she expressed.

"I believe he does. Please don't mention it to anyone. Even Mr. Deering doesn't know who commissioned Mr. Sargent."

"I'm very discreet," said Marion. "I can keep a secret."

Julia gave her a smile filled with uncertainty. Sharing anything confidential was troublesome enough for her, having Marion as the co-conspirator, really alarmed her. The deed was done. How many people would look at her with a judging glare the next morning? That was up to Marion.

A tremendous storm erupted at around seven o'clock the next morning. Towering clouds rose above the bay with a loud thunder. Julia got out of bed and looked at the gloomy sky from her bedroom window. An abrupt and violent rain began to fall. Through the thick veil of rain, she discerned a form, like a figure, standing at the far end of the garden. It stood still. Julia pressed her face to the glass, and strained to get a clearer image of what she was witnessing. Perhaps a gardener, she thought. Yet, why would he not seek shelter? A long, drawn-out rolling thunder echoed above Vizcaya, as the impressive sound increased. The figure stood there, indifferent to the rain and the powerful gusts of wind that violently shook the earth and the trees.

Julia jerked back from the window all of a sudden. She stared at the figure for a split second, and quickly put on her silk dressing gown.

She rushed out of her bedroom, and descended the stairway as fast as she could, crossed the courtyard and ran into the poring rain. "Clarence!" she shouted, as she ran toward him. The powerful thunderstorm and lightning strikes covered her voice.

Drenched and out of breath, she stared vacantly at the empty steps, on which a minute ago, she thought Clarence stood. Julia burst out crying. She began to wail, softly at first, then she broke down with a loud cry, and fell on her knees. She could feel the sting of the rain on her back, through the thin material of her dressing gown. How long did she remain there? A minute? An hour? She did not know, but when James Deering placed his umbrella above her, the rain had only increased, and Julia was in great danger of catching pneumonia.

"My dear Lady Julia, what are you doing here?" he asked. "It's a good thing I saw you." He helped her up, sheltering her under his umbrella. Her soaked garment stuck to her skin, and the suggestion of her naked body made Deering look away.

"I'm sorry," Julia said, holding back her tears, her hair in her face.

"Don't be sorry. We need to get you inside quickly, and get you to drink something hot, fast."

She held on to him, sheltered by the umbrella, as the rain showed no sign of slowing down.

"I'm terribly sorry," she uttered again.

Deering, much too considerate to ask anything personal, refrained from asking why Julia was out in the storm, crying. His nonexistent fatherly instincts, seemed to make an entrance with Julia, and he rejoiced inwardly at his newfound affection.

Both soaked to the skin, Julia and Deering headed to their own bedrooms, with instructions for Julia to have a hot bath and a cup of tea.

After the housekeeper had attended to Julia, she left her room and told her that she ought to have a hot bath as soon as possible.

While her bath was running, Julia stood by the window again. The rain had finally stopped and she looked at the central basin, overflowing onto the paths on its sides. The absence of sunlight, gave a strange glow to the garden, as if it came from within the ground. Vizcaya, like the compassionate, caring mother, endured Julia's torment through tears of rain. A corner of the sky was set alight in shades of coral and vermillion, and an intensely colorful rainbow ignited above. Julia began to cry again, and she began to shake.

"I wondered where Lady Julia is?" pondered Deering, as some of the guests sat at the breakfast table. Several hours had gone by since he brought Julia back inside. No one seemed to have laid eyes on her since the night before. Deering became concerned, seeing the late morning hour.

"I'll check on her," said Marion.

"Would you, Miss Marion? Thank you."

Marion walked to Julia's bedroom and knocked on the door. "Julia. Julia, are you awake?"

Deering had left the breakfast room and stood behind Marion. "Well? No answer?"

"No. Why are you so concerned all of a sudden?" inquired Marion, who could not understand Deering's keen vigilance.

"I'm going in," said Marion. "Something's wrong." She softly turned the door knob and opened the door. The curtains were drawn and the room was plunged into obscurity, though one could make out the shape of someone under the bed covers. "Julia. Julia," called out Marion as she approached the bed. Deering was not far behind, worried. Marion lifted the blanket and saw Julia lying there, her hair still damp. She was asleep.

Deering notice that Julia was shaking, and he placed his hand on her forehead, to see if she ran a temperature. "She's burning up," he said, fearful and feeling responsible for his guest. "I think she's going to need a doctor."

Marion felt Julia's forehead as well, and agreed with Deering.

Julia opened her eyes. She searched about the room, as if she was expecting to see someone. She knew this was the exit from this life she had been wishing for. This was the moment. A few hours of suffering, and circumstances will change and fate will be on her side again, smile at her again, beyond time. Death had the sweet aroma of her lost happiness, and she welcomed it. She knew now that the figure in the garden was Clarence, calling her to cross over. Julia had no doubts. Doctors or no doctors, her state of mind was lucid, even if her body and her health were in decline. He was not an illusion, from some concocted wish made for an impossible joy, no, Clarence was here, at Vizcaya. She had seen him just a few hours ago.

Deering became really worried. A decent doctor, with the latest techniques at his disposal, would be hard to find. Jacksonville, in the north of Florida, was the only city large enough to have such a doctor. Anywhere else would be a waste of time. "I will call Jacksonville. We must have a doctor here soon," uttered Deering, with deep anxiety in his voice.

It was not until the next day that a doctor finally arrived at Vizcaya. Julia's fever had spiked to an alarming temperature. The house had never known a sick person, and the maids, other servants and housekeeper, became caregivers. Julia laid in bed, all make-up gone and pale as a winter dawn. She appeared at peace.

The doctor told Deering that there was very little he could do, unless she was moved to a hospital, where perhaps a technique called antiserum therapy could be performed. That avenue was quickly rejected, as the nearest hospitals were in Key West, or Tampa; an arduous journey for either of them. Rest and herbal teas, were the only things that could be done, with the hope that Julia was strong enough to recover.

After admiring the house and accepting a five-hundred-dollar payment in cash, the doctor was driven back to the railroad station in Miami.

"Well, that's all we can do," said Deering, sitting in The Courtyard. He hated the fact that he was at the mercy of time, with absolutely no power to make any change, regardless of his wealth. He was very fond of Julia, and it distressed him to see her in such a state. Sargent, who joined him at the table, looked somber as well. He was very much looking forward to painting the beautiful Julia, yet now, the commission seemed uncertain. He would paint her at no cost if it meant a speedy recovery and she became well again. He genuinely felt inspired by the young woman, as a model.

Other guests inquired about Julia throughout the day. Marion seemed to be the main caregiver though, bringing soup and tea to the bedroom. She sat by Julia's bedside and wiped the sweat off Julia's forehead with fresh towels at regular intervals.

Julia opened her eyes. She saw Marion by her side, and felt her hand caressing her hair. "Thank you," she murmured.

"You need to rest," said Marion, happy to see her patient wake up at last, and talking.

"I wanted to go to him," moaned Julia, "I wanted to go to him," she repeated, closing her eyes again in semi-consciousness.

"You scared everyone," answered Marion, not entirely understanding the meaning of Julia's words. "It looks like you're going to recover," she smiled. "Mr. Deering will be very happy." Marion stood up quietly and left the room.

The news of Julia on the mend made its way around the whole estate, from the house to the farms across the street. Deering even thought of having some fireworks display, perhaps in a night or two, in celebration. Sargent too, was pleased. He so wanted to visit Julia in her bedroom, but such an action would be contrary to all sense of decorum.

Julia was well enough to get out of bed. She walked the length of the upper galleries, not quite ready to show herself downstairs. She closed the bedroom door behind her. She leaned on it as if to shut out the rest of the world. How could she allow anyone in now? Her eyes wandered aimlessly about the room. Various objects offered themselves, yet they lacked all interest, as the one so adored, so indispensable, was gone.

THIRTY ONE

Without an ID, or any kind of papers, Vincent was forced to travel by car. Charlotte, whose life lacked excitement, was more than willing to drive the twelve hundred miles to Miami. The roughly seventeen hours would be spent in Charlotte's very comfortable Range Rover.

About fifty miles were covered when the sun rose, like the inauguration of something new, something of an unknown origin that scared them both. Charlotte and Vincent were silent. The quiet sound of the engine marked the time. Vincent did not know what to expect in Miami. His beloved Vizcaya was like a terrified animal whose habitat had been destroyed. How could such powers, like the expansion of a world as a result of time, be expunged? The precious key in the depth of his pocket seemed like a worthless tool in a fight that would require a force not known to man. Everything around Vincent emphasized his despair; the very car he was driven in, the architecture along the interstate, all of it showcased his exile from another century and shone a light on his helplessness.

The monotony of the interstate allowed Vincent to relax. Delaying any kind of thinking about what he would have to do once in Vizcaya, was a must. He looked at Charlotte, who concentrated on the road. He felt a great sense of gratitude toward her, and realized that she really was the only friend he had. The entirety of his previous existence had been obliterated and everyone he knew deleted from the pages of his life. He returned his gaze on the highway. Richmond – 30 miles, announced the road sign. Vincent thought about the old lady in the Greyhound bus.

"I have absolutely nothing," said Charlotte, unexpectedly. "No husband, no boyfriend, no parents, no siblings and no children."

Vincent stared at her. A tear ran down Charlotte's cheek, which caught him off-guard. She wiped the tear, unemotionally, perhaps unaware of it, as if she had spoken to herself.

"Charlotte," whispered Vincent, looking at her and deeply impacted by the sorrowful comment. How does one respond and how does one battle despair? With what kind of weapon? Love? Lies? The mighty defender can lack conviction and Vincent had no wisdom to give.

After a quick stop for gas and some snacks, Charlotte took the wheel again.

"Are you alright driving," asked Vincent, who was really inquiring about his friend's state of mind.

"Yes, I'm fine."

"Good."

"You know what I was thinking?" she asked, as soon as they were back on the highway. "What if you can't get back to her? What if you're unable to break through... that... that barrier, you know... time. What then?"

"I'm not sure. It's something I try not to think about."

"Don't you think you ought to?" she replied almost immediately, like if she had planned her response.

Vincent kept silent. The focus of the conversation was heading on a path that led straight to a brick wall, with a cliff behind it, just in case.

"I have money, you know. More than I know what to do with," Charlotte said. The announcement, much out of character, shocked Vincent who felt very uneasy.

"Charlotte, you know how I appreciate everything you are doing for me, but this talk about money... that's not like you."

"It's not. It wouldn't be normally, but aren't you enjoying this trip? We could go anywhere you want. Just say the word," declared Charlotte.

Julia's compelling image manifested itself at that very moment. Vincent did not know if it was the result of his imagination. He detached himself from reality and sank into a trance that took him to the staircase in the courtyard of Vizcaya. There, he stood with her, barely able to breathe as she reached for his hand.

"Vincent! Did you hear what I said?" asked Charlotte. "I'm pulling into this rest area," she continued, exiting the road.

"Why are we stopping?" inquired Vincent, totally unaware of the crisis taking place.

"I've been poring my heart out, and you're stuck in a dream," said Charlotte. She parked the car. "You didn't hear a word I said."

"I'm sorry," replied Vincent, now mindful of the situation. Charlotte had a change of heart. The tediousness of the miles gave her time to reflect on her life, a life she did not particularly love, with the looming thought of an even worse outcome. "I did hear you, actually. I did hear your lament about how empty your life is. And I'm truly sorry. Sorry that I cannot do anything about it... sorry that you feel that way."

Charlotte leaned forward, her face on the steering wheel. "God, this is so hard!"

Vincent could only watch.

"I'm an accomplished woman, you know. But none of my skills matter to anyone... I'm a ghost, a little bit like my great-grandmother you're so fond of."

"You have friends, don't you?" asked Vincent, not really knowing what to say.

"Oh, yes, my friends... let's see... no, I don't have any." She sat up again, and looked at the people coming out of the restrooms. "I wish I was her, or her," she told Vincent, pointing out a couple of women heading back to their cars. "Anyone else, but me."

Vincent recalled the day Charlotte arrived in Boston for his mother's funeral. He remembered how keen she was to meet him, and used the memorial service as an excuse to make his acquaintance. "You don't really mean that," said Vincent. "Trust me, you never want to wish to be someone else."

"But you are," she answered. "That's all you've been wishing."

"That's true, but—"

"But nothing! It's alright. I understand." Charlotte looked at Vincent. "I mean, after all, you are not really Vincent Jones, are you? You are Clarence Jones, who by some perversion from the universe, came back to make my life even harder than it was." Charlotte started her engine. "Well, now that I made a complete fool of myself..."

Unspoken words often supply the soul with the arrows of regrets. Though love could not categorically be implied, Vincent did recognize that Charlotte was miserable. He never saw it before, at least not to that extent. Why is the heart so stubborn? he wondered, commiserating with Charlotte in many ways, since he, himself suffered from the same affliction. "You didn't make a fool of yourself," he uttered, as they headed south again.

"Is it bad to be resentful of a ghost?" she asked, smiling. "And you, what the hell are doing here? How on earth did you manage to end up here, now?" Charlotte continued, playfully and without any hidden agenda.

"I don't have the faintest idea." Vincent seemed anxious all of a sudden, like something he remembered. "I think I may have had that boating accident I told you about... I'm not absolutely sure, but I seem to have this weird reoccurring dream. I fall in the water. I can see the depth beneath me... it's dark, and something is pulling me under... and I wake up."

"That is scary," Charlotte said. "Dreams can be strange, well, they often are, so maybe, maybe they're telling you something. You could've died in a boating accident."

Vincent kept silent.

"Oh, my God! You're dead! Can't you see? You died in a boating accident," emphasized Charlotte. You're a ghost... essentially." She poked him in the shoulder, "Wait, no, you're real," she laughed.

"Ha-ha, funny. Essentially?" repeated Vincent, who enjoyed the banter. "So, how come you can see me?" he asked, mockingly, with the confidence of a twelve-year-old during recess.

"How do you know I see you?" Charlotte asked, prolonging the frivolous conversation.

Vincent laughed. "Oh, why can't it be like this, always?" he sighed, leaning his head back into the car seat.

Charlotte was quiet. The unexpressed answer was deafening, though she chose not to speak of it and showed no reaction.

In a short space of time, Vincent successfully estranged himself from previous comments, and contradicted his very own words when he denied Charlotte her affection and her love. He was a confused man, a condition not so unfamiliar with that gender when the opposite sex shows too much attention. He loved Charlotte's company. In simple terms, she made him feel good, alive. He loved her. Love. Why try to find another word for his feelings? She had much to give. A life of discontentment, suddenly given free reign and a trade for a life of exuberance and love, can make a convincing case. Why does one insist of things that may be, versus things that are? Perhaps for the same reason that one covets the bigger house across the street, of the prettier neighbor down the road. Vincent knew this. The odds, near

197

impossibilities really, of being able to get back to 1917, ought to compel him to realign his desires to a more realistic outcome; a life here, with Charlotte.

The 'Welcome to Florida' road sign arrived like a prophecy, a presage to a sinister conclusion to an otherwise cheerful journey. Vizcaya was a few hours away. Both Charlotte and Vincent, assumed their roles; Charlotte, who tried to change the unwritten rules of intimacy between friends, and Vincent, consumed by a strong suspicion as the miles went by.

Charlotte parked the Range Rover on the side of the road. She stared at the entrance of the estate, the intricate gateposts with the name 'Vizcaya' carved vertically on both sides, and she looked at Vincent. "Now, what?" she asked.

The entrance of Vizcaya seemed like an image from a folktale buried in the pages of some obscure book. Here, at this instant, none of it appeared real.

THIRTY TWO

"How did you go in last time?" Charlotte asked, as she glanced at the playful shadows from the trees that stood by the entrance. "How did you get to that secret door you talked about?"

"You're showing a keen interest in the detail all of a sudden," affirmed Vincent. "You don't want to know. Trust me."

"Why?" Charlotte looked at him. "What did you do?" she inquired, suspicious.

Vincent shook his head. "I was resourceful," he said, with a certain pleasure in his explanation. He could tell Charlotte's mind was actively engaged at identifying all possibilities.

"Resourceful," she remarked, looking at the main gate.

"I'd say, ingenious, actually," he grinned.

Charlotte shrugged. "Resourceful. Ingenious. I'm not..." Her glance returned to the entrance for a split second, before looking at Vincent again. "Oh my God, you broke in, didn't you!?" she exclaimed. "You did! That's so naughty of you."

"Naughty?"

"Yes, you're a naughty boy, Doctor Vincent Jones, or should I say Clarence Jones?"

"There was a hurricane, if you must know," answered Vincent, amused by the naughty boy comment.

"You broke into Vizcaya, a museum, in the middle of a hurricane. You're too much!"

"Please don't refer Vizcaya as a museum, I don't like it."

"I'm sorry. Though, it is a museum... but I know what you mean." They both returned their gaze to the entrance.

"She's there, you know," said Vincent. "She's right there, within that space."

"You really are in love with her, aren't you?"

Vincent nodded.

"Still, I can't believe you broke in," said Charlotte, shaking her head, yet rather entertained by the would-be scandalous revelation.

Vincent's memory, vague at times, was finally opening up its window into the most unreliable corners of his mind. The boating accident, thought to be a meaningless fragment of a potential memory from childhood, soared to the forefront of his mind. Clarence Henry Jones, the young tycoon, drowned. He was never found. Lost at sea, body and soul, adrift for eternity. Is that what happened?

"It doesn't seem real, does it?" said Charlotte. "Here we are, the traffic is... well, ridiculous... planes are flying over us... it is 2008, and you spoke to James Deering. You spoke to Sargent. Sargent!" she repeated with emphasis. "Please don't tell him I burned his painting, when you see him next." Charlotte smiled.

"Come with me." Vincent looked at her, the incredulity on her face. "Why not?" he continued.

"You know that's not possible."

"Why?" he asked.

"You belong there... I think. Well, you do, and that's all there is to it. As for me, I'd be a stranger, a stranger of the worse kind. More like an invader. Anyway, how do you know I wouldn't turn to dust as soon as I stepped through that passage of yours?" Charlotte shrugged. "Right?"

"A little melodramatic. Maybe not quite what would happen..."

"You don't know. I have no business being there, in 1917. Besides, Julia would scratch my eyes out!" Charlotte added with a chuckle.

"That would be the more realistic outcome," smiled Vincent.

"And then she'd find out I'm her great-granddaughter! What a saga! Definitely not an option."

"You speak about this as if it were a joke," said Vincent. "I think you should consider it."

"We should find a hotel," said Charlotte, dismissing Vincent's last sentence. "Tomorrow you can open up your book of life and see where the story takes you."

"Okay..." He liked the idea of being the protagonist of the story, a story that still remained to be written, or at least re-written.

The Ritz Carlton Hotel was out of the question this time, unlike all the previous visits. There were too many bizarre conflicts attached to it. They decided to stay at the Miami Marriott Hotel, only a fifteen-minute drive from Vizcaya. Charlotte was taking care of everything, and did not allow Vincent to thank her for any of the generosities she had shown. A short-lived awkward moment came when the girl at the reception was told that two beds were required; queen preferably. The choice of sleeping in the same room saved Charlotte about four hundred dollars, which she immediately said would come handy later at the hotel bar.

Later that evening, having celebrated life in all its aspects at the bar, Charlotte laid on her bed, and Vincent on his. Both were dressed. Both felt the intensity of the moment. Staying in the same hotel room, even if in separate beds, especially after an evening of drinking, can lead to some unwise decisions.

Vincent spoke first. "I wanted to thank you for everything you've done for me."

"None of that," replied Charlotte.

"Yes, but you must accept my gratitude. I am indebted to you," said Vincent, sitting up in bed. He rested his gaze on her profile, as she remained there, immobile. "So, what's the little girl's name? Your grandmother," he asked, quite unexpectedly.

Charlotte cast an erratic stare at the man before her. Was he really her great-grandfather? Had she been so far removed from the ordinary, that the question, though irrational, was justified? She kept staring at Vincent.

"Well?"

"Margaret. Her name is… was Margaret," said Charlotte.

"Margaret. Mmm… pretty name. Don't you think?"

"Yes… I guess so…" Charlotte answered. She watched Vincent lying back down on the bed, an expression of joy on his face. In these last couple of minutes, a hundred years slipped through the hourglass, and Charlotte's heart was changed. She understood the importance of aligning herself with the things that are meant to be, and not for the things she wished for.

"Vincent."

"Yes?"

"Do something for me," she finally said.

"Anything."

"Make my accident go away." Charlotte looked at him with a light in her eyes, as if he had the authority to change destiny.

"You know I can't do that."

"You can. Why can't you go to the future and save me?" she asked.

"It's not like that. I don't have a... a time machine, or some magic way to do that."

"I can't be in a wheelchair," she murmured in the silence of the room. "I just can't."

"I don't even know if the future can be changed, like that, at a drop of a hat." Vincent got up and started pacing the room. "I should've never told you," he said. "It's so unfair to you."

"Well, it's too late. You did tell me."

"That's why you should come with me. Nothing can happen there. You'll be safe in 1917."

"Are you crazy?"

Vincent sighed. "Yes..."

"You're a sweet man and I don't mean to be hard on you. You know how I feel about you..." Charlotte stated, revealing her sentiments again. However, she wanted to say more. "But if we are related, then you must know that it is impossible for me to be there with you. For more than one reason."

"Of course, you're right."

"I'm going to sleep now," said Charlotte. "I'm tired. Tomorrow we will access the inaccessible. Good night, great-granddad," she smiled. "You really should tuck me in."

Vincent approached Charlotte's bed. He bent down and kissed her on the forehead. She looked at him, her bright eyes locked onto his, in this first true contact with the supernatural. "About your accident... I'll do my very best," he whispered. "Sleep well."

"Yes. You, too," she answered, troubled by a peculiar emotion that she could not define, as he walked away from her.

Vincent stood by the window, looking at Miami skyline. He tried to visualize the fishing village Miami once was. "You should see how perfect this place was. Uncomplicated, calm..." he reflected out loud. He looked over his shoulder. Charlotte was asleep. He thought about Marion Davies, the time they both stood on the east terrace. To say that everything had changed, was very much an understatement. The world as it was, may as well be on another planet. Perhaps all of it was a fabrication of the most horrific kind. Perhaps. It felt so surreal at times. The life he was given as Vincent Jones, would forever be an enigma. There are things that cannot be rationally explained, things that belong to another dimension, far beyond human understanding. It is best to leave such matters alone. Vincent was allowed to glimpse into the afterlife with another chance at happiness, for no apparent purpose. Why? Why is the willingness to stand on the edge of a precipice taken as evidence to show the presence of love?

THIRTY THREE

Life had reached its full cycle. Something has to die in order to be reborn, like the waves that continuously wither on the sand only to return more powerful. Vincent laid on his bed and took another look at Charlotte. She slept peacefully. This was the last time he would lay eyes on her. All afternoon he had felt a presence, something compelling, exciting. Vincent knew that the entrance into the other realm was open, and this was his appointed day. "I'm ready," he uttered and closed his eyes for the last time as Vincent Jones.

A long mountain range suddenly appeared in the far distance, running from east to west. It began to move and the summits curled over, crashing onto themselves. A profound sense of horror devastated Vincent, who realized that it was an immense tidal wave, hundreds of feet high, and that it was coming his way. The gigantic surge moved at a slow pace, like a tremendous and unstoppable creature consuming everything in its path. Instantly, Vincent was transported to the edge of a vast and bottomless hole. He saw water and flames churning and lapping below, like in a furnace. He looked up. The tidal wave disintegrated into oblivion, though the water rose all around him. Vincent lost his footing and he fell into the dark water and it pulled him downward. The sunlight above became dimmer and dimmer, as Vincent sank deeper, unable to make it back to the surface.

"Vincent! Vincent!" cried Charlotte, who witnessed the panic on Vincent's face. "Wake up!" She shook him by the shoulders and she felt the icy touch of something pushing her away from the bed. She just stood there, petrified and unable to come to his help. Charlotte watched Vincent's inert body slowly dematerialize, like some sorcerous ritual ceremony was happening. She moved further back into the room, her back to the wall, terrorized. Everything that was said in those last days, possessed that air of fantasy, the inventions manufactured by susceptible minds. This, she could scarcely assimilate. Charlotte stood silent, staring at Vincent's empty bed as the sunrise brought in a new day. She remained that way for a long time, fearful of the reality and fearful of what she could not understand.

A letter, written on the hotel notepad, rested against the lamp on the bedside table; the silver key next to it. Charlotte noticed it. She wiped the tears from her face and picked up the note.

Dear Charlotte,

I'm sorry but I have to leave. I'm not sure how or when exactly, though I know it will be tonight. I just know it. I don't think I will return to 1917 in the same manner as I did before. You may witness some strange happenings, yet do not fear, no one is going to hurt you. Whatever is coming here... is coming for me.

I realize how difficult it has been for you to separate fiction from reality, though believe me when I tell you that nothing has ever felt so real to me. I am Clarence Henry Jones, and perhaps your great-grandfather, as ridiculous as that may sound. Now, I need to return to her, to your great-grandmother; Julia.

I leave this little key; my only possession and the only object that I valued in this world. It has magical powers!

My dear Charlotte, I will do my utmost to rid you of your misfortune. I promise.

Until we meet again, and this time you will know me.

Vincent/Clarence

Ps: I won't tell Sargent you destroyed his masterpiece, and who knows, perhaps I can change that, too!

Charlotte folded the small note, a vague smile on her face and stared at the key. She looked at Vincent's bed, the space he occupied. She slowly sat down on her bed, reflective about her life. Much was given, and much was taken away. Like a demanding creditor, Charlotte's life would return more burdensome, for it is nothing else than a curse to have glimpsed into the future. She knew that. Though given the choice, Charlotte was unsure of herself and which road she would take; the one marked certainty or the one marked fortuity? How to know? She was only conscious of one thing; both roads were travelled on much too fast.

Vincent's absence was already being felt. She missed the man, his intellect, his companionship. Charlotte's own failed opportunities disturbed her now more than ever. A light shone onto the width and length of her existence, and she did not like what she saw. And now, the ever-present torment of what lay waiting in the dark corners of the preordained, haunted her.

"Was everything satisfactory?" asked the man at the hotel reception.

"Yes, thank you. Everything was perfect," answered Charlotte as she checked out, hiding her grief behind sunglasses.

"We hope to see you again."

Charlotte paid the bill and her car was brought to the front of the hotel. Unsure where to go, she began to drive in the direction of Vizcaya. The need to feel closer to something she could not even describe, increased with the miles as Vizcaya drew nearer.

She drove through the main gate and continued behind another car to the parking lot. Several other visitors headed towards the small kiosk where tickets can be purchased. Charlotte followed. She walked onto the driveway that leads to the house and stopped. She had not been to Vizcaya in years, perhaps twenty years. The magnificence of the architecture took Charlotte's breath away. So, that's where you are, she thought. I don't blame you.

The estate was not very crowded and Charlotte found herself alone in the courtyard. She looked up, remembering Vincent's description of the roof and looked up towards the galleries. She noticed the small and delightful columns that ran the full perimeter of the space. Why did she wander around Vizcaya, envisioning the past, searching for the impossible? Shadows from another life, dwelled in each of the rooms. No matter how hard she wished it to be, Charlotte did not belong here.

There was one more room she had to see; the bedroom named Espagnolette, with the secret passage.

Charlotte stood in the bedroom. Vincent had told her where the hidden door was located and where to look for the thin groove of the opening. She just needed to see it, before leaving. A couple of people walked in, unaware of Charlotte's tribulations. She played with the silver key in the depth of her purse for a few seconds, and left.

Some people ran towards the house and others towards their cars, as thunder reverberated in the distance. After all it was July, the rainy season and nothing could change that, not the absence of a loved one, nor the passage of time.

THIRTY FOUR

Clarence opened his eyes and dared not move. He cast a vacant stare at the embroidered linen ceiling canopy and felt the softness of a bed beneath him. There was a cool breeze coming from the open window and a scent of jasmine about the room. His body felt like it had been tossed around in a giant spinner, and he made every effort to recall what had happened to him. Gradually, his memory began to unlock the likeness of what it captured, like sketches drawn in another room, in another time. He felt his body throughout, looking for any injuries and found none. Vincent Jones died and Clarence Henry Jones rose from the bed and approached the open window. A wonderful emotion penetrated his spirit, his entire being, palpable as he beheld the gardens of Vizcaya.

"I'm here," Clarence murmured as a mockingbird observed him from the top of a nearby marble goddess. "Hi," he said to the small creature. "Good morning." The bird wiped his beak against the stone and kept a wary eye on Clarence.

The grounds of Vizcaya began to fade out, slowly taking on other forms. Clarence felt the floor pulling him in, as to hold him there. He wanted to shut his eyes, anxious about more fearsome activities and was unable. The sky was in full rotation and its speed seemed to increase as days became nights, and nights, days. Then everything stopped. Darkness. The soundless rhythms of a dream. Like the interlocking pieces from a puzzle, an image emerged. A faceless young boy sat beneath a Christmas tree. He opened the only present under the tree; a box, a mahogany box, filled with the oddest items for a four-year-old child. The boy looked up at his parents and witnessed his father's sudden disappearance, while his mother aged to an elderly woman within seconds. The boy ran out of the room and down a long hallway as he changed into a man. The corridor seemed to have no beginning and no end, yet the man kept running, holding the mahogany box in his hand. Another man stood in his path, obstructing the way, but he passed right through him. This man was wearing a black dress and his eyes, full of tears, were outlined with dark paint. Still, the man holding his precious box kept running, until he finally came to the end of the passageway. He pressed his forehead against the wall, exhausted from the journey. Lights rushed by, as from a high-speed train. The wall cracked, collapsed onto itself and in an instant the man was teleported in the moving train opposite a young woman. Her face hid in the shadows and her body, suspended in mid-air, rocked in cadence with the train. She held her stomach with both hands, specifying where a child would grow, though she displayed no trace of a pregnancy. Another woman riding a horse bareback next to the train track, appeared; her long hair blowing freely in the wind. The horse was galloping, yet only a great void could be seen below him.

Clarence desperately tried to free himself from the vision he was forced to endure before he recognized the man with the mahogany box. Vincent Jones stared him in the face. Both he and Clarence stood in a vast empty edifice. Tall columns, a thousand feet high, lined two sides of the structure and several vaulted ceilings reached far into the sky. A cold wind launched from the north, came through the broken stained-glass windows. The violent gusts blew the last remaining leaves trapped in the dark corners of the empty space as a third figure appeared from the depth of the room; a woman. Vincent no longer was present. Clarence watched the figure come forth. Her face was indistinct and the deep shadows from the columns intermittently plunged her into obscurity. Though he strained to take a step in her direction, he seemed to be unable to move. She had to come to him. The last column was the last obstacle and the likeness of Julia emerged out of the darkness, into the light. Clarence extended his hand in an attempt to touch her, and saw her face lit up by an intense brightness coming from within her.

The soundless visions ceased as quickly as they began and Clarence found himself standing in the same bedroom in front of the window at Vizcaya again. The blue sky and the sway of palms brought a certain assuredness, a sense of reality. The mockingbird held his gaze on Clarence before flying away. Not a minute, not even a second of time had elapsed. A gardener crossed the main alleyway, on his way to the other side of the garden. Another joined him. Clarence felt like the nightmares, the years of assuming someone else's life, were over. The tormented existence built on delusions, ended. Clarence Henry Jones lived again, free to do and love whomever he wished. His rebirth was no more mysterious than the resurgence of a flower from the desolation of winter, or the aspiration to love and be loved. The warm air from the outside made Clarence feel alive and he took in a deep breath of sea air.

The absolute quietness in the house was noticeable all of a sudden. Clarence tiptoed to the bedroom door and was about to open it, when he became aware of his nakedness. Well, that would explain why that mockingbird was staring at me, thought Clarence. The only garment in the empty wardrobe was an embroidered silk dressing gown, in shades of dusty rose, with long kimono style sleeves. It smelled like it had been soaked in some exotic fragrance. Clarence realized that he was in a different bedroom than his previous visit. What else had changed? He put on the gown and stepped out of the room, looking like the lover, who caught off guard by a jealous husband, has to make a quick getaway. He leaned over the balustrade to peek into the courtyard. A group of about thirty people were looking up in his direction, as if they had been waiting for him, expecting him. They started to sing happy birthday to Clarence, with a look of bemusement and stupefaction which slowly caused everyone to gradually stop singing. James Deering raised his champagne glass, shaking his head, though not without a smile. Obviously, a birthday party was given in honor of Clarence and this was not the grand entrance everyone expected. Clarence had no choice but to make his way downstairs, utterly confused about when in time he had returned.

"Delightfully eccentric," said one of the women, an empty cigarette holder to her brightly painted lips, as Clarence joined the gathering. "I love your gown."

"It's not—"

"Mr. Jones, you do surprise me!" exclaimed Deering, who had witnessed far worse an offence in his time. "Well, happy birthday," he smiled.

"Thank you, Mr. Deering, but really you shouldn't have," uttered Clarence, still confused. He looked for a familiar face among the noisy crowd, drinking, talking and laughing. He looked for Marion Davies and he desperately searched for Julia. "I hope... I do hope I didn't make everyone wait for too long," said Clarence, fishing for some kind of chronology, while making sure the belt was tied properly around his waist.

"No. Not too long," answered Deering, perplexed.

The answer did not help. "I don't see Miss Davies," Clarence declared.

"Miss Davies?" asked Deering. I don't believe I know a Miss Davies."

"Right. Sorry, my mistake."

Deering turned his attention to another guest.

A young man approached Clarence. "Happy birthday, Mr. Jones," said the guest. His outfit was flawless, as was the red silk Ascot neck tie, done to perfection.

Clarence was distracted by the fact that he had no idea about the month or the year he found himself in. "Thank you," he finally answered the young man, absorbed by his quest to find a friendly face.

"Are you in the thirties club now?" inquired the young man. His courteous way of asking someone's age, confounded Clarence who was utterly unprepared to answer such a question. "I gather you're from Pittsburgh?" he continued, seeing the impassive glare on Clarence's face. "I belong to a small group of friends—"

"I'm sorry," interrupted Clarence, "I do not know how old I am, nor do I wish to know… and this… this attire is an accident. I don't… I'm sorry."

"My apologies," replied the man, who excused himself.

A little ashamed of himself for his lack of patience, Clarence grabbed a glass of champagne. It was becoming painfully evident to him that this was an alternate Vizcaya. He mingled with the guests around the courtyard, suffocated by the thought of yet more hostilities. What other sacrifice would be asked of him? What would he have to relinquish? Clarence wondered if he would ever be at this juncture, where good and bad are both clearly marked. This path leads to Julia, this one does not. Why does it have to be so hard?

The party grew in noise and crowd, it seemed. No one appeared shocked or curious about Clarence's outfit. No one seemed to care. It is as if he walked among ghosts again.

Much too embarrassed to ask what day or year this was, Clarence approached one of the butlers. "Do you know where I can find a calendar?" Clarence asked.

"There's one in the kitchen, sir," answered the man. "Would you like me to get it for you?"

"No, thank you, I'll be fine." Clarence made his way to the kitchen. Maids and cooks stared at him, like the lunatic guest from the big city. The younger maids giggled, though soon everyone returned to the task of preparing food. A 1915 calendar with a Boston harbor photograph, laid on the wooden countertop. The October page was marked with a note '*Birthday party - Mr. Jones*', on the 22nd. Clarence had his answer. He stared at the calendar page and with a heavy heart walked to the window that overlooks the east terrace. His gaze fell on the incomplete barge and the scaffoldings on its side.

Clarence grieved. A year and a half would have to pass to get to April 1917. He stared at the men hard at work on the stone mermaids.

THIRTY FIVE

Marion Davies was like the memory of a yearning too vulnerable to sustain. She walked among the flowers and her voice still echoed in the walls of Vizcaya, yet her silence revoked that truth. Clarence remembered her words about the ship of stone being under construction when she visited. He also recalled the fact that Julia was a guest at the same time. However, that reality could no longer be trusted. The continuity of time, as previously experienced, had been drastically altered.

The long train journey back to Pittsburgh would give him plenty of time to think. The last palm trees dotted the Florida landscape before entering Georgia, and Clarence felt the ache of separation from his first-class car. Pittsburgh had nothing to offer his heart.

An elderly couple kept staring at him from across the aisle. Clarence gave them a gentle smile, and returned to watching the drastically different scenery from his window. The hills were a grim reminder that Vizcaya was just a dot, somewhere to the south.

A cold wind rushed through Pennsylvania Station when Clarence arrived in Pittsburgh. Clarence Henry Jones, the entrepreneur, was eager to go back to work. He felt that the busier he would make himself, the faster time would pass. The cold November day energized him and he was happy. All that remained was the boating accident dilemma. That day was never made clear to him. As Vincent, he returned to Vizcaya in April 1917, which gave him about eighteen months. A year and a half, which during that time, he would have to anticipate death. Cheat death.

The steel mill, which Clarence began with another partner, had become very lucrative. Over two hundred employees worked around the clock, three hundred and sixty-five days a year. Contracts from all over the country and some from abroad were being honored, quickly. A chauffeur took Clarence directly to his offices on Congress Street.

Much faster than he wished, Clarence's life returned to normal. Work kept him busy at an incredible pace. His perspective from two different spirits living in the same body, gave him perhaps the outlook of a philosopher. His kindness and calm demeanor were also noted by his coworkers.

Two weeks before Christmas, Clarence received an invitation. The Carnegies were entertaining, and such an opportunity to mingle among Pittsburgh's elites was not to be missed.

Clarence paced the bedroom of his apartment, as if staying mobile would allow him to think more clearly. He looked out of the window several times, like he was expecting a visitor. Some snow had already settled on the ground. Julia were the only three syllables on his lips and he repeated them out loud, trusting in the impacts of the spoken word. A passing thought for Vincent agitated him. He sensed that other being, hidden within him for eternity. That person never meant to exist and like a prisoner serving a life sentence, Vincent Jones would never see the light of day again.

When Clarence went to bed that night, memories came flowing in. He got out of bed, quickly, exhilarated at the prospect of the Christmas party; Julia was there, then, and she would be again. She had to be.

THRITY SIX

Quite a few people were arriving at the Carnegies. Clarence observed the silhouettes in the crowded house from the street and the many Christmas lights and decorations throughout.

He made his way into the main room, dressed in an immaculate formal tailcoat. The party was in full swing and happy noises gave Clarence some joy and revived his spirit with the hope that Julia would be in attendance.

Mrs. Carnegie spotted Clarence from across the room. "Are you Mr. Jones?" she asked.

"I am, Mrs. Carnegie. Thank you so much for inviting me."

"Please call me Louise. I've been keeping an eye on your career, Andrew and I, both have. You've made something of yourself, young man."

"I'm honored, thank you."

"Andrew says you remind him of himself. We started with nothing, you know."

"I know. Mr. Carnegie was a great inspiration to me. Please give him my best wishes. Is he here tonight?"

"No, he's not feeling well. The invitation was his idea," said Louise.

Clarence reached for Louise's hand. "Thank you, Louise. From the bottom of my heart."

Louise returned to her many guests. Clarence walked around the room, admiring the space. He did not recognize anyone, and perhaps even worse, no one recognized him. He emptied his glass of champagne. The room was filled with strangers and a slight awkwardness tried to sneak into his head. However, one person could change that. One person. He surveyed the crowd, delaying the uncompromising fate. He had made a mistake in coming here. The obvious threatened Clarence with more hardship. She was not coming.

"This is Lady Julia," said Louise, who appeared out of nowhere.

Barely able to breathe, Clarence approached. She was here. The loud call from Clarence's heart was but mere desire, compared with the force pushing upward from somewhere in the depth of him. Photographs, portraits of any kind, cannot claim a shred of that mind-altering fervor when actual life is manifested. Julia's very essence enveloped him, to hold him in its wonderful grasp. Images of Julia extending her hand in front of the barge at Vizcaya, obsessed him.

"Julia…" Clarence's words seemed to forsake him and he stopped in mid-sentence. He stared at her, his spirit questioning hers, but to no avail.

The expression on Julia's face denoted perplexity.

"Lady Julia. How do you do," Clarence said finally, saluting the woman who he still hoped would forever change the course of his life.

"Mr. Jones is a young entrepreneur, I dare say," continued Louise.

"I'm very happy to meet you," replied Julia.

Clarence was crushed. What kind of scheme did the universe concoct, he speculated. What had been removed from what was initially granted? "What brings you to Pittsburgh?" Clarence asked, as calmly as he could.

Louise excused herself to attend to other guests that were arriving.

"I have family in Boston. I'm just passing through," said Julia, removing her gloves.

"I hope you won't be in too much of a hurry," Clarence smiled. "Would you like a drink?" he asked, anxious to keep her close to him.

"No, thank you, I can't stay long."

Clarence, conquered again by the dazzling young Julia, dove into the blue of her eyes, losing himself to the allure of her.

"So, what is it that you do, exactly, Mr. Jones?" she asked.

"Is it possible that we've met before?" Clarence asked, attempting to shake up a revised and intrusive destiny.

"I don't believe so. I was in California for a while and this is my first visit to the east coast."

"I'm in the steel industry," said Clarence. "Nothing very creative," he added.

"Well, that's not strictly true," she said, "one has to be creative in other ways, perhaps, yet creative all the same."

"I like that," Clarence declared. "I like that very much."

"I was told Mr. Deering would be here this evening," Julia asserted. "Do you happen to know him?" she asked, her eyes wandering about the room.

Clarence feared that the conversation had reached its limit. "I do. I believe he is coming."

"I would love to see his new house in Florida. Vizcaya, I think it's called."

"Yes, Vizcaya. It's magnificent." Julia's attention was back on track. "I'm sure you'll get an invitation," Clarence said, knowing full well fate was on his side. James Deering had no choice but to invite Julia.

"Oh, you've been there?" she inquired.

"I have. Mr. Deering has been kind enough to ask me to stay there, on two occasions. It's not quite finished yet, but I believe it will be spectacular when it is."

"I'm told it's the most perfect house," said Julia.

"It is more than that." Clarence had to do something drastic, or she would walk away. "Lady Julia, I…"

"Yes?"

"I… I think I can get you an invitation to Vizcaya," he quickly said, before making a fool of himself in front of all of Pittsburgh's high society.

"I would love that."

What a relief, thought Vincent.

"Thank you," uttered Julia, looking into Clarence's eyes, which caused his entire being to crumble inside, though he kept his composure. "I leave tomorrow for England," she explained, "and I'm not sure when I'll be back. Probably not for a year." Her demeanor changed to a more melancholic one. Her words, like ribbons of the most precious silk, drifted, uttered with sadness. Clarence took them as a small victory for the battles ahead.

"Perhaps you can give me an address… I could write to you, you know… about Vizcaya." Clarence's voice cracked at the request. Julia noticed and smiled.

He had to let her go. He had to say goodbye. Nothing of what he had imagined would happen, took place. Clarence sat in his office the next day, meditating about his life. She didn't know me, he told himself. How is that possible? "How am I to wait?" he said out loud. April 1917 was more than a year away. And then, what? She may not even be able to come, he continued in his deliberations. Clarence thought about writing a letter. He was anxious to correspond with her. Now? No. She was probably boarding her ship, he thought. "I think it's a bit premature," he murmured, looking out of his office window. "Lady Julia. Julia," he repeated, blowing steam on the window glass.

"Alright. I have to wake up now," he muttered to himself. "Sixteen months! What's that? Nothing," he continued.

Clarence's secretary knocked on his door. Mr. Deering was calling.

THRITY SEVEN

It has been said not to wish life away. Many things have been said about the dreaded uncertainty of the future, yet the thought of tomorrow is enticing. Why? Things unknown seem to awaken the desires scattered in our dreams. It is true that wisdom is not given until it is perhaps too late. Those later years, all knowing, all willing, arrive much too fast and only remorse lingers, like unmovable boulders. Remorse of once wanting to rush time, even though the knowledge of such an impossibility ought to appease. But, no, one marches on, ahead of time it seems, though it is quite the opposite; time is always winning that race.

Clarence watched his steel mills become number ones in the country, thanks to the hard work of many. His fortune doubled in the year that followed Julia's departure. He slept no more than five hours a night, if he was able to fall asleep at all. The first few months proved to be very difficult. Clarence could not comprehend the machinations he was subjected to. What purpose did the life he led as Vincent served? Was it all to do with the boating accident, his untimely death? He lived as Clarence Henry Jones now and Julia was meant to recognize him at the Christmas party. She did not. He wrote countless letters to her, one a week, though he only posted three. His declarations of love seemed childish and frivolous at times. Julia replied to one letter, saying that she had met Mr. Deering in London and was looking forward to come to Vizcaya. She did not give a date for her visit, and Clarence hoped that April 1917 was the magic month. She did however ask Clarence to drop the title when addressing her. *Just Julia*, she wrote, *no Lady, please.* Clarence held on to those words like the sweetest poem ever put to paper. He felt foolish reading her rather short letter, time and time again, and he sensed a trace of prudence on her part. The length of the letter meant much to Clarence, primarily that Julia's heart was not willing to reveal anything quite yet. With that make-believe confidence, Clarence was able to live a fairly normal life, awaiting her arrival.

Christmas of 1916 resembled the previous one, with several parties to attend, snow that fell right on schedule and the endless nights and the loneliness of an empty home. Everything was the same as Clarence walked home from a business dinner, except Julia was thousands of miles away. The new year could not arrive fast enough for him. Four months to go. Four months. James Deering had extended his invitations to come to Vizcaya, and Clarence returned there twice in the last ten months. The house was almost finished. The barge was completed, finally. Deering had met Marion Davies during the summer and Julia was coming. Everything was on time and in line for a triumphant visit in the spring.

A more clement weather returned to the north east, and Pittsburgh dried its streets under a glorious sun. Clarence packed his leather suitcase and sat on his bed. The Julia of the future, when she pursued Vincent, was the one Clarence sought now. The same one it seemed who stood in front of the barge, reaching out for him, before it all vanished. The Julia with a daughter. The Julia in love. Am I ill-fated, cursed? Clarence wondered. To presume otherwise was becoming more and more vague, and subject to much disillusion. What then? Devise a plan to rescue her from herself? A plan? "What am I doing?" he asked himself, avoiding the mirror above the chest of drawers. He closed the suitcase and accidently caught his reflection. He did not really know the man in the mirror. There were only a few memories of his own life. Dr. Vincent Jones, it seemed took the larger part of his remembrances, leaving little to discover. Clarence saw what the future had in store, the good and the bad. The expansion of great cities and the amazing course of technological advances. He remembered everyone and everything; Sarah, Charlotte, the world's conflicts and his work in the arts. As Clarence, he felt like a young child whose life has been roughly outlined with all good intentions, with a few locations marked 'danger'. Clarence approached the mirror. He stood still, looking at himself, expecting to suddenly get a revelation. Nothing. "Who the hell am I?" he whispered, making sure that his own lips moved.

The tiresome long train journey back to Miami empowered the dreamer to wander. Though Vizcaya was the reward at the end of the line, some creativity of the mind brought hope to Clarence, however impractical the notions may be. His mind was on Julia. He thought of little else.

As the train was about to leave the station, a heavy-set gentleman walked in Clarence's direction. He sat across the aisle from Clarence.

Both men looked out of the window. A rain shower that lasted for five minutes seemed to cool off the atmosphere for a bit.

Several hours had gone by. The monotony of the journey, interrupted by many stops, demanded a certain endurance, with Vizcaya as its prize.

Clarence's travel companion across the aisle dozed off and was awake now. The intriguingly familiar face confounded him. A well-used artist's wooden box, sticking out of one of the man's small luggage, caught Clarence's attention.

"I'm sorry, I don't mean to bother you, but are you an artist?" Clarence inquired.

"I am."

"That's wonderful. I would love to be able to paint beautiful things."

"Are you, yourself an artist?" inquired the man.

"Unfortunately, I am not."

"Some of the best subjects are not necessarily beautiful," the man replied. "One has to be... selective, if you will."

"I'm Mr. Jones. Clarence Jones," said Clarence extending his hand.

"John Sargent. Delighted to meet you."

Clarence's amazement was difficult to hide. Sargent. The watercolor. Sotheby's. A rush of memories flooded Clarence's head, who could not believe the timing. Of course, the self-portraits! No wonder his face spoke to me, thought Clarence.

Sargent saw the expression of Clarence's face at the mention of his name. "Perhaps you've heard of me?"

"I have. I have." Not a mention of the watercolors could be made, since none had been painted yet. Clarence was equally conscious that

Sargent would end up staying about two months at Vizcaya, as his mind was getting clearer and clearer. Many things that laid buried in his subconscious, were coming to light. Among many events, the very personal discussion with the great artist when they met in that other dimension. "Are you on your way to do a portrait?" Clarence asked, mindful it was not the case.

"I'm going to stay with a friend of mine, Mr. Deering," said Sargent.

Clarence was familiar with that 'other' Deering, James's older brother, Charles. However, any indiscretions could lead to disaster and he played along. "In that case we are both heading to Vizcaya."

"No, I'm going to stay with Mr. Charles Deering. His estate is not far from Vizcaya. So, you are a guest of Mr. James Deering. Well, I'm certain I will pay him a visit. I hear he built a splendid house."

"I think you will find Vizcaya… irresistible," added Clarence, emboldened by sheer historical facts.

"I look forward to seeing it. Mr. Deering's chauffeur will be picking me up," said Sargent. We can easily drop you off at Vizcaya, if you like."

After many more stops, the first palm trees began to appear. One could feel the humidity in the cars now as the thickness in the air announced the tropical climate of Vizcaya. Miami was a few hours away.

"Mr. Sargent," voiced Clarence. "May I ask you a question?"

"You may."

"It's about a commission. A portrait."

Sargent hesitated. Portraiture was something he had almost relinquished in the last few years. "I'm not really doing many portraits now, I've taken very few commissions recently."

"Would you consider making an exception?"

"Who's the subject?"

"A lovely young girl. I believe you will be struck by her beauty."

"Is that so?"

"Indeed. Will you consider it?" Though Clarence barely recalled the actual painting, he knew that Sargent would accept the commission. Clarence was also aware that the portrait was destined for destruction by fire.

After a slight hesitation, Sargent agreed. "I will. When can I meet this charming woman?" he asked.

"She's coming to Vizcaya. Soon. Her name is Julia. Lady Julia."

"Then, I shall meet this Lady Julia and I will give you my answer."

"Thank you. I look forward to your visit."

Sargent became curious about the potential subject of the commission. Lady Julia. He thought it was a good title. Yet, he became more interested in the human side of the story, a story that Clarence had barely shared. The blood of an artist is galvanized by deep emotions, outbursts of joy and deep pain that governs all decisions.

"Lady Julia, you say. You seemed to be transported to another celestial sphere when you speak of her," said Sargent.

"I have to plead guilty on that score. You noticed."

"It was hard not to," smiled Sargent. "You obviously have feelings for this young woman."

"I do."

"Then, I'm sure we can come to an agreement."

"You don't know what this means to me. Thank you so much, Mr. Sargent."

THIRTY EIGHT

Julia sat at her desk. She studied the photographs of her family on top of it. Her eyes lingered on those happy gatherings at the beach, and on the more intimate times she shared with her parents. Those paper figures displayed the journey of her life. She looked at the only image she possessed of her fiancé, Captain Andrew Hastings. Julia appeared so happy next to him. She grieved his loss for a long time, and was inconsolable when her daughter was born, deprived of one parent. She held a small silver frame with the image of her deceased younger sister, lost to pneumonia at age twelve. She remembered feeling helpless as death came swiftly for the young girl. Julia hated the world for a while. She swore never to squander time, and she prayed that time would not swallow her up. The two untimely deaths prompted her to go to America with her young daughter, Margaret. Her time in California proved to be an unhappy stay and after a few months, Julia headed home via Boston, which is where an aunt lived. The invitation to the Carnegies' Christmas party was an unscheduled event. At times, she wished she had not gone.

Julia had given Clarence just enough thoughts as to not forget him, and yet, she wished they had never met. Her life was in England. His life was in Pittsburgh. I liked his eyes, she said to herself, and glanced at the large expanse of lawn through the open window. The scent of roses lingered in and out of the room as the wind kept changing direction. Rain was definitely in the forecast. Clarence's letters were placed on top of a book, and Julia tried not to look at them, though she made no effort to hide them.

A fine drizzle fell. Julia grabbed a piece of paper with her name and the name of her estate embossed on it; Lady Julia, Trentham Hall. She began to write.

February 23, 1917

Dear Mr. Jones,

As I sit in front of my window and admire the gardens, I cannot help but imagine what that wonderful house, Vizcaya, must be like. You know us, British people, we are spoiled with such a rich history, though I believe this estate, buried in the depths of the Florida swamp, is quite a miracle of architecture.

Julia stopped writing. How did she truly feel about this man? She had seen things in her dreams that bothered her. She did not know him when they met at the Carnegies' Christmas party, yet her dreams conflicted with her memory. Clarence Henry Jones, and dreams of a passionate kind, brought her much struggle and had her wonder at night before going to sleep.

The nanny came in at that moment to say that Margaret was asleep, down for her afternoon nap.

After thanking the young girl, Julia returned to her contemplations. The drizzle had stopped and a timid ray of sun was attempting to pierce through the cloud cover. *What is it that I like about this man?* Julia asked herself.

She picked up her pen again...

I trust this letter will find you well, and... "and what?" she said out loud. Julia put the pen down and closed the window. She decided to go back to her letter when she figured out what to say, and more importantly, how she felt.

The next morning, Julia went for a long horse ride around the estate. The Lake District is known for its great beauty, and Julia enjoyed the cool morning and the delight of England's last weeks of winter. She let her horse rest for a while. The views around her, worthy to be captured on canvas, inspired her. She dismounted her horse and walked the little path that led to one of the smaller lakes. The calm was healing. A gentle breeze disturbed the water ever so slightly, breaking up the reflection of a huge oak tree on the other side of a stone bridge. Julia thought of Clarence at that very moment.

Cousins and other family members, including Julia's mother, were arriving for lunch and Julia wanted to finish her letter to Clarence. In fact, she thought of nothing else since coming back from her ride.

She sat at her desk again and began to write...

I trust this letter finds you well, and that you have forgiven me for not writing to you more often. I was engaged to a very honorable man for a while, I say for a while because my fiancé was killed in France, in the field somewhere in Verdun. Who knows when this dreadful war will end? Sometimes I fear it will go on forever. It seems every male figure in my life has been taken away from me. My own dear father passed away just about two years ago. I am surrounded by women!

I have a little girl, she is the joy of my life. Yes, I am a mother, though not many people know that. Her name is Margaret. She was born after her father died.

I met Mr. Deering during his stay in London, and he extended an invitation to visit Vizcaya. I plan to be in the United States in the spring, God willing. I believe the month of April would be the more suitable time to be in Florida. I would like to think that you will be there, also.

Most sincerely,
Julia
PS: you may write to me if you like

THIRTY NINE

Julia's letter was forwarded from Pittsburgh to Vizcaya, as instructed by Clarence, should any correspondence from England arrive. He sat in the tea house after the morning mail was delivered, anxious to be alone. The letter was written five weeks before it made its way into Clarence's hands. He clung to every word, reading each sentence, each phrase, following with his finger as he if was learning to read. The length of Julia's second letter pleased him enormously. The details about her life made him sad, yet the comments about the male figures gave him so much hope, that he let out a shout of joy. A few words put to paper can alter the course of mankind, though more significantly it can imply the greatest gift given to humanity, and that is, the complete devotion to another. To Clarence, this piece of paper represented the love letter he had been waiting for. Julia was thinking about him. He dared to hope that like him, she experienced the void and yes, a few sleepless nights. He wanted to run to the house and talk about his good fortune to anyone who would hear him; Lady Julia was in love. The miles separating them were just numbers, meaningless numbers and in a few weeks she would be here. Clarence cast a gaze on Biscayne Bay. The water, like a vast desert of glass, showed not even a trace of a breeze. The gigantic tower of a cumulus cloud mirrored in a perfect symmetry, caught Clarence's attention. The sheer might of nature amazed him once more. He felt like a tiny creature at the mercy of something way too powerful to contend with. Perhaps it was God. Perhaps. His mind fled the shores of Florida, holding the precious letter in his hand. This time, he felt the heavens granted his wish. Julia was coming in a matter of hours, of days. What difference would it make if all the clocks of the world stopped? None. She was coming to him.

FORTY

One lazy day followed the next at Vizcaya. Deering entertained his guests like they were royalty. Sargent, as planned, was staying indefinitely as Deering's special guest. His watercolor renditions of the estate impressed everyone, art lovers or not. Of course, Sargent was looking forward to meeting Lady Julia, and her scheduled arrival in about two weeks, beguiled him. Clarence, too, could scarcely keep calm. Deering noticed it.

The late afternoon light cast its gilded hues, and Clarence enjoyed nature's display of excellence from the east terrace.

Deering sat next to him, a brandy in his hand. "Everything alright?" asked Deering, without a trace of sarcasm.

"Very much so."

"Good. Good."

"I don't need to tell you what it means to be able to come here. I believe this is my favorite place in the world."

"I'm delighted you feel this way," replied Deering.

"A truly magnificent estate," said Clarence, looking out to the bay. "And this barge… what a sight, what a marvel of architecture."

"You seemed a little… anxious," said Deering.

"Anxious?"

"Yes. As if you were expecting something to happen. It wouldn't be because a certain Lady Julia is making her way here, would it?" he suggested, while looking into the distance.

"What makes you say that?" inquired Clarence.

"My dear Mr. Jones, it's quite alright. She is a ravishing creature, and something is telling me she's very much looking forward to seeing you again."

Clarence's face came alive. "She told you this?" he exclaimed, without holding back any of the feelings he had kept suppressed for far too long.

"Well, let's say it was implied. I think she is very fond of you. She spoke well of you when we met in London," said Deering, sipping his Napoleon brandy.

The world could do no wrong now. Life took a sharp turn, and the path to complete bliss became free of thorns, of landslides. "Thank you for telling me this," uttered Clarence, who was at a loss for more exalted words.

"Mr. Jones, I drink to your happiness," said Deering, emptying his glass. "We all need to be happy, I suppose even those of us who don't deserve it."

Sargent approached at that moment, also with a glass of brandy.

"Ha, Mr. Sargent, will you join us?" Deering asked.

"I most certainly will."

"Have you done a watercolor of the view from the other side of the terrace?" asked Clarence, trying to define a timeline in his head. The watercolor in question was the one he purchased as Vincent Jones and the one he admired, which led to that wonderful conversation with the great artist.

"I have not, but I've been thinking of doing one," replied Sargent.

"It will be outstanding."

"Thank you Mr. Jones," said Sargent.

"What a delightful afternoon this is," uttered Deering; a sentiment echoed by his two guests.

Biscayne Bay shone under a more muted light as the sun cast long shadows onto the east terrace. Another day had gone by.

The sky was riddled with stars. Clarence opened his bedroom window and stared at the vagueness of the night. The garden became like a solemn domain of remembrance, as silhouettes of statues appeared like ghostly figures, passing through from one world to another. Thoughts from a different mind it seemed, assaulted him, like particles of fragile images that once were. Something afflicted Clarence, though he could not define it. A memory, or perhaps it was a dream, something seemed to haunt him. He was aware of certain facts, yet not all of them made sense, and some disclaimed others. Vincent Jones was imbedded in the inner core of his being, yet many details were linked to his life, and only his life. Visions of unknown faces staring at Clarence, questioning his purpose, alerted him. He tried to remember life, the one lost somewhere beyond the boundaries of this time. He kept staring into the night, fearing he may recall something that would eradicate all hope.

When Clarence eventually went to bed, the confines of the bedroom began to emerge. A pale light slowly put on the colors of the walls, of the tapestries. He watched the glow of the new day, accompanied by the first chirping of a bird. The hours spent awake did not resolve anything. His mind clashed with reality, with everything he knew to be true. A gust of wind rushed through the open window like an uninvited visitor, which brought Clarence out of his meditations. He got up and ran a bath.

Deering sat in the courtyard. He lowered his newspaper when Clarence came down the stairs. "Good morning. Did you sleep well?" he asked Clarence.

"Good morning. I did, thank you."

"I must apologize for my behavior last evening. You and Lady Julia have a right to privacy, so please accept my apologies."

"You're too kind. But honestly, it felt rather good to be able to talk about it."

Deering nodded. "Marion Davies will be arriving later today," he told Clarence. "You are acquainted with her, correct?"

"Yes, I… I did meet her once. Though she may not remember me," Clarence added, not convinced the young film star's life and his, merged at all.

"I am certain she has not forgotten you," said Deering.

"Yes…"

Deering returned to his paper and Clarence made his way to the breakfast room upstairs.

A brass band began to play on the Casino mound, south of the garden. Clarence looked at all the women, the men and the children, all thrilled to be here, settling in for a leisurely day spent at Vizcaya. People had already arrived in great numbers. He recalled that once or twice a year, Deering opened the estate to the general public. A dreadful sensation overcame Clarence. The future. Visions of Vizcaya, the museum, passed before him like a sinister cortege. Struck by a sudden overbearing grief, Clarence walked to the garden. He needed the happy noise from the visitors. He needed to clear his mind of anything to do with himself, with Julia. A flock of bluebirds cut through the sky above the bay and Clarence watched the 'V' formation fly in the direction of Miami.

"You wish you were one of them?" The voice came from behind Clarence.

Marion Davies stood there, looking delightful. Clarence turned around. "Good morning," he said with a smile.

"Hello Mr. Jones. Apparently we've met before, Mr. Deering tells me." Deering waved at them from the house. "I don't remember you. Though it's strange… I feel like I knew you, there, when you turned around. Can you explain that, Mr. Jones?" asked Marion.

"I cannot," said Clarence, who saw this as yet another bundle of misfortune.

"Well, let us not be concerned by such details," she uttered. "Maybe it will come to me."

The festivities of the day came like an amnesty in the valley of Clarence's tribulations. He welcomed Marion's presence, even if she did not remember him. For a short while, the length of a day, frivolities replaced the disquietude. Clarence's enthusiasm returned, like a wild and euphoric horse galloping free, released from its harness.

FORTY ONE

Lady Julia was killed in a boating accident. The news was telephoned from England. Deering put the receiver down, in shock. He remained in the small phone booth, that so many people had admired as a modern curiosity when Vizcaya first opened. He just sat there. A maid walked by and noticed him. She could tell that something dreadful had happened. He signaled to her to stay there and wait. Eventually Deering came out of the small space and told the maid to find Mr. Jones.

Deering walked to his beloved courtyard, perhaps to be somewhere in a position of strength. He waited. The inevitable afflicted him profoundly. Deering, a man of great leadership in business, used to face and deal with influential people, now felt utterly inadequate.

Sargent came in from the garden, having just completed another watercolor. He walked to Deering.

"I have been informed of the worst news," Deering mumbled.

"What is it?" asked Sargent, who could tell his host was distraught.

"Lady Julia—"

"You are looking for me, Mr. Deering?" Clarence's smile quickly turned to a frown. The expression of Deering's face showed nothing but grief. Marion who followed Clarence from the garden, stood still.

"Yes, I am, Mr. Jones. I'm afraid I have some very bad news," said Deering. I just received a telephone call from England." A slight hesitation marked the gravity of the next sentence. "Lady Julia had a boating accident. I'm afraid she is dead. I am terribly sorry."

Sargent had to sit down. Marion ran outside, in tears. Clarence just stood there, in the middle of the courtyard, silenced by an immense sorrow.

"I am so very sorry," repeated Deering.

So, that was it. All this. This opulence, this prosperity, all of it, for nothing. For this. Clarence climbed the steps to the upper galleries, under the watchful eyes of Deering and Sargent.

Vizcaya it seemed had betrayed Clarence, and he sat on his bed and cried tears of self-reproach, remorseful for not being more impulsive. He cried for the things that will never be, for those irretrievable moments, that first wondrous kiss. The faded memories he feared the most, ended up being the accurate ones. The ones that did not include Julia. The ones that propelled him aimlessly throughout eternity.

The bedroom with the secret passage was unoccupied at the present. Clarence made his way to the door where everything began. After making sure that no one was coming, he opened it and stepped in the long passageway that led to the other door, the one he unlocked with the silver key. It was the first time he walked to it, coming from this side of time. He stared at it, wondering about what lay beyond; 1917 or 2017?

Having excused himself for dinner, he looked for Marion. She sat on one of the marble benches in the garden. The last rays of sun weaved through the thick foliage above, adorning her with a crown of light in her blonde hair.

"I came to say goodbye," Clarence told her.

"You are leaving?"

"Yes. I don't have any reasons to be here now, but I wanted to see you before my departure."

"I wish you could stay. Must you go so soon?" she asked, somewhat disheartened.

"I am broken-hearted, if you must know."

"Oh, Clarence, I am so sorry."

This was the first time Marion called Clarence by his first name. The sudden change endeared him to her.

Marion seemed confused. "I was wondering why Mr. Deering broke this dreadful news to you. You knew Julia?"

"Yes. Though at times I wonder…"

Marion gazed at the man in front of her. She could not comprehend why she held such esteem and fondness for him. "Were you in love with her?" she asked candidly.

"Yes. I still am."

"I am truly sorry. She was a wonderful woman."

Clarence could not bring himself to speak about Julia in the past tense. "Anyway, it was a great pleasure to get to know you. You are the most memorable woman I met here," Clarence said to a perplexed Marion. "And I love your films. All of them."

She watched him go, unsure if anything was kept concealed in her memory. "Goodbye," she shouted.

Clarence turned around. He waived.

The empty mahogany box now contained Julia's letter, and Clarence wrote a short note which he also placed inside. He decided to mention the fact that there were several other keepsakes in the box, though he did not know exactly what they were. Somewhere in the future, someone would know, he pondered.

All the items in this box belonged to Clarence H. Jones, but they also were the property of Dr. Vincent Jones. I did stay at Vizcaya. I was a guest of James Deering on several occasions, but now in peril of losing my life, I have to get back to 2017. All is lost. Julia has been taken away from me, just as I was about to hold her in my arms. I do not know what else I am supposed to do. My head is about to erupt with deceptive memories, memories that I cannot trust, nor take for granted.

April 10th 1917
C. H. Jones

Late that night when everyone was asleep, Clarence roamed the house, silently, like a thief, a ghost. He looked through all the rooms, whispering Julia's name. He sat in the darkness of the dining room, willing her to come to him, to haunt him again. Visions of Julia drowning disturbed Clarence intensely. She called for him in her distress, but her cries were not heard. She fought with all her might as the sea took her. No one was able to rescue her, no one. Nothing was left to Clarence, only the hope of her spirit returning to him. He closed his eyes. At that very moment, Clarence wished for death to sweep him away. He had never yearned for anything so vehemently before. Unable to think coherently, he covered his face with both hands, before slowly sliding them down to his chest. Both hands clasped together, Clarence implored the silent witnesses, the spirits of the long departed, to let Julia go free. In his longing to behold the impossible, he manufactured and imagined Julia's silhouette in the dark corner of the dining room. She stood there, like a dream from a different night. He began to talk to her, apologizing for his failure to come to her rescue, and declared his love to her. He knew that for at least two years, they had shared a passionate love affair, however, none of it figured in the archives of his time. Another Clarence, in another universe, loved Julia and held her in his arms. How cruel is fate, and the unknown purpose of what takes place during the course of a lifetime? Clarence could not even revive the sensation of her bare skin, the touch of her lips, the taste of her mouth. In an instant of lucidity, Clarence asked why she pursued him during all his years as Vincent Jones. Why was she so incessant and so determined to bring him here, to Vizcaya?

Two hours went by before Clarence returned to his bedroom. Thoughts about death tormented him. At about two o'clock in the morning, he returned to the unoccupied bedroom, and opened up the door to the secret passage. The dark tunnel-like corridor, narrow and coarsely built, awaited Clarence's arrival, it seemed. He held the mahogany box in his hand, like the precious element that would soon dismiss all his doubts. A couple of steps taken inside the passageway, only increased his fear. The light from the bedroom gave enough luminosity for him to continue, which he did, a step at a time. Then, a profound apprehension stopped him. He had toyed with the inexplicable, with the very atoms of a life split between two eras; one on the shores of a time which had yet to be, the other, here. Now. How much agony was due for the gain of such knowledge? The cost was high, for sure. Clarence as Vincent, and Vincent as Clarence, both sampled the taste of what is essentially eternal life. Was death now scratching at Clarence's window, like an invisible creature demanding to come in? How accepting one can become. Dying was the path to Julia. Death would reunite us, thought Clarence. His mind wrestled with possibilities, and another face became visible among the chaos. He could not quite discern the features. Who did the face represent? A demon? An angel?

At the end of the passage now, Clarence placed his hand on that second door. Pushing it was easy enough. There it was, standing in the way of deliverance, in whatever form. So, why the fear? Perhaps it was more disillusion than fear; the boundless years spent seeking that which is hidden. Julia. Vizcaya. Two enigmas far too complex to analyze. Both were lived and loved. Both had vanished, swallowed up by the relentless procession of time.

Clarence looked at his hand on the wooden surface of the second door. Beyond it, the twenty-first century awaited him. Was he certain of it? No. Like the first time, he hoped that the crossing to that other dimension, was open. As Vincent, he knew it. As Clarence, he had misgivings that 2017 was on the other side. Facing a guest of James Deering in that other bedroom, once the door opened, could be embarrassing to say the least. And if it was 2017, then what? His corpse, like the ancient remains of a dead man falling at the feet of some tourists, would stir the world of science. Vizcaya's fame may benefit from such a discovery. More and more images relating to Vincent's life came forth in the last couple of minutes. He was Vincent again. This is the only reasoning that made sense. Vincent. His time at Vizcaya had passed. He took a deep breath, pushed the door open and stepped into the room.

FORTY TWO

The bedroom was empty. Vincent stood still, anxious about the new unknown. His perceptions were intact. The smell of fresh linen was gone, so was the scent of jasmine. Instead, a dusty odor seemed to dominate. Clarence noticed that the intensity of the tapestry, the carpets had drastically diminished. Gone was she, the Vizcaya of his aspirations and the promises of a love that knows no end. The unmistakable aura of Vizcaya, the museum, had returned.

Clarence had morphed back into Vincent. The mahogany box was no longer in his hand, and the door had closed behind him. It was locked. None of this shocked him, though the disappearance of his box really pained him. He checked his pants and shirt; everything seemed fine. All he had to do is find out today's date. He took a few steps, when he felt something in his pocket. The wallet had reappeared. He quickly opened it up. The driver's license read 'Vincent Jones' and gave his New York City address. Credit cards were there, as well.

A noise, like a rumbling sound, seemed to hover above. Vincent walked to the gallery and leaned over the balustrade. The courtyard below was deserted. Vizcaya was deserted. The sound outside became louder and Vincent made his way downstairs and stood in the middle of the courtyard. The glass pyramid above brought him to tears, but beyond it, the day it seemed was going to bring havoc. There were no doubts. Vincent had reverted to the very day he left. Hurricane Irma raged. This was September 10th, 2017. He looked up at the glass roof again, in complete wonder of the day. The silent fountain on one side, grieved him, deeply affecting him. Deering's small and elegant cast iron tables covered with embroidered tablecloths had disappeared, like everything else that mattered here. The remaining shell of Vizcaya, which entertained and amused the well-intentioned tourists throughout the years, saddened Vincent. He cast a spiritless eye to the upper galleries, his mind on Julia. He knew that she would never return to him. He will look over his shoulder in the years ahead, expect and wait for her to suddenly appear, but he will not find her.

Vincent discovered the same broken window he used to enter the house. He shook his head in disbelief. A few minutes had gone by, and a hundred years had passed. The destruction had not quite begun. The storm had yet to come to shore.

The east terrace really broke his spirit. The barge, like a fragment, a shadow of what it was, sat in choppy waters covered with algae. The defaced mermaids, vandalized by time, held up the ruins of the ship made of stone. How sad. How tragic. And within the space of a handful of hours, more, much more damage would have to be endured. Marion's face came to him, like a frail image drifting in the storm. She would be stunned by all this; her youthful zeal shattered.

The extent of the damage caused by Irma will be catastrophic, and Vincent took one last look at the grounds. Battered by the increasing wind and rain, he made his way toward the exit, stricken with sorrow for what he had lost.

FORTY THREE

A little less than eighteen hours later, Vincent landed at JFK Airport, in New York. Television sets throughout the terminal showed Irma's devastation in Florida. Vizcaya was under attack. Everything Vincent held dear, faced devastation.

Vincent stepped out of the taxi and looked up at his building, not knowing why, perhaps to see if anything appeared different. He walked in the lobby.

"Good afternoon, Dr. Jones," said Grant.

Vincent observed Grant. There were no words to adequately express how he felt at this particular moment. His mind wandered, as flashbacks from his previous visit rallied it seemed, to confuse him.

"Hello, Grant."

"How was your trip, sir?" asked Grant, somewhat baffled by Vincent's reaction.

"My trip?"

"To Florida."

"Oh, yes… that trip. Good. It was a good trip."

"Well, it's nice to have you back."

"Thank you. Tell me, how long was I gone for?"

"I think you were gone for a week."

"A week. Alright, thank you."

Vincent walked to the elevator and pressed the button to his penthouse. He turned around. "You've been here all of the time, right?" he inquired, just to make sure.

"Every day."

A simple nod was given and Vincent entered the elevator. He felt his pockets and realized his did not have his keys with him. He asked Grant to use his pass to open the penthouse, which he did, and left Vincent.

The familiarity of the apartment appeased Vincent's spirit, though he scrutinized the main room, mistrustful of his very own perceptions and still not entirely healed of the Julia syndrome. He put his carry-on bag down and noticed the conspicuous absence of the Sargent watercolor. He searched for it throughout the whole penthouse, and finally went into the master bedroom. The wrinkled sketch he drew in the London hotel, laid on the bed, like a farewell gesture. Vincent stared at the drawing, afraid to touch it. The piece of paper had supernaturally materialized here, from thousands of miles away. Vincent was stunned. He studied the two figures he had depicted, the unknown which brought such uneasiness in his life; a woman with a child. The extraordinary events that led to this hour, removed all fears, though more evidence of the objectives for such happenings, continued to be a mystery. Julia had been here. She had to be. Vincent looked around the room, anxious. Sargent's painting was gone, that much was clear. The drawing was carefully picked up and taken downstairs. A laptop sat on the kitchen countertop, an empty glass by its side. A bunch of dead flowers in a vase half filled with water, appeared to be not much more than a week old. Everything appeared normal. All artworks were hung in their allocated spots. Still amazed, Vincent placed the drawing on his desk and sat down in the very inviting armchair, exhausted. And now what? Vincent wondered. What surprised him, was the fact that he could recall everything and everyone. Truly, only a week had gone by. He began to enumerate names and places in his head; Sarah, Charlotte... Lena. Lena, the sweet nurse who saved him from destruction. Where was she? On the French Riviera, after her winnings? He felt certain that she had kept her job, her calling, as a nurse. Wonderful Lena. And Charlotte. Would any of those people know him, remember him? Vincent's eyes fell on his black leather address book. He grabbed it and sat down again. Unfortunately, not every phone number was listed. Without his cell phone, the task of finding people would be a tough one.

The sound of the front door opening, startled Vincent. He looked toward the entrance. The door opened and Vincent's clone walked in. The two identical figures, one in the doorway, the other in the armchair, stupefied each other.

Both men looked at each other. Both could see the horrible expression on the other's face. Both remained silent.

Finally, Vincent rose from the armchair and spoke. "Are you real?" he asked the other. "Am I really seeing you?"

"I am."

"You're not some apparition… hallucination, are you?"

"I am as real as you are… I think. How long have you been back?" Vincent inquired, as he remained by the front door.

"I'm not so sure," Vincent declared. "I'm not so sure you are real." He walked toward the other, his double, astonished at the circumstance, yet not afraid. "How did you get the keys?" he asked, examining the authenticity of his features. A luminosity appeared to shine from within the man who stood by the door. The two stared at each other, amazed at all the deceptions. "One of us cannot be real. One of us doesn't belong here."

"I have the key to my own penthouse," said Vincent, showing the set in his hand. "That has to make you the impostor. Right?"

Vincent felt certain that the man standing in his doorway was unreal, a substitute lost in another dimension, the realms of time. He noticed a glow on his skin when he spoke. "What's on the bed, in the master bedroom?" he asked.

"A drawing. I saw it this morning."

"Do you know who drew it?"

The question seemed to be a puzzling one. The hesitation was proof. "It's of Julia and her daughter, isn't' it?" The name Julia hummed like the soft ripples on a stream, affecting both men equally.

Vincent took a step back, as the man who claimed the same identity gradually took on invisibility. He slowly became quasi-translucent, and a great fear marked his distorted face. The set of keys fell to the floor. "I am sorry," the man uttered in a barely audible whisper. "I don't know what happened. I tried. I don't understand what I was supposed to achieve."

"What do you mean? Is it Julia? Did Julia come to Vizcaya? Did she?" Vincent urged the man.

"Yes."

Nothing else was worth knowing. The fantastic, the incertitude, all of it was carried away, ravaged by one syllable.

The void in front of Vincent and the set of keys on the marble floor, gave him that sense of anemic victory, one undeserved and misconceived. What strange and capricious happenings had taken place? In which universe and physical world did Julia dwell? Not mine, thought Vincent. How can it be? "I could have encountered you," he said and sat back in the armchair. "Instead, I missed you by a hundred years." He leaned back and eventually fell asleep as different theories flooded his mind.

A night sky filled the large bay windows of the penthouse. Vincent opened his eyes. A few ordinary hours had passed and he turned the television to the Weather Channel. Disturbing images of Irma's path of destruction in Florida, were being shown. He watched, numbed to the desolation, resolute to remain unaffected by events that cannot be reversed.

Feeling some sort of balance for the first time, Vincent ordered a pizza on his computer and opened a bottle of wine. He casually kept looking through the address book, sitting at his countertop, sipping his wine. He thumbed through the pages to the letter 'C', looking for Charlotte's name, then to the letter 'M' for Montagu, Charlotte's last name. Not a trace of her to be found. Vincent closed the book, frustrated. He remembered her so clearly. Both times she had impressed him with her spirit, her vitality. In or out of the wheelchair.

The pizza arrived. Vincent smiled at the fact that he had not eaten what he would call junk food, for an eternity. An amusing thought for James Deering and Vizcaya's fine meals, entered his head.

Tomorrow he would attempt to contact Charlotte. After all he knew where she lived, and just as he introduced himself to her in 2008, he would again.

After the short flight to Philadelphia, Vincent took a taxi to the address he recalled. The taxi driver exited the main road and drove down the little lane to the point where Vincent asked him to stop. An empty field, and grass waving in the wind, mystified Vincent at first. Yet after reflection, he understood that which he knew to be real, no longer was. It became evident to him that the world he left behind, had profoundly been modified.

"Are you sure you have the right place?" asked the taxi driver.

"I'm not sure of anything."

"My GPS doesn't show a house anywhere," said the man.

"I know. Take me back to the airport."

FORTY FOUR

Little by little, life in New York City returned to what can be said was normal for Vincent. A whole week since Irma struck had slipped away, almost unnoticed. Cell phone in his pocket, on his way to Sotheby's, Vincent stopped by what used to be his favorite pastry shop. The store window was filled with photographs of properties for lease and sale. Another new reality. Vincent walked away, wondering what other surprises this 2017 had in store.

Sotheby's, fortunately remained the same. People who knew Vincent, wished him a good morning, as did one of the directors, James Mendoza.

"Hi," said James, as Vincent entered the back galleries.

The shock on Vincent's face was hard to miss, though he tried his best to hide it. "Trac... James," he mumbled.

"Well, good morning to you, too."

"James. James. My old friend," exclaimed Vincent, and he gave him a big hug, as if the two were reunited after a long war.

James stared at his college friend. "Are you alright?" he asked.

"You know... I really am," replied Vincent.

James was convinced. "Boy, do I have a surprise for you!" he said. "Follow me."

"What is it?"

"You'll see."

James pulled a wall panel, holding several drawings and paintings coming up for auctions. "Look at this," he said, pulling out Sargent's watercolor from Vizcaya.

"Oh, my God! It's here," murmured Vincent, unable to contain his joy. "I thought it was... never mind, it's here."

"What do you mean, it's here."

"Nothing."

"I thought of you when it came in. Beautiful, isn't it?"

"Who's is it?" inquired Vincent, his eyes on the painting.

"A Lady... something..." said James.

"Montagu?" The name was the obvious one.

"That's it. Charlotte Montagu."

Vincent shook his head in utter disbelief. "When is the sale?"

"In two weeks, I think. I'll have to look it up. You'll bid for it, right?"

"I think I must," smiled Vincent.

"Good. Good. I don't know why, but I'd hate for anyone else to have it. Do you think that's crazy?"

Vincent felt a great sense of gladness. "Not at all." He noticed that the frame was original. He thought of Sarah and her rage when she threw the painting against the column.

"It's a wonderful piece," said James.

"It is. Did you meet her? Lady Montagu."

"I did."

"How was she?"

"What do you mean?" James asked.

"How did she look?"

"Great... I guess." James looked into Vincent's eyes. "How long have you known me for?" he asked. The implication solidified Vincent's notion about his friend sexual preferences.

"Five minutes?" he replied, smiling inwardly. Vincent was hesitant and scared to ask the next question.

"What?" wondered James. "What is it?"

"Was she in a wheelchair?"

"A wheelchair? Why would you ask such a weird question? No, she wasn't in a wheelchair."

Vincent began a long dreamy smile.

"You've been acting really strange. Are you okay?" questioned James.

"I really am. Things are becoming clearer every day."

Both men walked to the front galleries. "Lovely drawing by Augustus John," pointed Vincent, in a much more cheerful mood. "Alright, I'll see you later. There's somewhere I have to be."

On the way home, Vincent marveled at what transpired. James had finally followed his heart and Vincent's belief that he had played a role, however insignificant, gave him more hope. Going through that secret passage had proved to be like the wages of a thousand lifetimes. Previously unforeseen happiness, now seemed but a step away.

Vincent knew what he had to do. He recognized the need to go back to England, to Sargent's grave. He had to return where it all began. And maybe, maybe, Julia would show herself one last time, and he would welcome her.

FORTY FIVE

A cold wind announced the approach of an early winter. Vincent stood in front of Sargent's headstone for the second time. A bunch of fresh white roses laid at the base of the stone. He knelt down, touched the dew on the petals and looked to see if he could spot someone. No one seemed to be around.

And here were those words again, like the speech of a wretched man, sublimely ignorant of things that are dazzling, elegant - *John S. Sargent RA - Born in Florence Jan12th1856 - Died in London April 15th1925.*

Why read the words, again and again? What did they mean, exactly? Precious little. Vincent stood within the same sphere as Sargent, sat at the same dinner table and spoke freely about his passion for the artist's work. Now, nothing. Now, desolation. Time, truly is the enemy, annihilating the vile and the sublime, without any exemptions. At least Vincent was known to Sargent, even if it was for a brief moment in time. That was the real miracle.

The wind stopped and an even colder air moved in. A groundskeeper told Vincent that the cemetery was closing in forty-five minutes. Vincent instinctively surveyed the grounds, waiting for another miracle to happen. He noticed a person in the distance, walking toward the exit. Such few visitors, he thought. Death is not an attractive concept, yet it is the inherent aftermath of all living things. Acceptance is crucial.

Vincent walked away from the grave, not quite convinced that coming here was justified, when he felt compelled to stop. Absolute silence. She was here. Julia was here. Though not visible this time, he could sense her presence. He closed his eyes to see beyond the tangible, beyond death. An inner voice, loud as a call for help, resonated in Vincent's head. It was Julia's voice, violating what is ingrained in the laws of nature. She asked for forgiveness and spoke of love that never stays dormant. I will be with you; Vincent heard those words as surely as he stood on these sacred grounds. He felt her touch on his face and he quickly opened his eyes, only to see the empty space around him. He waited. The loss of a loved one holds the power to gravely wound, but Vincent rejoiced. This, he felt was the last time Julia would appear to him, or at least make her presence known, and yet his spirit was filled with laughter. He did not fully understand why. Vincent took a few steps, heading toward the exit. He turned around one more time, and replayed the images of when he first visited Sargent's grave; the woman who wore an embroidered dress, a woman of another era, a few moments ago… a hundred years ago.

FORTY SIX

The auction room was packed. Vincent arrived late and had to sit at the very back of the room. Several items were already sold, though the Sargent was kept for last. Holding his auction paddle close to his chest, Vincent tried to catch a glimpse of Charlotte, who said she would attend the sale. He looked for a blond head among the crowd.

A small drawing by Andrew Wyeth was placed on the easel, ready for auction. It fetched twenty thousand dollars. A couple more drawings by lesser artists did not make the reserve price. The auctioneer finally announced the Sargent watercolor. He explained its history, Sargent's stay at Vizcaya and spoke about the rarity of such work. The room was buzzing with excitement. The auction began. The dollar amounts quickly rose from a hundred and twenty thousand to two hundred thousand. It kept climbing incrementally, five thousand dollars at a time. Vincent spotted at least two interested parties. Now at two hundred and forty-five thousand dollars, the painting had increased by twenty-five thousand, from that first auction. Vincent was under no illusion, this day had nothing to do with the past. He showed his paddle.

"Two hundred and fifty thousand," said the auctioneer, who knew Vincent well. "Any more bids?"

Vincent closed his eyes in the complete silence of the room.

"Two hundred and fifty thousand," said the auctioneer. "Fair warning. Any more bids? Anyone? Selling at two hundred and fifty thousand dollars… anyone else? Sold!"

What strange journey this was; a strange and full circle. But Vincent had only one desire now; meet Charlotte. He stood up, anxious to see her, to recognize her. People who knew Vincent congratulated him on his purchase. Some of the crowd left, while other groups remained in the room, talking.

James approached Vincent. "I'm so happy it's yours," he said. "I felt it should belong to you. You know, with your history with Vizcaya and all that."

"Thank you," answered Vincent, peaking over James's shoulder, still looking for Charlotte.

"Oh, I guess you should meet Lady Charlotte. Come, I'll introduce you. She's right over there. She was nervous about the sale," added James.

Vincent followed his friend to the front of the room. The only woman Vincent could see had dark hair. She sat with her back turned to them, looking at her catalogue.

"Lady Charlotte," said James, "this is the buyer, Dr. Vincent Jones."

Charlotte turned around. Astounded, dismayed, Vincent felt a rush of blood to his head and an unexpected bliss that amazed him. Julia, in the flesh, sat in front of his very eyes. Or was he being deceived by an inquiring fervor?

"How do you do," she uttered with a soft smile. "Congratulations."

James excused himself, saying he had some business to attend to.

"How do you do. Thank you," mumbled Vincent, spellbound by the woman who bore an absolute resemblance to Julia; shockingly so.

"May I sit down?" asked Vincent. "You have a minute?"

"I have. Please," she said, pointing at a chair.

"I am sorry to deprive you of such a wonderful work of art," said Vincent. "Though I can assure you, it has found a good home," he declared, attempting not to unwittingly lose himself in her gaze.

"I'm very glad to hear it."

"Have you had it all your life? I don't mean to be—"

"That's fine. Yes, it's been in my family for years. It was given to my great-grandmother by Sargent himself."

Vincent listened to every word, like the softest music. Each word was like a note, and each one became more and more glorious as she spoke.

"She was a guest at Vizcaya. I'm sure you're very familiar with that house," continued Charlotte. "You've been, right?"

"I have." Charlotte's presence conquered whatever was left of Vincent's powers of deductions. If he had the courage, the innocent foolishness to declare his love, he would take her by the hand. Her questioning eyes only delaying her very own affirmations.

"You must forgive me, Dr. Jones, but I have to go."

"Of course, of course. I'm sorry I held you up."

Charlotte stood up, and the marvelous truth warmed Vincent's heart. A hundred years had to be re-written, shuffled around, to arrive at this day, this moment.

"I'm very happy to have met you," said Charlotte.

I can't let her walk out of my life, thought Vincent. Quick, think of something... anything, he pondered. There're so many things you could ask her, like do you like Sargent... do you like Sargent? What kind of a question is that? Idiot. Ask her if she's enjoying New York City. Ask her to the Met. Ask her to dinner!

Charlotte extended her hand. "Goodbye. And congratulations, again."

"Have dinner with me," Vincent said with great haste, as if his brainpowers were about to shut him down. The broadcast of such a declaration made him feel incredibly awkward all of a sudden.

"When?" she replied, to Vincent's wide-open heart.

"Now. Tonight."

Charlotte laughed. What is it about a laugh that promotes indescribable joy within the confines of our world? What is that inscrutable chemical reaction that brings love? A glance from afar. A face. The wonderful complexity of another soul.

"Why do you want to have dinner with me?" she inquired, playfully as they both walked toward the exit.

The truthful answer was because each have been waiting for the other. The truth was Vincent had loved Charlotte from the very beginning. He loved her spirit, her strengths and her weaknesses. Julia's physical attributes were just an added element, the apex of the once insurmountable odds. None of this could be said, at least not yet. Vincent shrugged, like the teenager whose vocabulary lacks the more refined words. "I just do." He looked at her. Her presence was soothing.

"Good enough," she replied.

York Avenue bustled with people. The city noises brought a certain realism to the withdrawal Vincent indulged in within the walls of Sotheby's. Thoughts of Sargent and Vizcaya were quickly crushed, once outside. "You don't live here, do you? Where are you staying?" he asked Charlotte.

"Actually, I don't have a hotel. I wasn't planning to stay in the city tonight. I live in Wyoming. I'll find something."

"Wyoming?" said Vincent.

"I run a quaint little inn. The roof requires fixing, well... it needs to be replaced, actually," she giggled. "That's why I'm selling... sold the Sargent."

"I see." Vincent felt guilty all of a sudden, and bad for asking Charlotte to dinner. "Are you sure you can stay?" he asked, ecstatic inside that she would change her plans and accept his dinner invitation. An invitation, after all with a total stranger, as far as she was concerned.

"Yes, I'm sure. I'll see you tonight? Here's my card," she said, "that's my cell, call that number. The other one is the landline."

Vincent took the business card. "I'll give you a call. Maybe around seven?"

"Perfect," she answered and waved a taxi.

Vincent watched the yellow cab disappear in a sea of cars. Julia had made an entrance back into Vincent's life, under the most extraordinary circumstances. What woman in history has possessed the near-identical features of her great-grandmother? To such an extent. Not one. Ever. Though oblivious to it all, Vincent watched the traffic and people passing by. He looked at her card - *Charlotte Montagu, Lady Julia Inn, Sheridan, Wyoming.*

The penthouse seemed derelict of all its virtues. In this ivory tower, entrenched in his miniature universe, Vincent felt alone. Alone, like never before. He put down the Sargent watercolor with a nonchalance that surprised him. He stared at the painting. Yes, it was fantastic. Yes, he had coveted it from the moment Sargent showed it to him. Or was it the time after, when he first bought it? Did it matter?

A long shower helped Vincent settle down. As the afternoon opened its window to the night, Vincent became even more excited. He poured himself a small whiskey. Charlotte's card laid on his desk, like a symbol of hope, a new conviction. The number was dialed. Jittery, he waited for her voice.

"Hello?" Charlotte answered.

"Hi, it's Vincent. Dr. Jones," he felt compelled to add, and regretted it right away.

"I am so sorry, I won't be able to have dinner with you."

"Oh. Alright. Is everything—"

"I'm fine. Just a small emergency at home."

Vincent could tell by the noise that Charlotte was in a moving car. "You're on your way to airport?"

"Yes. I realized I didn't have your number, or I would've called you. You're not listed."

"I know. I'm sorry." The communication was lost. "Hello? Hello? Damn." Vincent paced the room, wondering if he should call again, right away. What was the polite thing to do? It felt wrong not to, yet he hesitated. He was about to dial again, when Charlotte called.

"Stupid phones," she exclaimed. "I'm at JFK now. Well... again I'm sorry. I really was looking forward to seeing you again."

"I was too. Look—"

"Goodbye Dr. Jones."

"It's Vincent, please."

"Vincent."

A long silence ensued, a silence much too long for two people who did not want to meet again. Neither one, it seemed, wished to end the call. Similar phone conversations with the Charlotte from another time, lingered. This pleased Vincent, and he knew that Charlotte felt the same. Though the foundations of many lives were altered, Vincent was certain that Charlotte's spirit had remained intact through it all.

"I have to go through security now," said Charlotte.

"Look, this is going to sound... I don't know... hasty, but—"

"I'd like to see you again," Charlotte uttered suddenly. "Oh, God, tell me that's what you were going to say."

"It is," Vincent replied quickly, happy, relieved.

"I tend to do that. Embarrass myself."

"Don't ever change. You don't know how happy I am, right now," said Vincent, who felt like he had been given wings.

"Strange, isn't it? A few hours ago, we had never met," she said dreamily. "And now..."

FORTY SEVEN

With Charlotte back in his life, the rhythm of Vincent's days beat to the thoughts of her. A collection of events, like the pages of a diary overflowing with memories, kept him awake at night. A part of him adhered to her. He stared at the ceiling, the companion of his sleepless nights, yet the name on his lips this time could be uttered without preconditions.

A belated dawn fought the cloud cover above the city. Idle since his return to 2017, regarding not only his identity, but the identities of others, Vincent spent the morning looking through documents, records of his existence. His mother's death certificate gave him a strange sense of peace. He stared at it, his mind on that 'other' Charlotte, the one in the wheelchair. It was senseless to do so; far greater governance oversaw the renovations of all lives involved. However, he missed her. He missed her most dreadfully.

Vincent opened his laptop, a freshly brewed cup of coffee in his hand. He typed 'Sheridan, Wyoming'. "Sheridan, Sheridan," said Vincent, "where the hell are you?" he said out loud, looking at the map. The 'Lady Julia Inn' website took him on a beautiful virtual journey of the grounds. Several buildings sat on the property, including a large stable. The main structure, dating from the late 1800's, looked like a well-preserved mansion with two imposing turrets. According to the website, it was one of the last remaining stately houses in the area. Vincent clicked on all the available images. A grand staircase in the entry held his attention, along with a stained glass, a marble fireplace and carved ceilings. A small crowd posed under the wrap-around porch for a picture. Some stood while others sat. Vincent noticed a woman in a wheelchair and he stood up, quickly, overwhelmed by an eerie feeling. He stared at the photograph from a safe distance. No, he thought. It can't be. His perfect world was crumbling yet again. He sat down and zoomed in on the image. Charlotte's smile warmed his heart, though Vincent's confusion reached its limits and he let out his frustration – "What the hell is happening!? Who am I?" he screamed. He shook his head, waiting for an answer in the hush of his kitchen. An answer from whom? From what? "Maybe I'm hallucinating again. Maybe none of this is even real. This room, this… this body," he said, looking at his arms, his hands.

After two large Scotch whiskies, Vincent paced the room, a reminiscent habit from earlier days when his mind and the supernatural realms fought against one another. He searched for something genuine in the penthouse, something he could claim as evidence of his life. The drawing from the London hotel offered such help. Vincent held it up in his hand, like the proof of a previous life. His phone rang.

"Hello?" Vincent answered, still looking at the drawing through the moisture of his teary eyes.

"Vincent, it's Charlotte."

Vincent wavered before answering. "Who are you, really?" he asked, finally.

"It's me. Charlotte? Charlotte Montagu?"

"No." Vincent's thoughts wandered, struck by increasing doubts, underscored by the effect of alcohol. "I mean, who are you? And what have you done with the real Charlotte?"

"Excuse me? Who is this? Is this Dr. Vincent Jones?"

"It is. But you are not *the* Charlotte Montagu," he went on. "Are you?"

"What on earth do you mean?"

"You have dark hair."

"So?"

"So, you can't be *my* Charlotte," he stammered. "And you're walking."

"I'll call back when you're sober," she exclaimed. "You are talking sheer nonsense," she added and hung up.

"Yes, that's right, take the easy way out," he said out loud. "And I'm not drunk," he whispered to himself. "Why should I be drunk? Everything is fine and dandy. Life is peachy."

The twenty-five-year-old Glenlivet Scotch had amended all of Vincent's conversation the previous evening. Charlotte must think me a fool, he thought. However, the photograph on the website spoke volumes. How could it be explained? Vincent opened his laptop again to double check. He studied the image one more time, hoping to catch a detail, something that would give him a time frame. He zoomed in on a young man wearing a T-shirt with 'Class of 2013' printed on it. Vincent closed the computer, his mind engaged with a myriad of speculations. The connection between Julia and Charlotte was blurry, to say the least. Though well-seasoned now on the paranormal, Vincent could not comprehend what was unfolding before his eyes. He walked to the bay window and admired the day. Central Park looked very inviting and he decided to take a stroll. Fresh air was needed.

The early November temperature required a coat; however, the sun was very much present and a lot of people took pleasure of the day. Vincent thought about hurricane Irma, and the damage on Vizcaya. He knew that a fundraiser would soon have to be organized and he looked forward to donating money again. He held his phone, debating why calling Charlotte was a bad idea. A text from James popped up at that moment. An important exhibition on Sargent's work was opening in a week at the Chicago Art Institute. Vincent became very excited.

Sotheby's held several more auctions, and Vincent was called upon to authenticate different works of art. It kept him busy. Though he joined some of his colleagues for drinks on two occasions at the local bar down the street, Vincent was socially inept. He found himself wallowing in a never-ending conundrum, unwilling to be in a crowd, and lonely in a gloomy penthouse. A full two weeks had gone by since that fiasco call with Charlotte. Many times, Vincent dialed her number and every time he lost his courage. Perhaps she was a lost cause, too. He had her affection when they first met, that day after the funeral. It could have easily matured to love, a great love. He had her knocking at his heart, and he pushed her back. Charlotte accepted him again, after Vincent returned to her, like a hooligan. She took him in, endorsing his claims about Vizcaya and its secrets. The offer of love was made one more time, and one more time it was refused. A trip to Miami had to be taken, and Charlotte drove a depleted Vincent, both physically and spiritually to the entrance of his beloved house. Charlotte did not stand a chance. Julia stood in the way. The ephemeral dream that she projected, remained intact and lit up a great fire into Vincent's imagination. Later, a terrified and helpless Charlotte was witness to Vincent vanishing in that Miami hotel room.

The Art Institute welcomed a very enthusiastic crowd to the Sargent exhibition. His work was highly acclaimed, and a show of this magnitude was not to be missed. James and Vincent made the trip together to Chicago.

The show was beautifully arranged. Some of Sargent's famous paintings were shown, but also some lesser-known examples were on display, like several watercolors, which pleased Vincent. The small painting of Charles Deering, which is part of the Institute's permanent collection, was mentioned by James, as pure mastery and genius.

"His work is amazing," said James, as he studied the painting of Charles Deering closely. "Look at this, just a few strokes and there he is… Charles Deering in the flesh."

The painting was dated 1917. Vincent stared at the date, like a hidden code from a forbidden story. His mind travelled through the painting, and he sat under the royal palms by the tea house, awaiting lunch to be announced; James Deering and Marion Davies by his side. He felt the warm breeze on the back of his neck, coming from Biscayne Bay.

"Vincent!" whispered James, who noticed a couple of impatient people waiting behind Vincent. "Come on," he gestured him to follow.

"Sorry."

"We'll come back to it if you want."

They entered the next room and Vincent abruptly stopped, dumbfounded. Julia's face confused him at first. Her nostalgic gaze seemed like a fictitious concept, born out of his longings, awaken by the exhibition. "Are you seeing this painting, too?" Vincent asked his friend.

James frowned, looking at Vincent with concern. "Yes," he said casually, "it's a fairly well-known painting. In fact, and you'll be interested in this, it's a portrait of Lady Charlotte's great-grandmother. Lady Julia."

Vincent was speechless. He recognized the mahogany box Julia held in her hands. Unmistakably, it was his. Both hands were held flat, one under the box, the other on top, as if protecting it. Sargent had clearly painted the initials C.H.J. on it, no doubt at Julia's request. Why did she select that particular item to be immortalized with her? Vincent came within three feet of the painting as he approached an altar, and stared into Julia's eyes. The full-length portrait hung in front of him. It was not destroyed by fire. Not in this version of his life. Nothing of Charlotte's previous life, or accounts, existed. The little girl, the dress catching fire, all that had been cancelled, like a bad idea, a footage from an unwanted scenario.

"Classic Sargent, isn't it?" said James.

"Fabulous," Vincent uttered, and read the museum label on the wall.

Lady Julia Montagu
Oil on canvas, 1917
Private Collection

Vincent continued reading.

Lady Julia was a guest of James Deering at Vizcaya. In 1917, Sargent was commissioned to paint her while staying at the estate. The client remains unknown. Lady Julia died tragically in a boating accident, off the coast of Scotland, a few months after the painting was completed. She was twenty-eight years old.

"Sargent was commissioned on the train, on his way to Miami," said Vincent. "Clarence Henry Jones commissioned the painting."

"What are you talking about?" asked James.

"Nothing. I hate when people don't do their research properly."

James read the museum label. "Private collection, of course," he moaned. "All the great art is in private collections." He read on. "Ooh, that's a shame. How tragic, she died so young," he said, turning to Vincent.

"I know."

James looked at the painting again. "What a beautiful woman she must've been. Look at her, it's like she's about to speak." He noticed the wooden box in Julia's hands. "That's interesting," he said. "Look at the box she's holding… same initials as your great-grandfather's. Weird."

Vincent walked away from the painting, dispirited. They *are* my great-grandfather's initials – Clarence Henry Jones."

"I don't understand," answered James.

"It's too long of a story. I'll tell you later."

James shrugged. "By the way, have you heard from Lady Charlotte?" he inquired, as they wandered around the rest of the room.

"I have not. Why do you ask?"

"No reason, it just looked like you two had a nice chat the day of the auction."

"We did, but I haven't heard from her since."

The weekend spent in Chicago brought a mixture of joy and misery to Vincent. He felt like everything he came into contact with was clearly doomed to self-destruct. What discoveries had to be assembled to make sense of all this? What was being taught? The questions stormed his intellect, relentlessly, as the plane touched down at JFK Airport.

FORTY EIGHT

Thanksgiving.   Another day.   Despite Dr. Jones's numerous invitations to all kind of events, none of them were for a family gathering.   Money was always the rationale.   Whose fault was it?   His, probably.   'Antisocial behavior can drastically affect your health and lead to loneliness'.   That, ought to be the warning on every road sign. And as he sat at the countertop with his microwaved turkey diner, Vincent's heart was tested one more time.   He felt the full force of what it meant to be without a loved one.   He did not like it.   In fact, he hated it.   He despised his life, the wealth that brought him nothing but pain. He looked around the penthouse with scorn, disgusted by what it represented.   The Sargent watercolor became an object of torment, a conglomeration of trust and abandon.   Vincent bitterly regretted his relentless wishes to go to the bowels of Vizcaya, and himself become a shadow of the past.   He pushed away the plate of cold food, and buried his face in his hands.   It was true, what has perhaps always been said, that genuine wealth is of a spiritual kind.   Charlotte's silence afflicted him.   He so wished for his phone to ring.   He so wished for her name to appear on the screen; a name he wrote in all caps.   He wondered what she was doing at this moment.   She had to be visiting family somewhere, friends, definitely.   She was not thinking of him.   She was happy, at peace.   Why should she be considering him at all?   If she formed an opinion, the word 'negative' would come to mind.   Vincent had made a terrible impression on her, given her an adverse and non-redeemable sentiment.   The inn was probably the destination for many tourists, unable to be with their loved ones at Thanksgiving.   Yes, Charlotte was most likely busy entertaining her guests, and snow was probably adding to the magic.

FORTY NINE

Vincent woke up to a thunder storm. Fierce lightning ripped across the sky, as nature displayed her strength. The power was out, and intense flashes of white lights erratically turned the bedroom from night to day. Vincent carefully made his way downstairs and watched the awesome performance through the bay window. Barely a few months ago, he would have expected Julia's presence at a time like this. Not anymore. His reality was contained within the space of a small world now. Absurd dreams of being another, somewhere far away, seemed foolish. No matter how constant he was in his search for logic, the answer always led to a dead end. Yet, Vincent lived as Clarence Jones, for whatever reason. That Christmas party at the Carnegies' was real, Julia was real. Vincent understood now, he knew that he was never allowed to pass beyond a certain point in time.

The storm passed and the early morning hours allowed a faint coloring to emerge in the penthouse. Vincent who fell asleep on the couch, opened his eyes to the new day. He stood up, decidedly. His mind was made up. Charlotte refused to call, so he would go to her. Simple. Go to Wyoming and beg for forgiveness. Right? Vincent sat on the couch, shot down from his cloud by the destructive spirits of fear. Perhaps take a trip, he thought, a work-related trip, or visit Mount Rushmore. Sheridan must be close by, he continued in his thinking. She could have lost my number, he said to himself, trying to rationalize what ought to be obvious. "Idiot, she hasn't lost your number! Deleted it, maybe. She just doesn't want to see you!" he said out loud. "Accept that, and you'll be fine," Vincent told that inner voice that turned best friend and advisor, in times like these.

The first images of the damage caused by hurricane Irma on Vizcaya, were released online. As an important donor, Vincent was privy to more data, which came in the form of emails from Vizcaya's Board of Directors. The cost was in the millions of dollars. Vincent scrolled through the pages of photographs on his laptop. He felt anger for that inexorable fury which are foolishly given people's names. The flooding was extensive and the gardens were a sad sight to behold. The long process of restoration had begun, as Vizcaya wept over its wounds like an injured child. Meditations about 1917 broke through the flimsy barricades Vincent had built to protect his sanity. The existence of Sargent's portrait of Julia, still amazed him. The lives of so many, running parallel but on very diverse planes, were beyond comprehension. The universe and all its mysteries had determined such courses. Vincent could only oblige.

One link took him to the next, reading about people's impressions of the estate. The word 'magical' was notably used. A short article about Marion Davies popped up. An autobiography about the silent film star, a book Vincent was unaware of, was being sold on eBay by a private seller. Vincent quickly entered the eBay site, and bought the book, simply titled 'Marion Davies, An Autobiography'. A detailed photograph showed her signature on the first page. Vincent was anxious to receive the book. He was fond of Marion and was curious about reading her journey through life in her own words.

Vincent felt exonerated, his unintended alliance with the spiritual world having ceased. Marion Davies, James Deering, Sargent, all were linked to his life, in an extraordinary way. And Julia. Her name was instilled in the depth of him, forever cherished, like a sweet agony that he was unwilling to free himself from. The strange activities and manifestations had stopped. Julia crossed to the other side, never to return.

Marion's book arrived a couple of days later. Vincent made a cup of tea and sat at his desk. He smiled at the photograph on the cover, representing Marion as he remembered her. He thumbed through the book, opening the pages that contained photographs; all those black and white memories, now lost in the pages of a book. The first chapters covered the early days, as expected, and the struggles of becoming a film star were many. He wished he had asked her about those difficult times. She would have told him. Vincent was surprised to find a section dedicated to Vizcaya. Though the paragraph was short, it surprised him. She never spoke about the house as someone who was captivated by the experience. He began to read…

Mr. Deering was the most generous host in the world, and nothing was extravagant enough for his guests. I was invited to Vizcaya twice. The first time was in the spring of 1916. The stone barge was still under construction in those days. I remember it well, though it's been more than forty years. The lazy days spent eating and drinking, were a relief from the madness of Hollywood, even in those days!

My second visit took place the following spring. This I remember with much more clarity. I arrived a few days before a certain gentleman. I have never forgotten the first time I saw him. He was so good looking, though he appeared somewhat lost, maybe a little shy as well. I stood by his bedroom door (no, I didn't go in!), and he turned around and saw me. I like to think I made an impression on him, because we became inseparable during the next two weeks. I fell in love with him, though I never told him. He was a sweet man, different than anyone I ever met. He was like a little boy in the presence of the painter, Sargent, filled with wonder in his eyes. I think there was something he was not telling me... like a secret.

I remember the day I asked him to come to California, to spend a little time with me. He looked as if he was anxious about something and he just smiled. He left one day, and I never heard from him again. I never went back to Vizcaya. Even if I had the chance to, I think I would've turned it down. I guess I just wanted to remember it with him there. I will love you until my last breath Mr. J.

Vincent leaned back in his chair. How fertile is the mind! Teeming with the circumstances of life, it becomes selective in its crusade to reconcile the bitter and the sweet. Marion was of the delightful kind. She possessed that youthful joy, irresistible to her audiences and the casual onlookers. She hid her sorrow well. Vincent closed the book and thought about that era again, the cycle of her days; the volatile happy moments and the lasting heartaches. Marion's whole life was defined between the two covers of this book; a few pages that marked her time on this earth. Who remembered her? Not many people. In another hundred years, she would be totally forgotten, as if she had never existed. That idea saddened Vincent and he began to meditate on his very own future.

FIFTY

"I was thinking about you this morning," said James, as Vincent walked out of the elevator at Sotheby's.

"You were?"

"Yes. I read something about the cost of that hurricane... Irma, and I thought about Vizcaya. I don't know why. You're the weirdo when it comes to that house."

"True. I am. What about Vizcaya?" asked Vincent.

"Just thinking about it. Your love for Sargent, the whole thing, really. I don't know, I guess I feel kind of sad. Is that odd?"

"No, it's not."

"By the way, I've been trying to call you," said James. "Why don't you answer your phone? I left like three voicemails." The two walked in the storage galleries. Vincent's expertise was required to authenticate and appraise a drawing attributed to Holbein the Younger, the 16th century German artist.

"I didn't get a call from you," exclaimed Vincent.

"Check your phone."

Vincent opened his phone and could not detect any missed calls. Not being particularly skilled with technology, he showed James what he could see.

James Laughed.

"What?"

"You really are useless when it comes to this," James said, taking the phone from Vincent's hands. "That's funny, you don't have any notifications. Something must be wrong with your phone. Oh, look, it's on airplane mode."

"What the hell was it on airplane mode?" Vincent asked scrolling through his voicemails. There were a few numbers, though he only wanted to see a specific one. And there it was. Area code 307. Charlotte had called several times. He counted four times, and she had left two voicemails. The first one said that she was sorry for hanging up on him, and that she felt stupid afterwards. The second voicemail was more personal. She spoke about the limited time they spent together, and how she wished for a chance at having another date with him. Her goodbye left Vincent imagining that more wanted to be said, but she just added that she was looking forward to hearing from him soon. "God, what must she think of me?" lamented Vincent, who stared at his phone. "I'm such a fool."

James had made his way to the alleged 16th century drawing. He stood in front of it. "Well, do what you do best," he uttered. "Here it is."

Vincent had stopped a few steps behind. "I have to call her, right?" stated Vincent.

"Call who?"

"Charlotte. Charlotte Montagu."

"She called you? I thought you said—"

"Forget what I said. I'm an idiot. She called me a million times and left two messages."

"You must've made quite an impression on her," said James.

Vincent shook his head. "She must think I'm ignoring her. I can't stand it. What do I do?" he questioned his friend, hoping for an answer that would satisfy him. However, Vincent sought another kind of reaction, one that would grab him by the shoulder and take him to her.

"Whoa, you are in love with this woman, aren't you?" asserted James.

"You know... I am. And I've been in love with her for years. A hundred years," he told James.

"You are crazy."

"Damn right. But my God, it feels good!"

"I'm happy for you. I really am," said James. "Now, do something about it. Don't just go off, dreaming."

"I'm going to Wyoming." Vincent began to walk away.

"Excuse me," said James, grabbing Vincent by the arm, "the Holbein."

"Oh, yes. Sorry."

After the long process of carefully taking the delicate paper out of the frame, the drawing was examined and studied. Vincent determined it was an original. The sale would bring a lot of money.

That evening, Vincent motivated himself with various arguments as why he should or should not go to Wyoming. A small piece of luggage laid opened on the bed.

His phone rang. The unexpected area code 307, startled him. "Hello," he answered bashfully.

"Dr. Vincent Jones?"

"Charlotte, I am so sorry I missed your calls. Truly. I just got your mess—"

"Are you Dr. Jones?"

The sudden formality put Vincent on guard. He took a deep breath. "Speaking," he replied. "Is this Charlotte Montagu?"

"It is. How do you know my name?" she asked, surprised. "This is really weird and I'm not sure why I'm calling you."

Vincent listened, anticipating some rationality from Charlotte.

"I had a strange dream," she continued, "a very vivid dream that I should call a Dr. Vincent Jones. This area code… you are in New York City, right?"

Vincent listened to every word, convinced that Vizcaya had not quite revealed all of her wonders. "I live in New York, yes. I… well, this is odd. So, you weren't here a few weeks ago?"

"No. I haven't been to New York since… a long time," she said, after a short hesitation. "Why do you ask if I was in New York?"

"You do live in Wyoming, correct? In Sheridan."

"Now, you see, how do you know this?" she asked, puzzled. "Who are you? I know we've never met. How did I get your name, and dreamt this, this strange dream? I even had a note on my kitchen table, in my own writing no less, reminding me to call you."

Charlotte could not see the smile on Vincent's face, as she tried to make sense of all this; the last miracle from a certain Lady Julia. He understood now. He realized what was at stake; his complete and utter happiness. Julia planned this all along, from the very beginning. The years searching, agonizing, all were formed to come to this conclusion. How many battles it took, how many roads meandering through rocky grounds, how many deserts, to arrive unscathed here?

"I think we should meet," said Vincent, bursting with joy and impatient to see her.

Charlotte did not respond. Her breathing told Vincent that she felt anxious about this phone conversation. "Why?" she said softly, after the silence.

"What else did you see in your dream?" asked Vincent.

"This is crazy. I don't know…"

"Tell me."

"There's this house. It's in Miami, and… well, we were there… you and I."

"Vizcaya. That's the house, right?"

"Yes." This time Charlotte's behavior changed to a less questioning tone. "I'm sure you've been there," she stated, as Vincent heard the sound of dogs barking.

"You have dogs?"

"Yes, yes, I do. Three."

"I love dogs," said Vincent, eager to win Charlotte's heart. Vincent was never brought up with dogs, and he certainly did not care for them that much. Yet, he was very willing to mend his ways. A very different Vincent was born. "What are their names?" he questioned with heightened interest.

"Lulu, Ripley and Daisy. They're my girls and they're great company. I don't think meeting is a good idea," Charlotte said all of a sudden.

"I could just be a casual guest at your inn," he told her.

"Of course, you know I own a hotel. What else do you know?"

"A few things…"

"Well, that sounds a little too weird for my taste," she shot back. "I think I better hang up."

"Oh, no, please don't. I'm quite harmless, really. You did have a dream about a Dr. Jones, and I am he."

"And what is it that you do, exactly?" she inquired, a little calmer now. "What are you a Doctor in?"

"Art history, mainly." Vincent wanted to know more about the dream. He felt sure that Julia had infiltrated her great-granddaughter's subconscious. "Can you tell me more about your dream?" he asked.

"I have to go," Charlotte said, "it was really more of a nightmare, and I don't want to talk about it."

"I'm sorry."

"I guess I can't stop you from coming here, if that's what you wish to do. Goodbye, Dr. Jones, I'm sorry. Maybe I'll see you here."

"Goodbye." Vincent's face lit up with a big smile, in awe about everything that transpired in the last twenty years of his life. A flow of memories came to him from his early childhood, when the first apparitions began. More reflections surfaced from the past, when he continually felt threatened by some supernatural powers, before Julia divulged her identity. And then, Vizcaya. Vizcaya and the transcendent dreams of her; the cancellation of everything Vincent knew to be real, to lose himself in the year 1917. All that, had to be told to someone. Surely, that someone was Charlotte.

FIFTY ONE

United Airlines, flight 5140 landed at Sheridan County Airport. Vincent made sure to take his phone off of airplane mode. The local time was 3:04 p.m. A strong wind, which the pilot had to deal with, blew the freshly fallen snow in small white twisters. The blue mountains in the distance sharply outlined the horizon, as a crisp afternoon air settled any polluting residue.

The holiday season gave Vincent much to think about; Christmas and the New Year's festivities were spent alone. He very much wished to live his life in a more meaningful way. This, to him, meant being with Charlotte. He had to make her fall in love with him all over again. How to make that happen? He had no idea.

"Where to?" asked the cab driver outside the airport terminal.

"The Lady Julia Inn, please. You know where it is?"

"Sure thing. The nicest place in the whole county."

"How far is it?"

"Fifteen, twenty minutes. The roads are clear, so it's not too bad."

Vincent watched the winter landscape. Snow tends to make everything beautiful, though this place held a natural charm that would inspire any artist. He thought about some of the world's great snow scene paintings, by the likes of Claude Monet, Alfred Sisley and other impressionists.

"First time here?" inquired the cab driver.

"Yes. First time in Wyoming," answered Vincent.

The taxi turned in a narrow road. "It's just up this way," said the driver.

"Thank you."

"How long are you staying for, if you don't mind me asking."

"I'm not sure. It may be a very short stay… though I hope not."

"Lady Montagu is a wonderful woman. My wife used to work at the inn, before she got the cancer."

"Oh, I'm sorry. Is she…?" hesitated Vincent.

"She pulled through. They got it all, but you know how that goes. Anyway, here we are." The car pulled in front of the main entrance.

The photographs did not do justice to the imposing house. The Christmas decorations were still in place, which gave the mansion a jovial atmosphere. Multicolored lights reflected onto to snow, and Vincent felt like he had just landed in another world. A world where words like 'tacky' and 'gingerbread house' bring redemption to the arrogant.

People with children were coming and going throughout the property. A large barn, which had been turned into a country store, seemed to be the center of animation.

Vincent paid the taxi driver and entered the lobby. The large staircase that he saw on the website led to the upper galleries. It reminded him a little bit of Vizcaya. The lobby was fairly crowded. Vincent could see a dining room at the back, and it looked like tea was being served.

"Hello," said the young girl behind the front desk. "Will you be staying with us, or you're just here for the day?" she asked.

"No, I'd like a room, please. I do hope you have one, it looks like you're very busy."

"Yes, it's our busy time. Do you have a reservation?"

"A reservation? No. I do not." Vincent looked around, like a lost child.

"I'm sorry, I don't have a room available. There are other places in town, though I can't guarantee a room. Sorry."

"Well... that's my own fault," said Vincent. "Is it possible to meet the owner? Lady Montagu."

"If you like, but she'll tell you the same thing."

"No, that's not what I meant. I need to talk to her about something."

"Let me see if she's in." The girl dialed a number. "What's your name?" she asked Vincent, while she waited for Charlotte to answer.

"Vincent Jones."

The girl quickly put the phone down. "Mr. Jones, we've been expecting you," she exclaimed. "I do have a room for you. Charlotte gave strict instructions. She knew you'd be coming. She didn't know when, but she wanted to reserve a room for you."

"Well, I'm speechless," said Vincent.

"She's giving you the nicest room in the house. The Lady Julia Room. The best."

"Thank you. I don't know what to say."

"Say nothing," giggled the girl, who showed impeccable white teeth and a colorful tattoo of a butterfly on the side of her neck. "You can thank Charlotte in person later."

"I look forward to meeting her."

"She's wonderful."

"It's what I hear," replied Vincent.

The girl handed Vincent the key to his room. "Do you need help with your luggage?"

"I'm fine, thank you."

"Dinner is served between six and eight," she added, "and breakfast is from six to nine."

"Thank you."

The room did not lack elegance, and the charm of the original mansion was strikingly evident. A series of four Audubon pictures hung on the wall, above the bed. The fine prints represented very colorful birds. A subtle wallpaper with a white rose pattern further emphasized a delicate feminine touch. Vincent gazed at the small reproduction of Sargent's portrait of Julia, which held a special place above the marble fireplace. "The Lady Julia Room," he uttered, standing in the middle of the room. He felt alive. He felt impervious to any suspicions he knew would soon crop up.

A table by the main fireplace was also reserved for Vincent in the busy and lively dining room. A group of people sat nearby, enjoying a drink in front of the fire. A small boy waved at Vincent as he sat down, and he waved back. The short menu boasted the fact that everything was organically and locally grown. The wine list impressed Vincent as well, though whoever Charlotte may claim to be now, he had full confidence her taste for the more refined remained unchanged. He looked around the room, searching for her. He really had no concept of her appearance. Did she even seem like the Charlotte from before? Vincent looked up every time someone entered the room. He understood why she would be hiding from him. Perhaps she had a spy seated just a table away; an absurd idea, which he quickly dismissed.

A waitress approached Vincent's table. "Good evening, my name is Candice," she said softly. "I'll be your waitress this evening." She stared at Vincent before she spoke again. "Charlotte was called away, and she apologizes for not being here," she declared with haste. "Would you like something to drink?"

"Did she say anything else?" he asked, not entirely believing the excuse.

"No, that's all she said."

"Well, if you do speak to her, tell her that I thank her for her being so kind. The room is fabulous, and I think I'll stay indefinitely. I will pay, of course. Tell her that."

"Okay," said Candice, who seemed at a loss.

"I'll have a bottle of the Lorenzi Estate Cabernet Sauvignon, please."

"Excellent choice."

After dinner, Vincent strolled towards the country store. There were fewer people around now and the temperature had considerably dropped. The snow-covered ground seemed to fade away into the distance, in shades of deep purple into the night.

FIFTY TWO

"That's him." Candice told Charlotte.

"I know."

Both women peeked through the curtains of a window from Charlotte's private suite. Vincent entered the store. Charlotte watched him.

"Why don't you want to see him?" Candice wondered. "He seems very nice."

"It's just too weird," Charlotte replied, her stare firmly locked on this man who was making himself known again. The excitement of a new attachment, intimate or not, was real. She felt a strong attraction towards him, which mystified her. The intense dream left her wondering.

"I've got to go back to the kitchen," said Candice. "You're okay?"

"Oh, yes. I'm fine. Go."

The young waitress left. Charlotte turned the lights off in case Vincent looked up. She kept her eyes on him as he appeared and disappeared behind various stands. Perhaps she will be brave tomorrow. Perhaps she will show herself and tell him how silly all this was. And this dream, this odd dream, well, was it really that clear? Did it really show Vincent Jones? The more Charlotte tried to defend her efforts to discard such a concept, the more powerful it returned. Every night, the same images flustered her. She went to sleep, fully expecting to be taken to some illusory rooms, shocked to find herself lying down, hand in hand with an intimate friend, a mysterious man. Such absolute providence was met with mixed feelings. Charlotte's sentimentality fought the cynicism of an intransigent heart. She was ready to give, and give wholeheartedly, yet she feared her own enthusiasm. The foundation of this potential relationship, even a platonic one, was very flimsy. It felt like a mistake, at least it did at times.

FIFTY THREE

Large snowflakes slowly fell to the ground. Nature muted all sounds. The virgin snow outside was not defiled by a single footstep. Vincent wiped the condensation on the window, and gazed at the serenity of the landscape. An infinite nostalgia veiled his senses and he thought of Vizcaya when a little girl suddenly ran out in the snow, wearing a bright red coat. A woman followed her. Vincent observed the happy scene. He felt at peace here, the same peace he found at Vizcaya. In fact, he could not remember another place that compared with these two locations; Vizcaya and The Lady Julia Inn. He considered his thoughts. Both places were linked to one another by two names; Vizcaya and Julia. It was an unbreakable bond that would overcome the test of time. Vincent would seize the day. He knew Charlotte was here, avoiding him, even against her better judgment. Was it too much to hope that a trace of the 'old' Charlotte had remained hidden in that rejuvenated soul? Nothing was impossible, however critical the situation may seem. Julia was orchestrating this, and Vincent laid all his hopes at her feet.

During breakfast, young Candice, who was not on duty that morning, approached Vincent's table.
"Good morning, Candice," said Vincent. He cut into a Belgian waffle.
"Good morning."
"Did you convey my message to Charlotte?" he asked.
"Kinda," she said, chewing gum.
"I know she's here. Why is she avoiding me?"
"I don't know," Candice said. "You two are weird," she continued. "Anyway, if you want to see her, she's always in the stables at sunset. Don't ask me why, I guess she likes to talk to her horses, or something."
"Will she be there tonight?"
"Yes, I think so."
"Thank you."

"Don't let her know it was me who told you."
"I won't. Don't worry."

Vincent sat on the wooden bench at the back of the stable. He stood up and sat down again, several times, rehearsing a few lines he prepared for Charlotte. His level of anxiety was high. He counted the horses in their stalls, eating. There were four. He checked twice; there were still four. Why am I so nervous? Vincent asked himself. The sun disappeared behind the mountain, painting an orange glow far reaching in the sky. One of the horses stuck its head out of the stall. Vincent was going to approach it, when someone entered the stable.

"Hello, can I help you?" asked the voice coming from the far end of the barn. A woman in a wheelchair approached, followed by three dogs. "This is not open to the public." She switched some dim lights on.

'Charlotte,' mouthed Vincent. A surge of memories, previously stored away like some discarded files, collided with the analytical side of him. Charlotte was here. The very same woman whose advances he reluctantly ignored.

"Dr. Jones," Charlotte declared, trying to avoid Vincent's eyes. "It's very inconsiderate of you to be here," she uttered.

"Why?" he asked, in a pleading tone of voice. "And how did you know it was me?"

Charlotte wavered on her answer. "I just knew it was you," she said, looking at the horse in the first stall.

Why don't you want to see me?" Vincent asked.

"Because."

"Because you're in a wheelchair? I already knew that," he said, looking at her.

"How could you have possibly known? Unless Candice told you." She pulled up the blanket covering her legs.

"You're cold."

"A little," she replied. "Well, now that you're here…"

"We can talk." Vincent looked at her and finally pointed at one of the dogs, roaming around the stable. "So, you have three dogs and four horses," he stated. He rolled his eyes, realizing the debacle of such an asinine observation. He saw the beginning of a smile on Charlotte's face.

"Yes," she replied, "that's Lulu, over there. She follows me everywhere." She looked for the others, but they had wandered off.

"I would so love to have dinner with you, or at least a drink," Vincent quickly added. "I need to talk to you. Please." He came closer to her. He could see her clearer now. She appeared the same, except this time Vincent noticed a slight resemblance to Julia, depending how the light shaped her face. She displayed some of the features he saw in her great-grandmother. Perhaps those characteristics were always there, though he may have been blind to them.

"I guess we could go have a drink in my apartment," she said.

"I would very much like that. May I?" he asked, placing his hands on the wheelchair and offering his help.

"Thank you."

Vincent pushed Charlotte around the back of the house. He noticed all of the additions that were made in order for it to become wheelchair accessible. An elevator was installed especially for her. It led directly to her apartments.

"I'm lucky," she said, "at least I have full use of my upper body. Some people are not so fortunate."

Vincent listened to Charlotte talk about her physical weakness, and he recognized the Charlotte he left behind, the British girl with the 'must carry on' attitude.

The Sargent charcoal drawing of Julia surprised Vincent. He looked at it as they came in the sitting room. He nodded with a smile, accepting anything logical or nonsensical as being legitimate now. "It's here," he just said, pointing out the drawing.

Charlotte watched, as Vincent walked around her suite. "Would you like a drink? Scotch?" she asked.

"Please." A photograph of Charlotte riding a horse hung above a small antique desk. Vincent recognized her right away.

"That was a long time ago," Charlotte exclaimed. She poured two drinks. "Please sit down." She sipped hers. "I haven't been entirely honest with you. That is to say, I haven't been honest at all." Charlotte stared at Vincent. "I thought about you… every day, after you literally disappeared from that hotel room in Miami!"

Vincent rushed to Charlotte and fell on his knees. "Ooh, Charlotte, so you do know who I am."

"I returned to Vizcaya many times after that day. I looked for you though I don't even know what I was looking for, or what I was supposed to find, if anything."

Vincent listened. He held Charlotte's hands in his, and watched the tears run down her cheeks. Charlotte's confession gave him peace and her tears, hope.

"I found several letters Julia had written, letters I had no idea existed," she continued, "and I searched for a clue. She wrote about someone who I guess was your great-grandfather, Clarence Henry Jones. But I didn't find anything. I knew you were there with her, and I just wish… I just wish…"

"I was never with her."

"But I thought…"

"Oh, I tried, trust me, but it wasn't meant to be. And I know better now."

Charlotte's countenance changed to a happier one. "And then a series of crazy dreams," she continued, "like it was meant to be a message. I saw that barge, that gorgeous stone barge. I was standing there and you came to me."

"This was in your dream?" asked Vincent, perturbed by the similarity of that day Julia arrived at Vizcaya. "What happened next?"

"I don't quite know. You vanished. That was the last time I had that dream."

"And New York? You didn't go there, did you? The sale of the Sargent, that wasn't you, right?"

"No."

"Julia," said Vincent, shaking his head, amazed. She was there. I met her, spoke to her…"

"How did she get hold of that painting?" inquired Charlotte. "How?"

Vincent grinned at Julia's ingenuity. "She stole it from me!" he exclaimed. Vincent kissed Charlotte's hands. He held them and explored their beauty, and observed again the absence of any ring. She let him. She liked the touch of him. She liked the touch of another human being. She dared to bring Vincent's hand to her lips. Charlotte felt her entire body quiver. They gazed at one another, their eyes blurring out everything else. Vincent caressed her face and Charlotte pulled her wheelchair away all of a sudden.

"I just don't think this is going to work," she said, holding back her tears. "Let's not pretend to be what we are not. Look at me." She spoke with a great tenderness, and looked at the man she had long wished to be with. "It's not fair to you."

Vincent stood up. Charlotte was his last chance at happiness. He had to fight for her, get away from the source of his own delusions and find clearer waters. There, he would discover peace, a peace like he has never known. That was Julia's masterful composition. The silver key, the secret passage, 1917, all of it was intended to rearrange the often flawed design of the universe. Vincent had loved Charlotte before he met her that day at his mother's funeral. The silent proclamation had been written long before then. "Charlotte—"

"Wait. I want to return something to you." She lifted her thick blond hair at the back of her neck, unlocked a little chain and took it off; Vincent's silver key was hanging on it. "I wore it as a pendant," she said.

Vincent was at a loss for words. "You kept it," he murmured, eventually, struck by a sudden desire to kiss Charlotte.

"You told me it was the most precious thing to you. And, there's this," Charlotte said, as she rolled herself to her desk, and produced the mahogany box. "I assume those letters carved on it, are your great-grandfather's initials?" said Charlotte.

"My God! You have it," uttered Vincent. "Yes, they are. I'm not going to ask you how it ended up in your possession."

"Good, because I don't have the faintest idea. One day it wasn't here, and the next, it was." She handed it to Vincent. "I've never been able to open it. No one could figure out the combination."

Vincent smiled and sat down next to Charlotte. "It's Vizcaya," he said laughing, as he turned each letter on the lock to read V.I.Z.C.A.Y.A.

"I tried that, but it wouldn't open," said Charlotte.

"Really? That's odd."

Charlotte watched Vincent turn the last letter. "I guess yours is the magic touch."

"There are a few things in here that mean a lot to me," he said and he opened the box. Vincent looked bewildered.

"What is it?" inquired Charlotte.

"The letter, the comb, it's all gone."

"The comb?"

"I think it belonged to your great-grandmother. I know… don't ask," said Vincent. He took out the single item; a faded out, handwritten letter.

"Who is it from?"

"I'm not sure," replied Vincent, unfolding the delicate paper. They both read it:

Dearest Charlotte,

I write to you as a spirit, as my life was cut short at the age of twenty-eight. Vincent's great-grandfather and I were fortunate to have been in love, even if it was only for a short time. Do not waste another day. Vincent Jones had to learn a valuable lesson. In the end it was all for the love of one woman. Can that be possible? The love of one human being?

Surely, the answer is an obvious one.

Julia

"It's from your great-grandmother," said Vincent staring at the note.

Charlotte looked at him. As before, she could not find fault in his character. She had loved Vincent from the beginning, from their very first conversation. The cynic will ask how can one be attracted to a total stranger, a voice on the other side of the world? Very easily. Very easily, indeed. What is more lasting, the heart, the essence of one, or the physical virtues which more often than not, lead to a maze built on misery? "I love you, Vincent," Charlotte whispered, as if she whispered the words to herself.

He looked into her eyes. "I love you," he whispered back, with all his heart. And she let him kiss her. And it was everything she imagined, as he wrapped his arms around her. It was as if a veil had been lifted, a dark cover that blocked out the light that indicates the quietest way.

"I think we have a lot to talk about," Charlotte said, though really speaking to and warning her own heart.

"Maybe we should say good night," Vincent replied. "I'll see you in the morning? I'm not going to be able to go to sleep, you know that, right?"

"Me, neither."

"Good night, Lady Charlotte," he smiled and walked to the front door. The three dogs were lying down on the couch, taking the full length of it.

"My rescue animals," she said.

"They're lucky they found you."

"Maybe it's the other way around," answered Charlotte.

Vincent nodded. "I look forward to the new day."

"Goodnight, Dr. Jones," she answered.

FIFTY FOUR

Vizcaya. Just three syllables, yet so much is contained within that name. How can a house be more than a house, and have such sovereignty, such spirituality? Where to find comparable charm and an elegance unrivaled, in the world? Vizcaya is stone and spirit. The casual onlooker will miss her inner beauty, her powers. Sargent understood her. His soul lingers in her fabulous gardens, in her courtyard. James Deering is right there, too, for those who know how to feel. Marion Davies's shadow roams with a never-ending dance. Clarence Henry Jones. Julia. You will find them, too, if you believe.

Vincent sat in his car, confused and listened to the soft rain. He held the key in his hand. Snow in Sheridan became rain in Boston in an instant, as Vincent was teleported without warning. He should be used to it, yet this time it was unexpected. The parking lot of the very familiar church was filled with cars. He realized that he was in Boston, when he heard a knock on the window and a voice call his name.

"Doctor Jones. It's Charlotte. Charlotte Montagu." She stood under an umbrella and smiled at Vincent. It was a smile of sheer exuberance, impromptu and true.

Vincent was stupefied at the sight of her. He rolled the window down.

"I'm sorry. This is probably a bad time for you. Not very thoughtful of me. I just wanted to say hi," she told a baffled Vincent, and began to walk away.

"Wait." Never did a smile illuminate a face so sweetly. Charlotte walking. Beautiful, bright Charlotte. He stepped out of the car, and they both noticed that the rain had stopped.

She folded her umbrella. "I know a funeral is not the best time to meet, but I assumed you wouldn't mind if I just said hello. I'm sorry for your loss." She looked at Vincent. "I thought your eulogy was wonderful. Different."

"It was really about a house," he declared, still utterly amazed at the miracle.

"Vizcaya, right?"

Vincent nodded, captivated by Charlotte's spirit, the entrancing energy she so freely offered.

"I thought that much. I love that house and I know you do, too."

"Have coffee with me," Vincent said quickly, afraid the mirage would disappear. He looked for Dimitri, the chauffeur, anybody who may be waiting for Charlotte. He did not see anyone.

"Are you sure?" she asked. "What about all those people?"

"As sure as you stand here," he answered. "I don't care about any of them. Is that bad?"

"No," she laughed.

He opened his car door for her and invited her in. "I know just the place," he told Charlotte, thinking of the café when they first met.

Her bright smile comforted him.

"I know we've spoken on the phone, but have you ever had that feeling about someone… like you met before?" she asked Vincent.

"I most certainly have," he replied, his spirit still in Sheridan at the Lady Julia Inn.

"I was so looking forward to meeting you, though I feel like I've known you forever. Strange, isn't it?" she uttered, and kept looking at him.

"I feel the same. I am so happy you came to my mother's funeral," said Vincent, "I can't begin to tell you how happy I am."

"I wouldn't have missed it for the world," she answered.

Vincent was at peace, knowing that Charlotte had returned to him. He looked forward to getting to know her all over again and listening to her talk about ordinary things, like her three dogs and her life in Sheridan. He could not help but marvel at her sight.

And that smile, that wonderful smile again, telling Vincent that the endless night had come to an end. He listened to Charlotte, the sound of her, like the peaceful murmur of a brook finally meandering in the aridity of his soul. And he thought about the words Julia had written a hundred years ago, or perhaps it was just the other day - In the end, it was all for the love of one woman. Can that be possible? The love of one human being?

Made in United States
Orlando, FL
24 November 2021

10698573R00154